WORLD OF WARCRAFT®

WAR CRIMES

A NOVEL BY
CHRISTIE GOLDEN

GALLERY BOOKS

New York   London   Toronto   Sydney   New Delhi

Gallery Books
A Division of Simon & Schuster, Inc.
1230 Avenue of the Americas
New York, NY 10020

First Gallery Books hardcover edition May 2014

GALLERY BOOKS and colophon are registered trademarks of Simon & Schuster, Inc.

For information about special discounts for bulk purchases, please contact
Simon & Schuster Special Sales at 1-866-506-1949 or business@simonandschuster.com.

The Simon & Schuster Speakers Bureau can bring authors to your live event.
For more information or to book an event, contact the Simon & Schuster Speakers
Bureau at 1-866-248-3049 or visit our website at www.simonspeakers.com.

Jacket design by Alan Dingman
Jacket art by Slawomir Maniak/Blizzard Entertainment

Manufactured in the United States of America

10 9 8 7 6 5 4 3 2 1

Library of Congress Cataloging-in-Publication Data

ISBN 978-1-4516-8448-3
ISBN 978-1-4516-8449-0 (ebook)

To Sean Copeland,
Historian Extraordinaire,
for his unfailing good cheer, swift and helpful responses,
and total enthusiasm and support for my work.
Thanks, buddy!

PANDARIA

SHADO-PAN
MONASTERY

MOGU'SHAN
TERRACE

TEMPLE OF THE
WHITE TIGER

ONE KEG

KUN-LAI
SUMMIT

ISLE OF
THUNDER

VIOLET RISE

PROLOGUE

Draenor.

It was the birthplace of the orcs, and for so long, the only home Garrosh Hellscream had known. He had been born there, in Nagrand, the most beautiful, most verdant part of that world. There, he had suffered through the red pox, and bowed his head in shame at the deeds of his father, the legendary Grommash Hellscream. When Draenor had become tainted with demonic magic, Garrosh had blamed that legend. He had been ashamed to carry Hellscream blood until Thrall, warchief of the Horde, had come to show Garrosh that although the elder Hellscream might have been the first to accept the curse, Grom had given his life to end it.

Draenor. Garrosh had not returned since he left, full of the heated fire of pride and a fierce love for the Azeroth Horde, to defend his new home against the horrors of the Lich King.

And now, it would seem, he was back.

But this world was not as he remembered it last, pulsing with fel energies, the wild creatures fewer and sickly. No, this was the world of his childhood, and it was beautiful.

For a moment Garrosh stood, his powerful body, adorned with the same tattoos that had decorated his father's skin, stretching as he turned his face to the sun, his lungs inhaling the clean, sweet air. It was impossible—but it was so.

And in this place that was impossible, another unthinkable thing happened. Before his very eyes, his father's image shimmered into shape out of nothingness. Grom Hellscream was smiling—and his skin was brown.

Garrosh gasped—for a moment no warchief, no hero of the Horde, no valiant warrior, but a youth beholding a long-dead parent he had never thought to see again.

"Father!" he cried, and fell to his knees, overwhelmed at this vision. "I have come home. To this, our birthplace. Forgive me for ever doubting your true nature!"

A hand dropped onto his shoulder. Garrosh looked up into Grom's face, the words still tumbling from him. "I have done so much, in your name, and my own name has become beloved of the Horde and feared by the Alliance. Do . . . do you know, somehow? Can you tell me, Father—are you proud of me?"

Grom Hellscream opened his mouth to speak. A metallic, clanging noise came from somewhere, and Grom vanished.

Garrosh Hellscream awoke alert, as he always did.

"Good morning, Garrosh," came the pleasant voice. "Your breakfast is prepared for you. Please—step back."

If his jailers had waited but a moment longer, Garrosh would have known the answer to the question that had haunted and driven him all his life. If only he could throttle the infuriatingly composed pandaren for such an intrusion.

Garrosh, clad in a robe and hood, contented himself with presenting an imperturbable expression as he rose from the sleeping furs, stepped back as far as possible from the metal frame and glowing violet octagonal windows of the cell, and waited. The mage, wearing a long robe decorated with floral designs, stepped forward and began an incantation. The glow faded from the windows. She moved back and the other two pandaren—identical twins—approached. One brother watched Garrosh closely while the second slid a meal of tea and assorted buns through an opening level

with the floor. As the guard rose, he motioned that Garrosh was
free to take the tray.

The orc did not do so. "When will my execution be?" Garrosh
asked flatly.

"Your fate is still being decided," one of the twins said.

Garrosh wanted to hurl the food at the bars, or preferably, lunge
faster and farther than anticipated and crush his smirking tormen-
tor's windpipe with a single massive hand before the little female
could intervene. He did neither, moving with calmness and control
to the furs and sitting down.

The mage reactivated the imprisoning violet field, and the three
pandaren then left, ascending the ramp. The door clanged shut behind them.

Your fate is still being decided.

What in the name of the ancestors did that mean?

1

"It looks too peaceful and beautiful to be the prison of someone so horrible," Lady Jaina Proudmoore mused as she approached the Temple of the White Tiger. She, the blue dragon Kalecgos, Ranger-General Vereesa Windrunner, and King Varian Wrynn rode in a cart drawn by a steady-footed yak, whose fluffy fur indicated the beast had been freshly bathed. In acknowledgment of the honored status of the passengers, the cart had been upholstered with silk cushions in vibrant shades, though the travelers did bounce a bit when a wheel hit a rut.

"Better than he deserves," said Vereesa. She fixed her gaze on Varian. "You should not have stopped Go'el from killing him, Your Majesty. There is no other justice for that monster than death, and even that is more merciful than what he has done."

The ranger-general's voice was sharp, and Jaina couldn't blame her. Especially as she completely shared Vereesa's sentiments. Garrosh Hellscream had been responsible for the destruction—no, that was too kind, too clinical a word for what he'd done—the *obliteration* of the city-state of Theramore. The deaths of hundreds, all occurring in the space of a heartbeat, could be laid at his feet. The then-warchief of the Horde had contrived to trick several of the Alliance's finest generals and admirals into assembling at Theramore, where they planned for the sort of warfare that involved an honest fight. Instead, Garrosh had dropped a mana bomb, its power magnified by an artifact stolen from the blue dragonflight, into the heart of the city. Everyone, every *thing* in the bomb's blast radius had died. Jaina shook her head to clear the awful memory of precisely how some of them, people she loved, had been killed. Jaina Proudmoore would never again be the lady of Theramore.

A gentle touch on her arm brought her back to the present. Jaina looked up at the blue dragon Kalecgos, who had been the one good thing to come out of the disaster. He and Jaina might never have found one another if he had not come to Theramore asking for her aid in recovering the Focusing Iris. If the tides of war had brought Jaina a loving companion, they had borne away that of Vereesa Windrunner. Rhonin, the archmage who had held Jaina's present title of leader of the Kirin Tor, had stood at the heart of the city, pulling the mana bomb to himself in order to magically contain the blast as best he could. In the process, he had forcibly pushed Jaina through a portal to safety. Jaina, Vereesa, the night elf Shandris Feathermoon, and a few of her Sentinels had been the only survivors.

The leader of the Silver Covenant had never—likely *would* never—truly recovered from the loss. Vereesa had always been strong and outspoken, but now her words were barbed, and a hatred cold and bitter as the ice of Northrend dwelt in her heart. Thank the Light, the ice thawed when she spoke to her twin sons, Giramar and Galadin.

Not so long ago, Varian might have risen to the bait and grown angry with Vereesa for her open condemnation of his choice. Now he merely said, "You may yet get your wish, Vereesa. Remember what Taran Zhu promised."

After Varian had prevented Go'el—formerly hailed as Thrall, once warchief of the Horde and now leader of the shamanic order known as Earthen Ring—from dealing Garrosh the death blow with the mighty Doomhammer, Garrosh had been delivered into the paws of the pandaren, a people whom both Horde and Alliance trusted, and who had endured their share of harm at Garrosh's hands. Taran Zhu, lord of the Shado-pan, had assured them that Garrosh would be tried, and justice would be meted out to all. The orc was presently imprisoned in the cellars beneath the Temple of the White Tiger, under heavy guard, and two days ago word had come from the celestial Xuen's own emissary: *We request your presence at my temple. Garrosh Hellscream's fate shall be decided.*

Nothing more.

Every Alliance leader had received the same letter, and Jaina saw some of them at the foot of the hill, getting into similarly refurbished carts for the trek up to the temple. Queen-Regent Moira Thaurissan, one of the three joint leaders of the dwarves, appeared to be arguing with an unruffled pandaren, pointing with annoyance at the cart. No doubt she did not find it "suitable" for her royal self.

"I remember," said Vereesa, "and it seems to be important to the celestials. And if it is so cursed important, why were we not allowed to just fly to the temple? Why waste time with this cart?"

"We are here by their invitation," Kalec said. "If they are willing to wait until we arrive by this method, we should be, too. It is not that long a ride."

"Spoken with the patience of a dragon," Vereesa said.

"I am what I am," he replied, seemingly unperturbed by her comment. Yes, thought Jaina, he was indeed what he was, who he was, and she was glad of it, though much yet remained for them to sort through in their relationship.

She tried to settle back into the embroidered cushions and enjoy the slow ride up the curving path. Pandaria exuded remarkable peace and offered beauty wherever one's eye fell. Cherry trees exploded with pink blossoms, a few fluttering about as the wind swayed the branches. Statues of white tigers guarded the first graceful gateway, and the path began to grow steeper. As the cart made its steady way forward and the cold pressed in, Jaina was grateful for the heat of the various braziers they passed, and wrapped a cloak more tightly about her slender frame. The earth bore first a scant dusting of snow, then drifts as the altitude increased. Jaina became aware of a profound sense of lightness, and all at once she understood. She well knew the import of casting a spell with focus and purposefulness, and it was suddenly clear to her that in their own way, the celestials were giving their guests a chance to do precisely that. By taking a leisurely cart ride up the mountain, skirting the outlying exterior structures, and being exposed to beauty and peacefulness the entire way, Jaina and her companions had the opportunity to set aside the duties of their everyday world and arrive mentally fresh. She permitted the air, scented with the subtle fragrance of the cherry blossoms, to cleanse her mind.

She and Kalec were seated so they faced backward, so Jaina didn't see what twisted Vereesa's beautiful visage into a scowl and thinned Varian's lips as the cart halted before the first of the swaying rope bridges. The high elf's hand automatically went to her side, and then curled into a fist as she remembered they had been asked to bring no weapons to the temple.

"What are *they* doing here?" Vereesa snapped, then answered her own question. "Well, Garrosh *is* their former leader. I suppose they would be present when his fate is announced."

Jaina turned in her seat, looking up at the courtyard of the temple proper, and her eyes widened slightly. Her gut clenched as she was reminded of Garrosh's tactic at Theramore—assembling the greatest Alliance military tacticians in one place—as it seemed that the invitation the Alliance leaders had received was extended to the Horde as well. The blue-skinned troll Vol'jin, of course, was here. Varian's counterpart as the new warchief. Would he be better than an orc? Worse? Did it matter? Not even the former warchief Thrall, who now went by his birth-name of Go'el, could curb the Horde's hunger for violence, and he had tried.

Even as she thought about him, her gaze found the orc shaman. At Go'el's side was his mate, Aggra, who carried a small bundle.

Go'el's son.

Jaina had heard Go'el had become a father, and there was word that Aggra was again with child. Once, Jaina would have been invited to hold this little one, but that time had passed. Go'el was surveying the crowd, and his eyes, as blue as Jaina's own, met hers.

Anger and unhappiness surged through her, and she looked away.

Seeking distraction, Jaina turned her attention to the tallest of the leaders, Baine Bloodhoof. Save for Go'el, Baine was the only Horde leader Jaina had ever been able to think of as a friend. Garrosh had first slain the tauren's father, Cairne, and then stood by while the Grimtotem tauren attacked Thunder Bluff. Unable to get aid from the Horde, Baine had turned to Jaina for help against Magatha, which Jaina had been glad to give. Baine had returned the favor by warning her of the impending attack on Theramore. Of course, Baine had assumed it would be an ordinary battle. He had not known of the stolen Focusing Iris, or the deadly purpose Garrosh had planned for it. In Jaina's opinion, any debts between them had been paid.

She spotted a few others too: Lor'themar Theron of the blood elves, with whom she had recently, albeit under duress, negotiated; and the obnoxious goblin Trade Prince Jastor Gallywix, sporting his ridiculous top hat.

A pandaren clad in the robes of a monk bowed in greeting as they exited the cart. "Honored guests," he said. "You are welcome. Here there will be only peace, as you attend the first ever gathering of *all* the leaders of Azeroth. Do you promise to abide by this rule?"

"I thought we were here to see justice done," Vereesa began, but Jaina laid a hand on her arm. Vereesa bit her lip, and said nothing more. Since the murder of her husband, Vereesa had gravitated to Jaina, and the leader of the Kirin Tor was the only one who seemed able to pour oil on the churning waters of Vereesa's loathing of the Horde.

"You understand that there is not peace in our hearts," Jaina said to the monk. "There is pain, and anger, and a desire for justice, as Vereesa has said. For my part, however, I will offer no violence."

The other three answered in kind, although Vereesa uttered the words with difficulty, and the pandaren invited them to follow him up the swaying rope bridge and the massive central staircase, and into the coliseum.

Aysa Cloudsinger, among the first of the pandaren who had joined the Alliance, stood at the entrance to the temple, and the newcomers bowed to her. Her eyes sparkled with pleasure at seeing them. Aysa had settled in Stormwind City, and Jaina had not seen her since the monk's arrival some time ago.

"I knew you would come," Aysa said, bowing to each of them in turn. "Thank you."

"Aysa," Varian said. "Can you tell us what is going on?"

"All I know is that those who lead the factions of Alliance and Horde were requested to come here peacefully, and that the August Celestials have made some sort of decision," she said. "Please—enter the temple in silence, and stand with your fellows in the center area, on the left. The celestials will arrive soon." Her normally modulated voice was higher than usual, betraying the strain and concern she felt. That was not a good sign, but they all nodded agreement.

Quietly, Jaina asked, "Is Ji here?" Aysa's stride faltered. Ji Firepaw was the first pandaren to ally with the Horde, as Aysa had chosen the Alliance. It had divided them until Garrosh had turned on Ji, who had come perilously close to execution. That the two cared deeply for one another was obvious, but what would happen between them now was not so clear.

"He is here," Aysa said. "For now, we are together, and this time is precious to us both." She offered no more, and Jaina did not press her. The archmage hoped that perhaps this trial would make Ji realize that the Horde was the wrong side for him to have chosen.

The Temple of the White Tiger was vast. Here, in the cavernous arena that was at the center of the temple, pandaren monks trained, the disciplined practice under Xuen's watchful eyes turning them into masters of their martial art. Despite the size, somehow the temple did not feel oppressive. Perhaps it was because despite the copious amount of seats, no one gathered here to witness death— only skill.

The entrance was in the south, directly opposite a huge, brazier-flanked throne in the seating area. Banners were on display in the west, north, and east. On the floor was a ring of six large, self-contained decorative bronze circles, with a substantial, slightly re-cessed seventh in the center. The illumination came from blazing lanterns that hung from the ceiling, and the daylight streaming through the open doors of the entryway.

Others were there before them. Varian's son, Prince Anduin, strode up to them and embraced his father. Jaina was happy to see the ease and affection with which the two interacted, as opposed to the strain of their relationship not so long ago. Anduin, who had been in this land longer than any of them, put a finger to his lips, and they nodded their understanding.

In silence, as requested, they moved to join High Priestess Tyrande Whisperwind, representing the night elves, and the general of the Sentinels, Shandris Feathermoon. Velen, the ancient leader of the alien draenei, inclined his head in greeting, and An-duin went to stand with his teacher and friend as others filed in. Genn Greymane, king of Gilneas, entered along with High Tin-ker Gelbin Mekkatorque. They were followed by Moira, Muradin Bronzebeard, and Falstad Wildhammer, the triumvirate that spoke for the dwarven kingdoms.

Greymane had opted for his worgen form. The choice spoke vol-umes. It both acknowledged to the Horde present that at least some of the Alliance understood what it was like to taste the more primal side of nature, and told his fellow Alliance members that he was not ashamed of it.

On the right-hand side of the room, the Horde representatives had gathered, and Jaina's lips thinned as she regarded them. Go'el was now accompanied by his old friend and advisor Eitrigg and another elderly orc—one whom Jaina remembered. Varok Saurfang. His son Dranosh had fallen at the Wrath Gate. Dranosh had been reanimated by the Lich King, only to finally fall again—a true death this time. Varok looked to be a hard-bitten warrior, but he was also a father who mourned a worthy son.

Beside her, Jaina heard a swift intake of breath, and she followed Vereesa's gaze.

A slender, graceful figure had entered the Temple of the White Tiger. She looked at first glance like an elven archer, but there was a sickly blue-gray tint to her skin, and her eyes blazed red, as if they were the only outlets for an unquenchable fire.

Sylvanas Windrunner, Dark Lady of the Forsaken and sister to Vereesa, had arrived.

aine Bloodhoof normally found Pandaria to be second only to Mulgore in its ability to soothe his heart and mind. As a warrior, he respected the skill and prowess displayed by those who fought in Xuen's temple. And yet, he was filled with an inner anxiety.

It could be argued that the first great wrong Garrosh did against any member of the Horde had been against the tauren—the death of Baine's beloved father, the great and deeply missed Cairne Bloodhoof. There was no doubt in Baine's mind that Cairne would have emerged victorious from the true, fair, one-on-one fight which the mak'gora was supposed to represent. Cairne had not been slain by a superior blow, but by poison, applied to the blade without Garrosh's knowledge.

But Garrosh had known that Magatha, the shaman who had "blessed" the blade, was against her own people, and he should never have trusted a tauren who did not remember and honor her roots. And thus by treachery, the best of the tauren had been murdered. Perhaps it was inevitable that while Garrosh had been innocent of that particular betrayal, he had become stunted, dark, capable of the atrocities that no one denied he had committed. First Theramore had been annihilated, a memory that still haunted Baine's dreams, and then the Vale of Eternal Blossoms, which struck personally at Baine's deep love and reverence for the Earth Mother.

The vale had been created by the titans, an almost impossibly lush, beautiful place of growth and harmony. Sealed off after the ancient mogu race had been defeated, the vale had been tended to by careful guardians. Only recently had the Alliance and the Horde won the right to enter. And, mused Baine bitterly, it had taken an even shorter time for Garrosh Hellscream, in his lust for power, to destroy something that had lasted for untold millennia. The blossoms in the vale had not proven to be "eternal" after all. They were gone, nothing but a memory, although new life—and new hope—had come to the vale once the sha had been truly defeated.

Baine trusted the celestials. He believed in their wisdom and fairness.

So why was he so agitated?

"I once told Garrosh he gonna know exactly who fired the arrow that pierced his black heart. I be knowing what makes you champ your tusks, if you had them."

Baine started. Vol'jin had moved so quietly the tauren had not even heard the troll step beside him.

"It is true," Baine said. "It is difficult to reconcile my father's teachings of honor and justice with what I personally prefer to see happen today."

Vol'jin nodded. "As they tell us at Brewfest, get in line," he chuckled. "But if we be wanting a clean start, we gotta do what Varian says. Garrosh done enough damage alive. We don't want to have a martyr for the remaining orcs to carry on his wicked ways. Whatever the celestials decree, nobody got a leg to stand on to say anything."

Baine glanced over at Go'el, Eitrigg, and Varok Saurfang. Go'el had taken his son, Durak, from Aggra, holding the child securely and with ease. Baine knew that, having lost his own father to violence, Go'el was determined to be actively involved in the child's rearing. Cairne had been such a present father, and the sight unexpectedly moved Baine. Fathers and sons . . . Grom and Garrosh, Cairne and Baine, Go'el and Durak, Arthas and Terenas Menethil, Varok and Dranosh Saurfang. Surely this recurring theme was a reminder from the Earth Mother of the connections that ran so deep, and how they could manifest great good or great evil.

"I hope you are right," Baine said to Vol'jin. "Go'el is the one who put Garrosh in charge, and Saurfang holds deep anger."

Vol'jin shrugged. "They be orcs, and orcs of honor, all of them. It's *that* one who makes me think twice. Ain't nobody knows more of hate than the Dark Lady. And she like her hate dished out icy cold."

Baine regarded Sylvanas, who stood proud and alone. Most leaders had brought other prominent members of their races with them; he himself stood with Kador Cloudsong, the shaman who had been such a comfort to him during dark times, and Perith Stormhoof, his most trusted Longwalker. Sylvanas was hardly ever glimpsed without her Val'kyr, those undead beings who once served Arthas and now served—and had saved—her. But it seemed for this event at least, Sylvanas scorned company, as if her own powerful, raging presence was more than enough to see Garrosh dead without anyone else's assistance or permission.

His eyes flitted across the arena to where the Alliance representatives were gathered. Young Anduin and Lady Jaina, with whom he had once sat and—the memory made him smile sadly—shared a cup of tea. There was one beside her who looked eerily familiar, although she was a living, breathing high elf. This must be Vereesa Windrunner—sister to Sylvanas and the missing Alleria.

Wounds were being ripped open everywhere today, it would seem. But even as Baine wished for the celestials to come and deliver their announcement, the fur along his arms lifted, and his heart felt suddenly, strangely lighter.

Four shapes appeared in the doorway, silhouetted against the light. As they strode into the arena, Baine realized that though his heart and spirit recognized these beings as the August Celestials, to his eyes they had utterly changed. He had always before beheld them in the guise of animals, but it seemed that today, they had chosen to adopt different incarnations.

Chi-Ji, the Red Crane, bringer of hope, had assumed the appearance of a slender, thin-boned blood elf. His long hair was a shade of fiery red, and what Baine had taken for a golden cape proved to be folded wings. Xuen, the White Tiger, whose temple this was, embodied controlled strength in the fluid movement of his pale blue human body, his hair and skin streaked with black and white stripes. Baine was honored to see that the indomitable Black Ox, Niuzao, had chosen to appear to mortal eyes as a tauren. He moved his white head as he surveyed the visitors with radiant blue eyes, every clop of his glowing hooves seeming to echo. The wise Jade Serpent, Yu'lon, had taken what initially struck Baine as the most peculiar incarnation of all—that of a pandaren cub. Even as he thought this, Yu'lon's magenta eyes found his, and she smiled. It was true wisdom, he realized, to appear so gentle and appealing that all would want to come to her.

The four celestials made their way to the north, where Xuen normally sat holding audience. Baine felt calmness and clarity that had been missing descend upon him. He exhaled, closing his eyes briefly in gratitude simply for their presence.

Everyone was still, waiting eagerly for word.

But the celestials did not speak. Instead, they turned to look expectantly at a figure that had just entered the temple.

He wore dark leather armor, and an image of a snarling white tiger adorned his right shoulder. A wide hat and a red cloth across the lower part of his face would have concealed his identity had not everyone present known whom to expect. Taran Zhu, leader of the Shado-pan monks, bowed awkwardly, grimacing slightly, and approached the center circle with a supple stride that belied his age

and his rotundity. He bowed again, once to each of the mighty, silent beings, then regarded those gathered.

"Welcome," he said. "Today, I speak for the celestials, and I say to
you, we receive you with grateful and humble hearts. I would ask
you all to take a moment and acknowledge this sight, never before
seen in this world. All those who serve as leaders in the Horde, and
all those who speak for the peoples of the Alliance, are gathered here
today. No one among you carries a weapon, and I have instructed
that a dampening field be put in place to prevent any untoward use
of magic—even the summoning of what you call the Light. All of
you are here for a united purpose, just as you have joined together
for greater purposes before. Please—for a few breaths, look at your
dear friends, and your honorable enemies."

Baine looked first to Anduin, a face he knew would not be twisted
in hate. His eyes moved to the stern visages of the dwarves, the furry
mien of Genn Greymane. Vereesa looked as if she was clenching her
teeth as well as her small, strong fists, and he wondered if Jaina knew
how easily her own unhappiness and resentment could be seen. As
the minute of reflection stretched on, Baine saw some tense features
relax; others seemed to grow more impatient. On both sides.

Taran Zhu continued. "Below us, in a prison well guarded, resides
the one whose fate you have come here to learn: Garrosh Hellscream."

Baine swallowed, straining for the words. He could feel the tension in the air, smell the anger and fear and anxiety. But the placid
monk would not be rushed.

"You were told that Garrosh Hellscream's fate would be decided
today. This is completely true. The celestials do not lie. But neither have they revealed everything to you. After much discussion
and meditation, they have come to the conclusion that Hellscream
should not be tried solely by them. All have suffered because of
Hellscream, not just Pandaria, although its people suffered indeed."
He placed his paw on his midsection, where Gorehowl had bitten
deeply not long ago. "Therefore, you deserve to be involved. His

guilt is beyond question, but we will hold a fair and open trial to determine his fate, one that both Horde and Alliance will conduct, with the possibility of a reduced sentence—perhaps even liberty."

Uproar.

Baine couldn't decide who was shouting more loudly, the Horde or the Alliance.

"Trial? He bragged about what he had done!"

"He deserves death! He has brought it to so many!"

"Let's put *all* the Horde on trial!"

"We know what he's done! The whole world knows it!"

Xuen's eyes narrowed slightly and his voice rang out, bell pure and sword sharp. *"There will be silence in my temple!"*

He was obeyed. Satisfied, he nodded to Zhu to continue.

"The August Celestials do not disagree that Garrosh Hellscream is guilty of terrible, grievous acts. I repeat—that he committed crimes is not in dispute. What must be decided now, however, is the manner in which these crimes are to be addressed. It is not *that* he must be accountable. It is *how*. And the only way to do this is through a trial. In this way, you, Horde and Alliance both, and any other voices who have aught to say will have a chance to be heard."

"And yet the celestials will still be judge, jury, and executioner, will they not?" This came from Lor'themar Theron. Baine had no doubt that the blood elf's ability to "work together" had been tested to the limit.

"No, friend Lor'themar," said Taran Zhu. "The celestials have indeed offered to be the jury, but are amenable to other ideas. I would be honored to serve as fa'shua—as judge. The celestials are wise beings, and wish true justice, and I have come to know many of you who stand before me now. Duly elected representatives from the Alliance and the Horde shall serve as Accuser and Defender, according to ancient Pandaren law."

"He is already guilty—you said so yourself," said Vereesa. "How can there be a Defender and an Accuser then?"

"The Defender will argue for a more merciful sentence. The Accuser, of course, will argue for a more stringent one. You may select whom you will, and the other side has one veto."

"I personally veto these entire proceedings!" snapped Genn Greymane. "Garrosh Hellscream led the Horde against our people and slaughtered them like a butcher. If we agree to have a trial, let's have a real one, for every leader in the Horde. At best, they stood by and let it happen; at worst, they joined in or"—and here he shot Sylvanas a venomous look—"even instigated their own attacks!" A chorus of angry agreement arose. Baine was sorry to see that Jaina appeared to be among the dissent.

"That would take quite awhile," said Taran Zhu calmly, "and not all of us have long lives."

"The Alliance," spat Gallywix, "shouldn't be involved at *all*. Garrosh should be tried by his peers, to ensure he makes proper compensation to those of us he wronged."

Mekkatorque laughed without humor. "Monetary compensation, you mean!"

"That would be an acceptable form, yes," said Gallywix.

Taran Zhu sighed and raised his paws for silence. "The leaders of the Horde and Alliance must decide. Are the terms as I have presented them agreeable to you, Warchief Vol'jin, and you, King Varian Wrynn?"

Troll and human regarded one another for a moment; then Vol'jin nodded. "Celestials seem to have a better view on things like this than us who be down in the middle of it, and you be honorable, Taran Zhu. I prefer to be getting a voice and not having a decision just handed out. Horde agrees."

"So does the Alliance," said Varian at once.

"You will be taken to a place where you may choose your Defender and Accuser," replied Taran Zhu. "Remember—one veto only for each side. Choose wisely and well."

Ji Firepaw, who had been standing off to the side, now approached

Vol'jin and bowed deeply. "I will take you to one of the side temples, where there will be braziers." His broad, furred face split in a grin and his eyes twinkled. "And refreshment."

The pandaren was as good as his word. Fifteen minutes later, Vol'jin, Go'el, Aggra, Baine, Eitrigg, Varok Saurfang, Sylvanas, Lor'themar Theron, and Jastor Gallywix sat on a carpet that, while not ornate, insulated them from the chill of the stone. Meat and drink were provided, and the promised braziers warmed the air.

Vol'jin nodded at the food. "Talk be wiser when bellies be full," he said. The food was consumed, and of course, this being Pandaria, there was plenty of beer to wash it down with. Once everyone was settled, Vol'jin wasted no time getting down to business.

"My orc brothers and sister, you know how much I be respecting you. But I think if we want to have Garrosh defended by an orc, we be making sure the Alliance gonna veto us."

Go'el nodded. "It is deeply regrettable that Garrosh has fallen so far that he has brought a whole race with him in the eyes of others. Nothing an orc Defender can say would be taken seriously, for good or ill."

Baine disagreed. "On the contrary: I believe it might be good for everyone to see an orc behaving with honor during so public an event. Eitrigg is known for his calm manner and wise head."

But the old orc was shaking that wise head even before Baine had finished speaking. "Your words mean much to me, High Chieftain, but Go'el is right. I, and he, and Saurfang will have our chance to speak if we wish. Taran Zhu has promised us, and I believe him."

"I will defend Garrosh," said Sylvanas. "It is well known that he and I disagreed. The Alliance could never accuse me of going soft."

"You be a great Accuser for Garrosh, that much be true," Vol'jin said. "But we be looking for a *Defender*."

"Come now, Warchief," Sylvanas said. "No one here wants to see Garrosh leave this place for any destination other than the executioner's block! You know this! You yourself once said—"

"I know what I once said better than you, Sylvanas," Vol'jin said, his voice a low warning. "And you were not the one being left for dead with a slashed throat. I know what all of us here suffered under his rule. But I also know that the celestials be looking for as close to a fair trial as mortal beings can give. I think there be only one proper choice for the job. Someone respected by both the Horde and the Alliance, who has no love for Garrosh but who never gonna lie, or do any less than his best."

He turned to Baine.

For a blissful second, Baine simply thought that the troll was turning to him for his opinion. And then he understood.

"*Me?*" he bellowed. "By the Earth Mother, Garrosh slew my *father!*"

"You make the warchief's point for him," said Lor'themar. "Despite the wrongs Garrosh has done you personally, you were loyal to the Horde until such time as you believed he was harming it too. The Alliance has plenty of spies, and you have a good history with the lady Proudmoore."

Baine turned to Go'el, his large eyes pleading with the orc to intervene. Instead, Go'el smiled. "The tauren have always been the heart of the Horde. If anyone can defend Garrosh and be listened to, it will be you, my friend."

"I don't want to defend him—I want what you want," Baine snapped. "Garrosh has earned death a hundred times over."

"Make them listen," came a voice that had hitherto been quiet. It was deep, strong despite age, and a sharp thread of pain ran through it. "There is no challenge in flinging a list of atrocities at Garrosh's head," said Saurfang. "The test will be who can make the judge and jury truly listen. To hear you speak for calm consideration when all know how you suffer—only you can do that, Baine Bloodhoof."

"I am a warrior, not a priest! I do not fill my mouth with soft, pleasing words or play on heartstrings."

"Garrosh is a warrior too," Go'el said. "For good or ill, you are as close to a fair representative as we can muster."

Baine champed his teeth and turned to Vol'jin. "If I could be loyal to the Horde and my warchief when that title was held by Garrosh, I can certainly be loyal to you, who have always been worthy, Vol'jin."

"I be not ordering you," Vol'jin said, placing his hand on the tauren's shoulder. "You need to follow your heart on this."

Things were not turning out the way Sylvanas Windrunner had desired. Not in the slightest.

First, she had hoped—as every member of the Horde, even softhearted Go'el, obviously did—that they had been called here to decide which of them would perform the coveted task of slaying Garrosh. Preferably slowly, and while inflicting a great deal of pain. Varian Wrynn had already averted that pleasant outcome for too long, and to hear that the celestials wanted an all-out *trial* was ludicrous. Even they and Taran Zhu admitted that Garrosh was guilty. The very notion of "justice" and "not acting out of revenge" was far too nauseating to be worth the time and effort expended. Sylvanas reflected that the only saving grace was the hope that she might at least be able to speak and add her truth to the sky-high mound of evidence of Garrosh's shortcomings. She was also pleased that Taran Zhu was the pandaren chosen as fa'shua. He was, she mused, probably the only pandaren who would accept a death penalty; most of the others she had observed would have simply bundled off Garrosh and poured beer down his throat till the orc drunkenly sobbed that he was sorry.

She did not expect to be chosen as the Defender, and knew that Vol'jin was right to say that she would make a better Accuser, if nothing else.

But Baine?

The most placid "warrior" she had ever seen, bred from a race of gentle people?

Madness, all of it. Baine had more of a reason than even she to wish Garrosh dead. The orc should have been Baine's own personal Arthas, and yet she knew the tauren would, if he accepted, probably argue so well that everyone would want to give Garrosh flowers instead.

Baine's ears drooped as he sighed heavily. "I will undertake this task," he said, "though I have utterly no idea how to achieve it."

Sylvanas had to exert a conscious effort to keep her lip from curling in a sneer.

Ji poked his head in. "The Alliance has chosen their Accuser. If you are ready as well, we can reconvene in the arena."

They followed him back up the snow-dusted trail. The Alliance representatives were already there, and turned to regard their Horde counterparts. Taran Zhu waited until everyone had arrived, then addressed the two groups. "Each of you has made your decision. Warchief Vol'jin, whom have you selected to defend Garrosh Hellscream?"

Defend Garrosh Hellscream. The very words were an offense.

"We choose High Chieftain Baine Bloodhoof of the tauren people," Vol'jin said.

"Alliance? Do you have any objection?"

Varian turned his dark head to look at his fellows. No one spoke; indeed, as Vol'jin had predicted, many of the Alliance seemed pleased. To Sylvanas's disbelief, Varian's spawn even had a small smile.

"The Alliance accepts the choice of Baine Bloodhoof, who is known to be honorable," Varian announced.

Taran Zhu nodded once. "King Varian, whom does the Alliance put forth to serve as Accuser of Garrosh Hellscream?"

"I will serve in this capacity," Varian replied.

"Absolutely not!" Sylvanas retorted. "You are done ordering us about!" She was not alone; other angry voices were raised in protest, and Taran Zhu had to shout to be heard over them.

"Peace, peace!" Despite the literal meaning of the word, his voice was commanding, and the cries subsided to mutterings and then dwindled. "Warchief Vol'jin, do you exercise your right to reject King Varian as Accuser?"

Varian had few friends among the Horde. Many distrusted his apparent personality change, and even his refusal to occupy Orgrimmar had won him only grudging acknowledgment. Humans were the enemy, would *always* be the enemy, and Sylvanas could see that the Horde's displeasure with the trial in the first place would only become the sourer if they had to watch Varian speak as Accuser. It seemed as though Vol'jin saw this, too.

"Yes, Lord Taran Zhu. We gonna exercise our right to veto," he said.

Oddly, the Alliance didn't try to argue them out of it. Sylvanas was on alert at this reaction, and her mind seized upon the truth of the calculated trick even as the name of the Accuser was announced.

"Then our selection as Accuser will be High Priestess Tyrande Whisperwind," Varian said smoothly.

Tyrande Whisperwind. Of all the races, even humans, the night elves hated the orcs the most. Rightly so, given their love of nature and the orcs' desire for building and war materiel. Sylvanas was initially outraged, then found herself wondering for a moment if this really was as bad a choice as it seemed. Most of the Horde would have preferred to accuse Garrosh rather than defend him, as Baine's reluctance had demonstrated.

But as Tyrande's glowing eyes swept over the Horde, Sylvanas saw no empathy for their plight. Tyrande was a priestess, but she had also fought her share of battles.

Taran Zhu continued to speak, describing how Pandaren law dictated the trial's points of order and in what manner they would unfold, but the Banshee Queen turned a deaf ear to him.

"Well played, Alliance," she murmured in her once-native language.

"They only fronted Varian, knowing we would veto him, so they could get someone even more determined in his place, in case any of us had lingering affection in our hearts for Garrosh," came an answering voice in the same tongue. "I do not think they quite understand that we hate him as much as they do."

Sylvanas looked over at Lor'themar, lifting an eyebrow. The sin'dorei leader had always been polite but coldly resentful whenever Sylvanas had approached him to forge unity, keeping his precious dignity even when coerced. Did this conversation in Thalassian signal a shift? Was he perhaps smarting from being overlooked for leadership of the Horde?

"She has no love for Garrosh," Sylvanas continued.

"She has no love for the Horde, either," countered Lor'themar. "I wonder if Vol'jin will regret not taking Varian when we had the chance. I suppose we must wait, and watch."

"As we ever do," said Sylvanas, curious as to how he would respond to the implied partnership. He did not seem to hear it, instead bowing to someone on the Alliance side as the various representatives filed out. Sylvanas turned to see who it was.

Of course—Vereesa and Lor'themar had encountered one another recently. Her sister's courtesy toward the blood elf leader surprised Sylvanas. She was even more surprised when, after acknowledging Lor'themar, Vereesa deliberately met Sylvanas's eyes for a long moment before turning away.

It was the first time the Windrunner sisters—two of them, anyway—had seen one another in years. It would naturally be somewhat emotional to Vereesa to see Sylvanas again. But there was neither bitterness nor sorrow in Vereesa's face.

There was only grim resolve and a peculiar sort of . . . satisfaction? And Sylvanas had no idea why.

3

B aine's chest loosened as he set hoof once again on good Mulgore soil—he had felt constricted the entire time he was in Pandaria. He took a deep breath of the clean, fragrant night air and sighed it out.

The shaman Kador Cloudsong was waiting for him. "It is good to have you home," Cloudsong rumbled, bowing deeply.

"It is good to *be* home, even for so brief a time—and for so somber a task," Baine answered.

"The dead are always with us," Cloudsong intoned. "We may grieve that we do not have the joy of their physical presence, but their songs are in the wind, and their laughter in the water."

"Would that they could speak to us and give us advice, as they once did." The thought made Baine's chest ache again, and he debated the wisdom of deliberately reopening this old wound. But he trusted that Cloudsong would have dissuaded him had the shaman believed his request unwise.

"They do speak, Baine Bloodhoof, though not in ways that we are used to hearing."

Baine nodded. His father, Cairne, indeed, was always with him. Baine and Cloudsong were together at Red Rocks, the ancient site where fallen heroes of the tauren were sent to the Earth Mother and Sky Father via cleansing flame. Set a slight distance away from

Thunder Bluff, Red Rocks was aptly named, a naturally occurring formation of red sandstone. It was a peaceful and reflective site, where one could step out of the world of Thunder Bluff into a place that served as a transition between that world and the next. Baine had not been here since he had said farewell to Cairne. Now, as then, Cloud-song was beside him, although this time it was just the two of them. Looking due west, Baine could see Thunder Bluff in the distance, silhouetted against the star-crowded sky, its bonfires and torches little stars all on their own. A small fire burned in the direction of the east here on Red Rocks as well, adding warmth and a comforting glow.

Fire. He turned back and looked at the pyre platforms, empty now of bodies awaiting ritual burning. Only ashes would remain, and even these would be taken by the singing winds and scattered to the four directions. Even though they had a lasting home now in Thunder Bluff, the tauren chose not to bury their dead. Their death ritual bespoke their origins as nomads, and if their beloved ones were freed to the wind and fire, they could wander in death as in life if they chose.

"Did you have sufficient time for preparation?" he asked Cloud-song.

"I did." The shaman nodded. "It is not an overly complex rite." Baine was not surprised. The tauren were a simple people, and had no need of elaborate words or strange, difficult-to-obtain items in their ceremonies. What the good earth provided was almost always sufficient. "Are you ready, my high chieftain?"

Baine gave a pained chuckle. "No. But let us begin, even so."

Clad in leather made from the hides of beasts he himself had slain, Cloudsong began to stamp his hooves in a slow, steady rhythm as he lifted his muzzle to the eastern sky.

"Hail to the spirits of air! Breeze and wind and storm, all these you are, and more. Tonight, we ask you to join this our rite, and whisper wisdom from the great Cairne Bloodhoof into the waiting ears of his son, Baine."

It had been a still evening, but now Baine's fur was ruffled by a gentle zephyr. He pricked his ears, but all he heard was a soft murmur, at least for the present. Cloudsong reached into his shaman's pouch and withdrew a handful of gray dust. This he scattered on the ground as he walked, forming a curved line to link east and south. Normally the material so utilized would be corn pollen. But that was for ceremonies that involved life. This ritual was of the dead, and therefore the gray dust was composed of the ashes of those who had been sent to the spirits on this site.

"Hail to the spirits of fire!" Cloudsong faced a little blaze, lifting his staff to honor it. "Glowing ember and flame and inferno, all these you are and more. Tonight we ask you to join this, our rite, and warm Baine Bloodhoof with the strong courage of Cairne Bloodhoof, his beloved father."

The flame shot up high for a moment, and Baine felt fierce heat from the wall of fire. Having made its presence known, the fire subsided to its more temperate state, crackling as it burned gently.

Now Cloudsong turned to the west, invoking the spirits of "raindrop, river, and tempest" and asking them to bathe the tauren high chieftain in memories of his father's love. Baine's heart thumped painfully for a moment, and he thought, *Tears are made of water too.*

The spirits of earth were made welcome next—soil and stone and mountain, the very bones of the honored dead. Cloudsong asked that Baine be able to draw comfort from the solid land of his people, to which Cairne had brought them all. Here Cloudsong closed the sacred circle, outlined with the gray ash. Baine felt the energy shift within the space, thrumming with power. It reminded him of the sensation he experienced when a storm was coming, but this also felt unusually calm.

"Welcome, Spirit of Life," called Cloudsong. "You are in our breath with air, our blood with fire, our bones with earth, our tears with water. We know that death is merely the shadow of life, and that the ending of things is as natural as the birth of them. We ask that you join this, our rite, and invite one who walks in your shadow to be with us this night."

They stood in silence in the center for a moment, their breathing rhythmic and steady. After a time, Cloudsong nodded and invited Baine to sit at the core of the empty pyres, facing Thunder Bluff. Baine did so, continuing to breathe deeply and stilling his galloping thoughts. Cloudsong handed him a clay goblet, filled with a dark liquid that reflected the starlight.

"This will grant a vision, if the Earth Mother wills it so. Drink." Baine raised the goblet to his mouth and tasted the not-unpleasant flavors of silverleaf, briarthorn, earthroot, and something else he could not identify. He returned the goblet to the shaman. "Do not drowse, Baine Bloodhoof, but rather look upon this land with soft eyes," Cloudsong urged. Baine obliged, letting tension leave his body and his eyes unfocus.

He heard the soft, regular *thump-thump* of a hide-skin drum, emulating the sound of a tauren heart. He did not know how long he sat and listened to Cloudsong, only that he was deeply relaxed, and felt peace within his heart as it beat time to the drum.

Then, gently, he was made aware of a presence. Cairne Bloodhoof smiled down upon his son.

This was a Cairne that Baine had never known—the mighty bull in his prime, his eyes sharp and keen. He held his runespear; it was whole again, as was he. Cairne's massive chest rippled with muscle as he lifted the spear in salute.

"Father," breathed Baine.

"My son," Cairne said, his eyes crinkling in affection. "To walk between your world and mine is difficult, and my time brief, but I knew I had to come when your heart is so troubled."

All the pain that Baine had buried deep inside, that he could not express, could not even permit himself to feel lest it interfere with his duties to the tauren people he led, came pouring out like a flash flood.

"Father . . . Garrosh killed you! He denied you the right to die with honor! He stood by while the Grimtotem and I fought like— like beasts in a pit, while he awaited the victor! He violated the land, lied to his own people, and Theramore . . ."

Tears ran down Baine's muzzle, tears of grief and anger, and for a moment he could not speak. The twin emotions choked him.

"And now, you have been asked to defend him," replied Cairne. "When all you wish is to put your hoof on his throat."

Baine nodded. "Yes. You spoke out against him before anyone else had the courage. Father . . . should I have done so? Could I have stopped him? Is . . . is all the blood he has spilled upon my hands too?"

He was surprised by the question, but the words came of their own volition. Cairne smiled gently.

"The past is past, my son. Borne away, like blossoms in the wind. Garrosh's choices are his alone, as is the responsibility for his actions. Always, you follow your heart, and always, you have made me proud."

And at that moment, Baine knew the answer Cairne was about to give him. "You . . . think I should do this thing," he whispered. "Defend Garrosh Hellscream."

"What I think does not matter. You must do what you feel is right. As you have ever done. What was right for me, at that time, was to challenge Garrosh. What was right for you, at other times, was to support him as leader of the Horde."

"Varian should have let Go'el slay him," growled Baine.

"But he did not, and so we are here," said the young-old bull placidly. "Answer this, and you will know what to do. If it grieves you that I was slain by treachery, can *you* then do anything but strive for perfect truth and integrity, even—perhaps especially—when it does not come easily? Can you not do your utmost to honor this role that has been given you? Dear son of my blood and my heart, I believe you knew the answer before ever you came."

Baine did. But the knowing pained him.

"I will take up this burden," he murmured, "and I will defend Garrosh to the best of my ability."

"You could do no less and still be you. You will be glad of it, when it is all over. No, no," he said, lifting his hands in protest when Baine tried to speak. "I cannot tell you what the outcome will be. But I promise—your heart will be at peace."

Cairne's image began to fade. Baine realized this, stricken that he had wasted this precious opportunity complaining like a mere youngling when his father . . . his *father* . . . !

"No!" he cried, standing, his voice cracking with emotion. "Father—please, do not go, not yet, please not just yet—!"

There were so many things Baine wanted to say. How terribly much he missed Cairne. How hard he strove to honor his father's memory. That these few moments meant the world to him. Too late, he reached out imploringly, but his father walked in the shadow of life, not the sun of it, and Baine's grasping hands closed only on empty air.

Cairne's eyes grew sad, and he too reached out, only to vanish in the next breath.

Cloudsong caught Baine as he fell.

"Did you find the answers you sought, High Chieftain?" asked Cloudsong as he handed Baine a goblet filled with cool, clear water. Baine sipped, and his head began to resolve.

"The answers I sought? No. But I did get the answers I needed," he said, smiling sadly at his friend. Cloudsong nodded his understanding. The not-silence of the night, the song of crickets and the sigh of the breeze, was broken by a familiar hum as whirls of bright color took shape.

"Who dares interrupt a ritual?" growled Cloudsong. "The circle has not yet been released!" Baine got to his hooves while the shaman strode over to the opening portal. A slender high elf stepped through. He looked fairly typical of the race, with sharp, elegant features, long, flowing golden hair, and a decoratively trimmed tuft of beard gracing his chin. He beckoned urgently to Baine.

"High Chieftain, my name is Kairozdormu. Taran Zhu has sent me to escort you to the Temple of the White Tiger. Please, you must come with me."

"You are interrupting a sacred ceremony—" Cloudsong began.

The elf gave him an irritated glance. "I'm terribly sorry to be disrespectful, but we really must hurry!"

Baine's eyes fell to the tabard the elf wore. Brown with gold trim, it had an insignia in the center of the chest: a golden circle inlaid with the symbol of infinity. It was the tabard worn by Timewalkers, and Baine decided to hazard a guess. "I did not know your flight continued to wear this," he said. "I thought your power over time—"

Kairozdormu waved a long-fingered, impatient hand. "The story is long, and the time is short."

"Amusing phrase, coming from you. Is there some dire timeways catastrophe afoot?"

"Much more prosaic a reason—this portal won't stay open forever." He suddenly chuckled. "Well," he amended, flashing white teeth in a wry grin, "theoretically it can, but that's neither here nor there in this *particular* moment. High Chieftain Baine, if you please?"

Baine turned to Cloudsong. "I thank you for everything, Kador. But duty calls."

"In an elven accent, it seems," said Cloudsong, but bowed nevertheless. "Go, High Chieftain, with, I am certain, your father's blessing."

The meal was light and simple: pine nut bread, Darnassian bleu cheese, and fresh lunar pears, all washed down with moonberry juice. Here in the temple of her beloved Elune, Tyrande told Archdruid Malfurion Stormrage of the events that had occurred earlier in the Temple of the White Tiger.

She had been pleased to learn that Taran Zhu had appointed a mage for the purpose of portaling those involved in the trial. Yu Fei was a sweet-faced pandaren whose silken robe was crafted with the hues of water, which matched the single unruly lock of hair that demurely hid one blue eye.

"Chu'shao Whisperwind," Yu Fei had said, using the Pandaren term for "counselor" and bowing deeply as she introduced herself, "I am honored to send you home until your duties require you here. Do not hesitate to call upon me if you need my assistance."

"Love, are you certain you wish to undertake this task?" asked the archdruid. Feathers that now grew from his arms, reminders of millennia spent in the Emerald Dream, brushed the tabletop as he poured her a second cup of moonberry juice. Tyrande realized she had grown used to the changes that had affected Malfurion during his long slumber: the feathers, the feet that now were more like a nightsaber's than an elf's, the length and thickness of his great green beard. No outward appearance could change the beauty of his inner heart to her, though. He was, and would ever be, her beloved.

Malfurion continued, "You do not know how long the trial will take, or indeed, where it will take *you*."

Tyrande sipped the drink, cool and sweet as the forests at night. "The eyes of the world will be on this trial, my heart. And," she remarked, smiling, "you are more than capable of taking care of anything that should arise in my absence. I will be able to return home every night to be with you, which is a blessing from Elune herself. As for where it will take me"—here her voice hardened slightly—"it is likely I will have to do very little, save present the evidence. Garrosh has had few who have loved him these many moons past, fewer still now that his brutal rampage has been stopped."

His face was somber as he searched her eyes. "I did not ask how you would fare in the trial, but rather, what it would do to you."

Tyrande was surprised and slightly perplexed. "What do you mean?"

"You are a high priestess, devoted to Elune, who champions

enlightenment and healing. And when need be, you are fierce in battle. But you will be working with words, which are slippery and fickle things, not your beautiful heart. And you will be inciting hatred and a desire to condemn, not enlightenment."

"In the end, the facts that I present will provide enlightenment and understanding, and condemning Garrosh appropriately will eventually bring healing," she said. He still looked troubled and opened his mouth to reply, but before he could speak further, a female voice came from outside the pavilion where Tyrande and her mate were taking their meal.

"My lady?"

"You may enter, Cordressa."

A slender hand lifted the gauzy flap, and the Sentinel poked her midnight-blue head in. "You have a visitor. She says she has come on trial business, and the matter is urgent."

Malfurion raised an eyebrow in query, and Tyrande shook her head, as surprised as he. "Of course, Cordressa. Show her in."

The Sentinel stepped back, holding the pavilion flap, and indicated that the mysterious visitor could enter.

The guest was a gnome with silver hair rolled up in twin buns on either side of her slightly freckled face. Wide green eyes sparkled with pleasure as she greeted Tyrande and Malfurion.

"Archdruid, High Priestess—so nice to see you both again! Terribly sorry to bother you, Chu'shao, but I fear it's quite important."

Chu'shao. Of course, that was another title Tyrande now bore, for at least a time. "Certainly, Chromie." Tyrande smiled, sinking gracefully into a kneeling position before the bronze dragon Chronormu so they might look eye to eye. At the mention of the dragon's name, the Sentinel quietly dropped the pavilion flap to give them privacy. "How may I help?"

"The celestials have something they'd like both you and Chu'shao Bloodhoof to utilize as you present your cases. It's easier just to show you. Would you mind coming with me, please?"

4

Upon his arrival at the Temple of the White Tiger, Baine bowed to Yu Fei, thanked her for portaling him there, and turned to the leader of the Shado-pan.

"Greetings, Lord Taran Zhu. Kairozdormu has brought me as you requested."

Baine glanced about as he spoke. The Temple of the White Tiger seemed even more cavernous at night. Moonlight and lamps provided some illumination, but even so, the upper seats were shrouded in shadow. Baine noticed that furnishings appropriate for the trial had been brought in. There were three areas—one for him and Garrosh, one for Tyrande, and one for the fa'shua and witnesses. The Accuser and Defender sections were identical, with rectangular tables, covered by a crimson and gold cloth, and simple chairs. One section was set up in the circle located in the west; the other, with two chairs, in the east. Baine assumed this side was for him and Garrosh. The tables had empty pitchers and glasses, along with ink, quills, and parchment neatly arranged, presumably for note taking.

Taran Zhu, however, would be seated on an elevated dais in a chair that was more ornate than the others, but nowhere near as lavish as the throne high in the north part of the spectator area. Beside the chair were a small gong and mallet. On the floor in front of

Taran Zhu's seat and slightly to the left was the witness chair, with a little table where an empty pitcher and glass now sat.

This much Baine had been told to expect. But there was another set of tables and chairs, placed to the side and slightly behind Taran Zhu's chair, which bore an item draped with a black cloth.

"May I ask what that is?"

"It is the reason why I have asked you here at this hour," said Taran Zhu, providing a perfectly fine explanation while providing none at all. He forestalled Baine's next question by holding up a paw. "When Chu'shao Whisperwind has arrived, all will be revealed. Patience."

"I was pulled away from a ritual ceremony on the grounds that time was of the essence. I'm certain you can appreciate that, right now, I have little interest in patience," Baine replied.

Taran Zhu gave the bronze dragon standing beside Baine a reproachful glance. "Yu Fei could have reopened the portal a few moments later, Kairozdormu. She would not have minded. I know you are not as familiar as your Alliance counterpart with the ways of the younger races, but you must learn to respect them."

Kairozdormu looked discomfited. "I am sorry. You are correct. She has the advantage over me. I trust Chu'shao Bloodhoof will accept my apologies and help me to know better the tauren ways."

Baine was only slightly mollified. The dragon hadn't interrupted the key part of the ceremony, but the elements also did not abide not being properly thanked for their presence. He decided to let it go and focus instead on something else Taran Zhu had said. "Alliance counterpart . . . ?"

"As Kairozdormu is here to work with you, so another bronze dragon will be advising the Accuser. They will arrive shortly."

Baine looked again at the mysterious covered object, at the now-empty seats that would soon be crowded with onlookers. When his gaze fell upon the table and two chairs in the Defender's area of the arena, despite what he told his father he snorted at the thought of not only having to defend Garrosh, but being forced to sit next to the orc every day during the trial.

"Something troubling you?" Kairozdormu lounged in what would be Baine's chair, his hands clasped behind his golden head, and looked at the tauren quizzically.

"Many things trouble me, Kairozdormu, but you cannot do anything about them," Baine answered.

"Don't be too sure about that. And call me Kairoz, please."

Two figures—one tall, one short—now entered the arena. Tyrande Whisperwind inclined her head gracefully. "Good evening, Chu'shao Bloodhoof. Lord Taran Zhu, I hope we have not kept you waiting long."

The gnome accompanying her turned to Baine. "Hello, High Chieftain. It's good to see you again!" She gave him a quick smile and went to speak with Kairoz.

"High Priestess Tyrande, High Chieftain Baine," said Taran Zhu, "thank you both for coming. I will get right to the point. More important than what happens to Garrosh is the necessity of having a trial that all agree was fair and just. Otherwise, the risk is run of either Garrosh becoming a martyr, and having many of the Horde fight to hold aloft the beacon they believe he has dropped to them, or a public perception of too much leniency, in which case the rift between Horde and Alliance will only be widened."

"My task is an easy one, Lord Zhu," the night elven high priestess said in her musical voice. "I am certain the evidence will speak for itself."

"And while all know I have no love for Garrosh, I would sooner die than dishonor a charge I have been given," Baine said, his voice deep with the beginnings of affront. What was Taran Zhu getting at?

"No disrespect is intended," Taran Zhu said. "Well do I know that neither of you would resort to trickery or deception. And yet, there would be rumors that such was the case."

"That is regrettable," Tyrande agreed, "but inevitable."

The bronze dragons exchanged smiles that were almost, but not quite, smirks. "In an ordinary trial, yes," said Kairozdormu. "But this is no ordinary trial. You are familiar with the Hourglass of Time?"

It was a rhetorical question. The Hourglass—enormous, beautiful, and able to reverse time itself—had been created by Nozdormu, the former Aspect of Time. Nozdormu had foreseen his own corruption and transformation into a being called Murozond, and had given those who would fight and defeat Murozond the use of the Hourglass to aid them in their battle.

Baine and Tyrande shared awkward glances. Word had reached them both that anyone attempting to assist Nozdormu had been confronted by dark, twisted echoes of themselves. It was not a comforting thought.

"We know of the Hourglass," said Baine curtly.

"Well, ever since Murozond's defeat, I have been . . . well . . ." Kairoz paused, groping for the word.

"Tinkering," said Chromie.

"Tinkering, yes," agreed Kairoz. "Magically. I've been exploring the Timeless Isle. Utilizing a few grains of the Sands of Time contained in the Hourglass, and combining them with ground particles of the epoch stones found on the isle, I have crafted an artifact I call the Vision of Time. It's quite a marvelous little thing, really, if I do say so myself. Its abilities are different from the Hourglass. It cannot turn back time as the Hourglass can, but Chromie and I can direct the Vision to provide a display of any single given point in time— any important moment—as it truly was. I've even been able to get some glimpses into the future."

"How?" asked Baine, glancing up uneasily at the still-cloaked item.

"It can create a precisely controlled rift in time."

"Do you not run the risk of changing history?" asked Tyrande.

"Not at all," said Kairoz. He looked proud of himself, and, Baine thought, rightfully so. "As I said, I have altered the intrinsic makeup of the Sands of Time we will be using. The Vision of Time won't actually *manifest* the events. Nothing will be here physically—only the sights and sounds will be able to come through the rift."

"Also, it only works one way," Chromie added. "There is absolutely *no* risk of changing anything."

"Let me show it to you," said Kairoz. He grasped a corner of the black cloth and, with a dramatic flourish, whipped it off.

The Vision of Time was an hourglass with two dragons crafted of metal—quite literally bronze dragons. Each twined around a globe. They circled nose to tail, and so exquisite was the craftsmanship that they appeared to be merely drowsing.

"The sand in the top globe is not falling," said Tyrande.

"It will commence doing so when Chromie or I activate the Vision," Kairoz said. "There's a finite amount of sand in the upper bulb. Each of you will be permitted a certain number of hours to use during the trial. You'll be able to choose which historical moments you wish to present as irrefutable evidence, and the duration of each display will count toward your total."

"In other words," said Tyrande, "there is no need for witnesses."

"I wouldn't go so far as to say that," Kairoz said. "You'll have to choose your moments wisely, and witnesses can help—or hurt—a case with more than simple facts. Chromie has been chosen to advise you, High Priestess, on the strategy of integrating them into your presentations, and I will be working with you, High Chieftain."

"So," Baine mused. "No lies, no exaggerations, no difficulties if a witness is unable to precisely recall an incident."

"The unvarnished, unaltered truth," Chromie agreed. "Over which there can be no debate."

"Oh, there certainly could be," Tyrande said. "Motive, inner thoughts, other plans—"

Chromie held up her hands. "Don't give your tactics away, High Priestess!" she urged.

"How will we know which moments to choose?" Baine asked. "Will we be able to see them ourselves before we show them to the court?"

"Of course," said Kairoz. "As for which ones to choose, that's why you have us. You tell me or Chromie what sort of point you wish to make, and we will assist you in locating the perfect moment."

"Why don't we retire to Darnassus and have a discussion about how best to use the Vision to support your position?" asked Chromie.

"You speak wisdom, Chromie. Lord Zhu, do you require anything further of me?" Tyrande asked.

"You are free to leave with your advisor, Accuser. As are you, Defender," Taran Zhu said. "Now, from this moment on, the two of you and I will not see one another, nor will we exchange any words, until the trial begins. Peace be with you, and may the wisdom of the celestials carry you both as you discharge your duties with honor and diligence."

He bowed deeply and held the pose for a moment, though it was clear the motion pained him physically, and Baine felt the respect and gratitude emanating from the monk.

Tyrande, too, bowed to them all, and left with Chromie. She still moved with her usual languid grace and power, but there was a subtle eagerness in her steps that betrayed her excitement.

"Well, *she* certainly seems pleased with my contribution," said Kairoz, standing beside Baine, looking after them.

"She is right to feel so," Baine replied.

"And you do not?"

Baine gave him a contemplative look. "All here tonight know well that the pure, unvarnished truth will not reflect positively on Garrosh. And as my duty is to defend him, whatever my personal opinions, this feels more like a gift to the Accuser than anything else."

"Come now," Kairoz replied, smiling. "Don't give up just yet. Even pure, unvarnished truth can be interpreted differently in certain lights. Your right to ask me to display particular interactions is not limited just to what *Garrosh* has done and said, you know."

"An interesting perspective . . . I must say, I am intrigued. Let us return to Thunder Bluff, you and I, and you will tell more on how I might make the best use of this Vision."

It shouldn't have felt like a celebration, and Jaina Proudmoore knew it. The eve before a trial where the verdict would surely render an execution, the ending of a life? No, of course it should never feel so.

But it certainly did.

She could tell others shared the sentiment, though no one seated at the table tonight would raise a toast to a death well deserved—at least, not openly. But postures were straighter than they might otherwise have been. Voices were lighter, and there was even laughter—something Jaina had almost forgotten. There was contentment in her heart that had not been there for some time, and she dared to hope that now—finally—the horrors of war were over, at least long enough for her to take a breath, mourn the dead, laugh with the living, and truly begin the gentler tasks of learning about being in a relationship with someone so different from her, yet so true.

The feeling of peace, so tentative for so long, grew in her as she looked at the faces around her, sharing this meal at Violet Rise. Kalec (of course), Varian and Anduin Wrynn, Vereesa Windrunner.

Even as she was grateful for their presence, she felt the absence of the fallen. Attuned to her, Kalec gently squeezed her hand.

"You miss them," he said softly, and she did not bother to deny it.

"I do," she said. "They should be here—Pained, and Kinndy, and Tervosh."

They had spoken quietly, but little escaped elven ears. "Yes, they should," said Vereesa. "They, and Rhonin, and so many others."

Anduin looked troubled at the hard tone of Vereesa's voice. "I feel certain that with the celestials as jury and Taran Zhu as judge, justice will be done."

"Yes," said Vereesa. "Baine was an odd choice to defend Garrosh, but one I have no quarrel with."

"Baine is honorable," Anduin said, "and there is no doubt in my mind he will endeavor to do the job to the best of his ability, despite how he feels personally."

"But I do not think it is a task he is relishing," said Kalec.

"True," said Varian. "As opposed to Tyrande's task, which I think everyone in the Alliance coveted."

"Except you," Jaina pointed out.

"I'd rather watch this play out," Varian replied. "If I simply wanted Garrosh dead, all I would have needed to do was stay silent while Go'el swung the Doomhammer."

Vereesa's lips thinned, but she said nothing. Jaina couldn't blame her; she herself had mixed feelings about Varian's intervention.

"You did the right thing, Father," said Anduin. "This will be a difficult trial, but who knows what good it may do in the long run? It will put an end to things more firmly than a simple execution— whatever is decided."

Would it? Jaina wondered. Would it put an end to her nightmares, to the sudden flaring of hurt in her heart when she remembered afresh not only that friends had died, but *how*? She thought of Kinndy, crumbling into a pile of violet dust as Jaina touched her. She realized she had been holding a fork so hard her knuckles had turned white, and her fingers ached as she deliberately placed down the utensil. She looked at the meal of roasted fowl, and macabre humor made her smile as she picked up a drumstick and regarded it.

"Wouldn't it be convenient if Garrosh choked on a bone at dinner tonight, and saved everyone a great deal of trouble?" she said, keeping her voice light. "I hear there is a lovely cake for dessert, if anyone's saved some room."

5

Day One

T he crowds—and the security for them—were unlike anything Jaina Proudmoore had ever seen. She was grateful for Varian's guards, who helped clear a path through the milling throng that swirled about the entrances and enabled Jaina, Kalec, Varian, Anduin, and Vereesa to reach their reserved seats.

All the leaders of each Horde race were likewise gathered, their colorful clothing and skins and generally raucous presence a sharp contrast to the almost stoic Alliance seated across from them. The August Celestials had wisely placed members of factions that had no allegiance to either Horde or Alliance in the middle seats, a physical buffer lest things become heated. Jaina was surprised to see in that section a certain elven-looking female, her red tresses crowned with thorns. Her face was lovely, yet etched with an expression of ethereal sorrow. Jaina's heart ached in sympathy.

"Alexstrasza," she said softly.

"I would she had not come," Kalec sighed, easing into a seat beside Jaina. "This can only be painful for her."

It seemed to Jaina that Alexstrasza, the great Life-Binder and former Dragon Aspect, would be above such things as trials and the younger races' method of justice. She had always behaved with dignity, courage, grace, and compassion, even when faced with inconceivable horrors and deep personal loss. Her sister, the green dragon Ysera, sat beside her, holding Alexstrasza's hand and looking about with a childlike air of curiosity and wonder.

"Alexstrasza needs to be here," said Jaina. "Not for the trial. For herself. Just like I do."

"Wrathion's here too," said Anduin. "I invited him to come, to watch, and listen, and make up his own mind as to what was the best for Azeroth. I'm glad he decided to do so."

Jaina followed Anduin's gaze, curious for her first look at the being who often went by the soubriquet of the Black Prince. Few knew of him; fewer still knew of his true identity.

"Well, then," said Jaina, keeping her voice soft for Anduin's ears only, "looks like all the flights are represented."

Wrathion was, as far as anyone knew, the only uncorrupted black dragon in existence.

Sired by Deathwing, he had escaped the vile touch of the Old Gods thanks to intervention while still in the shell. Although he had been fortunate in that respect, Jaina had to admit that his life had not been idyllic. The red dragonflight, under Alexstrasza's command, had sought a way to purify the black dragons. One red dragon, Rheastrasza, had resorted to extreme measures in an effort to fulfill that charge. Rheastrasza had kidnapped a female black dragon and forced her to lay eggs. With the cooperation of a gnome inventor, Rheastrasza had managed to purge a single egg of the madness that had tormented the entire flight. Deathwing had not been pleased and had destroyed the egg—or so he thought. Anticipating this, Rheastrasza had swapped the purified black dragon egg for another, sacrificing not only her own life but that of her unhatched child.

Wrathion, though still in the shell, had been fully sentient and keenly aware of what was transpiring, aware also that he would be raised and closely watched by the red dragonflight for perhaps his entire life. His "liberty" came when his egg was stolen by rogues, and he hatched and remained free of red dragon influence. How he had escaped his captors was a mystery, but here he was, alive and quite sane.

Anduin and Wrathion had met and become friends of a sort in Pandaria, though, as Anduin admitted, that friendship was mainly focused on how different their outlooks were. Wrathion's "age" was hard to define. If it was judged by actual years of life, then he was a toddler of two. But as he was a dragon, he was possessed of an innate intelligence and wisdom, and his appearance was that of a youth approximately Anduin's age.

Jaina had, throughout Anduin's life, often felt maternal toward him, and was uneasy about his new friend. On the one hand, Anduin had few equals his own age. On the other, Jaina had her concerns that Wrathion might be, as the phrase went, a "bad influence." Oddly enough, the reason wasn't that he was a black dragon. Before the horrors of his madness perverted him, Neltharion—better known as Deathwing—had been the Aspect of Earth, wise and protective. It was some of the things Anduin had reported Wrathion as saying that concerned her. She noticed that the Black Prince sat as far away from Alexstrasza as possible. Given his history, she couldn't blame him.

He looked largely human, though dramatic, with his darker skin and unusual outfit of baggy pants, tunic, and a turban. He was flanked on his left side by an orc female, whose face seemed set in a perpetual glower, and on his right by an equally menacing-looking human female. He gave Anduin a smile and turned his glowing eyes, the sole thing that indicated his true form, to Jaina. He inclined his head and graced her with a smile as well, but one that suggested he found something humorous. Jaina wondered what amused him.

Pandaren guards stood close by, still and patient as a serene mountain lake, but well able to explode into swift action in less than a heartbeat should it be required. If violence did erupt, it would be bare-handed; Jaina felt the presence of the magic-dampening field like an oppressive fog, and weapons were forbidden.

"This looks familiar," Varian murmured.

"What does?" Jaina inquired.

"That," he said, and Varian nodded at the seats starting to fill with spectators. "That's the same look I saw when I fought in the gladiator pits. They're thirsty for blood."

"They will not get it today," said Vereesa. She did not have to add, *But if there is justice, they will by the end of this trial.*

"They'd better not," said Varian. "Everything will be lost if this dissolves into chaos. Including far too many lives."

Jaina turned her attention to the floor. Baine and Tyrande were already present. Each sat in a chair at his or her respective table, waiting. That did not surprise Jaina. What did surprise her was that there were two others also awaiting the arrival of Taran Zhu, the celestials, and Garrosh. Jaina recognized Chromie, the extremely powerful bronze dragon who opted for the least threatening appearance possible, but did not know the handsome high elf to whom Chromie was speaking. Both wore the brown tabard of their order and sat beside a small table set off to one side, atop which perched a covered object.

Just as Jaina wondered why two bronzes were present—and apparently in an official capacity at that—a pandaren dressed from head to toe in long, formal robes entered. He carried a polearm that bore the standard of the Shado-pan. He slammed down the butt of the weapon three times, and the crowds quieted, settling into their seats.

"Respect for the rule of law is dear to the pandaren people. Law is the means by which wrongs can be righted, and by which balance can be restored. This is a historic occasion, as, for the first time in our long history, outsiders will be participating. In the search for righting the wrong, we traditionally name the one who is on trial, and the one or ones who seek justice. And so, with all solemnity, we open the judgment upon Garrosh Hellscream for wrongs against the people of Azeroth. Please stand to acknowledge the August Celestials, who will listen with open ears and hearts to the testimony presented here, and to show respect to he who will judge the lawfulness of the proceedings, lord of the Shado-pan, Taran Zhu."

Everyone obeyed, getting to their feet. Chi-Ji, Xuen, Niuzao, and Yu'lon entered the balcony, all seeming to move without effort. Their grace and beauty, as always, made Jaina's breath catch, even in these new forms. She had asked Aysa about it. The pandaren had told her that it was a gesture of respect to the Horde and Alliance. They were exquisite and unique, not just in their appearances, but in the energy that seemed to emanate from them. Taran Zhu might be more accessible, as he was a mortal being, but even he was imposing, and his posture bespoke controlled power and peace. He ascended into the fa'shua's chair and, picking up a small mallet, struck a gong three times, letting the echo subside before he spoke.

"You may be seated," he said, his clear, quiet voice carrying even in the enormous chamber. "Before the Accused appears, I will advise all present that I will tolerate no disturbance of this trial. Anyone who violates this rule will be held under guard until the trial's completion. Also, to suit the uniqueness of this situation, there will be a unique manner of presenting evidence."

He nodded to the two bronze dragons. They got to their feet and whisked away the concealing cloth, revealing an hourglass.

Jaina understood what they would be doing before they even began to speak. Their voices, explaining how this Vision of Time artifact would work, faded away, and a dull roaring sound filled her ears. For a moment, she couldn't breathe; for a moment, she was drowning again, just like when—

The pain of her hand being tightly gripped brought her back to the present. Breath came in, and she gasped quietly as it flooded her lungs. The roaring ceased, though Jaina could still hear her heart thudding, swift as a rabbit's. She turned to Kalec, who watched her keenly, concern on his beautiful face. She licked dry lips and nodded, mouthing *I'm all right.*

He looked uncertain, but relaxed his grip. Jaina took several slow, deep breaths. The bronze dragons had finished their explanation and stepped back.

Taran Zhu nodded to the guard. "You may bring in the prisoner."

The effect of those six words was galvanic. Everyone in the room was suddenly alert, their eyes focused on the door that led to the outside, and to the lower chambers.

Garrosh Hellscream entered, flanked by six guards—two Horde, a troll and a tauren; two Alliance, a night elf Sentinel and a draenei vindicator; and two of the largest, most muscular pandaren Jaina had ever seen. Garrosh's distinctive armor—adorned with the tusks of the demon slain by the orc's illustrious father, Grom—was gone. He wore only a belted cloth tunic and simple shoes. The fabric had obviously not been cut for him and strained against his massive shoulders and chest. Dark tracings, like webby fingers, competed with the tattoos on his brown skin—the legacy of the sha. Chains, each link bigger than Jaina's hand, bound him at the neck, wrists, and feet, reducing his long stride to a halting shuffle exaggerated by his damaged leg. His face was impassive, and he displayed neither a cowed stance nor a prideful one.

For a moment, the silence was absolute, broken only by the clank of the chains and the tramp of the guards' boots.

Then chaos erupted.

Waves of people—both Alliance and Horde, and even some nominally neutral parties—rose in their seats, some rushing down to the balconies to scream epithets and shake their fists. Although Jaina disliked the dampening field as much as anyone, she was grateful for it now. She realized she did not want Garrosh to be killed out of hand by an angry mob. She wanted him to hear and—thanks to the bronze dragons—to *see* all he had done. The devastation he had caused. The hate he had engendered. She wanted him to know how severely *all* of Azeroth had turned against him.

And, she realized with a burst of shame, if she couldn't kill him, she didn't want some unknown, furious crowd member to have the honor.

The pandaren response was swift. Most of the guards stationed in the seating area were monks, whose own bodies were weapons, and the protestors were quickly subdued and removed from the arena. Garrosh's guards all drew their weapons and closed ranks about him, their backs to the orc and their calm faces turned to the crowd.

Other than the guards, the only ones who seemed unruffled by the outburst were Taran Zhu, the four celestials, and Garrosh Hellscream himself. The orc's brown, tattooed face might as well have been carved from stone for all the emotion it revealed.

Taran Zhu's voice carried a stern warning: "You have now all witnessed what happens should you disrupt this court. Those who have done so will be held under guard for the remainder of the trial, at which time they will be released. Anyone who further disturbs this most solemn event will join them."

He nodded, and the guards around Garrosh returned to their flanking formation. Garrosh was led before Taran Zhu's dais, where he halted. The two massive pandaren took up sentry positions behind him. Jaina knew that the only movement they would display—barring another outburst of violence—would be the slow blinking of their eyes. The remaining four guards bowed to Taran Zhu and filed out. Taran Zhu looked down at the orc for a moment. "Garrosh Hellscream. You have been charged with war crimes, and crimes against the very essence of sentient beings of Azeroth, as well as crimes against Azeroth itself. You are also charged for all acts committed in your name, or by those with whom you have allied."

Garrosh merely stood there, silent and still.

Taran Zhu continued. "The charges are as follows: Genocide. Murder. Forcible transfer of population. Enforced disappearance of individuals."

The list of the heinous crimes alone was powerful enough to

make Jaina tense. She glanced over at where Vol'jin and the other Horde leaders sat. She had heard of the treatment of trolls under Garrosh—and what the orc had tried to do to Vol'jin himself.

"Enslavement. The abduction of children. Torture. The killing of prisoners. Forced pregnancy."

Anduin winced, and Jaina could not blame him. She thought of Alexstrasza and the horrors that had been perpetrated upon the Life-Binder personally and the red dragonflight in general. Kalec was very still beside Jaina. She looked up at him, meaning to offer him comfort, and instead found him looking down at her. He knew what was coming, and slipped an arm around her.

She braced herself.

"The wanton destruction of cities, towns, and villages not justified by military or civilian necessity."

The Vale of Eternal Blossoms.

Theramore.

"What say you to these charges, Garrosh Hellscream?"

Garrosh did not reply, and for a wild second, Jaina wondered if maybe, just maybe, hearing the charges so bluntly laid out before him would move the former warchief. She had heard of his anger at an underling who had slain innocents in his name, knew that the one thing even Garrosh's enemies must give him credit for was a passionate devotion to his race. And, at one time, he had also been given credit for honor.

She stared at Garrosh, hardly daring to blink or even breathe, not knowing if she wanted him to break down and ask forgiveness for his atrocities or to stand firm—so that they could kill him with impunity.

And then Garrosh smiled, beginning to slowly applaud, although the chains about his wrists hampered the gesture.

"The show has barely commenced," he responded, sneering, "and already I give it a standing ovation. This promises to be more entertaining than the Darkmoon Faire!" His contemptuous laughter rang through the hall. "I will not say that I am guilty, for that denotes shame. Nor will I protest innocence, for I claim no such. Let the comedy begin!"

For a second time, audience members leapt to their feet, seemingly willing to climb over one another in order to wrap their bare hands around Garrosh Hellscream's throat. Jaina had no memory of placing her own hands on the arms of her chair and lifting herself halfway out of her seat until she became aware of Kalec and Varian, one on each side, almost forcibly holding her down.

"Do not rise, beloved," Kalec whispered urgently, and she realized she was about to add her own shouts of outrage to the cacophony. Sweat broke out on her forehead as she commanded herself to sit, fists clenching.

Meanwhile, Taran Zhu had lost his patience. He struck the gong several times, and barked orders in Pandaren. More members of both Horde and Alliance were hauled away to spend the rest of the trial confined to muse upon their unruliness.

Once relative calmness was reestablished, a composed Taran Zhu regarded Garrosh. "Since your words do not change the original intent of this trial, we will proceed as planned." He nodded to Garrosh's guards, who escorted him to the empty chair beside Baine, where he would sit for the duration of the trial. Despite his chains, Garrosh appeared to lounge, defiant and smug, and Jaina hated him with an intensity so bright and burning it made the mana bomb he had dropped on Theramore look like a candle's flame.

6

While Garrosh's venomous words and arrogant attitude were not unexpected, Anduin found that he was disappointed nonetheless. Most would be surprised at his sentiments; Anduin personally had been attacked by Garrosh, and had barely survived.

Toward the end of his time as warchief of the Horde, Garrosh had become increasingly obsessed with accumulating spiritual and magical means to overcome the Alliance—no matter the cost. Anduin could scarcely credit some of the things that Garrosh was rumored to have done, but he had seen other actions with his own eyes. Garrosh, unlike Varian, had chosen to use the dark abilities of the sha—deadly and terrifying physical manifestations of negative emotions—to empower his troops.

Garrosh had stolen a mogu relic known as the Divine Bell to accomplish this task. When rung, the bell emitted pure and unremitting chaos. There was, as with all things in Pandaria, a way to balance the bell—the Harmonic Mallet. Anduin had reassembled the broken artifact and, in a confrontation with Garrosh, had used it to strike the bell, turning the sound of discord into true harmony.

He had thwarted Garrosh, and the enraged orc had swung at the bell with his axe, Gorehowl, shattering the mogu relic.

And Anduin's bones.

The ache rose again, in each part of his body that had been crushed by the bell's broken shards crashing down upon him. The pain came briefly when he shifted position, and manifested in a different, deeper way when he recalled the incident. Velen had told him that the pain probably would never disappear entirely, and there was a good chance it would increase with age.

"The body does not completely forget the harm done to it, and each of your bones has its own memory," he had said. Then the ancient draenei had smiled, adding, "And thank the Light, you, dear young prince, will live to listen to those memories."

That was enough for Anduin. And, he reflected, as the mallet had wrought harmony out of discord, so too could sentient beings. Anduin believed this in the very depths of his soul. It was something that the draenei and even the naaru believed, and they were wiser than he. The Earthen Ring, which had done so much to help the world recover after the wounds Deathwing had inflicted upon it, was composed of shaman of all races. They had united with the Cenarion Circle to restore the World Tree Nordrassil. Cooperation was possible; he'd seen it. Every individual was unique—and could grow.

The trial had barely begun. If the list of his crimes had not moved Garrosh—except to boasting—then perhaps the bronze dragons' ingenious contribution to the proceedings would do so.

The young prince felt bad for Baine Bloodhoof, whom he still considered a friend. He remembered the night he and the tauren had sat in Jaina's parlor, after Baine had been forced to flee for his life during the Grimtotem uprising. Anduin admired Baine for taking on the responsibility of defending the orc who had slain his father. Anduin glanced up at Varian for a moment, wondering how his father would behave if he were in Baine's place. He hoped Varian would rise to the occasion with as much dignity.

Tyrande Whisperwind rose from her table and walked to the center of the arena. She was clad in a flowing robe that could be described by the pedestrian adjective "white," but was so much more than that—subtle hues of lavender and blue and pearl and silver united in a garment that managed to be both simple and elegant at the same time, as was she. Anduin had met her before, and of all the Alliance leaders—and even some of the Horde—she intimidated him more than any other. It was not that she was overbearing or haughty. On the contrary, she had been kind and gracious.

Anduin saw in Tyrande the very essence of what was beautiful in the radiant moon goddess she worshipped, and in the cool night woodlands her people so loved. And when she had spoken to him the first time, at the service for Magni Bronzebeard, he had trembled at the kind touch of her hand on his cheek in a gesture of comfort as sincere as it had been profound.

Now, Tyrande looked up at the faces in the gallery for a long moment, not speaking, as if gathering her thoughts, then lifted her glowing gaze up to the four August Celestials.

"It is my right as Accuser to speak first to the jury, and to those assembled," she began. Her voice carried, but was melodic rather than strident. "This right is so granted because the Accuser must prove her case. But I am almost tempted to let the Defender speak first, because Chu'shao Baine Bloodhoof has chosen to accept a much more difficult task than I."

She began to walk with graceful steps, her long blue hair flowing down her back, her lavender face turned up toward the onlookers. "For Garrosh Hellscream has done me a great service this day. Not only does he admit to the lengthy list of heinous crimes with which he is charged, but he boasts of them, and offers insult to this court. No one in this temple—indeed, I would venture to say no one in Azeroth—has been untouched by the deeds of this single orc."

Now she looked at Garrosh, and though her face changed only subtly, Anduin could see the loathing in it. "My task, an honor and a somber joy both, is to offer proof that Garrosh did everything of which he is accused, and more. I intend to show you that he did these deeds with full knowledge of the anguish, suffering, and destruction they would cause."

She paused, and turned to the table where Chromie and Kairoz sat. Her hands to her heart, she gave them a deep bow. "I offer gratitude to the bronze dragonflight, for now my tool is no longer the dull repetition of words to which we would eventually become inured—but the actual *sight* of how these events played out. You will watch Garrosh Hellscream plot. You will listen to him lie. And by the end, you will witness him betray."

Garrosh offered no interruption. Tyrande was setting the tone for the Accuser's strategy, and it would be a brutal one. She would be relentless, and Anduin would have thought that Garrosh would be unable to keep his mouth shut. But he did.

If Tyrande was disappointed, she did not show it. Her delicate nostrils flared, and she again looked up into the crowd. Her voice was gentler, filled with the same compassion Anduin recalled from their first meeting.

"I know that some of these sights will be horrific, and that many of you personally suffer from what Hellscream has done. To you, I offer my sincere regrets for the pain I must cause. But I believe that you would suffer more if I failed to do everything in my power to bring this . . . *orc* . . . to true justice."

Now she bowed to the four great beings, who were still as stone but whose presence could be felt throughout the arena. "August Celestials, you are kind as well as wise. I give both qualities my respect. And I urge you to give us this true justice of which I speak. To find Garrosh Hellscream, former warchief of the Horde, guilty, on *every single abominable count,* of crimes against Azeroth—its individuals, its races, and the world itself—and to press for the fullest possible punishment: death. *Shaha lor'ma* . . . Thank you."

Anduin let out a breath he hadn't realized he had been holding. Applause was not permitted; if it were, he was certain that the vast majority of onlookers would be clapping and cheering their approval. Garrosh, however, remained visibly unaffected by her poignant and powerful words.

Once Tyrande had taken her seat, her color high and her pose straight as an elven arrow, Taran Zhu nodded.

"Thank you, Chu'shao. The Defender may now speak."

Baine did not radiate the calm yet barely contained energy of Tyrande. He rose slowly, with dignity, bowed deeply to the August Celestials, then turned to face the spectators.

"The Accused, Garrosh Hellscream, spoke of this trial being a 'show.' As I do not wish it to be perceived as such, or as a comedy, as he referred to it, I will not insult anyone's intelligence by claiming that Garrosh Hellscream is innocent. Nor will I run the risk of scorn by attempting to convince you that he is simply misguided, or misunderstood. I shall not ask for pity, or for anyone to overlook the crimes of which he stands accused. And I will get one important matter out of the way now."

Baine stood tall, his massive chest expanded with a full breath, reminding all present that he was a warrior, a high chieftain, and a son of a high chieftain. "Garrosh Hellscream killed my father. Most of you know this. Yet here I stand, not out of any fondness for Garrosh as an individual, choosing to defend him. Why? Because, Fa'shua Taran Zhu, August Ones, and fellow Azerothians, like the rest of you, I too want the 'true justice' of which my esteemed night elf colleague spoke so eloquently. And also because it is the *right thing to do.*"

He began to walk, looking up at the audience as if daring them to contradict him. "We will not be as Garrosh was to us. We will not put our wants or needs first. We will not think with heated fury of slaying, of vengeance, of restoring to our races glory perceived to be lost. We are better than that. We are better than *him.*" He pointed a finger at Garrosh Hellscream, who now sat with an amused smile curving around his tusks.

"And *because* we are better, we will listen, and use both our minds and our hearts to reach a verdict that generations to come will agree was indeed true justice." Baine looked toward the Alliance stands, and he caught and held Anduin's gaze for a moment before turning to Varian, then Jaina Proudmoore.

Jaina was frowning, displaying the little crease that marred her brow when she so furrowed it. Anduin usually saw that crease when she was concentrating, but now he realized she was not pleased with what Baine was saying.

"Our challenge—mine, and that of the August Celestials, and indeed, of all present—is to keep both those minds and hearts open. It is the wise heart, not the broken one, which must be called upon. If you truly do not wish for Garrosh to 'get away with it,' as I have heard some voices mutter, if you honestly crave justice, then you must spare his life. While one exists, one can change, and one can begin to do something to mend what he has shattered. Thank you."

He bowed and returned to his seat.

Baine's opening speech was met with stony silence. Anduin was unsurprised. The tauren's battle was not only uphill; it was practically a vertical climb.

"We will take an hour's respite, then resume later this afternoon with the first witness," Taran Zhu stated. He struck the gong and rose. Everyone in the amphitheater stood as well, and then the talking began, the buzz of excited conversation, some angry, some gleeful, all of it—*all* of it—anti-Garrosh.

Anduin tried to catch Baine's eye, but the tauren walked over to speak with Kairoz, his movements measured and his face grim. Anduin watched him for a moment, wishing it were possible for him to go to the tauren he considered a friend to offer his support. One day, perhaps. His gaze traveled to Garrosh, and he stiffened.

The orc was looking right at him.

His expression was unreadable. Anduin felt his palms grow moist and his chest tighten under that cold scrutiny, and his mind flashed back to the moment when he had confronted Garrosh.

Striking the bell, transforming chaos into harmony. Turning to Garrosh, telling the orc what the mallet had done. Garrosh's fury.

Die, whelp!

And then—

A hand came down on Anduin's shoulder and he started, coloring when he realized it was only his father.

"Are you all right?" Varian asked, then followed his son's gaze. He made a low noise of displeasure. "Come on. Let's get something to eat. You don't have to look at him if you don't want to."

Despite the reactionary fear that had spurted through his body at the eye contact, Anduin found he actually didn't mind looking at Garrosh. Baine's words were still ringing in his ears and heart, and Garrosh was not gloating. Indeed, the orc now inclined his head in a gesture of respect before rising to follow his guards as he was led away for his own meal.

"I'm all right, Father," Anduin said, and added, "Don't worry. You did the right thing."

Varian knew what he meant. The king looked after Garrosh, his lips thinning.

"I'm not so sure, now. I'm not sure at all."

They assumed her dead, and Zaela, warlord of the Dragonmaw, preferred to keep it that way.

At first, she had been far too close to that state to have had any choice in the matter. She had been shot off her proto-dragon, Galakras, during the Siege of Orgrimmar, plunging seemingly to certain death. Astonishingly, she survived the fall. Her injuries were grave, but her will was strong. Determined to spit in the face of death, Zaela had flung a smoke bomb to distract her enemies and half-stumbled, half-ran to safety before collapsing. She had pushed her recovery, fueled now by a certainty that she had been spared for a purpose. And that purpose was to save Garrosh Hellscream, who was presently on trial for his very life.

She and many of the Dragonmaw had retreated to the now-abandoned Grim Batol, where they had once enacted the greatest moments of their history—thus far. There, Zaela and others had recovered in secrecy. Zaela operated out of the very room where the great Life-Binder, Alexstrasza, had been tortured to breed new red dragon mounts for the Dragonmaw. Even now, Zaela was heartened daily by regarding the deep furrows an agonized Alexstrasza had clawed in the very stone of the mountain, by standing next to an enormous chain that had once forced the dragon matriarch to bow her red head.

Word had reached her that Vol'jin's "Horde" had searched the Twilight Highlands, looking for her, and that there was a price on her head. They had never thought to look for her here. Such an oversight was, Zaela was certain, entirely due to the fact that Vol'jin was a troll. An orc warchief would have known to search Grim Batol. Regardless, it was not to be their permanent home. They needed to be on the move, and soon.

Now she looked out at what remained of her clan, and her heart was full. "My Dragonmaw," she said, her rough voice brimming with emotion, "you followed me against the fel orc Mor'ghor who once led us, knowing that the proud orcish race should never be sullied by such corruption. You followed Garrosh Hellscream, whose only goal was to keep the Horde strong, pure, and powerful. For that dream of a true Horde, he now languishes in prison, defended by a *tauren*, his fate to be decided by Pandaria's celestials. My spies there report that we still have a few days left to save our glorious warchief."

Her eyes went from one to the other, knowing they would feel as she would, yet regretting what was likely inevitable. "You are trained. You are ready. But still, we are small in number. You are aware, as am I, that we may fail, and that none of us might survive. But I would rather die in battle for a noble cause than continue to hide, even here. Shout if you are with me!"

A roar went up. Every one of them shook their weapons, opened their throats, stamped their feet. She laughed fiercely and joined in their war cry. "By the ancestors! Perhaps by will and heart alone we will triumph!"

As she spoke, she saw movement in the entryway. One of her scouts hastened to her, and she saw he clutched a scroll. He dropped at her feet, panting. "My warlord—I have run all the way—an intruder—he bids me bring you this!" He thrust out the scroll, slightly crushed from being held too tightly.

Growling in irritation, and to disguise her worry, Zaela cracked the seal and read:

Greetings to the Warlord Maiden!

Heads have been bowed low, but not yet severed from their bodies. While the warchief lives, there is still hope in the fierce hearts of all those who believe in the true Horde, as it once was and yet will be again.

If you share that hope, if your heart beats for the glory of the orcish people pray grant me admittance, and we will speak. I can be of great help.

A Friend

"A friend," she repeated, staring down at the courier. "An orc, I assume?"

His eyes wide, the courier shook his head vigorously. "No, my warlord. It . . . he's a *dragon!*"

7

G o'el used the respite to clear his head. He had brought the wolf Snowsong with him to Pandaria, and was glad of some time to simply ride and think. The friend who had bonded with him ages ago was older now than she had once been, and so he no longer rode her into battle. But she was still strong and healthy, and in rare moments they both enjoyed a spirited run. They headed out of the temple grounds and along the curving road that twined through a spare landscape that reminded him a great deal of Durotar.

Strapped securely to his breast was his infant son, Durak. The comfort of his father's warmth and beating heart soothed the boy. He dreamed deeply as Go'el coaxed the wolf into an all-out run toward One Keg, a small village that lay at the base of the Howling-wind Trail. The orc's spirit was calmed by the feel of this little life nestled against him, and the sweet-scented wind caressing his face.

Tyrande had spoken the truth. She could win the trial simply by showing up each morning and letting the facts speak for themselves. But this new element of being able to display scenes from the past troubled him. If words could be twisted, then surely images could be.

His thoughts went to the angry initial cries of some in the Alliance who wanted to put the entire Horde on trial. Go'el was certain that chief among those tried would be he, for the crime of giving Hellscream so much power. It could have all turned out so differently. Go'el had wanted Garrosh to admire his father, and so Garrosh had—but he had admired the wrong things. And now, all of Azeroth was paying for Go'el's gamble on Garrosh's strength of character. He himself wondered how much of the blame could be laid at his own feet. Garrosh had done so much damage—not just to those whose lives he had ended or broken, but to the Horde he claimed to champion. Go'el sent out a prayer to the elements for swift, true justice. Garrosh had done enough harm. As long as he lived, Go'el believed, he would continue to do so.

He lifted one hand and pressed Durak more tightly against him. The past could not, should not be changed. The future could. And Go'el knew that so much—perhaps everything—hinged on what happened in the courtroom.

He made a silent vow to himself, dipping his chin to brush the top of his son's head. He would do whatever he must to safeguard that future. No matter the cost.

"Chu'shao, you may summon your first witness."

Tyrande nodded. "May it please the court, I call Velen, Prophet and leader of the draenei people, to speak as witness."

Go'el clenched his jaw. Beside him, cradling Durak, Aggra inhaled swiftly. "From what I knew of her, I would have thought better of this elven priestess," she said to her mate. Her voice was quiet but angry. "It would appear that if the orcs hate the night elves, the feeling is indeed mutual."

"We do not know what she intends." As he spoke them, he knew the words were as much for himself as for Aggra.

"I think we can make a good guess," Aggra replied.

Go'el didn't answer. He watched Velen, alien and unspeakably ancient, who had once shown kindness to a youngling named

Durotan, stride with grace and dignity to sit in the witness chair. He was bigger even than the tallest draenei Go'el had seen in person, but seemed somewhat slighter than those massively muscular beings. He wore no armor, only a relatively simple garment of soft, swirling, white-and-purple robes that seemed to float of their own accord as he moved. His eyes glowed a soothing shade of blue, framed by deeply etched wrinkles. Short tendrils banded with gold protruded through Velen's beard. The white length fell almost to Velen's waist, and reminded Go'el of the crest of a mighty wave.

Baine, too, was watching Velen carefully, and Go'el knew the tauren well enough to see that his muscles were gathered in anticipation of movement.

Go'el himself had once written down the history of his forebearers. It had been a piecemeal documentation of the events, as so few remaining orcs remembered them clearly. Demonic blood had flowed through their veins, fueling their hatred while making clear thought difficult. When Velen had reemerged in Azeroth, his people— unsurprisingly, Go'el thought with a stab of sorrow and bitterness— had chosen to bond with the Alliance. Until the day that true peace and trust came to Azeroth, Go'el would never have the chance to sit down and ask Velen questions, as his father had done. And he knew that while the Alliance and Horde had banded together to take down Garrosh, that orc had likely rendered any such a future impossible.

"Prophet Velen," began Tyrande formally. "Truth only in this place, truth ever in this place. This is the charge of the Pandaren ancestors, whose law we follow, seeking balance."

"Whose law we *honor*," prompted Taran Zhu, gently.

Tyrande colored slightly and corrected herself. "Apologies, Fa'shua Taran Zhu. Whose law we honor, seeking balance. Do you give your word?"

"I do give my word," Velen answered immediately. His voice was resonant, but warm and kind even in those few words. He folded his hands in his lap and looked at Tyrande expectantly.

"Prophet, I am sure everyone in this court today recognizes you as one who has been witness to atrocities ere now," Tyrande began.

And there it is, thought Go'el. *She will now proceed to paint us all black—or red, with the stains of blood spilled in years gone by.*

Baine sprang to his hooves. "With respect, I protest," he called out. "Fa'shua, we are here to judge the actions of one orc, not all of them."

"With respect, Lord Zhu," replied Tyrande, "the Defender spoke earlier of Garrosh's great love of his people. It is my desire to acquaint the jury with the history of these people. The celestials know much, but they do not know of Draenor, and their understanding of the orcish mind and history will be vital to any decision we can expect them to render."

"I agree with the Accuser," Taran Zhu replied, and Baine, his ears flattening slightly, inclined his head in acceptance of the ruling and took his seat.

"Thank you," said Tyrande, and continued. "Prophet, will you briefly identify yourself?"

"I am Velen, and I have led my people to the best of my ability for millennia. We fled from our homeworld of Argus to escape the demonic Burning Legion. We arrived in Draenor centuries ago, and made it our new home. From there, as I am certain you all know, we came here, to Azeroth."

"Were you made welcome in Draenor?" Tyrande asked.

"We were not unwelcome," Velen said. "The orcs and the draenei coexisted peacefully for a long time."

"Would it be accurate to say that you and the orcs lived alongside one another in Draenor for centuries with only a little interaction, trading peaceably, each race respecting the other?"

"Yes, that would be accurate."

The high priestess looked over at Chromie, who nodded and slipped from her chair. Kairoz remained seated, watching alertly. "May it please the court, I wish to present the first Vision of Velen."

Chromie hopped up onto the table, the limitations of her chosen height making it impossible for her to reach the Vision of Time otherwise. No one, however, dared laugh at a dragon, even if that dragon looked pleasant and cheerful. Chromie moved her small hands with the deftness of the gnomish race she liked to emulate.

The eyes of the carved dragon coiled about the top bulb snapped open.

A soft, startled murmur rippled through the chamber. The dragon lifted its head, shook itself as if awakening from slumber, and moved its foreclaws to grasp the bulb below it. The sands within the top bulb began to emit a golden illumination that matched the dragon's eyes. Sand trickled down into the waiting bulb below, its guardian still immobile, still made of lifeless bronze.

With Chromie's own eyes glowing as she used the magic unique to her flight, she splayed a small hand. A misty tendril the hue of the sand emanated from it, twisting its way to the center of the great amphitheater and twining in on itself like a snake, shaping and reshaping until forms could clearly be distinguished. Color began to bleed across the forms, the radiant bronze tones shifting to paint the larger-than-life figures in realistic hues.

Two young orcs stood, their brown skins covered with sweat and dust. Their mouths were slightly open and their eyes wide as they stared up at a draenei warrior clad in gleaming metal plate armor. He looked concerned, and the boys wore expressions of shock, but not fear.

Go'el knew who these youths had to be.

Memories crowded on him: the wonder and pride when he first learned of his true heritage from Drek'Thar. The joy of "meeting" his parents in one of the alternate histories of a malfunctioning timeway, and the heart-cracking anguish of being forced to watch them die. Now, as a parent himself, his gaze roved hungrily upon the boyish features of his father. And as he turned to reach out to hold his own son close, he saw that Aggra was already moving to place Durak in his arms. Their eyes met and locked in a moment of wordless love and understanding; then Go'el, cradling Durak, looked back at the tableau.

"Prophet," said Tyrande, "can you tell the court what we are seeing here?"

Velen sighed, and his shoulders stooped slightly. "I can," he said in a melancholy tone. "Though I did not witness this moment myself, I recognize all three."

"And who are they?"

"The draenei was a dear friend—Restalaan, the captain of the Telmor guards. The young orcs are Orgrim, later known as Doomhammer, and Durotan, son of Garad."

"Were such interactions common?"

Velen shook his head, his tendrils moving with the gesture. "No. This was a first. We traded with the orcs, but had never met their young ones."

"And what happened to lead up to this?"

"The boys were fleeing from an ogre, and a group of draenei came to their aid. My captain of the guards, Restalaan, was impressed that they were from different clans, yet were friends. We knew enough of their ways to know this was unusual. It was too late for them to travel home safely, so Restalaan sent runners to notify their clans and invited them to stay as our guests until morning. He thought I might be interested in meeting these two. I was. I had dinner with the young orcs, and found them to be intelligent and of good character."

Go'el remembered Drek'Thar telling him of this meeting. The old orc had not witnessed it personally, but he had been told of it. He was glad Drek'Thar was not here to relive this moment from the past, before so much darkness had come.

"The city you speak of, Telmor—was it easy to find?"

"No," Velen replied. "It was hidden by both magic and technology. The boys would never have found it had we not made them welcome."

"May it please the court, I would like to present the second Vision of Velen." Tyrande nodded to Chromie. Chromie, her hands looking as if they wore gloves of honey-colored light, gestured. The scene before them dissolved, and another one appeared. The Sands of Time in the hourglass again began to fall, grain by glowing grain, and before Go'el's eyes, a second tableau came to life.

"Here we are," the image of Restalaan said. He dismounted from a cobalt-coated talbuk and knelt on the earth, moving aside some leaves and pine needles as if looking for something. His questing touch uncovered a beautiful green crystal, and he placed his palm gently upon it.

"Kehla men samir, solay lamaa kahl."

The forest around them began to shimmer. For an instant, Go'el wondered if the Vision of Time might be malfunctioning, then realized the figures themselves remained steady. The young Durotan gasped. The shimmering increased, and then suddenly, where there had once been dense woodlands, there was now only a large, paved road that led up the side of the mountains.

"We are in the heart of ogre country, though it was not so when the city was built so long ago," Restalaan said, rising. "If the ogres cannot see us, they cannot attack us."

"But . . . how?" asked Durotan.

"A simple illusion, nothing more. A trick of . . . the light. The eye cannot always be trusted. We think what we see is always real, that the light always reveals what is there the same way at all times. But light and shadow can be manipulated, directed, by those that understand it. In the speaking of these words and the touching of the crystal, I have altered how the light falls on the rocks, the trees, the landscape. And so your eye perceives something entirely different from what you thought was there."

Restalaan chuckled warmly. "Come, my new friends. Come where none of your people have ever been before. Walk down the roads of my home."

The scene froze, then disappeared. The grains in the top half of the hourglass ceased to fall. The bronze dragon resumed its original pose and, closing its glowing eyes, returned to the state of a simple ornament. The one curled about the bottom bulb, however, awakened and stretched, then placed its own claws protectively around the bulb it was designed to guard.

"Restalaan revealed to Durotan and Orgrim the secret of how the draenei protected their city. Did the two boys keep that secret?" Tyrande quietly asked.

Go'el knew the answer.

"No," Velen responded, pained.

"What happened?"

Velen sighed deeply. He looked over to the Horde side of the arena, searching out Go'el. When the Prophet spoke, it was as if he were speaking only to the son of the little boy he had once made welcome, not to a raptly attentive audience.

"Years later, the orcs were deceived by Ner'zhul, and then betrayed by Gul'dan. I truly believe that Durotan felt great remorse over—"

Tyrande smiled gently, even as she cut him off. "Your compassion does you credit, Prophet, but please, simply state the facts as you know them."

Aggra looked stricken—and angry. "She will not even let him speak what is in his heart! Why does Baine not protest?"

Baine stayed silent, though his ears were flat, betraying to Go'el his dislike of the proceedings. "Because Tyrande is correct in asking what she does. Baine will have his say, beloved. Do not worry." But Go'el could not deny that he shared his mate's anger.

Velen nodded. "Very well. The simple facts are that Durotan led a force of orcs against Telmor years later."

"Thank you," Tyrande said. She turned to look at those assembled, her gaze sweeping the stands and coming to rest upon the four celestials. "I must warn the court that what you will see will be violent and disturbing. But such is the nature of betrayal and slaughter."

Again, Baine did not protest. Go'el realized bitterly it was because once again, Tyrande was correct.

To her credit, though, the Accuser looked unhappy at what she was about to do. Nonetheless, she said, "I present a third Vision of Velen—the taking of Telmor by the orcs."

The grains of the Vision of Time began to fall once again, and another scene appeared. Go'el looked upon a Durotan he could now recognize, grown to adulthood. The leader of the Frostwolf clan wore what his son instantly knew to be the battle harness handed down through ten generations of clan leaders, even though he had never seen the armor before. Crafted of heavy plate mail connected by chains, it bore the images of two white wolves facing one another on its front. *It should have been mine*, Go'el thought. *It should have, one day, been Durak's, if fate had so willed it.*

But fate had not, he reminded himself. The harness had been lost to time; Orgrim had thought it scavenged or destroyed by the elements. And he himself had reached adulthood as a human's prisoner. The Horde, especially under Garrosh, had much to answer for, but so did the Alliance.

Durotan and several other battle-ready orcs stood in the same "forest" as seen in the previous Vision. Orgrim, looking much like Go'el remembered him, stepped beside his friend, watching as Durotan searched for something on the ground. Go'el knew—he was certain everyone knew—what it was.

Durotan rose, holding an exquisite emerald-hued gem in his palm.

"You found it," said Orgrim. Durotan nodded, lifting his gaze from the stone to the faces of his colleagues.

"Get into position," Orgrim said to the other orcs. "We have been fortunate that there has been no advance warning."

Durotan hesitated for a moment, then spoke the deadly words.

"Kehla men samir, solay lamaa kahl."

The illusion that had protected Telmor slowly disappeared, revealing the wide, paved road that stretched ahead as if in obscene invitation.

All at once, it was as if the entire arena had transformed into a battlefield. The scale was massive, almost overwhelming, as the orcs, mounted on armored wolves, weapons at the ready, screamed their battle cries and charged. The Vision focused on them, following them as the great beasts they rode added their own howls to the cacophony, and the dusty, thundering group was in sharp and brutal contrast to the tranquility of the city. Then individual images replaced the panoramic sweep of the Vision. Here, a handful of draenei simply stopped in their tracks, clearly too astonished to even attempt to flee or defend themselves. There, swords and axes severed horned heads from bodies so swiftly that confused looks still lingered on the blue faces. Indigo blood spattered everywhere, decorating armor and brown skin. It clotted in the wolves' fur, and the beasts made tracks as they ran.

Screams of terror and pleas in the lilting draenei tongue joined the chorus of killing. Durotan's people thundered on, the tide of warriors followed closely by the then-new warlocks, who peppered gathered clusters of terrified, unarmed draenei with fire, shadows, and curses.

Some of the orcs turned into the buildings, pursuing those who had foolishly entered seeking shelter. A mere few heartbeats later, the warriors emerged covered with blood, racing down the steps in search of their next targets.

But now the citizens of Telmor had defenders. The draenei guards fought back with magics far beyond the comprehension of their enemies. Silvery white, azure, and lavender light countered the sickly greenish yellow of the warlock magic. It obscured the hand-to-hand fighting, but Go'el's attention was firmly fixed on his father. As if following Go'el's gaze, the Vision focused on Durotan and the one who had just attacked him with a sword that glowed with blue energy.

Restalaan.

He shouted something Go'el didn't understand, seized Durotan, and hauled the orc off his mount. Surprised, Durotan didn't react in time and hit the ground. Restalaan brought his sword down just as Durotan grabbed his axe.

Durotan's black wolf whirled to defend his rider, his massive teeth seizing the draenei's arm. The glowing sword fell from Restalaan's hand, and Durotan's axe sliced down, through armor into flesh. Restalaan dropped to his knees, and the wolf bit harder while blue blood poured from the axe wound. Durotan struck a second time, ending what must have been agonizing pain. And so Restalaan, who had befriended Durotan and showed him his city's secrets, was slain.

Go'el thought this surely had to be the end of the gory display, that Tyrande had more than made her point. He glanced over at her to see that she stood with her arms tightly folded, her eyes fixed on the horrifying images that had manifested in this court on her command. She gave no sign that she was done, and the carnage continued.

Orcs rampaged through the city in the Vision. Go'el realized with a sickening feeling that the death of Restalaan, gut-wrenching as that had been to witness, was only the prelude to what Tyrande had in store.

8

The corpses were so numerous that orcs sometimes stumbled over them as they raced toward a fresh kill. The fighting was at close quarters, and Durotan, as bloodied as any of his comrades, slashed and stabbed and struck with both speed and accuracy. So present, so real was the violence that when Go'el saw what was about to happen, he shouted out a warning. He was not alone.

Someone charged Durotan as he fought. Go'el watched in impotent horror.

The girl was still mostly a child, with only a hint of womanly curves that would never have the chance to fully flower.

It was his father's training, Go'el realized, that prevented Durotan from cutting the girl in half. Go'el knew the effort and skill it must have taken, could feel his own muscles tighten in empathy as Durotan twisted the axe's arc. The girl had no such qualms, and threw herself at the massively armed and armored orc, beating at his leg with her clenched fists and nothing else. Her defiance as she flung herself into a path she had to know was fatal was perhaps one of the most courageous things Go'el had ever seen.

But Durotan did not strike down the draenei child. Go'el knew that he never would. But another did, and Go'el felt the sting of tears of shocked outrage as the girl stopped, her glowing eyes going wide, her open mouth gushing blood. She had been run through from behind. Her killer shoved the spear to the side, and the body was forced to the earth. He put a foot on the girl's still-twitching corpse and tugged his spear free, grinning up at the sickened Durotan.

"You owe me one, Frostwolf," the Shattered Hand orc said.

The scene froze, lingering on the sight of the murdered girl, and then faded.

In his mind's eye, Go'el saw another scene play out—one he had himself experienced. He had only recently escaped from beneath the boot of his "master," Aedelas Blackmoore, and was being tested by the Warsong clan. A human boy had been brought before him— one even younger than the tragic draenei girl.

"You know what this is," Iskar had said. "They are our natural enemies . . . Kill this child, before he grows to be of an age to kill you."

"He is a child!" A terrified little boy, nothing more, and Go'el's heart raced at the memory.

"If you do not . . . you may rest assured that you will not leave this cave alive."

"I would rather die than commit such a dishonorable atrocity."

And Hellscream—Grom Hellscream, the wildest, most vicious of the orcs, the father of Garrosh—had stood by that decision.

"I have killed the children of the humans ere now," Grom had said to Iskar. "But we gave all we had fighting in that manner, and where has it brought us? Low and defeated, our kind slouch in camps and lift no hand to free themselves, let alone fight for others. That way of fighting, of making war, has brought us to this."

Tyrande was doing exactly what Aggra and Go'el had feared— taking the truth and twisting it. This cold-blooded murder of a little girl was not what—not who—the orcs were.

But there was no reprieve from the horror. Almost immediately, another scene appeared. It was clear that this was sometime later that same day. The orcs were covered in gore. The once-beautiful rooms in which they now stood had been savaged, littered with broken chairs and other objects.

"What of any draenei we find alive?" a voice asked of Durotan.

"Kill them," Durotan said in a rough voice. "Kill them all."

The scene froze, then slowly faded. The sands in the hourglass ceased to glow.

"No further questions, Lord Zhu." And Tyrande, head held high, jaw set in barely concealed anger, took her seat in an amphitheater that was filled only with stunned silence.

Anduin stared, his mouth open in shock. He knew about this part of history, of course. Many did, to some extent, and living with the draenei as long as he had, Anduin had learned more than most. But he now realized how very much the draenei had spared him by choosing not to reveal their personal stories about that dark day. His hands were clammy with sweat, and he found they trembled.

Velen looked older, sadder, and Anduin understood that even now the compassionate Prophet was grieving for both the fallen draenei and the orcs who had butchered them. Anduin had lived among the draenei long enough to understand that. The victims had died innocent. The orcs had to live with the consequences of their actions.

"I would spare you war if I could, my son." Anduin looked up at his father. Varian's face showed grim sympathy. "It is an ugly thing. And what we have just seen is war at its worst."

Anduin's mouth was too dry for speech, so he could not counter his father. He agreed that war was ugly, but what they'd just witnessed was not war. War was between two sides, matched, armed, prepared. What had happened to Telmor could not be graced by that name. It was nothing more—and nothing less—than a slaughter of innocents. Still somewhat dazed, the prince looked over at the Horde section. None of them, not even the orcs, seemed pleased by what they had seen. It was not necessarily the violence that disturbed them, but that there was no "glory" there. Anyone could butcher an unarmed populace.

Baine waited for a moment, then rose with deliberation. He inclined his head in a gesture of respect. "I am certain that what you just witnessed was painful to you, Prophet, and I regret that the Accuser deemed such a gratuitous display necessary."

"With respect, I protest!" shouted Tyrande.

"I agree with the Accuser. The Defender will refrain from telling the witness what he is thinking."

"Certainly, Fa'shua. It was wrong to assume. I apologize. Can you please tell us what you did think of what we just saw, Prophet?"

"There is no need for an apology. If you put words in my mouth, Chu'shao Bloodhoof, they were only the words I would have chosen," said Velen. "It was indeed painful to behold."

"Can you tell the court what, exactly, pained you?"

"The needless deaths of innocent people, children among them, of course."

Baine nodded. "Of course. Is that all?"

"No. I am also pained to remember that one whose nature was noble and true was compelled to act against it by his superiors," Velen replied.

"You speak of Durotan?"

"Yes."

"You do not think he enjoyed the slaughter?"

"With respect, I protest," said Tyrande. "The witness cannot possibly know what Durotan was thinking."

Baine was obviously expecting this, for he seemed unruffled as he turned to Taran Zhu. "May it please the court, I would like to display a portion of what the Accuser has introduced into evidence—a specific moment that Chu'shao Whisperwind opted not to show."

"Proceed," said Taran Zhu.

Baine nodded to Kairoz. The bronze dragon rose, towering over Chromie, and with deft flicks of his fingers coaxed the sands to stir to life. Once again, the image of Durotan, his wolf, the young draenei, and her killer shimmered into being. The awful moment was frozen, the girl's mouth spouting blood, the spear thrusting through her body.

Anduin wanted to avert his eyes, but forced himself not to. Where was Baine going with this?

Then the figures moved, the girl falling and convulsing as the orc withdrew his weapon. "You owe me one, Frostwolf," he sneered.

Tyrande had ended the display at this point, moving forward to Durotan's damning statement, *"Kill them. Kill them all."*

But in this instant, everyone with eyes could see the expression of horror on Durotan's face as he stared down at the corpse of a murdered child. And everyone with ears heard his long, broken howl of despair, rage, and remorse. The Frostwolf orc lifted his head, and Baine snapped, "Stop. Right there."

Tears gleamed on the brown face, and all knew how seldom orcs wept. Durotan's tusked mouth was open in a now-silent keening. The arena, too, was silent.

The image faded. After a long moment, Baine resumed.

"Can you please tell the court how you feel about orcs today, Prophet?"

"With respect, I protest," said Tyrande.

"I agree with the Defender," said Taran Zhu. "The witness may answer."

Velen was slow to do so, and his voice was ragged with sorrow when he found the words. "I am glad that they were able to overcome the curse of drinking the blood of Mannoroth."

"Are you aware who freed the orcs from that curse?"

"Grom Hellscream, the father of Garrosh," replied the draenei.

"So you are saying that you believe people can change," mused Baine. "Even Grom Hellscream."

"I do believe it. With all my heart."

"Even *Garrosh* Hellscream?" pressed Baine.

"With respect, I protest!" cried Tyrande a fourth time. "Once again, the Defender is steering the witness."

Baine turned to Taran Zhu with a mild mien. "Fa'shua, the Accuser introduced this line of thought with her own evidence," he said.

"I agree with the Accuser," said Taran Zhu. "Defender, you will not ask the witness to speculate. You may rephrase."

Baine nodded. "In summation, then, in your experience, the orcish people have wrestled with a great challenge and overcome it. Have they changed who they are?"

"Yes," said Velen. "I know, more than most, how powerful demonic influence can be." His voice was ancient and sad.

"I have no further questions," said Baine.

Tyrande, however, did. Her beautiful face was almost cold as she approached the draenei whom she herself had brought in as a witness. "I have only one more question, Prophet. And please answer simply, with no opinion. Had Durotan and the others partaken of Mannoroth's blood when they descended upon Telmor?"

"No," the draenei replied.

"Their minds were their own? *Durotan's* mind was his own, his choices his own?"

The answer was reluctant. "Yes."

Tyrande could not quite conceal a look of triumph. "Thank you. No more questions."

Taran Zhu called for an hour's respite, wisely sensing that the spectators needed to remove themselves from the courtroom and clear their minds of what they had seen, or else more would join the ranks of those "restrained" until the end of the trial.

Anduin himself made his apologies to Jaina, Kalec, and his father, claiming he needed to stretch his still-healing legs and get a breath of fresh air. What he really wanted to do was escape. The respite was too brief for him to return to his favorite spot in Pandaria, Mason's Folly. Long-ago stonecrafters had carefully carved a set of steps that led to nothing, save a striking vista. No one knew what the original purpose of the stairs had been. Anduin loved the idea of stairs that led only to beauty, and found the place serene. Now he had to make do with a point on the temple grounds, away from the main area.

It was a small overlook, an offshoot of the section usually reserved for the monks and Master Lao. For the duration of the trial, they and the grummle blacksmith, Black Arrow, had been asked to stay away from the temple during the day, so Anduin had the solitude he craved.

The mountain air was bracing and crisp, and Anduin's feet left bootprints in a light dusting of snow. Massive chains encircled the vista point to protect the unwary from falling. To the west rose the mountains, ancient and snowcapped, their colossal peaks draped with smoky mist and piercing the clouds. To the east Anduin saw two of the smaller pagodas, embraced by cherry trees and guarded by a statue of the mighty Xuen.

The view directly ahead, to the south, like the painting of a true master, contained both the peace of the temple and the vastness of Pandaria. Not for the first time, Anduin experienced a tug of protectiveness, and wondered why a place so alien to him and all he had known felt so much like home.

"Do you wish solitude, or may I join you?" The silky, youthful voice behind him was familiar. Anduin smiled as he turned to Wrathion, standing in the archway.

"Of course, though I doubt I'll be good company."

"High Priestess Whisperwind, or should I say Chu'shao Whisperwind, is certainly starting strongly," Wrathion said, stepping beside Anduin. Hands clasped behind his back, he peered out at the vista as if he were actually interested in the view. Anduin knew better.

"That she is," he replied.

"And yet, she is telling us nothing new," Wrathion continued. "Everyone already hates Garrosh. Why bring up an event that happened even before his birth? It is a curious tactic."

"Not really," said Anduin. "She's showing us that the orcs can't hide behind the 'we drank demon blood' excuse. Garrosh is completely untainted—by that, at least." Garrosh was not untainted by a desire for power, or a callousness toward the suffering of others so all-consuming Anduin couldn't even begin to fathom it.

"And yet he did such terrible things," mused Wrathion, frowning and stroking his small tuft of beard thoughtfully. "Still . . . painting an entire race with so broad a brush will only backfire if she persists. Nuance is required."

"You always think nuance is required." The irritated comment passed Anduin's lips before he could stop it. He folded his arms tightly and shivered. The arena had been warmed by braziers and body heat, and he'd forgotten to bring his cloak with him. He realized, too, that the scene with the murdered girl had unsettled him more than he had thought.

Wrathion only laughed, the cold air turning his breath to mist. "That's because I'm right. Nothing is set in stone, Prince Anduin. A race with which one allies today may be an enemy tomorrow." He made an expansive gesture toward the mountains. "Even the earth itself shifts. Fire blazes and then subsides to embers. The air is still and then becomes a whirlwind, and the oceans and rivers never cease their movements. There is no such thing as a hard-and-fast truth."

Anduin pressed his lips together. Wrathion wasn't right. He couldn't be. Some things *were* universal, unchangeable. Some things were *always* wrong. Like the murder of innocents.

"If nothing is solid, how can anything be built that lasts?" Anduin asked. It was meant as a question, but it came out as a weary plea.

"There are degrees of solidity," Wrathion pointed out. "While rock and water both can shift if you try to build a house upon them, you are much less likely to end up swimming if you choose the former as your foundation."

Anduin was silent for a moment. Thoughts raced through his

head. None of them were pleasant, and all of them ran deep. Finally, he turned to the dragon prince and asked quietly, "Wrathion? Do you think of us as friends?"

Wrathion actually looked surprised at the question, and that amused Anduin a little. He tilted his turbaned head to one side and pursed his lips, pondering the query.

"Yes," he said at last. "As much as I can have a friend, at any rate."

Anduin smiled ruefully at the amendment. "Then . . . can we just . . . stay here in comfortable silence for a while? As friends?"

"Why yes, of course," Wrathion said.

And so they did.

9

"**P**lease tell us your name and your trade," said Tyrande. The second witness she had called was an orc. He was of middling years, stout, with skin that was an unusually pale green. He sported a bushy black beard, perhaps to compensate for a completely bald pate. "I am Kor'jus, and I grow and sell mushrooms in Orgrimmar."

"What is the name of your shop, and where is it located?"

"It's called Dark Earth, in the Cleft of Shadow."

Tyrande began to walk, or rather glide, so elegant were her steps. Her arms were folded and a furrow of concentration marred her high forehead.

"Dark Earth," she repeated in an overly dramatic intonation. "Cleft of Shadow. Sounds rather ominous. Or maybe . . . forbidden. Something that might attract unwanted attention from the warchief, perhaps?" Her voice was almost, but not quite, confrontational, and Kor'jus bridled.

"My mushrooms have graced the tables of two warchiefs," he snapped. "That is the only attention I have had from them until recently."

"May it please the court, I would like to show the jury this event that Kor'jus speaks of."

Once again, Chromie activated the Vision of Time, and an image of Kor'jus, kneeling and harvesting mushrooms, appeared. He was facing away from the door, intent on his work, and did not see the visitors lifting the curtain. Even so, perhaps sensing them, Kor'jus frowned, and turned.

"Stop here, please," said Tyrande, and Chromie halted the scene. "Kor'jus, can you please tell us who these orcs are?"

"I only knew one by name, but they all were members of the Kor'kron. The Blackrock orc—the one with three fingers on one hand and that scar all across his face—that is Malkorok. Or was, at least."

The identification was necessary only as a formality; most of those assembled recognized the late leader of the Kor'kron. Gray-skinned and covered with red war paint, Malkorok, for many, had come to epitomize the worst of what the Blackrock orcs were known for. Oh yes, he was recognized, and despised.

"Thank you. Chromie, please continue."

"Read the sign," said the image of Kor'jus. "The shop doesn't open until tomorrow." His hand tightened on the small knife he had been using.

"We're not here for mushrooms," Malkorok said, his voice soft. He and four other orcs moved into the shop. One of them drew the curtain. "We're here for you."

Only now did Kor'jus look uncertain. "What have I done?" he asked. "I am a fair merchant. There can be no complaints against me. Warchief Garrosh himself eats my crop!"

"It is because of the warchief that we are here," Malkorok said, advancing one step, then another. Kor'jus stood his ground. "You speak against him so—perhaps one day your mushrooms are not so carefully harvested, eh?"

Understanding dawned, and Kor'jus scowled. "The Horde is not made up of slaves. Each member is of value! I can speak against my warchief's decisions without conspiring against him!"

Malkorok exaggeratedly tilted his head and tapped his chin, as if actually considering this. "No," he said, "I don't think you can."

He seized the mushroom grower's wrist in his three-fingered hand. Even maimed, Malkorok obviously had a powerful grip, for Kor'jus dropped the knife and gasped. Casually, clearly relishing his task, Malkorok wrenched his victim's arm backward. It broke with an audible snap. The other four rushed in, perhaps fearful of losing their own chance for sport, laughing cheerily as if they were indulging in a drinking game rather than pummeling an outnumbered opponent into a pulpy mass.

They used only their fists, and went for what would hurt rather than what would kill: the face, legs, and arms. One of the Kor'kron landed a solid punch and Kor'jus's nose crunched, spraying blood and mucus. His head snapped back and teeth flew at a second punch, and when the overzealous orc went for a third, Malkorok stopped him.

"If we kill him, he can't show people how afraid he is," the leader of the elite guards reprimanded.

Kor'jus lifted his chin and watched the Vision display his own beating with a steady gaze. As well he might—though the fight was five highly trained Kor'kron against one shopkeeper, Kor'jus held his own for several minutes before, inevitably, he dropped to his knees. His face was hardly recognizable, and he breathed in sharp, pained gasps. One final kick sent him curling up tightly, but even then he resisted crying out.

The Kor'kron were barely winded, and clapped one another on the back as they left. When they were gone, Kor'jus lifted his head, spat blood and more teeth, and fell unconscious.

The scene faded. Kor'jus was now breathing quickly, angrily. Tyrande resumed her questions. "Kor'jus, to the best of your knowledge, was this attack on you by the Kor'kron the only one of its kind?"

"No," the orc replied. "There were others. Beaten as badly as I, or worse."

"You were *extremely* badly beaten," said Tyrande. "It is a wonder you did not die."

"With respect—" Baine began.

"I withdraw the last comment, Lord Zhu," Tyrande said, interrupting the Defender with a look of weary patience. "Please tell the jury what you mean by 'or worse.'"

"I refer to the explosion at Razor Hill Inn awhile ago," Kor'jus replied.

"Razor Hill is not exactly known for its decorum," Tyrande said, and chuckles ran the length of the auditorium. "Surely violence there—even an explosion—could be explained away by disgruntled customers, not the Kor'kron."

Despite the amusement displayed by the audience, Kor'jus's expression stayed somber. "I was there. I was at the inn in order to avoid Orgrimmar as much as possible, so that I would not run into Malkorok." He laughed shortly. "Ironic, isn't it? He came in and started to threaten a Forsaken and a blood elf." Kor'jus looked uncomfortable. "I left once they arrived, unnoticed. I was lucky."

"Really? He threatened them? Physically or verbally?"

"He tried to intimidate them, at least at the beginning. I don't know what was said later."

Tyrande nodded. "Chromie, if you please? Let us see for ourselves exactly what happened."

Anduin had never been to the inn at Razor Hill, and saw nothing in the scene before him to make him want to have visited before it had been destroyed and rebuilt. It was dark, raucous, filthy, and likely foul-smelling. He noticed the bronze dragon Kairoz hiding a smile at some of the reactions that this particular tableau engendered.

Nonetheless, it seemed to be a boisterous place of good cheer, until the Kor'kron entered. They paused at the door, their hulking presences blocking out most of whatever light penetrated into the tavern's main room. Two patrons, a Forsaken and a sin'dorei, were drinking together, but looked up at the newcomers.

"Pause," Tyrande said. "These two Horde members are Captain Frandis Farley and Kelantir Bloodblade. Captain Farley was sent by the lady Sylvanas to command the Forsaken units that would serve under their warchief. The Blood Knight, Bloodblade, had previously served under Ranger-General Halduron Brightwing. Both, by all accounts, fought well in the battle against Northwatch Hold."

Anduin glanced over at the Horde area. Both Sylvanas and Halduron were leaning forward. Anduin had not heard of either Farley or Bloodblade, but judging by how their leaders reacted to their images, the two were held in high regard.

Bloodblade had hair the color of the sun and skin so pale as to look untouched by it. Even off-duty, she kept pieces of her armor on. Farley had been well on his way to decay before he had been reborn as a Forsaken, and Anduin wondered how he managed to indulge in liquid refreshment with a jaw that didn't seem likely to close.

Tyrande nodded to Chromie, and the scene resumed.

"Trouble," Kelantir said to her companion.

"Not necessarily." Frandis lifted a bony arm and waved. "Friend Malkorok! Are you slumming? The contents of a chamber pot are probably better than the swill this rascal Grosk serves, but it's cheap and I hear it does the job. Come, let us buy you a round."

Malkorok smiled. Anduin didn't like the look of it, and if her expression was any indication, neither did Kelantir.

"Grosk, drinks all around." The Blackrock orc clapped Frandis on the back so hard the Forsaken nearly fell forward on the table. "I might expect to find tauren or Forsaken here. But I must say, you look sorely out of place." He looked right at Kelantir as he spoke.

"Not at all. I have been in worse places than this," the paladin said, narrowing her eyes at Malkorok while the innkeeper, presumably the rascal Grosk, served them.

"Perhaps, perhaps," Malkorok said. "But why are you not in Orgrimmar?"

"Iron allergy," Kelantir said.

Despite the tension, Anduin grinned. He liked this Kelantir. She was brave. It was the sort of thing his friend Aerin, a gutsy dwarf, lost to the upheaval of the Cataclysm, might have said.

Malkorok seemed taken aback at first, then laughed.

"It does seem that you and several others prefer more rustic environments. Where is that young bull Baine, and his toady, Vol'jin? I had hoped to speak to them."

All eyes went to the new warchief and the Defender. They, of course, were seeing this for the first time, like most of those present, and looked slightly startled at the blatancy of the insult.

"I have not seen them in a while," said Kelantir. She plopped her boots up on the table, keeping her gaze steady. "I do not much involve myself with the tauren."

"Really?" replied Malkorok. "Yet we have witnesses that put both you and Frandis right in this very inn just last night, in close conversation with both the tauren and the troll, among others. They reported that you were saying things like, 'Garrosh is a fool,' and 'Thrall should return and kick him all the way to the Undercity,' and 'It was cowardly to use the mana bomb on Theramore.'"

"And the elements," another Kor'kron added.

"Yes, the elements—something about how it was too bad Cairne hadn't killed him when he had the chance, because Thrall would never utilize the elements in such a cruel and insulting fashion," Malkorok continued.

Kelantir's beautiful face was frozen. Frandis Farley dripped ichor on the table, holding his mug.

"But, if you say you haven't seen Baine or Vol'jin recently, then I suppose those witnesses must be mistaken," said Malkorok.

"Clearly," said Frandis, recovering. "You need better informants." He turned back to his drink.

"We must," Malkorok said agreeably, "for it's obvious to me that neither of you would ever say such things against Garrosh and his leadership."

"I'm glad you understand that," said Frandis. "Thanks for the drinks. Can I buy the next round?"

"No, we had best be on our way," replied Malkorok. "See if we can find Vol'jin and Baine, since, unfortunately for us, they are not here."

Fortunately for them, Anduin thought. *Their loa and Earth Mother must have been keeping them safe.*

Malkorok rose and nodded. "Enjoy your drinks," he said, then exited the inn with the other Kor'kron.

"That was far too close for comfort," Kelantir said, exhaling in relief.

"Indeed," said Frandis. "For half a moment, I expected to be arrested, if not outright attacked."

Kelantir looked around. "That is odd. Grosk is gone."

Frandis brought his jaw back into position for a frown. "What? With such a crowded inn? He should be hiring more help, not skipping out with several thirsty customers waiting on him."

And as the two locked gazes, Anduin knew. The hair at the back of his neck rose, and he wanted to shout out a warning. But this was not the present; it was the past, and it was too late, had already been too late by the time Farley and Bloodblade had realized what was going on.

The ill-fated pair leaped to their feet and raced toward the door. Ice crackled up to stop them in their tracks, and the scene went white. The sound of an explosion echoed through the hall, and then the Vision disappeared.

Tyrande stood in the center of the arena, looking up at where the celestials sat. It was hard to read them from this distance, but Anduin, who knew at least Chi-Ji well, knew that they had to be as distressed as anyone present. The night elf opened her mouth, as if to say something to the jury, then seemed to think better of it, shaking her head. She did not have to explain what exactly they had just seen. They all understood.

"No further questions, Fa'shua Zhu."

And she walked back to her chair in a huge coliseum filled with total silence.

10

Baine sat for a long moment. He hoped he exuded calmness; in reality, his anger was threatening his ability to question Kor'jus, so furious was he at what he had just seen.

He had, like nearly everyone else, suspected that the explosion at Razor Hill Inn had not been an accident, but of course there were no witnesses left to prove anything. As he understood it, Grosk had maintained that he knew nothing, and insisted that his departure had been a fortuitous coincidence.

No matter. He was not the one who had thrown first a frost and then a frag grenade into a packed tavern.

Baine silently prayed for control as he rose and went to Kor'jus.

"You had a narrow escape, it would seem," said Baine. "Malkorok and the Kor'kron had clearly decided that the time for simple beatings in order to discourage talk against Garrosh was over."

Kor'jus nodded. "You speak truth. I thank the ancestors that I live."

"No doubt Malkorok was doing what he had done in Blackrock Mountain," Baine continued. "Sniffing out those he perceived as traitors and summarily eliminating them as threats. You said earlier, I believe, that others were also targeted by this new, obsessive Kor'kron."

"Yes, I was far from the only one menaced."

"And did any of them ever hear Malkorok say that he had been directly ordered by Garrosh to . . . *menace* . . . anyone?"

Kor'jus scowled, his gaze flitting to the orc in question. Garrosh sat as if he had been carved in stone, his eyes flat and disinterested. "No. But I think it's clear—"

Baine held up a hand. "Just answer the question, please."

The scowl deepened, but Kor'jus said sullenly, "No."

"So you cannot tell this court that the Accused *ever* gave instructions to murder his own people for speaking out?"

"No," repeated Kor'jus, clearly struggling not to elaborate.

"Then it's entirely possible that Malkorok and the Kor'kron did this on their own, and that Garrosh did not even know about this incident? Or indeed, any such incidents? And that had he known, he might have disapproved and taken action against Malkorok?"

"With respect, I protest," said Tyrande.

"I agree with the Defender," said Taran Zhu. "The witness may respond."

Through gritted teeth, Kor'jus growled, "Y-yes. It's possible."

"I have no further questions." Baine nodded to Tyrande, who rose but did not move toward the witness.

"Fa'shua," said Tyrande. "I request that a segment of the opening statements be read back to this court. The portion where you addressed the Accused before leveling the charges."

"Granted," said Taran Zhu, nodding to Zazzarik Fryll, the goblin whose penmanship and neutrality had both been bought with a not-too-exorbitant fee. The goblin adjusted his spectacles on his beaklike nose and, small chest swelling with importance, rolled the scroll open.

"'Garrosh Hellscream,'" he began in a raspy voice. "'You have been charged with war crimes, and crimes against the very essence of sentient beings of Azeroth, as well as crimes against Azeroth itself. You are also charged for all acts committed in your name, or by those with whom you have allied.'"

WAR CRIMES   97

"Thank you," said Tyrande, and Zazzarik returned to where he had left off, his quill poised to continue.

"'For all acts committed in your name, or by those with whom you have allied,'" the night elf repeated, then gave a shrug. She looked to the celestials and said to them, "There are moments when I think things are so obvious, my presence here is not even necessary."

That got to Baine, and he leaped to his hooves in true anger. "The Accuser's comment is completely inappropriate!" he snapped, forgetting to use the formal phrase.

Tyrande smiled and held up a placating hand. "I withdraw the statement, Fa'shua, and I apologize to my esteemed colleague. I have no further questions."

"The witness may return to his seat," said Taran Zhu. Kor'jus rose and hurried back to the stands, relief radiating from him. Taran Zhu leveled his steady gaze upon Tyrande. "Chu'shao, I must urge caution in these proceedings. I would dislike being forced to reprimand you."

"Understood," said Tyrande.

Baine turned and looked back at Garrosh with narrowed eyes, then at Tyrande. "I request a ten-minute respite to confer with the Accused and my time advisor before the next witness, Fa'shua."

"So granted," said Taran Zhu, and struck the gong.

Kairoz approached Baine with a quizzical look. Still standing at her table, Tyrande gave the dragon a nod of acknowledgment. He grasped the chair she had vacated, giving her a wink and a smile.

"You'll have this back in no time," he promised the astonished high priestess, then pulled the chair alongside the chained Garrosh.

Baine said irritably but quietly, "Tyrande won't forget that."

"I don't intend her to," said Kairoz, keeping his voice equally soft. "By my reckoning, and I am always right about such things, we now have only seven minutes and eighteen seconds. Please speak, Chu'shao."

The tauren needed no further urging. He turned his attention full upon Garrosh, his nostrils flaring. "What in the name of the Earth Mother are you *doing*, Garrosh?"

"Me?" Garrosh chuckled. "Why, nothing at all."

"That is precisely what I mean. You are showing no remorse, no reactions—not even vague *interest* in these proceedings!"

Garrosh shrugged, and his chains jingled with an incongruously bright sound. "That is because I *have* no interest in the proceedings . . . *Chu'shao.*"

Baine swore softly. "Do you truly desire execution, then?"

"Execution? No. Death? If I were to die in glorious battle against the likes of this priestess charged with damning me . . . yes. I would most assuredly wish that."

"Your odds of being released and permitted to fight again decrease with each passing moment that you sit stoically in this chair doing nothing to help your cause!" Baine warned.

"I am no youngling to be told bedtime tales, Bloodhoof," Garrosh said. "I will *never* be permitted another battle, were I as long lived as this bronze wyrm."

"Life is full of surprises," Kairoz said unexpectedly. "But I will say, you certainly won't see battle if your head is on a pike like a skewered peanut chicken, being happily passed around from the gates of Stormwind to Orgrimmar and back again."

With the minutes ticking away, Baine sat for a moment, wrestling with his conscience. If Garrosh himself did not care what happened to him, why should he? *Surely honor is being satisfied,* Baine thought. *No one can say that I did not try to defend him well. And what if he is reprieved? What then?*

"Chu'shao Bloodhoof," said Kairoz in a warning voice. Baine lifted a hand to silence the dragon.

He knew he was defending well—better, likely, than the orc deserved. But could he meet his father in the afterlife and say, *I have come home, Father, and I have done the best I could?*

He knew the answer. Baine took a deep, resigned breath, and turned again to Garrosh. "Give me something to counter her with, Garrosh. I've had to create my entire case without any help from you."

"And you can see how well *that's* going," said Kairoz.

Baine gave Kairoz a withering glance. "Your confidence," he said, "is inspiring." He turned back to Garrosh. "If you will not talk to me, help me to defend you . . . Is there anyone you *would* speak to? Some warrior, some shaman who holds your respect?"

A strange smile curved around Garrosh's tusks. "Well, Chu'shao . . . there is . . . *one*," he said.

Still reeling from Garrosh's completely unexpected request of a confidant, Baine settled in beside the orc a few moments later. Garrosh's earlier smile had faded, and he once again wore the inscrutable mask he had donned for the proceedings thus far. Tyrande was running rampant over anything and everything Baine put forward. There was no one left alive that Baine could use to share the blame for what Garrosh had done, and there were few who would or even could speak well of him.

Tyrande's next witness was making his vow to uphold the honor of the court. Baine mused darkly that Kairoz's comments were on target. She had called another orc—one whom many present knew and respected. One whom Baine was not looking forward to questioning.

Varok Saurfang.

He sat in the chair, his mere presence charismatic and calm. Age spotted his green face, and time and sorrow both had etched deep wrinkles in his forehead and around yellowed tusks. Long white braids draped his still-massive shoulders, and his eyes were alert. Baine knew where this would be going, and his ears were pricked forward, hoping to find something, anything, he could use that could remotely help Garrosh.

"Please state your name," said Tyrande kindly.

"I am Varok Saurfang," he said in a deep voice. "Brother to Broxigar, father to Dranosh. I serve the Horde."

"Broxigar being one of the great heroes not just of the Horde, but of Azeroth, correct?"

Saurfang's eyes narrowed, as if he was suspecting a trick. "I and many others deem him so, yes," he replied.

"You yourself are regarded highly in the eyes of your people, and by the Alliance as well," Tyrande continued. Baine could hear genuine respect in the night elf's voice. "Many here know of the great tragedy that befell your son."

Varok's face grew carefully impassive. "Others suffered as well because of the Lich King's darkness. I have never asked for special treatment." The words were true—the brave Dranosh Saurfang had been slain at what had become known as the Battle of Angrathar the Wrath Gate, only to be drafted to rise again as an undead to challenge his father and other heroes of the Horde. But such horrors were tragically not uncommon. Many, like Varok, had been forced to oppose someone they loved whom they had already mourned once. The dark legacy of the Lich King lived on in the wounded hearts of the survivors, and in the Knights of the Ebon Blade, now an uneasy part of both Horde and Alliance society.

"I would like others to fully understand just what you endured, may it please the court."

Baine abruptly realized with a sickening jolt precisely which scene Tyrande was planning on displaying.

No. It didn't matter if Tyrande was being calculating or if she was acting from misguided compassion. He could not let her show—

Baine leaped to his hooves. "With respect, I protest!" he cried. "Varok Saurfang has suffered enough, Fa'shua, and what Chu'shao Whisperwind is suggesting is nothing but salt in the wound. I will not see him forced to endure the death of his son yet again!"

"What you will and will not see in this court is not your decision,

Chu'shao," warned Taran Zhu. "But I agree with you. The court recognizes that Varok Saurfang is a respected war hero and has undergone great loss, Chu'shao Whisperwind, but we do not see how that has a bearing on his interactions with Garrosh. The Lich King is not the one on trial here."

Color rose in Tyrande's cheeks. "I withdraw my request and offer apologies to the witness if it disturbed him."

Varok's jaw tightened, but he nodded curtly. The high priestess continued. "Would you agree that you are well respected, Varok Saurfang? That few, if any, would question your devotion to the Horde?"

"It is not for me to decide how I am viewed in the eyes of others," Saurfang replied. "For myself, I love the Horde with my whole being."

"Enough to die for it?"

"Yes, of course."

"Enough to kill for it?"

"Certainly. I am a warrior."

"Would you say that you and others used the Horde as a sort of . . . license to butcher?"

"With respect, I protest!" Baine shouted. "The Accuser's apparently obsessive focus on past events that have nothing to do with the Accused is verging on hate-mongering!"

Taran Zhu turned a calm visage on Tyrande. "Chu'shao, can you explain why this line of questioning has pertinence?"

"I am actually attempting to show that this witness is rational and responsible, Lord Zhu. Which is the farthest thing from hate-mongering I can imagine." She gave Baine an angry look.

Taran Zhu considered this, then said, "Very well. I'll allow it. The witness may answer the question."

"My answer is yes," said Varok.

"Do you presently condone that sort of behavior?" Tyrande continued.

"No, I do not. And I have said so."

"To whom?"

"It is no secret. I am not proud of what I did." Varok looked at Velen as he said this.

"Did you express this sentiment to Garrosh Hellscream?"

"I did."

Tyrande nodded. "May it please the court, I would like to show a Vision that I believe pertains to this. So noted," she added, with a look at Baine, "because I was requested to withdraw my first choice of Vision."

"The Accuser may introduce this evidence," Taran Zhu said. The by-now-familiar working of Chromie over the Vision of Time was followed by images solidifying in the center of the room.

For the first time, those assembled looked on Garrosh Hellscream not as he was now—captured and in chains, an emotionless expression on his face—but as he had been a few years ago, before the fall of the Lich King. When, mused Baine, his own father still respected the son of Grom Hellscream.

Even High Overlord Saurfang looked younger, thought Baine, realizing with a heavy heart how much the loss of that orc's only offspring had taken its toll.

Garrosh and Saurfang stood side by side at Warsong Hold in the Borean Tundra, gazing down at a large map on the floor. It was made of stitched-together hides, with miniature standards of Horde and Alliance marking the various strongholds, a toy zeppelin buzzing away, and painted skull faces representing the seemingly inexhaustible Scourge. Saurfang knelt, pointing out things as he spoke. Garrosh hung back, managing to look both disinterested and annoyed.

Saurfang was attempting to impress upon Garrosh the importance of supporting the troops in practical matters when Hellscream retorted with a dismissive gesture, "Shipping lanes . . . supplies . . . You bore me to death! We need nothing more than the warrior spirit of the Horde, Saurfang. Now that we are firmly entrenched in this frozen wasteland, nothing shall stop us!"

Baine noted the familiarity with which Garrosh addressed the much older, much more experienced orc, and he did not like it. Saurfang, however, was too smart to rise to the bait and pressed on.

"Siege engines, ammunition, heavy armor . . ." Saurfang replied. "How do you propose to shatter the walls of Icecrown without those?"

Garrosh smirked and drew himself up to his full height. "Propose?" he sneered. "I will show you what I propose!" He lifted Gorehowl and brought it smashing down on the figurines representing Valiance Keep. "There . . . now we have a shipping lane. And just for good measure . . ." Valgarde and Westguard Keep fell beneath his booted feet.

Saurfang said witheringly, "So the prodigal son has spoken! Your father's blood runs strong in you, Hellscream. Impatient as always . . . Impatient and reckless. You rush headlong into all-out war without a thought of the consequences."

"Do not speak to me of consequences, old one."

Baine's hackles rose, and apparently so did those of the Vision's Saurfang. He stepped closer to Garrosh and growled, "I drank of the same blood your father did, Garrosh. Mannoroth's cursed venom pumped through *my* veins as well. I drove my weapons into the bodies and minds of my enemies. And while Grom died a glorious death—freeing us all from the blood-curse—he could not wipe away the terrible memory of our past. His act could not erase the horrors we committed."

The image of Saurfang then looked away, talking more to himself now than to the younger orc. His eyes were haunted. "The winter after the curse was lifted, hundreds of veteran orcs like me were lost to despair. Our minds were finally free, yes . . . Free to relive all of the unthinkable acts that we had performed under the Legion's influence." He nodded, as if coming to a conclusion, and his voice became so soft Baine had to strain to hear it. "I think it was the sounds of the draenei children that unnerved most of them. You never forget . . . Have you ever been to Jaggedswine Farm? When the swine are of age for the slaughter. It's that sound. The sound of the swine being killed . . . It resonates the loudest. Those are hard times for us older veterans."

Velen had closed his eyes. Baine felt the focus in the room shift to the draenei, and heard some uncomfortable shuffling in the stands. He looked up at the celestials to see them raptly watching the Vision unfold.

The image of Garrosh shattered the somber mood with words that made Baine want to throttle him, words that went directly against what had just been shown with Durotan. "But surely you cannot think that those children were born into innocence? They would have grown up and taken arms against us!"

To Baine's surprise, Saurfang did not react to the suggestion. Instead he said in that soft, distant voice, "I am not speaking solely of the children of our enemies . . ."

That, at last, seemed to silence Garrosh. He simply stood, looking at Saurfang with a mixture of revulsion and pity. Saurfang shook himself, and when he turned to speak with Garrosh again, his voice was strong and firm.

"I won't let you take us down that dark path again, young Hellscream. I'll kill you myself before that day comes."

That was doubtless the gem Tyrande had been waiting for. A great war hero threatening to kill Garrosh before he'd let the impetuous youth plunge the orcs into another devastating war for no true reason.

The image of Garrosh replied, and Baine was startled at the change in the young orc. He spoke in a quiet tone of respect and almost wonderment.

"How have you managed to survive for so long, Saurfang? Not fallen victim to your own memories?"

Saurfang smiled. "I don't eat pork."

"Pause." The scene froze, and Tyrande let it linger there, etching itself on the minds of the jury and the onlookers, then nodded to Chromie. The scene vanished. Tyrande turned to Saurfang and gave a slight, sincere bow. "Thank you, High Overlord. Chu'shao—your witness."

Baine nodded, and he walked toward Saurfang. "High Overlord, I will keep this brief, so that you may spend no more time in that chair than necessary. You spoke of killing Garrosh before you let him lead the orcs down that dark path."

"I did."

"Was that a figure of speech?"

"It was not."

"You would actually kill Garrosh with your own hands?"

"Yes."

"And do you believe he has done so? Led the orcs down that dark path?"

"Yes. That is why I took up arms against him. After some of the things he did—" The old orc shook his head, disgusted, and gave Garrosh a venomous look.

"So you would be happy with the verdict that Chu'shao Whisperwind advocates—execution."

"No."

Murmurs rippled through the courtroom, but Baine felt quiet pleasure. He had been right about Varok. He allowed himself a brief glance at Tyrande and saw the kaldorei sitting up and watching attentively, hoping for some misstep. Baine intended to give her none.

"What *would* you like to see?"

Tyrande leaped to her feet. "With respect, I protest! The witness's personal preference is irrelevant."

"Fa'shua, I am attempting to clarify what the high overlord meant when he said, 'I'll kill you myself.'"

"I agree with the Defender," said Taran Zhu. "You may answer the question, High Overlord Saurfang."

Saurfang did not do so immediately. He gave Garrosh a long,

appraising look, then spoke. "Garrosh was not always as you see him now. He was, as I have said, reckless and impulsive. But I once would never have doubted his loyalty to the Horde. And even now, I do not doubt his loyalty to his people. But his crimes must be addressed. I vowed to kill him, and I would still uphold that vow. But I would not surrender him to others for execution. I would challenge him myself, in the mak'gora."

"Do you think he deserves a second chance?"

"If he defeated me—yes. That is the way of the orcs—the true way. Honor."

Baine could barely believe what he was hearing. "I do not wish to misunderstand you, so forgive my repetition. You do not want Garrosh executed by this court, but rather wish to challenge him in honorable combat. And if he won that combat, you would see him forgiven?"

"He would need to earn his reputation back, given that he has ripped it to shreds and trampled it into the angry earth," Saurfang snapped. "But yes. If he were a victor, then he should have that chance. He had honor, once. He could learn it again."

Baine could barely refrain from letting out a shout of delight. This, he understood. This, he could support, and moreover, it was fair. He thought of his father, dying in the mak'gora, and how Cairne would have approved, and knew in his heart he was on the proper track. Despite his anger toward Garrosh, Baine was in truth doing the right thing.

He gave Tyrande a triumphant look and announced, "I have no further questions."

And to his surprised pleasure, neither did Tyrande. When Taran Zhu sounded the gong to close the opening day of proceedings, for the first time since the trial had begun, it looked like Garrosh Hellscream might just, quite literally, keep his head.

11

Most would have assumed, when Shokia turned up in Hammerfall, that she was so disheartened at the fall of Garrosh Hellscream that she wanted to return to orcish roots. To come here—where Orgrim Doomhammer, another great warchief, had been killed—and vanish into obscurity, contenting herself with putting her astonishing sniper skills to work slaughtering enemy trolls and Alliance adventurers. Those who assumed that would be wrong, but it was a façade Shokia was happy to maintain. She was not retreating to lick wounds and mourn failure. She was an agent of someone who wanted what she did—a return to the glory of the Horde. Shokia was in deep cover.

Hammerfall had become an unofficial refuge for discontents who felt they had no place in the current world, and so her story was not questioned. And she had been content to wait for her orders, enjoying watching the heads of her enemies explode like thrown pumpkins through her scope.

Since the trial of Garrosh Hellscream had begun in Pandaria, however, she had grown anxious. When would her ally summon her to the field of battle? What would his instructions be? Who else shared their feelings?

"Wait for me to send you orders," he had said in that silky voice. *"I will not fail to do so, but only when the time is right."*

So when Adegwa, the tauren innkeeper, let her know there was a letter for her, she was hard put to contain her delight.

> *No doubt, your fingers itch to fire at our enemies. But first, you must accumulate allies. What follows is a list of those who will be helpful. Seek them out, and when you are gathered, I will send you further instructions.*
> *Meet the first one today, in Drywhisker Gorge.*

Shokia had packed her precious rifle, her few other belongings, mounted her wolf, and was at the gorge a scant five minutes later. She took up a position overlooking the trail, peering through the scope of her rifle, but did not have long to wait.

A black wolf, his pelt sleek and glossy, came into view. His rider crouched low over his back. The cloak hid her face, but billowed out sufficiently for Shokia to determine that her new comrade in arms was another orc female. Slowly, Shokia began to grin. She wondered if . . . She would find out soon enough.

The rider slowed, and the wolf began to pick his way up the trail. Without revealing her position behind a boulder, Shokia cried out, "Hail, wolf rider! Are you a friend of the dragon's?"

The orc came to a halt and shoved back her hood, revealing her strong face. "Under most circumstances, I am no friend to dragons," Zaela, warlord of the Dragonmaw, called back. "But this time—yes."

"Zaela! I had heard you had fallen in battle!"

"I fell, indeed, but I lived to keep fighting for our true leader. I came alone, as instructed, but what remains of my clan is ready for battle."

"Then," said Shokia, lifting the scroll, "let us gather more allies!"

Day Two

"I summon His Royal Highness Anduin Wrynn, prince of Storm-wind, to speak as witness."

Anduin had been dreading this moment. He'd always resented SI:7's code name for him, "the White Pawn," and had no desire to become involved in this case in any fashion, fearing that both sides would use him thus. His father had known, of course, but Jaina hadn't, and she looked surprised and a little concerned as Varian gave his son's arm a squeeze and Anduin then descended from the stands to the witness chair.

He was accustomed to royal events, and had even given speeches to throngs much larger than this one. But that was different. In those situations, he was a guest, or an invited speaker, or the respected host. He knew what to do, how to behave. This was completely new, and not a little unsettling. He caught Wrathion's eye as he took his seat. He could almost hear the Black Prince saying, *How very interesting!* The amusing thought calmed him.

Tyrande gave him a kind smile as she approached. "Prince Anduin," she said, "thank you for being here today." He thought it best not to remind her that it wasn't as if he'd had a choice in the matter, and merely nodded. "Your Highness, you are known throughout Azeroth as a proponent of peace. Is that accurate?"

"Yes," Anduin replied. He ached to elaborate, but remembered what his father had told him. *Stick to the questions. Don't volunteer anything. Tyrande knows what she's doing.*

"So it would be fair to say that you do not hate the Horde, or its races?"

"It would be fair, yes."

"You have worked with them on occasion, and urged mercy even in wartime, correct?"

"Yes, I have."

"Everyone here knows Garrosh Hellscream by name and reputation, of course. But you have had personal encounters with him, have you not?"

Here we go, he thought, and deliberately did not look at Garrosh. "I have."

"On how many occasions?"

"Two."

"Can you please tell the court about them?"

Anduin wondered why she didn't just show both encounters, given the unique tool she had in the Vision of Time. Perhaps she was saving her allotted minutes for something more lively than people sitting around talking. "One was in Theramore, at a peace conference. My father, Lady Jaina Proudmoore, and I were there, and Thrall brought Garrosh and Rehgar Earthfury, and some of the Kor'kron." He hadn't thought about that ill-fated meeting in some time; so many other things had happened. Anduin found himself looking at the chained orc, whose steady gaze made Anduin feel like an insect pinned to a board. Odd . . . Garrosh was the prisoner, not he, yet it was Anduin who came close to squirming in his seat.

"How did the conference unfold?"

"It was a bit of a rocky start," Anduin admitted. "But as things progressed, we started to find some common ground. Even Garrosh—"

"Can you elaborate as to what you mean by a 'rocky start'?"

"Well, first of all it was storming, so no one was in a particularly good mood. Everyone brought weapons—for the formal laying down."

"Who put down the first weapon?"

"Um . . . I did. My bow. That was the first time I spoke with Thr— I mean, Go'el."

"Did King Varian and the warchief follow your example?"

"They did. They learned they had more in common than they thought when they sat down to talk."

"What did Garrosh contribute to these peace talks?"

"Well . . . he didn't seem to understand that being a leader means sometimes thinking about things that aren't all that exciting. He interrupted when Go'el and Father were discussing trade. He kept talking about the Horde . . . just taking what it wanted."

Tyrande gave Garrosh a pointed glance. "I see. Please continue."

"Go'el and Father were starting to get along when word came of another attack by the Lich King. They agreed it needed to be addressed but were planning on resuming the conference, but then we were attacked by agents of the Twilight's Hammer cult. It all fell to pieces after that. Of course, that's just what the cult intended. They broke the attack down by races—the Horde members of the cult targeted the Alliance races of the summit, and vice versa. Garrosh was shouting about 'human treachery,' Father mistakenly believed that Go'el had hired an assassin, and . . ."

"History documents the rest, thank you, Prince Anduin." She paced deliberately, her back to him, her face turned to the crowd peering eagerly down. Anduin, too, glanced up at the spectators, and thought again of his father's comment about the gladiator pits. They *were* hungry for blood, he realized, and the idea both chilled and saddened him. His gaze went back to Garrosh, and there was weariness in the orc's posture that made Anduin wonder if Garrosh was thinking the same thing.

And if, finally, he might not want to fight it anymore.

"I would like to move on to your second . . . encounter . . . with Garrosh Hellscream."

He knew this was coming, of course, but was unprepared for the way he responded. It was as if no time had passed—as if only a moment ago, the great bell had fallen . . . He cleared his throat, and was displeased that his voice shook slightly when he spoke.

"It was a few months ago, before—"

Tyrande turned, smiling gently, but holding up a hand that forestalled further comment. "May it please the court," she said. "I do not need you to tell it, Prince Anduin. I would like to show it."

So that's what she wants to save the Vision for . . . "Do you think that's wise?" Anduin blurted. Too fresh in his mind was the awful screaming of the Divine Bell, and the effect that sound had on those with any kind of darkness in their hearts. The thought of replicating that moment horrified him. "What if it—"

Tyrande held up a hand. "Do not fear, Your Highness. I understand your concerns. I spoke with Chromie at length about this event, and she and I have already witnessed it. While these displays granted to us through the Vision of Time are remarkable, seeing and hearing the bell rung in this manner does not have the same effect as actually being in its presence."

"Thank the Light," Anduin murmured as he relaxed, exhaling in relief. His bones ached, abruptly and deeply. Neither he nor his body, apparently, would relish watching the events surrounding the Divine Bell play out. His palms were moist and he took a breath to steady himself, whispering a soft prayer. A gentle wave of healing energy washed through him, and the pain subsided somewhat.

"Now that you have been reassured, Prince Anduin, can you please set up the details of what we are about to see?"

He licked his lips and glanced up at the celestials. They did not show any reaction, but simply seeing them was calming to Anduin. Keeping his gaze focused on them and avoiding Hellscream, he spoke. "The mogu created an artifact that Lei Shen, the tyrant known as the Thunder King, called the Divine Bell. Its origins were violent and cruel, in keeping with the discord and horrors it would unleash when it was rung. Its tones fueled the anger and hatred of Lei Shen's warriors, lending them unnatural strength and power, while striking fear into the hearts of his enemies. Once the Alliance learned about it, the night elves hid it away in Darnassus. The idea was to keep it out of any hands that might misuse it—Horde or Alliance. Lady Jaina herself placed protective wards to keep it safe."

"It sounds like a powerful weapon." And of course, Tyrande knew it was.

"It was a double-edged sword," Anduin continued. "It took as much as it gave—perhaps more."

"What happened to the bell?"

"A Sunreaver agent, acting on orders from Garrosh, was able to bypass Lady Jaina's wards on the bell. He and several other Horde members stole it."

"From what you are telling us, it sounds as though this bell would have made Garrosh Hellscream unstoppable."

Without even realizing it, Anduin glanced over at Garrosh. His skin crawled at the expression on the orc's face, but the reaction was not from fear. The stillness Garrosh assumed was unnatural for him, whom Anduin always recalled posturing and bellowing. Anduin reached for a glass of water on the small table beside his chair before continuing.

"The pandaren had crafted the means to combat the ringing of the bell. They had made the Harmonic Mallet, which turns the bell's chaos to harmony. The mallet had been broken and scattered, but with help, I managed to find and assemble the pieces, and located an ointment to activate it. When it was restored, I headed out to confront Garrosh. I wanted to stop him before he rang the bell."

"Alone?"

"There wasn't time for anything else."

Tyrande nodded at Chromie, and what Anduin had been dreading began.

This time, though, Anduin had a chance to hear what Garrosh said before the human prince had reached him.

Garrosh stood, larger than life in the Vision, the one whom Anduin remembered, not this still-as-stone orc who sat in the courtroom watching with an emotionless visage. He was alone save for his champion, Ishi, on a platform off the Mogu'shan Vaults, facing the bell. It was enormous, much bigger even than the mighty orc himself. It bore the face of a grotesque creature on it, and its lower rim was studded with spikes. Garrosh grinned and roared in triumph, lifting his arms. He called out to his people, still lingering in the vaults, "We are the *Horde*. We are slaves to nothing and no one! With the Divine Bell, I will burn away any remnants of weakness within us."

Garrosh was trembling, Anduin realized, shaking with an almost uncontrollable passion and excitement as he spat out the names of the emotions he despised.

"Fear . . . despair . . . hatred . . . doubt. The lesser races are buried beneath their weight. But *we* will control their power. Together, we will destroy the Alliance and claim what is rightfully ours. Let our song of victory begin."

Despite Tyrande's words of reassurance, Anduin clenched his fists so tightly that his fingernails cut into his palms, and his brow was dewed with sweat. The dark song rang out, but he knew at once that the high priestess had been right—he heard the awful, discordant cry of the bell only in his ears, not in his heart or his bones. Gratitude left him weak for a moment as he watched and listened.

Anduin saw his image race toward the bell. He thought of himself as average-sized; his father, of course, was a particularly large human male, but Anduin had been used to that since his birth. But to see his form standing next to not only the then-warchief of the Horde but also the gargantuan bell made him realize how slender he was . . . how very breakable—

"Stop, Garrosh! You do not know what that bell is capable of!" His own voice—firm, certain.

Garrosh whirled, saw Anduin, looked past the prince, and then smiled as he realized Anduin was all that stood between him and victory. He threw back his head and laughed.

"So in the end, it is not Varian but his whelp who comes to face me. You run bravely to your death, young one."

Tyrande called, "Stop here," and the scene froze. Anduin blinked, coming back to the present moment. "That was indeed exceptionally brave, Your Highness."

"I, uh . . . not so brave," Anduin admitted. "I was scared to death. But I had to stop him, no matter what the cost."

Tyrande seemed taken aback, but then she smiled—sweetly, genuinely. "Ah," she said in a kind voice, "to proceed with what you knew was right even while afraid—that is courage indeed."

Anduin felt his color rise, but all he said was, "Well, it's the truth. He couldn't be allowed to continue."

Tyrande gave Chromie the signal to resume the scene.

"I will not let you do this. I swear to it," the image of Anduin cried out.

"Stop me then, human," Garrosh taunted, knowing Anduin couldn't physically prevent him from striking the bell a second time. Couldn't hold back that massive arm, couldn't even reach him or the bell fast enough. Garrosh proceeded to make a mockery of Anduin's threat.

Again the awful sound, terrible in its beauty, rang out, and this time the bell had a victim in Garrosh's champion.

Ishi cried out, his body contorting as the dark entities known in Pandaria as the sha, the very essences of hatred, fear, doubt, and despair, descended upon and *into* him. Even now, the sound of the orc's anguish made Anduin's heart ache.

"This pain!" screamed the orc, who had likely endured more of it than most could ever imagine. "I cannot control it!"

Both Anduins—the one in the courtroom and his image—watched, transfixed, as Ishi struggled. No doubt drawn by the screaming, Horde members began to emerge from the depths of the vaults. Ishi charged his own people, who were forced to fight him or be slaughtered themselves. "Pause," said Tyrande. "Prince Anduin—why did you not strike earlier, or now?"

"The mallet would only work once. A glancing blow would have wasted my chance. I had to wait till I could strike strongly and true. As for why I didn't do anything here—I didn't know what it would do to Ishi."

"You were concerned for the welfare of an orc champion?"

Anduin was puzzled. "Why shouldn't I be?"

Tyrande stared at him for just an instant before recovering. "Continue," she instructed Chromie.

Garrosh kept encouraging Ishi to "fight," to "master," to "use" the sha, while Ishi went through every conceivable negative emotion—doubting the Horde's strength, grieving the fallen, fearing his own death, which claimed him soon after. Ishi fell to his knees, his last thought of his duty, gasping, "Warchief! I . . . I have failed you."

Garrosh went to the dying warrior and said, calmly and brutally, "Yes, Ishi. You have."

And suddenly, Anduin was angry. Garrosh had forced the sha upon Ishi, and both he and Anduin had watched how hard the champion had struggled to dominate things that he simply couldn't. He'd given his life to try to please his warchief, and for all his effort and suffering, he had received the cruelest possible words from Garrosh. Now Anduin did turn his gaze upon the prisoner, feeling his face flush with the emotion, and clenched his jaw when Garrosh, curse him, actually let his lips curl in a tiny smirk of satisfaction.

His bones ached.

"Your interference has cost me a great warrior, young prince," the image of Garrosh was saying. "You'll pay with your life."

"That is where you are wrong, Garrosh." Anduin's own voice sounded impossibly young in his ears. He watched himself leap upward. He remembered praying silently with all his being to the Light, asking for peace, for this single strike to ring true. The image of Anduin brought down the hard-won mallet upon the Divine Bell, and saw a great crack mar the beautiful and dangerous-looking surface. Garrosh Hellscream reeled backward, stunned, barely able to keep his balance as the sound washed over and through him.

The then-Anduin turned, and hope shone brightly on his young face. He opened his mouth to speak—

Garrosh recovered, growled, "Die, whelp!" and charged—not at Anduin, but at the bell, which would never again summon sha with its call. The bell that fractured and fell upon Anduin in a rain of brass and agony. The bell that shattered his bones, which now ached so fiercely with remembered torment that it was all Anduin could do not to gasp.

The next thing he was to remember was waking up in the care of pandaren monks and his teacher, the kind and wise Velen, who had saved his life. What the Vision of Time now displayed was new to him, and Anduin forced himself to focus on what he was witnessing rather than the icy-cold ache of his body.

To his surprise, the Vision-Garrosh looked distressed, rather than pleased at having dealt a death-blow to the son of his great enemy. "There is much I do not know about this artifact," he muttered. "The weak-willed cannot control this sha energy, but I *will* master it."

No one dared speak to him. Even his own people stood silently by, doubtless wondering what would happen next. Garrosh roused himself. "At least the human prince is dead," Garrosh said. The words bit deep. "King Wrynn now knows the price of his continued defiance." He waved a hand dismissively, turning inward again, his massive brow furrowed. "Leave me. I have much to think about."

The scene faded. Anduin was glad to see the last of it, but Garrosh's words—and his expression—confused him. He glanced over at the orc, who wore the same expression as he had in the display—a furrowed brow of deep thought, but no hint as to the nature of those thoughts. Anduin gazed into those yellow eyes, and was pulled away from them only by Tyrande's voice.

"Chu'shao, your witness," Tyrande said, stepping back. She bowed to the prince of Stormwind, and her wonderful eyes were kind. Anduin gave her a ghost of a smile, then steeled himself. It was now Baine's turn to question him.

12

Baine inclined his head. Anduin thought he caught a faint echo of regret from the tauren, but if it was there, it was gone an instant later.

"We have all seen what you endured, Prince Anduin," Baine said. "For a while, rumors circulated that you were dead. I am very pleased to see that you survived."

"So am I," Anduin said, and a small titter rippled through the courtroom. Baine's ears twitched.

"You said earlier that you were frightened when you confronted Garrosh. How did you feel when you realized the bell was about to fall upon you?"

Anduin blinked and drew back slightly at the question, then recovered. "I . . . it . . . it happened so fast."

"Try to remember, please."

The prince licked his lips. "It's impossible to describe how terrified I was. And how . . . *betrayed* I felt. That sounds foolish, I know, to feel 'betrayed' by an enemy."

"Why did you come to confront Garrosh at all?"

"To prevent him from invoking the sha."

"Understood. But why?"

"Because . . ." Anduin paused. The obvious answer, of course, was that he wanted to stop Garrosh from using the sha as a weapon.

He'd talked his own father out of the same idea, persuasively arguing that the abominations would do more harm than good. Varian had seen the wisdom of it.

"I wanted Garrosh to understand just what he'd be doing," he blurted. "I thought if I could make him grasp the price he'd be paying for victory, he'd—well, he'd—"

"He would what?"

"He would see that it wasn't honorable. That it was—dark in a way I didn't believe *he* was dark. That sacrificing his people to those . . . things . . . wasn't the path toward any kind of victory worth having." The words tumbled from him, uncensored, unimagined until they passed his lips. But Anduin knew by the easing of pain in his wounded bones that it was the truth—and it was of the Light.

Baine's body quivered, ever so slightly, and he strode over to Anduin, peering at him intently. "When the weight of the brass pieces of the bell crushed you, I would imagine you were filled with fury. That when you awoke and faced an agonizing and long recovery, you wanted revenge against Garrosh for breaking every bone in your body, after you had come to him with help and wisdom."

Anduin said, very quietly, "No."

Baine pressed on. "You weren't in torment? Frightened that you might never walk again? Angry?"

"Yes, of course, all those things."

"But yet you say now, here, under oath, that you did *not* want revenge."

"That's true."

"That is a remarkable attitude. Why not?"

"Because it doesn't do any good. It won't unbreak my bones, or bring back the dead. It won't do anything but cause more damage." It came easier now, the flow of words, as easy as breathing, and as necessary to life.

"But certainly you do not wish Garrosh to do any of the things he has been charged with ever again, do you?"

"No." *No more torment, no more pain. We're here to help one another. To grow and prosper together.*

"Well, the Accuser insists that the only way to be certain that these terrible things won't happen again is to put Garrosh Hellscream to death. Is that what *you* want?"

"With respect, I protest! What the witness wants is not relevant to the verdict to be rendered in this courtroom!" Tyrande's voice was strained, and her movements were slightly less graceful than usual as she sprang to her feet. She shot Anduin a confused look.

"Fa'shua," Baine said, "most of Garrosh's victims are dead and cannot speak for themselves. Prince Anduin is one who has survived to tell us his thoughts. If we purport to be trying to obtain justice, I maintain that those who have been the most wronged should be allowed to express their opinions."

The pandaren eyed first Baine, then Tyrande. "You do understand, Chu'shao Bloodhoof, that this is a sword that can cut both ways? If I agree to allow this witness to speak such an opinion, then the Accuser's other witnesses may do the same."

"I understand," Baine replied, and now Tyrande's look of confusion transferred to Baine. Anduin wondered at the tauren's tactics—surely, he had handed Tyrande a powerful weapon in permitting a witness's opinion on the fate of Garrosh Hellscream. Baine was too intelligent not to realize that.

"Very well, this shall be admissible. Prince Anduin, you may answer the question."

"Please tell the court, Prince Anduin," said Baine. "Do you want Garrosh Hellscream to die for what he has done?"

"No," Anduin Wrynn said quietly.

"Why not?"

"Because I believe people can change."

"What makes you say that?"

"Because I saw it happen with my father." Anduin's eyes flickered to Varian, who looked surprised.

"Do you think Garrosh Hellscream can change?"

A pause. Anduin turned his golden head to regard Garrosh intently. Inside his heart was no fear, only peace. He took a deep breath, expanding himself so that the true answer could come.

"Yes."

Baine settled back and nodded. "I have no further questions." Tyrande looked at Anduin, then at Baine, then at Anduin again, and shook her head.

Anduin permitted himself a quiet sigh of relief as he rose and resumed his regular seat in the audience.

Sylvanas sat still as stone, the rage inside her belying her cool exterior. She could not believe the night elf's incompetence. If Sylvanas had been the Accuser, she would have had *many* questions for the young human prince, questions as silky and as dangerous as spider webbing with which to entrap him. Yet despite the fact that Garrosh Hellscream had *broken every single bone in Anduin Wrynn's body*, the child had piped up with testimony so hand-wringingly heartfelt that Sylvanas felt the mood in the entire chamber shift, and Tyrande had shaken her head.

"Court will take an hour's respite," said Taran Zhu, and struck the gong. As Baine left the floor, Sylvanas hastened to meet him, but Vol'jin had beaten her to it. The two were heading for the door, and the troll was actually congratulating Baine on his "fairness."

"No one gonna feel that Garrosh was treated badly by the Horde now, whatever else Tyrande springs on you. Mon, you could be calling the prince of Stormwind as a witness for the Defender!"

"Young Wrynn knows what is right," Baine rumbled. "He is forgiving. His word counts for much."

"More, apparently, than the word of the high chieftain of the tauren," snapped Sylvanas, falling into step beside them as they emerged outside. It was noon, and Sylvanas disliked the sun, but she was not about to back off.

Baine's ears flattened. "Be mindful of your own words, Sylvanas," Vol'jin said. "You don't know when you gonna have to eat them."

"Fortunately, I do not have to be mindful of what I say when all of Azeroth is watching, or else I might become as much a boot-licking Alliance sympathizer as—"

Baine did nothing so obvious as roar and seize her throat. He merely stopped in his tracks, gripped her upper arms, and squeezed. He was so gentle and precise in his movements and speech when off the battlefield that she had forgotten he was a warrior—and one of the finest the Horde could boast. He could, she realized belatedly, snap her arms like brittle twigs.

"I am not an Alliance sympathizer," he said in a deep, calm voice. "Nor do I lick boots."

"Let her go, Baine," said Vol'jin, and Baine obeyed. "Sylvanas—Baine be doing his job, the job that I, his warchief, asked him to take on. He does it with honor. There be nothing wrong with that. Don't you go acting like there is."

"I do not object to him doing his job well," said Sylvanas, recovering her composure. "I object to him doing it so well he might actually win!"

Baine chuckled ruefully. "You do not intend to, but you flatter me. I believe there is little danger of that," he said. "I have made those spectators who are hungry for slaughter pause and think for a moment, nothing more. And that is all to the good. One should never make the decision to take another life lightly—not in battle, not in the mak'gora, not in a courtroom. Now, if you both will please excuse me, there is some work I must do in preparation for the next witness."

He bowed to both of them, letting his body drop more deeply to Vol'jin than to Sylvanas, and departed. Kairoz was waiting for him, and Sylvanas realized he had watched the whole thing. Sylvanas wished she could claw the smirk off the dragon's handsome face. Why wasn't he suggesting more damning things to show?

Vol'jin shook his head and sighed.

"When you gonna be getting wiser instead of just smarter, Sylvanas?" he said, not unkindly.

"When the Horde itself grows wise enough to realize not to dish out mercy to those who have done nothing to deserve it," she replied. "Garrosh might have been a good choice for leader of the Horde for a short while, but once Thrall announced he was going for good, something else should have been done."

A smile played around the warchief's long tusks. "Like making a Dark Lady a dark warchief?"

Sylvanas shook her head. "Power in that capacity does not interest me. I would have thought you knew that, Vol'jin." It was the best kind of lie—one that had some truth to it. She was, indeed, not interested in wielding power in so blatant and crude a fashion.

He shrugged. "Who knows what you want, Sylvanas. Sometimes I don't even think you do." He jabbed a sharp-clawed finger at her. "Leave Baine be. He not gonna rob you of your kill. You just need to let it come in its own time."

He walked off, calling to one of the vendors for a quick bite to eat. Sylvanas watched him go, considering.

Her anger had not abated. It never did. Anger was to her now what breathing had been when her heart still beat. But it had changed, from hot and impulsive to thoughtful and controlled.

Vol'jin and Baine were not thinking clearly. They were too caught up in how their own people functioned, in what Horde members would want to see, and how they would perceive things. Even if they did take into account the Light-loving members of the Alliance, the verdict would never be in question.

But the jury was not made up of members of the Alliance and Horde. It was made up of beings who were completely impartial— and completely detached from the more visceral, transitory, intense emotions of the other races of Azeroth. Perhaps that detachment would stretch to being aloof from concepts such as "mercy" and "second chances," in which case she need not worry. Or perhaps it would distance them too much from white-hot vengeance and the unending ache of the deaths of people one had once loved.

Clarity came to her, calming and arrow-sharp. She could not take the risk that the celestials, "august" as they might be, would make the wrong decision.

Sylvanas would not let her "kill" come "in its own time," as Vol'jin had urged. She would take matters into her own hands, as she had done many times before. But how, precisely? It was possible she could accomplish it alone, but unlikely. Whom, then, could she trust? Not Baine, of course. Not Vol'jin. Perhaps Theron—he had seemed willing to talk. And Gallywix doubtless had a price.

There was still some time left before court resumed. She always thought better in her own realm, in the Undercity, beneath lowering skies and surrounded by the Forsaken, who entrusted themselves to her guidance. She would let them, let her home, inspire her.

She approached the mage assigned to the court, Yu Fei, and requested a portal. Just as Yu Fei had finished murmuring the words of the spell and an image of the Undercity appeared before her, another pandaren, whom she did not know, raced up.

"Lady Sylvanas," he said, "my apologies, but I was instructed to give this to you!" He pressed a scroll and a small package wrapped in blue cloth into her hands. Stepping back quickly, he bowed. Even as Sylvanas opened her mouth to inquire who had sent said scroll, the air shimmered around her and she manifested in her quarters.

They were spare, as befitted one who did not linger overlong in them. Sylvanas Windrunner no longer needed sleep as such, though she did come here from time to time simply to be alone and to think. She had few belongings: a bed hung with heavy, dark drapes; a desk with candles and writing materials; a chair; and a single shelf lined with a half-dozen books. Select weapons were displayed on the wall within easy reach. She needed very little else in her present existence, and she did not keep much from her past one.

Curious as to who might be sending her a missive and a package, and cautious about opening them, Sylvanas inspected the scroll thoroughly. She sensed no magic from it, nor did she notice any telltale signs that would alert her to poison. The scroll was sealed with red wax, but there was no identifying mark. Turning her attention to the package, Sylvanas noted that the blue cloth was an item commonly sold in all major cities. She shook it gently, and something clinked inside. Sinking down on the soft bed, she then removed her gloves, cracking the seal with a fingernail.

The handwriting was elegant, the lines few:

Once we were on the same side.
Perhaps we can be again.

Sylvanas narrowed her eyes speculatively, trying to think who this mystery person might be. The handwriting wasn't immediately recognizable, but it was somehow familiar. She had a rather lengthy list of people who had turned against her, or whom she had defied. Amused, she unwrapped the parcel and opened the small wooden box.

Her chest contracted, and she dropped the package as if it had bitten her.

The banshee stared at its contents, then rose and unsteadily made her way to her desk. Her fingers shook as she unlocked a drawer. Here, untouched for years, was all that remained of her past. There were only a few items: decades-old letters, arrowheads from significant kills, some other odds and ends, the detritus of a life.

And a small box.

Part of her urged her to throw the new gift inside this drawer, turn the key, and forget again. No good could come of this. And yet . . .

Holding the box, she returned to the bed. With unwonted gentleness, Sylvanas lifted the lid and gazed at what was inside. An adventurer had found this, several years ago, lying among the ruins of the spire where she had fallen. It had been returned to her. The memories it unleashed had nearly broken her then, and threatened to do so now.

Such a small thing, to have such power over the Banshee Queen: a simple piece of jewelry. Sylvanas picked up the necklace, letting the cool metal rest in her hand and gazing at the blue, winking gem that adorned it. Gently she placed it down next to the one she had just received.

They were a perfect match, save for the gemstones. Hers was a sapphire; this was a ruby. Different, too, Sylvanas knew, were the inscriptions.

She opened hers and read: *To Sylvanas. Love always, Alleria.*

Alleria . . . the second of the Windrunners to have left them. First had been their brother, Lirath, the youngest of them all, and perhaps the brightest. Then Alleria, lost beyond the Dark Portal in Outland. Then . . .

Sylvanas shook her head, reclaiming her composure. Of the Windrunner immediate family, she was certain of only one who yet drew breath.

Sylvanas opened the ruby locket, knowing what she would find, but needing to see it with her own eyes.

To Vereesa. With love, Alleria.

13

The note was written in bold print, brief, and to the point.

I will see you at home after court.

So few words, to make Vereesa so nervous.

Her sister was clever; no one intercepting this would know who had sent it, and even if they did, it seemed so harmless a message.

Except it wasn't. "Home," in this case, had a very dark meaning. Vereesa thanked Jia Ji, the pandaren courier who had so unwittingly borne messages that could potentially have started a war, rolled the scroll up till it was barely as thick as the quill that had written on it, and tossed it into a nearby brazier.

"Vereesa?" She started and whirled. It was Varian. "It's almost time to go back in. If you want some dumplings, best get them quickly."

He and Anduin were finishing up some spring rolls and heading toward the temple. Belatedly Vereesa realized that the brazier into which she had tossed the note belonged to a stout pandaren cook, who was busily stacking bamboo steamers atop one another and using chopsticks to delicately fish out perfectly formed dumplings. He smiled inquiringly at her, and she nodded, although food was the last thing on her mind.

"You'll like them. Anduin almost cleaned out Mi Shao yester-day," Varian said, grinning and ruffling Anduin's fair hair. The boy ducked sheepishly, looking his age for once.

"The human cub is growing stronger," Mi Shao said. "Pandaren food suits him. I am honored to provide both sustenance and plea-sure to one who understands my land so well."

"Try one of the little ones with seeds on them," Anduin urged Vereesa. "They're filled with lotus root paste. Amazing."

"Thanks," Vereesa said. "I will take two, please."

"So will I, on second thought," Anduin said. "You head on in, Fa-ther. I'll join you shortly."

"I will see you both in a few moments then," Varian said, pull-ing his son to him for a quick hug and then striding off toward the arena. Anduin watched his father go, thanked Mi Shao in the pan-daren's native tongue, and took a bite of the pastry. He closed his eyes in pleasure.

"These are *so* good," he said. Vereesa was fleetingly reminded of her own sons and their inexhaustible appetites, but her thoughts quickly drifted back to Sylvanas. She made no move to eat. As he chewed, he regarded her, then asked, "Are you all right?"

Vereesa's heart sped up. He was too damned perceptive . . . How had she betrayed herself? Did he already know about—

"Of course I am. Why would I not be?" She forced herself to eat a bite of the pastry. The exterior was soft and chewy, the interior sweet but not cloying. Had her stomach not been in knots and her mouth not been as dry as sand, she might have enjoyed the delicacy.

"Well . . . because of what I said in court. I know that you and Aunt Jaina aren't too keen on giving Garrosh a second chance. And I wanted you to know that I understand why. I do."

Relief made her feel weak. "And I understand why you feel as you do."

His face lit up, and at once she felt guilty for the prevarication. "Really?"

"You see the best in everybody, Anduin. Everyone knows that."

His expression sobered. "I know some people don't respect it. They think I'm too soft."

"Hey," she said, and caught his arm gently. "You stood up in a courtroom full of people who would eagerly kill Garrosh with their own hands, and you spoke on his behalf. Soft people do not have that kind of courage."

His irritation vanished, replaced by a winning smile. *The boy is going to break hearts one day. If he lives long enough.* "Thank you, Vereesa. That means a great deal, especially when it comes from you. And . . . honestly, it's a little surprising. I'm afraid I count you among those who'd like to kill Garrosh with their own hands."

"No, I would not. I believe in the wisdom of this trial, and I believe the celestials will do what is right."

"I'm—really glad to hear that."

As they walked together back to the courtroom, Vereesa felt a fresh rage at Garrosh Hellscream, for turning her into someone who would lie to a fifteen-year-old boy.

To their surprise, a pandaren guard was at the entrance, gently refusing everyone admission. Varian was talking to him, becoming more agitated, then finally turning away. He caught sight of Vereesa and Anduin approaching, and waved them to hurry up. His face was thunderous, and Vereesa felt sweat break out on her brow. Could he have discovered . . . ? No. If he had, he would be attacking her himself right now.

"What is it?" she asked, trying to sound curious and concerned, but not too much so.

"Court is closed for the rest of the day," Varian said brusquely. "Anduin, come with me. Vereesa, you can return to Violet Rise if you wish."

"Of course," said Vereesa. She did not do so immediately. On the pretext of finishing the bun, she lingered where she could look inside the temple. Taran Zhu, Baine, and Tyrande seemed to be waiting for Anduin and his father. Baine began to speak. Varian crossed his arms and set his jaw. Anduin looked confused as he listened, and unable to contain himself, Varian started shouting at Baine. Taran Zhu said something, and Varian turned to shout at him and Tyrande as well, while Anduin tried to calm things down.

"Ranger-General," said the pandaren guard. "Respectfully—this is not for your eyes."

She felt heat rise in her face, and nodded. "Of course. I apologize." She turned and walked away, wondering what new tactic Baine was going to employ to try to wring sympathy from the August Celestial jury for a mass murderer.

Vereesa clenched her fists and strode off. Twilight could not come swiftly enough for her.

"What's going on?" Anduin asked as he looked from Taran Zhu to Tyrande to Baine and finally to his father. His father's was the only expression he could read; Varian was extremely upset by something.

"Anduin," Varian said, "Baine has asked . . ." A muscle in his jaw tightened. "Light blind me, I can't even *say* it!"

Baine stepped forward. "Your Majesty, I wish to thank you for even bringing the prince here."

"Don't thank me yet," muttered Varian. "I'm this close to marching him back home to Stormwind."

"But—what—" Anduin began.

Baine flicked an ear. "I have been asked to make a request."

"Who asked—" Anduin started, but the words died in his throat. All at once he knew who, and he knew what. There was only one question. "Why?"

"I don't know why he wants to speak with you," Baine said, and his ear flicked again in obvious frustration. "Only that he does. He says you are the only person he will talk to."

"More like the only person who would talk to *him*," said Varian.

Anduin placed a hand on his father's arm. "I haven't said I would yet, Father." He looked at Taran Zhu. "Is something like this even allowed in the trial?"

"Under Pandaren law, I determine what is permissible in this trial, young one. Chu'shao Bloodhoof approached me some time ago, and I meditated on this. I instructed him to wait until after you had given your testimony. Both Accuser and Defender have waived their rights to ask you to testify any further, so both have something to gain and to lose."

"Being blunt," said Baine, "you are known as a kind and compassionate human, Your Highness. It would benefit my case if you were to befriend Garrosh and exercise your right to speak of it, and harm my case if you were to turn against him and speak of *that*. Chu'shao Whisperwind faces the same conundrum, only reversed."

"So why not just forbid it?"

"Because Garrosh is considering breaking his silence in court if you do so," said Tyrande. "That means I would get a chance to question him directly, and that could strongly help my case."

"And depending on what happens in your conversations, it could strengthen mine," Baine said. "As I said, it's a gamble."

"I cannot force Garrosh to speak in court, but I feel it would be an important thing if he did," Taran Zhu said, "no matter what happens. No one could say he did not have a chance to speak, then."

"So it's all on my shoulders," Anduin said. "You're really not giving me much of a choice, are you?"

"You don't have to do this," Varian said. "You know I'd rather you didn't. I think you've been through enough."

"Then why didn't you just say no, Father?"

"Because you're of an age to decide for yourself—and it's got to be your choice," Varian said. "As much as I wish it weren't. I had to bring you the option. You can see Garrosh, or never have to see him again, if you'd like."

That surprised Anduin, and he gave his father a small, grateful smile. He thought for a moment, trying to calm the flood of conflicting emotions.

He thought again of the bell's pieces crashing down on his vulnerable body, of the hate on Hellscream's face, and his bones ached in response. To never again see Garrosh, to sidestep a deliberate invitation to pain—oh, that *was* alluring. Garrosh had done nothing at any point to indicate anything but contempt and loathing toward Anduin, and there had been ample opportunities. The prince owed him nothing. He'd already spoken more kindly of the former warchief than anyone had any right to expect. He'd done enough to help save the life of someone who had been all too eager to take his.

And yet . . .

Anduin recalled Garrosh's reaction when he thought the prince dead. Not gleeful or gloating, as one might suspect, but contemplative. And the weariness in Garrosh's posture right here in the courtroom.

What had Garrosh been contemplating at those moments? What emotions was he experiencing, to reach out to a priest? Might he be feeling remorse?

The ache in his bones receded slightly, and Anduin arrived at a decision. He looked at the faces of those assembled, each one a different race and in a different relationship to him—his human father, a night elven heroine, a pandaren guardian, and Baine . . . tauren friend. Unexpected by anyone's reckoning, never spoken of—but true.

"Someone in trouble has asked me to speak with him. How, Father, could I say no, and still stand in the Light?"

Varian at first had insisted on accompanying his son, but Anduin, keeping his hope to himself, had refused. He also demanded that any guards present come no closer than the entryway, so that his conversation with Garrosh would remain private. Varian had argued against that for almost a solid hour, but to no avail. "I am being called upon as a priest in this," Anduin had said. "He must be able to speak freely to me, and know that what he says, I will keep in confidence."

With little graciousness, Varian finally conceded. He looked at Taran Zhu, Tyrande, and Baine in turn. "If any harm comes to Anduin, I will hold you all responsible. And I will then kill Garrosh myself, regardless of the repercussions, and damn these proceedings."

"Rest assured, King Varian, it is physically impossible for Garrosh to attack Anduin. Your son is completely safe, and I would not say it if it were not so," Taran Zhu replied.

Now Anduin stood outside the sectioned-off area below the temple. Two of Garrosh's guards, the Shado-pan monks Li Chu and Lo Chu, awaited him, flanking the door.

They bowed. "Welcome, honored prince," Li Chu said. "You show courage in facing your enemy."

Anduin's stomach was in knots, and he was relieved when his voice didn't betray his apprehension. "He is not my enemy," he said. "Not here, not now."

Lo Chu smiled slowly. "To understand that is to demonstrate that you are wise as well as brave. Know that we will be at the entry at all times, and will come the instant you call for us."

"Thank you," Anduin replied. Velen had taught him how to calm the spirit when agitated, and now he followed that advice, inhaling slowly for a count of five, holding the breath for a heartbeat, then exhaling to the same count. *"All things will be well,"* Velen advised. *"All nights end, and all storms clear. The only storms that last are those within your own soul."*

It worked . . . at least until he stood before Garrosh's cell.

The cell itself was cramped. There was room only for sleeping furs, a chamber pot, and a basin. Garrosh was unable to walk more than a pace or two in any direction, and even his limited amount of movement was defined by chains linking his ankles. The bars were thicker than Anduin's whole body, and the octagonal openings were sealed with a soft purple radiance. Taran Zhu had spoken truly. Garrosh Hellscream was imprisoned both physically and magically.

Anduin noticed all this only peripherally. His eyes went at once to those of the orc, who sat upright on the furs. The prince did not know what to expect—anger, pleading, mockery. But none of those were present. On Garrosh's face was the same pensive expression Anduin had seen immediately after Garrosh had "killed" him.

"Please do not touch the bars," Lo Chu instructed. "You may stay for up to an hour, if you wish. Of course, if you desire to leave sooner, simply let us know." He indicated a chair and a small table, upon which sat a pitcher of water and an empty glass.

Anduin cleared his throat. "Thank you. I'm sure I'll be fine."

Garrosh did not even appear to notice the guards, so intent was he on Anduin. The brothers, as they had promised, retreated to the far back of the room. Anduin's mouth went dry. He sat and poured himself some water to ease the desert in his throat, and took a deliberate, unhurried sip.

"Are you afraid?"

"*What?*" The water splashed. Anduin's bones suddenly ached.

"Are you afraid?" Garrosh repeated. The question was casually posed, as if the orc were simply making conversation. Anduin knew it for a verbal grenade. To either answer truthfully or lie would blow open a door to things Anduin had no desire to discuss.

"There's no reason to be. You are restrained by chains and enchanted prison bars. You're quite unable to attack me."

"Concern for one's physical safety is only one reason to fear. There are others. I ask again: are you afraid?"

"Look," said Anduin, ardently placing the glass on the table, "I came here because you asked me to. Because Baine said that I was the only person you agreed to talk to about . . . well, about whatever it is you want to talk about."

"Maybe your fear is what I want to talk about."

"If that's so, then we are both wasting our time." He rose and went for the door.

"Stop."

Anduin paused, his back to Garrosh. He was angry with himself. His palms were damp and it took every effort he could summon to refrain from shaking outright. He would not let Garrosh see fear in him.

"Why should I?"

"Because . . . you *are* the only person I wish to talk to."

The prince closed his eyes. He could leave, right this minute. Garrosh was almost certainly going to play games with him. Perhaps trick him into saying something he shouldn't. But what, possibly, could that be? What could Garrosh want to know? And Anduin realized that, afraid on some level though he might be, he didn't really want to go. Not yet.

He took a deep breath and turned around. "Then start talking."

Garrosh pointed at the chair. Anduin shifted his weight from one foot to the other, then took the seat with deliberate, casual movements. He lifted his eyebrows, indicating he was waiting.

"You said you believed I could change," Garrosh said. "What in this world or any other could make you think that, after what I have done?"

Again, no real emotion, only curiosity. Anduin started to answer, but hesitated. What would Jaina . . . no. Jaina was no longer the sort of diplomat he wished to emulate. He felt a flicker of amusement when he realized that for all his threats of murdering Garrosh, Varian had now become more of a role model for Anduin than Jaina was. The realization was both sad, for he loved Jaina, and sweet, for he loved his father.

"Tell you what. We'll take turns."

An odd smile curved Garrosh's mouth. "We have a bargain. You're a better negotiator than I expected."

Anduin let out a short bark of laughter. "Thanks, I think."

The orc's smile widened. "You go first."

The first point goes to Garrosh, Anduin mused. "Very well. I believe you can change because nothing ever stays the same. You were overthrown as warchief of the Horde because the people you led changed from following your orders to questioning them, and finally rejecting them. You've changed from warchief to prisoner. You can change again."

Garrosh laughed without humor. "From living to dead, you mean."

"That's one way of doing it. But it's not the only one. You can look at what you've done. Watch and listen and really try to understand the pain and damage you've caused, and decide that you won't continue down that path if given another chance."

Garrosh stiffened. "I cannot change into a human," he growled.

"No one expects or wants that," Anduin answered. "But orcs can change. You better than anyone should know that."

Garrosh was silent. He looked away for a moment, pensive. Anduin resisted the impulse to cross his arms, instead forcing his body posture to seem relaxed, and waited. A bright-eyed, coarse-furred rat poked its head out from under the sleeping furs. Its nose twitched, and then it ducked back out of sight. *The warchief of the Horde once . . . and now his cellmate is a rat.*

"Do you believe in destiny, Anduin Wrynn?"

For the second time Anduin was blindsided. What was going on inside Garrosh's head?

"I—I'm not sure," he stammered, his carefully maintained image of coolness dissolving immediately. "I mean—I know there are prophecies. But I think we all have choices too."

"Did you choose the Light? Or did it choose you?"

"I—I don't know." Anduin realized he had never asked himself that question. He recalled the first time he considered becoming a priest, and had felt a tug in his soul. He craved the peace the Light offered, but he didn't know if it had called him, or if he had set out in pursuit of it.

"Could you choose to deny the Light?"

"Why would I want to do that?"

"Any number of reasons. There was another golden-haired, beloved human prince once. He was a paladin, and yet he turned his back on the Light."

Outrage and offense chased away Anduin's discomfort. Blood suffused his face and he snapped, "I am *not* Arthas!"

Garrosh smiled oddly. "No, you are not," he agreed. "But maybe . . . I am."

14

The Ghostlands, it was called now. Once, the Windrunner family called it home. Vereesa had been invited back a single time before by Halduron Brightwing, to fight their mutual, ancient enemy, the Amani. It had made her soul-sick then, and did so again now. As she flew her hippogryph over the Thalassian Pass, her stomach muscles contracted and her palms grew slippery on the reins.

The Dead Scar. Twining its way through a once-beautiful land, leaving a trail like a slug where hundreds of undead feet had trod. No one knew if it would ever recover. It penetrated Tranquillien, aptly named no longer, dividing the Sanctums of the Moon and of the Sun, on into Eversong Woods and through Silvermoon, cleaving that wondrous city of song and story as well. Even from this height, she could see the legacy of the Lich King, dead things still shuffling, still killing.

Dead, but not dead. Like my sister.

No. Not like Sylvanas. She and her people had their own wills, their own minds. They could choose what they would and would not do. Whom they would and would not kill. And that ability was what had brought Vereesa back to the place of her childhood, where she had never thought to return.

Her eyes were dry, her senses dull with the constant press of pain that had begun with word of Rhonin's death and had not ever truly eased. She steered her mount to the west, and could not help but wonder if Sylvanas was enjoying the thought of Vereesa returning to Windrunner Spire.

Seeing it again brought a wave of fresh pain, new and sharp and adding fuel to her hatred. Orcs had not done this to her home, but orcs had taken enough from her—first her brother, Lirath, and then Rhonin, her great light. They desired to raze Quel'Thalas as thoroughly as Arthas later had.

As she drew closer, Vereesa's lip curled in a snarl. The spire—her family's spire—was crawling with walking corpses and transparent spirits.

Banshees.

The spirits drifted, seemingly as without aim in death as they had been full of purpose in life. Speckled in among them were hooded figures in red and black robes. Vereesa knew who they had to be. They were the human followers of the Deatholme cult that had sprung up after Arthas's incursion, using Windrunner Spire for some obscene and violent purpose.

Using my home.

Vereesa let out a wordless shriek, and all the impotent anger that had raged inside her since Garrosh's defeat surged forward at this welcome outlet. She nocked and let fly arrow after arrow. The first one caught the acolyte in the eye. The second and third pierced throats before the victims even registered what was happening. The fourth target turned a shocked face up to Vereesa, and his fingers flexed as he reached for a weapon; then he too was dead. Leaping off her hippogryph before it even had a chance to land, she attacked the fallen rangers, swinging a sword that glowed as it sliced through incorporeal flesh, sending them to oblivion and presumably peace, with more rage than pity. Vereesa winced as a banshee's howl shuddered through her body, but it only slowed her an instant before the specter's terrifying scream was forever silenced. The high elf added her own screams to the cacophony, jumbled phrases that said nothing but spoke bitterly of poisonous anger and pain.

Two more acolytes had the misfortune of being too slow in their spells. Vereesa charged them, slicing the head off of one and following through to bring the sword carving across the chest of another. As he fell, blood spurting, she thrust the sword down through his belly.

She caught her breath, yanking the sword free, looking about for any more enemies, living or undead, that might be converging on the spire. Vereesa was unconcerned about being recognized. Few enough living beings ventured out here anymore. A hooded cape was sufficient disguise if an intrepid blood elf dared approach the deserted place, and any acolyte that saw her would not live to report back.

The minutes crawled past. From time to time Vereesa heard again soft, mindless moans and sighs. She fought her adversaries back when their meandering brought them onto Windrunner property, ruined though it was. Mist, clammy and cold, clung to her skin. She began to pace back and forth, wondering if this was all some kind of cruel trick on Sylvanas's part.

Her sharp ears caught the faintest of sounds behind her and she whirled, bow ready, arrow nocked. Before she could let the missile fly, there was a splintering of her arrow's shaft, and the string twanged.

The archer, clad in black leather, had shot Vereesa's arrow right out of the bow.

The newcomer brushed her hood back. Glowing red eyes pierced the haze, and black lips twisted in a sardonic grin.

"Have a care, Sister," Sylvanas said, lowering her weapon. "I do not think you want to kill *this* banshee."

They walked along the gray sand, the sound of the waves easier to bear than the sighs and laments of the dead, though not by much.

Sylvanas thought the place full of ghosts, not only literal, but those of a family that once picnicked here.

"We are all that is left," Vereesa said, as if reading her thoughts. Sylvanas smiled a little. As the two middle children, they had always had a bond that set them apart from Alleria, the eldest, and Lirath, their only brother.

"A diplomatic choice of words," she said.

Vereesa had come to a halt, peering out across the North Sea. "First Lirath, murdered by the orcs. Then Alleria, vanished in Outland. Why did you pick this place, Sylvanas?"

"Why do you think, little sister?"

"To wound me. You chose a rendezvous site where the dead feel at home. Where the living are not welcome." Then she amended, "Unless they have evil intentions."

Sylvanas stiffened. "To wound *you*? Arrogant child!" She laughed without humor. "Did you not notice who clustered about you, sobbing and shrieking for their lives back? Those were *my* rangers! I *died* here!"

Vereesa winced. "I—I am sorry. I thought . . . you were used to . . . well . . ."

"Being the 'Banshee Queen'? The 'Dark Lady'?" Sylvanas spoke in an exaggerated tone. "It is better than rotting. At least now I have a say in what happens in the world."

"We have less of a say than we could have hoped," Vereesa said. She picked up a rock and threw it into the ocean, where it immediately vanished. "I do not know who you are now. You are not she who was my beloved sister."

I am . . . and I am not, Sylvanas thought, but said nothing.

"But you and I agree on one thing." Vereesa turned, her face flushed and her eyes blazing. "Garrosh Hellscream must die for what he has done. And it seems as though you, like me, do not trust the celestials to reach that same decision, or else you would not have come."

"I cannot disagree with you on any of those counts. And it was brave of you to attempt to contact me—especially if, as you have said, you do not know who I am now." Brave, and a bit reckless. Had the locket been intercepted, Vereesa would have been branded a traitor.

"I took a risk. It seemed worth it. I hope it was."

"You did not do so simply to have me sympathize with how wretched a creature Garrosh Hellscream is," Sylvanas said, folding her arms. "You must have a plan."

"I—well, not yet."

Sylvanas arched a brow, and began to calculate how long it would take to kill Vereesa.

"I wanted to tell you that we are not alone," said Vereesa. "There are others who think exactly as we do, and who would either actively help us or not stand in our way if we attempted to . . . to murder Garrosh."

"People complain and grumble, Sister, but few are willing to act. These allies you speak of will evaporate if they get a whiff of any danger to their persons or their reputations."

Vereesa shook her head earnestly. "No. They will not. I even have Lady Jaina's approval."

Sylvanas frowned. "Now I know you lie, Sister. Jaina Proudmoore may no longer be the dewy-eyed peace lover she was before, but she cannot possibly advocate an assassination. She might hope for Garrosh's death, but she would never act upon it."

"You are wrong. She wants him to die. Before sentence is pronounced. Save us all the trouble of a trial, she said. There are others too. Sky Admiral Catherine Rogers, for one. She hates the Horde, Garrosh most of all."

"I recall she is from Southshore," Sylvanas said. "I doubt she will want to work with the Banshee Queen of the Forsaken."

"She does not have to know. No one has to know. Just us."

Sylvanas fell silent, thinking. "We could wait to see if the celestials do the job for us first."

"No. If they do decide on *mercy*"—and Vereesa spat the word—
"we will not get another chance. We have to act while the trial is
going on. While both of our sides have access to him."

At that, Sylvanas laughed aloud. "Access? Have you seen how
heavily he is guarded, Sister? Even the most accomplished assassin
will not be able to penetrate that cell."

Vereesa smiled. It was still the face Sylvanas remembered, still
the same lips that had parted in shrieks of laughter when Vereesa
was a child. But the expression gave Sylvanas a glimpse into a cruelty she would never have expected her sister to display.

"No," Vereesa agreed. "Not an assassin. But even prisoners must
eat, must they not?"

Poison. No wonder Vereesa's thoughts had turned to her sister.

"And you wish a poison no one can detect—a poison that has not
been created yet."

Vereesa nodded.

"Perfect," said Sylvanas. "I am ashamed that it had not occurred
to me, actually."

"We will need to get someone to infiltrate the kitchens, or tamper with the food at its source," Vereesa continued. "Or else convince someone who is already trusted with preparing his meals.
We—"

"A moment, before you career off plotting and scheming, entertaining though that might be," said Sylvanas. "I have not said that I
will participate."

"What? You just said it was perfect!"

"Oh, it is. But I have suffered beneath the hand of a tyrant before,"
Sylvanas said. "And defied he who made me. Arthas raised me to
torment me, but he is gone and I am here. I defied Garrosh as well,
and I *will* see him dead." She spread her hands, indicating her body,
as strong and, in its own way, as beautiful as when she drew breath,
but blue-gray and cold to the touch. "And—I am Forsaken. You can
understand *my* reasoning. What is yours, little one?"

"I cannot believe you are asking me this!"

"I am, and I pray you, answer." Her voice was cold. "What did Garrosh do to make you decide upon this course?"

"What did he *not* do? He unleashed a horror upon Theramore that cannot ever be excused! And they died . . . terribly. It is sheer luck I was not among their number."

Sylvanas shook her head. Her locks had been pale blond in life, but appeared to be silver, and now they looked almost as white as her sister's. They were the moons, Alleria had teased, calling them Lady Moon and Little Moon, while she and Lirath—the eldest and the youngest—were the suns of the family, with their bright golden tresses. Alleria . . .

"That is not the reason."

"The orcs have ever been our enemies. Garrosh is the worst they have spawned that yet lives. Their history is littered with monsters and demonic barbarism. They took our baby brother from us, Sylvanas! And you *know* Alleria would have fought anyone for the honor of dispatching Garrosh herself. She would *want* us to do this."

Sylvanas pursed her lips. "While I agree with all you say, that is not the reason either."

Vereesa swallowed hard. "You do want to wound me. You want to see me suffer."

"I want to judge for myself the depth of your pain. It is not the same thing."

Vereesa was Alliance. She had married a human, had borne children with him. That had been her home, and she had a place there. What she said she now wanted went against the laws that the Alliance claimed to uphold—though, certainly, there were rogues and murderers and thieves enough among their number.

For a moment, Sylvanas thought her sister would refuse. The Windrunners had ever been strong willed. Vereesa's slender body was as taut as her bowstring, almost quivering with tension. Sylvanas waited with the patience of the dead—another gift Arthas had unwittingly bestowed upon her—for the fury she sensed boiling inside her sister to erupt.

It did not happen.

Instead of fire, Sylvanas saw water—tears filling Vereesa's eyes and spilling down her face. Vereesa did not even bother to wipe them away as she spoke.

"He took my Rhonin."

That was all. That was everything.

Sylvanas stepped forward and embraced her sister, and Vereesa clung to her like the drowning woman she was.

15

Day Three

"Warchief," said Tyrande, inclining her head.

It was still odd, thought Go'el, to hear someone else being addressed so. Not wrong—he had not a moment's regret in his decision, and ancestors knew that Vol'jin was worthy of the title—but . . . odd. He wondered if he would ever truly grow used to it.

Vol'jin's eyes were bright and held a hint of mischief as he replied, "High Priestess."

"You have been a leader of your people for many years, and before you, your father led."

"That be truth."

"Now, after Garrosh Hellscream's tyrannical reign—"

"With respect, I protest," said Baine, although it did not sound as though his heart was in it.

"After Garrosh Hellscream was defeated," Tyrande amended smoothly, as if there had been no interruption, "Go'el appointed you warchief. You now lead not just the Darkspear trolls, but all the various races of the Horde—even though you are not an orc."

"With respect, I protest!" shouted Baine, and this time he clearly did. "The witness's ability to lead the Horde is not a subject for debate in this courtroom!"

"Lord Zhu, I am attempting to prove the witness's credibility to the jury," said Tyrande.

"Find another way, Chu'shao," said Taran Zhu calmly.

"As you wish. Warchief Vol'jin, your people suffered greatly under Garrosh. So did you, personally. Can you please tell the court about this?"

"With pleasure," Vol'jin said, his voice deepening with banked outrage. "The trolls were the first of Azeroth's people to join the Horde when the orcs arrived in this world. We been loyal friends to the orcs, to Go'el. Go'el asked me to be an advisor to Garrosh, and I did everything in my power to be that. But Garrosh did not remember what good friends the trolls be to him."

"What specifically did he do?"

"He forbade my people to live where they chose in Orgrimmar. He forced them into a special area. He put the Echo Isles under martial law."

"Hardly the actions of a leader whose charge is to represent all the various races that compose the Horde," mused Tyrande.

"That be true."

"You exchanged words with him over your concerns, did you not?"

"More than once, yes."

"And he admitted to you that he had done this? Put your people in slums?"

"That he did."

"I would like to show the jury the first Vision from this witness," said Tyrande, and she stepped back to watch the unfolding scene. The troll leader and the warchief were in the throne room in Grommash Hold.

"Don't talk back to me, troll," Garrosh snarled. "You know who was left in charge here. Haven't you stopped to ask yourself why Thrall chose me instead of you?"

"Dere be no question why, Garrosh. He gave ya tha title because ya be Grom's son and because tha people be wantin' a war hero." It was true. Fresh from the aftermath of the defeat of the Lich King, the people were tired of war, but they still revered their war heroes. Go'el had thought the title, bequeathed for a short time, would help Garrosh learn to channel his energy. He had been so very wrong.

The image of Vol'jin was not yet done. "I tink ya be even more like ya father den ya thought, even witout da demon blood."

Garrosh snarled and stepped closer to the troll, quivering with barely restrained rage. "You are lucky that I don't gut you right here, whelp."

"Stop here!" Tyrande said sharply, and the two figures froze as if instantly embedded in ice. "August Celestials—there it is, right there. Garrosh Hellscream, warchief of the Horde, explicitly threatens Vol'jin with death." She nodded to Chromie, who moved her little fingers and resumed the scene.

"You are foolish to think that you can speak to your warchief in such ways," Garrosh said.

"Ya be no warchief of mine. Ya not earned my respect, and I'll not be seein' tha Horde destroyed by ya foolish thirst for war." Vol'jin was calm, precise, and cool, in contrast to Garrosh's almost rabid agitation.

"And what exactly do you think that you are going to do about it? Your threats are hollow. Go slink away with the rest of your kind to the slums. I will endure your filth in my throne room no longer."

The scene froze, then faded. Tyrande shook her head. "'Go slink away with the rest of your kind to the slums,'" she repeated. "That is an interesting way to treat and to speak of a race that has served the Horde so loyally for so long."

"I thought so myself."

"So, far from treating you as a respected advisor as Go'el had instructed, Garrosh ushered the trolls into areas he himself described as slums, and banished you from his throne room. He also threatened your life."

Go'el tensed. Vol'jin's almost casual demeanor grew serious. "He did more than threaten." He tilted his head back and exposed a raised scar, pale blue, where a would-be killer's knife had slashed across his throat. Go'el looked up at the celestials and saw them shift unhappily at the visible evidence of Garrosh's hatred.

Tyrande let the murmurs play out, then said, "I would like to show this despicable attack, and the role that Garrosh Hellscream played in it. Chromie?"

There was a universal rustling throughout the auditorium as nearly every spectator sat up straighter, leaned forward a little more. The story of what had happened to Vol'jin had spread throughout the Horde and Alliance both. Some were watching from mere prurient interest in the bloody details, but others watched to perhaps shake off lingering traces of disbelief.

"Warchief, could you please set the stage for us?"

"Of course. This be after the Horde landed on the shores of Pandaria. The Darkspears were not ordered to go with the rest of the Horde. I be thinking it a mistake to storm this place, but Garrosh was very happy to have a land . . . What did he say? . . . 'This land is rich in resources: wood, stone, iron, fuel. And people,'" he quoted.

"Wood, stone, iron, fuel, and people," mused Tyrande. "All listed as 'resources' in Garrosh's mind. So you are telling this court that you believe Garrosh intended to *enslave* the pandaren?"

A horrified gasp rippled through the room, and Baine leaped to his hooves. "With respect, I protest!" he shouted. "Any response would be the witness's opinion, nothing more, and there has never been any evidence that Garrosh desired to enslave an entire race!"

"No," Tyrande shot back, "one who treated the trolls so well would *never* do that!"

The two faced each other angrily, and Taran Zhu struck the small gong with more force than he usually displayed. "I will have order in this court! I will remind all present that any outbursts will result in confinement for the duration of this trial! Chu'shao Whisperwind, unless you can support this accusation, I suggest you change your approach."

"You did rule that a witness's opinion is admissible in court, Fa'shua."

Taran Zhu paused and then sighed. "That I did. Rephrase the question appropriately, then, please."

Tyrande turned to Vol'jin. "Warchief, what do you think Garrosh meant by those words?"

"I don't think he meant 'enslave' as Chu'shao Whisperwind be trying to say. I think he just wanted to have new recruits to fight. His war cry was, 'Storm the shores, and paint this new continent red!'"

"Red with blood, you mean? *Exterminate* the pandaren, not enslave them?"

"Chu'shao!" snapped Taran Zhu before Baine could even rise out of his chair. "You will cease putting words in the witness's mouth, or I will reprimand you."

Tyrande bowed and held up a hand. "Understood, Fa'shua. Please continue, Warchief."

"I think his intention was to make Pandaria a territory of the Horde. Lots of people to fight for the Horde, and the Horde color be red. That's what I think he meant."

"But you are not certain?"

"I can only tell you what I heard, and what my own thoughts be."

"Of course," said Tyrande. Not for the first time, Go'el was filled with respect for Vol'jin's integrity. It was only an opinion, and Vol'jin could have easily lied about it. But he had not done so. Still, Tyrande had raised the issue, and planted doubts, and neither the jury nor the spectators would stop wondering what Garrosh had really meant by those words.

"So . . . the Horde had arrived on Pandaria," Tyrande prompted.

"Without the Darkspears. I went to see Garrosh. He be all angry and speaking bitter words like before; then he seemed to reconsider."

"Thank you. Chromie?"

The little bronze hopped onto the table, activated the Vision of Time, and the scene manifested.

"This is the difference between me and you, Vol'jin," the then-Garrosh stated. "I won't let *my* people starve to death in the desert. I will stop at nothing—*nothing*—to ensure a proud and glorious future for the orcs and anyone with the courage to stand with us. Wait here."

He walked off a little ways and spoke softly with one of the Kor'kron, Rak'gor Bloodrazor. Go'el frowned, wondering why Tyrande did not let the jury hear that whispered conversation. Garrosh returned a moment later, smirking.

"There is something you can do, troll, to demonstrate your value to the Horde. A mission in the heart of this continent."

"I will go," Vol'jin said, adding, "but only as a witness for my people. Someone gotta keep you in check, Garrosh."

The scene froze, then faded to nothing. Tyrande turned back to Vol'jin. "Can you fill us in on what happened on this quest Garrosh assigned you and Rak'gor Bloodrazor?"

"We went in search of a saurok rookery," said Vol'jin. "The scouts had reported there was ancient magic in those caves. Garrosh be wantin' 'em checked out."

"And what did you discover?"

Vol'jin inhaled deeply, then replied, "They were . . . unnatural. Bloodrazor told me Garrosh had learned there be some kind of connection between the saurok and the mogu. He . . . was right."

Another scene appeared in the center of the arena. This time, Vol'jin, Bloodrazor, and a few others whom Go'el did not know were in a dark, damp cavern. The body of a massive saurok bled slowly into the stagnant, ankle-deep water. Eggs were everywhere—Vol'jin had found the rookery. A low growl escaped him, and when he spoke, his voice was deep and shaking—with outrage.

"Dese mogu . . . dey workin' wicked, dark magic here. Da saurok, dey not born—dey was created. Flesh shaped an' bent." He shook his head in revulsion. "Dis be the blackest of magics, mon!" He turned to Bloodrazor, his weapon raised, clearly expecting orders to destroy all the eggs.

Instead, the orc gave him a cruel grin. "Yes!" Bloodrazor exclaimed. "The power to shape flesh, to build warriors. This is what the warchief wants!"

Go'el tore his gaze from the unfolding scene to look at the reactions of the jury and spectators. As was usually the case, the celestials appeared impassive, but they were the only ones. The rest of those beholding this scathing indictment had expressions ranging from nausea to fury and every shade in between.

"Garrosh playing god?" shouted the image of Vol'jin, infuriated. "Making *monsters*? Dis ain't what da Horde is about!"

That, Go'el thought, was the phrase. The phrase that, even if unheard by anyone save those few comrades of Vol'jin, had been spoken and released into the world. It had guided Go'el, when he helped retake the Echo Isles for Vol'jin. It had enabled the troll leader to cling to life and claw his way back to recovery to defend the Horde that was his family. It was Varian's knowledge of that truth that had prevented him from doing what Garrosh wanted to do with the sha, that had caused the human king to refuse to take Orgrimmar and occupy it.

This is not what the Horde is about.

And it never would be.

But it was what Garrosh had wanted it to be, and the scene continued, unsparing.

Bloodrazor went to Vol'jin, and the troll glared angrily at him. The orc's nostrils flared and he made a face, as if he had smelled some horrible stench.

"He knew you were a traitor!" he snarled, and although Go'el knew it was coming, even he was startled by how swiftly the bulky, armored Kor'kron moved. The knife's arc was the briefest flash, and the blood spurted from Vol'jin's open throat as the troll collapsed.

The crowd gasped. The scene vanished.

"Zazzarik Fryll, would you read charges two, three, four, five, and seven again, please?" Tyrande asked the court secretary.

The goblin harrumphed, searched through several scrolls, and then proceeded to read aloud: "Murder."

Tyrande lifted a hand to interrupt him and he paused, blinking through his spectacles at her.

"Murder," she said, and held up her index finger. "Ordering a member of the Kor'kron to slice open Vol'jin's throat if he did not approve of Garrosh's barbaric plan. Continue, please."

"Um . . . Forcible transfer of population." The goblin looked at her expectantly.

Tyrande held up a second finger, ticking off the counts. "Forbidding the trolls—who are completely viable and respected members of the Horde—to live in certain areas."

"Enforced disappearance of individuals."

Three, now. "Sending Vol'jin out with Bloodrazor, knowing full well that it was likely Vol'jin would be murdered."

"Enslavement."

"Possibly of Pandaria. Certainly the saurok mutations were not volunteers."

"With respect, I protest," Baine said. "Garrosh is not responsible for what happened to the saurok."

"I agree with the Defender," said Taran Zhu.

"No, but the Vision of Time makes it clear he wished he *had* been responsible," Tyrande snapped, and Taran Zhu was forced to nod.

"I will allow the term 'an expressed desire for enslavement,'" the pandaren said.

"Torture."

"If we agree that Garrosh planned to do something similar to what happened to the saurok—warped. Twisted. Bent and violated. Beings were to be made this way for no other reason than one orc's whim."

She gestured. "In this single witness, we have evidence of fully half the charges of which Garrosh Hellscream is accused. *Half!* There are others who will speak of murder, and torture, and the remaining despicable acts Vol'jin has confirmed that Garrosh has committed. He—"

"Fa'shua," Baine rumbled. "If the Accuser has run out of questions to ask the witness and must now resort to oratory, may I have a chance to question him?"

It was a palpable hit—Tyrande's cheeks flushed a darker shade of purple.

"*Do* you have any more questions for the witness, Chu'shao Whisperwind?" Taran Zhu asked pleasantly.

"I do have one more scene I wish to present, Fa'shua, if I may. It is . . . extremely important. Only one person yet lives who has experienced it."

"By all means then, proceed."

Tyrande had recovered her composure and nodded calmly to Chromie.

Go'el was confused at first. Tyrande was presenting something that she had just shown: the scene of Garrosh insulting Vol'jin, then walking off to speak privately with Rak'gor.

But this time, everyone could hear what Garrosh said to his Kor'kron bodyguard.

"I have no doubt that you will be able to confirm my suspicion," the image of Garrosh said, for Bloodrazor's ears alone. "See how the troll reacts. If he approves, he may live. If he does not—he is a traitor. Cut his throat."

The scene froze. Tyrande walked forward, right up to the oversized image of Garrosh, his face caught in a smug leer. She looked from the Vision-orc to the true one.

In stark contrast to the almost caricatural, gloating Hellscream from the past, this Garrosh had little expression. His eyes, though, were fixed on Tyrande, not on the scene she had captured. Her back was straight, her head high. She was beautiful and terrible in her righteous fury, an implacable goddess of justice untempered by mercy and unfettered by compassion, her chest rising and falling with quickened breath, her heartbeat pulsing visibly in her long, slender throat. Go'el tensed, waiting for what he knew was coming. The impassioned speech. The outrage. The disgust at the depths to which the son of Hellscream had sunk. She would have no lack of supporters in her excoriation of Garrosh. The courtroom was about to be thrown into upheaval.

Finally, she spoke.

"So now, we know."

The words were uttered in a quiet voice that was heard throughout the shocked, silent room. She stared at Garrosh a moment longer. Then, with a curl of her lip that spoke more eloquently of contempt than anything else she might add, she turned her back on him.

"No further questions."

16

aine's mind was scrambling, frantic, desperately trying to come up with something that had even the faintest chance of undoing the damage Tyrande had just done to his case.

Vol'jin was Baine's friend. He had always respected the troll, and they had grown closer since Cairne's death. He had no desire to interrogate Vol'jin, question his interpretation of events, or try to discredit him to the jury. But it had been Vol'jin who had urged him to defend Garrosh in the first place.

"Warchief Vol'jin . . . you are a troll of honor, and both Horde and Alliance realize that. No one is disputing that this attempt on your life happened, or that the trolls were exiled to one of the less savory parts of Orgrimmar."

Vol'jin waited, expectant. "You are now the one bearing the responsibilities of warchief," Baine continued. "You have already been forced to make some extremely challenging decisions. Might I ask what your policy on traitors will be?"

"With respect, I protest!" Tyrande shot to her feet. "As you just ruled, Fa'shua, the witness's ability to lead the Horde is not a subject for debate in this courtroom!"

"Fa'shua," Baine said, "I am not questioning his ability. I am merely asking for his stand on policy."

Taran Zhu cocked his head. "I trust it is relevant to the case, Chu'shao?"

"It is."

"It had best be. I agree with the Defender."

"I've not had the opportunity to be dealing with anyone turning traitor on me," Vol'jin answered, adding, "yet." The subtly friendly expression was gone from his face, to be replaced by a look of wariness.

"I hope you never do," Baine said. "But you were willing to put Garrosh to death, for what he did to the Horde."

"I was."

"So you would be willing to put to death anyone who—in your opinion as warchief—betrayed the Horde?"

The tension in the room was thick, and for the first time since the trial began, it was not directed at Garrosh. Baine felt it, prickling at the nape of his neck, but knew he could not back down now.

"Yes, provided—"

"Just answer the question, Warchief. Please."

Vol'jin watched him searchingly, then said, biting off the word, "Yes."

Baine turned, relieved to not have to look at Vol'jin anymore, and nodded to Kairoz. He had been sitting quietly, his expression growing darker, clearly itching to use his abilities, and now he practically leaped up to operate the Vision of Time.

Baine blew air through his nostrils, resisting the urge to stamp restlessly as the scene manifested. It was Garrosh and Vol'jin in conversation, the same one that Tyrande had shown, but the night elf Accuser had ended the encounter prematurely. Baine wanted the jury to see how it played out. His tail switched anxiously as he watched.

"Ya be no warchief of mine," the image of Vol'jin said in his controlled voice. "Ya not earned my respect, and I'll not be seein' tha Horde destroyed by ya foolish thirst for war."

"Stop here," said Baine. He turned to face the August Celestials, regarding them intensely. "This is important, so I'm going to emphasize this. What you see right now, with evidence that we all know to be pure fact, is the following: a *subject of the Horde* has just told the orc who was *properly appointed by the sitting warchief,* and I quote, 'You be no warchief of mine.'"

With perfect timing, Kairoz delayed a moment to let the import of what Baine had said sink in, then resumed the scene.

"And what exactly do you think that you are going to do about it?" Garrosh shouted. "Your threats are hollow. Go slink away with the rest of your kind to the slums. I will endure your filth in my throne room no longer."

"I know exactly what I'll be doin' about it, son of Hellscream. I'll watch and wait as ya people slowly become aware of ya ineptitude. I'll laugh as dey grow ta despise ya as I do. And when tha time comes dat ya failure is complete and ya 'power' is meaningless, I will be dere to end ya rule swiftly and silently."

The scene paused. People shifted in their seats. "Vol'jin has called the duly appointed warchief 'inept.' He has said he 'despises' Garrosh. He threatens to 'end his rule.' What else can these words possibly be construed as other than treason? And what fate awaits traitors to the Horde, according to Vol'jin, its current leader?"

"With respect, I protest!" For the first time since the trial began, Tyrande seemed truly on edge. Baine had unsettled the perennially poised night elf. "The Defender is harassing the witness!"

"He is not addressing the witness at all," Taran Zhu said.

"What Vol'jin did or did not do, or said or did not say, is not pertinent!" shouted Tyrande.

"With all due respect, Fa'shua, I believe that it is," said Baine. "I believe that Garrosh felt threatened by Vol'jin and considered him a traitor. I believe it is possible that Garrosh felt his own life was in danger."

"I have heard discontent expressed, and annoyance and disrespect so far, Chu'shao," said Taran Zhu. "And a possible threat that Garrosh might not be leading the Horde. But Go'el stepped down peacefully. While Vol'jin is clearly an unhappy and disrespectful subject, I see no physical threat."

He could stop. He had made his point—that Garrosh could well have been acting within the law, and his right, to kill Vol'jin if he perceived the troll to be attempting to depose him. But Baine knew that wouldn't be enough. The August Celestials had seen Garrosh perpetrate violence against Vol'jin. They needed to see the other side.

Hating that it had come to this, yet doggedly determined to do his duty, Baine said, "I request permission to finish this conversation. I believe it is extremely pertinent."

Taran Zhu eyed them all, then nodded. "Proceed."

Baine could look at neither the real Vol'jin nor his image. He kept his gaze on the celestials as the Vision of the new leader of the Horde spoke.

"Ya will spend ya reign glancin' over ya shoulda and fearin' tha shadows."

Baine closed his eyes briefly.

"For when tha time comes and ya blood be slowly drainin' out, ya will know exactly who fired tha arrow dat pierced ya black heart."

"You have sealed your fate, troll," snarled then-Garrosh. He spat at Vol'jin's two-toed feet.

"And you yours, 'Warchief.'"

The image faded.

Silence. Baine still couldn't look at Vol'jin, and instead directed his attention to Taran Zhu. "I have no further questions for this witness, Fa'shua." And the pandaren nodded, regarding Baine with what seemed to the tauren like a hint of pity.

17

The door from the hall clanged shut behind Anduin, and per his specific request, he was alone in a room with a mass murderer.

Anduin poured himself a glass of water and drank. He noticed that this time, his hand didn't tremble quite so much. Garrosh, shackled as usual, sat on his sleeping furs, regarding the human prince.

"I would know your thoughts about Vol'jin's testimony," Garrosh stated.

Anduin's lips thinned. "If we're sticking to our bargain, you tell me something first this time."

Garrosh rumbled a deep, melancholy chuckle. "I will say to you then, that I believe today has put an end to any hope that I will walk out of this cell other than to my execution."

"No, it . . . didn't go well," Anduin allowed. "But what specifically makes you say that?"

Garrosh stared at him as if he were an idiot. "I threatened Vol'jin, banished his people, and tried to have him killed. Surely that is enough."

Anduin shrugged. "He threatened you as well, paid no honor to your title, and vowed to your face that he would kill you. He could easily have had followers ready to carry out the deed in Orgrimmar if he couldn't. Maybe you banished his people not because you hated them, but because you were afraid of them."

Shouting in rage, the orc was on his feet so fast Anduin jerked backward. At his bellow of fury, the Chu brothers entered and rushed forward.

"It's all right!" Anduin said, raising a hand and forcing a smile. "We are just . . . discussing things."

Li and Lo exchanged glances. Li regarded Garrosh with a slow, appraising stare. "It sounded like more than that." The orc was silent, but breathed hard and swiftly as his fists clenched and unclenched.

"It wasn't," Anduin said.

Lo said quietly, "Prisoner Hellscream, you will control yourself. Speaking with His Highness is a privilege, and one that will be revoked if we feel he is in any danger. Do you understand?"

For an instant, it looked as though Garrosh would attempt to burst through the bars to get at Lo. Then he sat down. His chains clanked. "I understand," he said, still angry, but in control.

"Very well. Do you wish to continue, Your Highness?"

"Yes," said Anduin. "Thank you, but you may go."

The brothers bowed and left, although Li gave Garrosh another warning look before he ascended the ramp out of sight.

"I would have killed you if there had not been bars between us," Garrosh growled softly.

"I know," Anduin replied. Oddly, he wasn't frightened. "But there were."

"Indeed." Garrosh took a deep breath and continued. "I was not afraid of some cowardly attempt on my life. I was *never* scared of Vol'jin."

"Then why did you not challenge him to a mak'gora?" Anduin shot back, recovering. "Why do something underhanded, something that goes against your own traditions, if you weren't afraid he'd beat you in a fair fight? That's the game cowards play. That's the game Magatha played."

"I thought you honorable, but you strike below the belt, whelp."

"I speak the truth, Garrosh. That's what's upsetting you, isn't it? It's not what others think about you. It's what you think about yourself."

Anduin expected another burst of fury, but this time Garrosh turned his rage inward. Only his eyes revealed his anger.

"I have never forgotten my people's traditions," he said, in a voice so soft Anduin had to strain to hear it. "I repeat what I said to Vol'jin. Were I free, I would indeed stop at nothing to ensure a proud and glorious future for the orcs—and anyone with the courage to stand with us."

"What if the Alliance stood with you?"

"What?"

"What if the Alliance stood with you? Is it truly the orcs' pride and glory that concerns you, or your own?" The words were not planned; they flowed out almost as if of their own accord. Even as Anduin spoke them, he realized their absurdity. And yet, something inside him whispered, *No, not absurd, not impossible. There can be peace.* No one need give up such a future. Unity, working together for the good of all—what else could inspire such true pride, bring such lasting glory?

Wasn't it this, and not killing, that made a hero?

Garrosh stared at him in utter shock, his mouth slightly open in disbelief.

Anduin's breathing was shallow as the moment stretched out between them. He did not dare speak again, for fear of breaking the spell.

Finally, Garrosh spoke.

"Get out."

The disappointment made every bone in the prince's body ache, as if they sung a dirge.

"You lie, Garrosh Hellscream," Anduin said softly, sorrowfully. "There *is* something you'll stop at. You'll stop at peace."

And without another word, Anduin rose, ascended the ramp, and knocked on the door. It was opened for him in silence, and he left, feeling Garrosh's gaze boring into his back.

Jaina was alone in her tent at Violet Rise, washing up for dinner. Located far to the northwest of the Temple of the White Tiger, Violet Rise was the base of operations of the Kirin Tor Offensive. Presently it also played host to Varian and Anduin, as well as several powerful magi, Vereesa, Kalecgos, and herself. She changed into a less formal robe and splashed water from a basin on her face. She almost felt like humming. Vol'jin's testimony had been damning. She had never interacted with the troll, and Light knew their kind had ever been dangerous to humans and other Alliance members even before there had been a Horde. It was amusing, in a way, to hear him talk about the variety of races under the Horde banner when one took into account the trolls' lengthy history of racial superiority. Nonetheless, she all but cheered at his words spoken in court.

"Jaina?"

"Kalec!" she said. "Come in."

He lifted the flap but didn't enter. Her good mood ebbed as she saw his face. "What's wrong?"

"Care to go for a walk with me?"

It was raining—it seemed it was always raining here—but Jaina said, "Of course." She stepped out of the tent slipping on a cloak as she did so, and he let the flap drop closed. Their hands met and clasped. Jaina told Nelphi, an eager young apprentice who helped out all the magi on Violet Rise, they would be gone for a little while, but not to delay supper if everyone else was ready.

They walked across the wide, paved square where the other magi were going about their business in the drizzle. Still hand in hand and in silence, they descended the great staircase, once trod by mogu feet, leading toward the water, picking their way across broken pieces of the trail. As they turned left through Shadewood Thicket, Jaina realized that Kalec was taking her down to the small patch of beach at the bottom of a winding path. The arcane guardians set here to keep watch paid them no mind, trundling about on their programmed duties of surveillance. Jaina focused on stepping safely across the rain-slicked, ancient paving stones, growing more certain that she would not enjoy the conversation they were about to have.

As she set foot on the narrow beach, Jaina could not help but be reminded of walking along a similar patch of sand, Dreadmurk Shore, outside of the walled city that was no more. She recalled seeing the blue dragon in flight, searching for a place to land, and remembered how she had broken into a run to meet him.

His face had lit up when he saw her. They had spoken of those who had come to aid her against the Horde. Jaina had expressed concern for the generals' personalization of the battle to come.

She recalled what she had said to him then: *"If anyone should be bitter and hateful, it should be me. Yet I hear the things some of them call the Horde—insulting, cruel terms—and I feel so much regret . . . My father didn't just want to win. He hated the orcs. He wanted to crush them. Wipe them off the face of Azeroth. And so do some of these generals."*

Anduin had been right. People *did* change. Now, she was one of those whom she had once mentally chided.

It had been then that Kalec had first hesitantly expressed that he wished to be more than a friend to her. He had promised to help her defend her home. *"I do not do this for the Alliance, or for Theramore. I do this for Theramore's lady."* And he had pressed a kiss into her palm.

They had grown closer when Kalec struggled against losing himself while under the influence of the artifact that had revealed the true story behind the creation of the Dragon Aspects. But the events of the recent months had again put distance between them, and he had only recently come to Pandaria. Now he regarded her, with love, but also with unhappiness, and she felt a chill that had nothing to do with the crisp air coming off the sea.

For a moment, she simply took in the sight of Alliance vessels in the water, and the beautiful, violet light of the topmost part of the tower. It hovered a good distance away from the levitation platform below. Sigils in the shape of the Kirin Tor's eye surrounded it, and to Jaina it looked almost like a lighthouse, a beacon in the storm.

Black humor made her chuckle. "First a swamp, then the rain. One of these days, we'll have to find a really nice beach."

When he did not respond with a quip of his own, she felt cold inside. She inhaled a deep breath and turned to him, taking both his hands in hers. "What is it?" she asked, though she was afraid she already knew.

For answer, he gathered her in his arms and held her tightly, resting his cheek on her white hair. She slipped her arms around his waist and breathed in his scent, listening to his heartbeat. Too soon, he gently disengaged and looked down at her.

"This war has taken so much from you," Kalec said. "And I don't just mean physical things." He smoothed a lock of hair that had fallen across her eyes, letting the single streak that was all that remained of her golden tresses trail through his fingers. "You've grown so . . ."

"Hard? Bitter?" She had to struggle not to let her tone of voice match the words.

He nodded sadly. "Yes. It's as if the process of wounding doesn't ever stop for you."

"Shall I list what's happened?" She spoke sharply, but didn't regret it. "You've been there for some of it!"

"But not all. You didn't ask me to come with you to Pandaria."

She looked down. "No. But that doesn't mean I don't—"

"I know," he interrupted gently. "I am here now, and glad to be, and I hope to continue to be with you, whatever comes. I want to help, Jaina, but you seem to like this dark place where your heart has landed. I watch you in court each day, and I see someone who is filled more with hatred than with love. Garrosh might have put you there. But you're staying in that place of your own free will."

She stepped back, staring at him. "You think I like this? That I like having nightmares, and feeling so angry I am about to explode? Don't you believe I have a right to be satisfied—no, no, downright *ecstatic*—that someone who did such horrible things is getting what he deserves?"

"I *don't* think you like it, and I *do* believe you have a right to your feelings. What worries me is that those feelings won't end with this trial."

A vein throbbed in her temple, and she placed a hand to it. "What makes you think they won't?"

"Remembering how eager you were to have Varian dismantle the Horde."

"I can't believe you—"

"Hear me out, please," he implored. "Think for a moment how you would feel if Varian did what Garrosh has done. Let's say he decided that the Alliance should consist solely of humans. He decrees that the draenei should only be allowed in Stormwind if they live in slums. He orders that Tyrande be murdered if she doesn't agree to create a legion of satyrs to fight in his army. The gnomes and the dwarves are tolerated merely as a labor force. He hears that some artifact is located in the most beautiful place in Azeroth, a place of great sacredness. He destroys it to get what he wants. He—"

"Enough," said Jaina. She was trembling, but couldn't identify the emotion. "You've made your point."

He fell silent.

"I didn't destroy Orgrimmar. And I could have. So easily," she said.

"I know."

"Do you remember when you told me you would stay and fight in the Battle of Theramore?" He bit his lower lip and nodded. "I was frustrated with the generals for their hatred of the Horde. And you asked me if I thought that hatred would make them unreliable commanders in battle."

"I do remember," he replied. "You also said that it didn't matter how you and they felt. And I said it *did* matter, a great deal—but defending the city was the most important thing at that moment. Just like defeating Garrosh was, when all of us—Alliance and Horde—were trying to take him down."

"So . . . you're telling me that now that we have, that he's standing trial . . . the differences between—between *us* . . . they matter again."

He whispered, "Yes."

Tears stung her eyes. "How much?" she said in a faint voice.

"I don't know yet. I won't until I see who we are at the end of all this. If you keep hanging on to this hatred, Jaina . . . it will devour you. And I couldn't bear to watch . . . to lose you to that. I don't want to lose you, Jaina!"

Then don't leave me, her heart cried, but she didn't voice it. She knew what he meant by the words, and they went far beyond a simple physical parting. This wasn't a lover's quarrel over something foolish. This was about who they were, at their very cores. And whether or not they could continue to be together if what their hearts most needed was in conflict.

And so Jaina didn't argue. She didn't promise to change, nor did she threaten to leave. She simply arched up, threw her arms around his neck, and kissed him with her whole heart. With a soft little sound of pain and love commingled, Kalecgos pulled her tightly to him, clinging to her as if he would never let go.

It was a beautiful evening in Silvermoon City. Thalen Songweaver, informally clad in stockings, breeches, and a linen shirt open at the throat, had the windows flung wide to let in the night air, and the gossamer curtains swelled and billowed softly. Faint sounds wafted up to his luxurious apartments in the Royal Exchange. He lay on his bed, smoking a hookah of black lotus and dreaming glory. The normally relaxing combination was failing him tonight. While his senses were dulled, the agitation remained, and his white brows drew together as he brooded upon the current situation.

Not so long ago, his position was one to be envied. He had provided aid in more than a single capacity to his warchief, Garrosh Hellscream: first, by pretending to be a devoted and trustworthy member of the Kirin Tor while reporting faithfully back to Garrosh, and second . . . well. Suffice it to say that history would forever remember Theramore not for how it was founded, or evolved, but for how it had been obliterated.

The thought made the blood elf smile as he idly fiddled with a miniature toy mana bomb, a small-scale replica of the one he had created. He'd given them out as a little thank-you to those of the Horde who had freed him from his Theramore prison. It was, he knew, in exquisitely poor taste, but was still vastly amusing.

Yet even reflecting on that moment of glory did not make him feel comfortable this evening. He sighed, rising and walking to the window. He leaned on the sill, peering out. While the auction house was open at all hours, the streets were quiet this time of night. Unlike their kaldorei cousins, civilized elves conducted most of their business with the sun smiling down upon them. If he'd wanted to see lively activity at night, he'd have taken quarters above Murder Row.

It had been going so very well. And then everyone had turned on Garrosh. Thalen's aquiline nostrils flared. Even his own leader, Lor'themar Theron, had refused to aid the warchief. Weaklings, all of them. Now Garrosh's fate was being decided by a bunch of talking bears and some glowing sort of . . . spirit beings, or whatever they were. Absolute madness.

He glanced back fondly at his lavish quarters. He suspected that soon wisdom would dictate that he vacate them. Theron had been too busy overthrowing the rightfully appointed warchief to bother with a lone archmage, but once they had all decided what to do about Garrosh, no doubt the sin'dorei leader would recall that little incident in Theramore, and elves like Songweaver—elves actually *loyal to the Horde*, imagine such a thing!—would become persona non grata. Who knew—if Theron kept cozying up to the Alliance, he might even call for executions.

Thalen's hand went to his slender throat, stroking it thoughtfully. He rather liked his head right where it was.

Such melancholy thoughts. Perhaps a drink at the Silvermoon City Inn would help ease him into slumber. He was just about to pull the windows closed, then paused as he saw two huge black wolves riding into the exchange. For a moment, he thought nothing of it, assuming the cloaked orcs were adventurers seeking to unload their most recent spoils at the auction house. But they rode past both the house and the bank, halting directly below his window. He saw now they were both females. One had the hood of her cloak down and was looking about guardedly. The other's hood hid the rider's features.

Unease warred with curiosity—his bane, Thalen mused sourly. *Ah well, bravado to the last . . .*

"Hail, friends or foes," he called down in a bright voice. "I am not quite sure which. Either you have come to arrest me, or you are my rescuers from that unpleasant imprisonment in Theramore come to visit me, as I invited you to do."

The hooded rider lifted her face. The sight was intended for his eyes only, and it was the proud visage of a gray-skinned orcish female. "Neither, but a friend nonetheless. We have come seeking your assistance in a matter most urgent and full of glory."

Zaela, the leader of the Dragonmaw clan, grinned fiercely up at him.

"Well, well," he said, "I thought you were—"

"I am alive and well, and I am pleased that you are also." His heart leaped at her next words. "As you said—someone rescued you once, when you languished in captivity. I think you might be the sort of person who would care to return that favor."

18

Day Four

Tyrande looked at Go'el, seated in the witness chair, and then laughed softly, shaking her head. Taran Zhu frowned.

"Chu'shao, do you need a moment?"

"No, Fa'shua, I ask the court's forgiveness. I was simply trying to think of how to introduce Go'el."

"Let him introduce himself," suggested Taran Zhu.

Tyrande lifted a brow, inviting the orc to speak.

Go'el looked up at the celestials, addressing them. "My name is Go'el. I am the son of Durotan and Draka, life-mate to Aggralan, daughter of Ryal. Father to Durak. I lead the Earthen Ring."

"Can you tell us more about the Earthen Ring, and what it does for Azeroth?" asked Tyrande.

"The Earthen Ring is an organization composed of shaman of all races," he said. "There, there is no conflict, only care for our world. Our present, overriding duty is to work with the elements to heal it from the destruction of the Cataclysm."

"But you personally did more than most shaman, after the Cataclysm," Tyrande continued. "You were instrumental in defeating the cause of the Cataclysm himself—the corrupted black Dragon Aspect, Deathwing."

"I was honored to help."

"You did more, World-Shaman Go'el, but for now, I would like you to tell the court about another name, and another title, you once held. Can you explain to us what your duties were prior to your heroic activities on the part of our world?"

"With the utmost respect, I protest," said Baine, clearly reluctant.

"Fa'shua, I am merely establishing the nature of the witness's character," said Tyrande. "By anyone's reckoning, Go'el is a truly remarkable individual."

"I do not disagree with you, Accuser, but please move on. Go'el, please answer the question."

"I was once known as Thrall, warchief of the Horde."

"An interesting name, 'Thrall,'" mused Tyrande. She had recovered from her earlier moment of confounded humor, and now walked leisurely around the courtroom. "Can you please tell us how you received it?"

"The word means 'slave,'" Go'el said. "My parents had been murdered. I was found by a human, Aedelas Blackmoore, who named me and raised me to be a gladiator. I later learned his intention was to use me to lead an uprising of the orcs against the Alliance."

"Obviously, you did not do so," Tyrande said. "What did you do?"

"I escaped Blackmoore and set about freeing orcs from internment camps."

"When was this?"

"A few years prior to the coming of the Legion."

Tyrande nodded. "You built an army of freed orcs, did you not?"

"I did."

"And what did you do with this army?"

"I led them against the control center for the internment camps, Durnholde Keep. I defeated Blackmoore and won freedom for my people. Eventually I led them across the ocean, to Kalimdor, and founded a new land and city—Durotar and Orgrimmar."

"Orgrimmar, for Orgrim Doomhammer, and Durotar, for your father, Durotan. A land and a city for the orcs," Tyrande said.

"It would be the new orcish homeland, yes," Go'el said.

"*Just* for orcs?"

"No. I found strong and brave allies in Sen'jin, leader of the Dark-spear trolls, and later in his son, Vol'jin. The tauren—I have openly said I believe them to be the heart of the Horde, and Cairne Blood-hoof was my brother. The Horde grew to encompass the Forsaken, the sin'dorei, a section of the goblin populace, and now it is also open to any pandaren who wishes to join us and believes in our ideals."

"Some believe these choices diluted the true Horde."

Go'el looked at Garrosh, who was seated in his usual place beside Baine. Garrosh gazed steadily back at him. "I believe that they have strengthened the Horde, not weakened it."

"When did you step down, and why?"

"It was shortly after the defeat of the Lich King," Go'el said. "Right after the Cataclysm shook Azeroth. I left for Nagrand, to study with the shaman there. To learn what was troubling the elements. The Horde needed leadership while I was away. Later, as I mastered my abilities, I joined with those who were working to calm the elements and save our world."

"You appointed Garrosh Hellscream to take your place, did you not?"

"I did." Go'el's jaw tightened, but his voice remained civil.

"What were your reasons?"

"Garrosh had acted well and with honor in Northrend. He was young, courageous, a symbol of hope and victory to a people ground down by war and the horrors of the Scourge."

"Did you have any misgivings?"

"I would have had one misgiving or another with anyone I appointed. I would have wondered, for instance, if the burden of leadership would be too much for those who were elderly. Or if the fact that they were not orcs would lead to discontent. There was no one perfect choice. Garrosh seemed to know his own limits, and there were many on hand to advise him."

Tyrande nodded to Chromie. "May it please the court, I would like to show a Vision depicting this thought process."

The scene took shape in the center of the arena, a moment Go'el recalled well.

"You will be returning soon?" Go'el blinked, surprised at the lack of confidence in the voice of the Garrosh in the Vision. He had truly forgotten how ill at ease Garrosh had once been with his heritage—and himself.

"I—do not know," Go'el saw and heard himself say. "It may take time to learn what I must. I trust I will not be gone too long, but it could be weeks—even months."

"But—the Horde! We need a warchief!"

"It is for the Horde that I go. Do not worry, Garrosh. I do not forsake it. I travel where I must, to serve as I must. We all serve the Horde. Even its warchief does so—perhaps especially its warchief. And well do I know that you serve it loyally too."

"I do, Warchief. You were the one who taught me that my father was someone to be proud of, because of what he was willing to do for others. For the Horde. I have not been part of it for long. But even so, I have seen enough to know that, like my father, I would die for it."

Go'el saw the looks of surprise on many faces in the temple as the Garrosh of the past spoke with such sincerity. For so long, the only Garrosh they had seen or heard tell of was the destroyer of Theramore. Go'el questioned Tyrande's wisdom in showing this; surely it would win sympathy for Garrosh.

"You have already faced and cheated death," Thrall said. "You have slain many of its minions. You have done more for this new Horde than many who have been part of it since the beginning. And know this: I would never leave without appointing someone able to take care of it, even during so brief a sojourn."

"You—you are making me warchief?" Such surprise on that young face . . .

"No. But I am instructing you to lead the Horde on my behalf until I return."

Garrosh groped for words. "I understand battle, yes. Tactics, how to rally troops—these things I know. Let me serve that way. Find me a foe to face and defeat, and you will see how proudly I will continue to serve the Horde. But I know nothing of politics, of . . . of ruling. I would rather have a sword in my fist than a scroll!"

"I understand that," Thrall said. "But you will not be without sound advisors. I will ask Eitrigg and Cairne, both of whom have shared their wisdom with me through the years, to guide and advise you. Politics can be learned. Your obvious love for the Horde?" He shook his head. "That is more important to me than political acumen right now. And that, Garrosh Hellscream, you have in abundance."

Still Garrosh seemed uncharacteristically hesitant. Finally he said, "If you deem me worthy, then know this. I shall do all that I can to bring glory to the Horde!"

"No need for glory at the moment," Thrall said. "There will be enough of a challenge for you without any extra effort. The Horde's honor is already assured. You just need to take care of it. Put its needs before your own, as your father did. The Kor'kron will be instructed to protect you as they would me. I go to Nagrand as a shaman, not as warchief of the Horde. Make good use of them—and of Cairne and Eitrigg. Would you go into battle without a weapon?"

Garrosh looked confused. "That is a foolish question, Warchief, and you know it."

"Oh, I do. I am making sure you understand what powerful weapons you have," Thrall said. "My advisors are my weapons as I struggle to always do what is best for the Horde. They see things I do not, present options I did not know I had. Only a fool would scorn such things. And I do not think you a fool."

"I am not a fool, Warchief. You would not ask me to serve so if you thought me one."

"True. So, Garrosh, do you agree to lead the Horde until such time as I return? Taking advice from Eitrigg and Cairne when they offer it?"

Garrosh took a deep breath. "It is my true longing to lead the Horde to the best of my ability. And so, yes, a thousand times yes, my warchief. I will lead as well as I can, and I will consult with the advisors you suggest. I know what a tremendous honor you do me, and I will strive to be worthy of it."

"Then it is done," Thrall said. "For the Horde!"

"For the Horde!"

"Stop here, please." The scene froze. Tyrande walked up to the still, enormous figures, looking carefully at the younger Garrosh. He looked happy and deeply moved. She then turned and looked at the present Garrosh, silent, chained, his eyes half shut as he stared back at her. She didn't need to say a word, Go'el realized. The contrast between the two versions of Garrosh Hellscream could not have been starker.

She shook her head, as if having difficulty believing the evidence of her own eyes, then resumed. "Please tell us what happened after you left—presumably for a brief time."

"The Cataclysm struck," Go'el said. "My shamanic abilities were needed more than I—than anyone—could have anticipated."

"So that kept you from returning? Your studies?"

"Initially. I then went to the Maelstrom, to aid the Earthen Ring in their efforts to calm the elements, as I said earlier. But after Deathwing exploded into our world, my skills with the element of earth, especially, proved to be important."

"I would say absolutely vital to his destruction," Tyrande said. She cast a quick glance in Baine's direction, no doubt expecting a protest, but there was none. "In the absence of the original, uncorrupted Neltharion, there was no Earth-Warder, is that correct?"

"Yes." Go'el shifted uncomfortably.

"And only you were strong enough to hold the element of the earth against Chromatus, and the Demon Soul against Deathwing, is that true?"

"Yes," Go'el said. "Even so, we would have failed without the help of many others from both sides. And I maintain that any other shaman capable would have unhesitatingly taken the risks upon himself or herself."

"But there was no one else capable," Tyrande pressed.

"No," Go'el said. He disliked being regarded, even temporarily, as an Aspect's equal, or given credit for any particular remarkable act of heroism when he knew bone-deep that any member of the Earthen Ring would have done the same if he or she could have.

"And after Deathwing's fall, you returned to the Maelstrom, where you continued your work, correct?"

"Yes."

"Even by then, word of what Garrosh was starting to do had reached your ears."

He shot her a searching look, then nodded. "Yes."

"Many feel you should have returned to lead the Horde once this started."

"Those who say so were not with me in the Maelstrom," Go'el said. "Any one of the Earthen Ring who served there can tell you that *no* one was dispensable."

"So, you were forbidden to leave?"

"No. No one was ordered to stay. We had to search our own hearts as to what was best. I still heard the call of the elements, and so, I knew I had to remain."

"Suppose you had not continued to hear the call. That you had been able to leave the Maelstrom. What would you have done? Would you have perhaps gone to Orgrimmar and told Garrosh to get off your throne?"

"By then he was the warchief. I had no authority to do such a thing. I was not even a member of the Horde, truly, by that point. I became the leader of the Earthen Ring, and it was there that my loyalties lay. Other leaders were in a position to make change, but I was not. I did not even know for certain if my old vision of the Horde was still what the people wanted."

"I am not sure I understand." Go'el knew she did, but he nonetheless welcomed the chance to speak something that had weighed on him.

"The world did not wait on my return," he said with a self-deprecating smile. "It changed. The orcs changed. My Horde changed. What was I to do—kill my fellow orcs until it was once again *my* Horde? Did I have any right to force the Horde to be what it was under my leadership? Did I even have a voice to protest anymore, if I had chosen another path?"

"If you had been asked—what would you have done?"

"I was indeed asked for help by Vol'jin. And the moment I received that request from my brother, I answered it with a full heart."

"What did you and those who followed you have to do to help Vol'jin and the trolls?"

Go'el did not answer at once. "Kill the Kor'kron who were holding the Echo Isles under martial law."

"Was that not acting against the will of the warchief?"

"It was. But regardless of who leads it, the Horde is, and always will be, family. This was not an outward defense or even an incursion against an enemy. This was the Horde attacking its own."

"And this is what made you decide to take arms against Garrosh."

"Yes. I could not stand idle when asked to aid my brother against one who should value him, not seek to kill him."

Tyrande smiled and inclined her head in a gesture of respect. "Thank you, Go'el. I have no more questions. Defender, your witness."

Go'el realized that, grueling as Tyrande's examination had been, it would be nothing compared to what was coming. His friend Baine, son of Cairne Bloodhoof, had risen. Go'el had seen what Baine had done to Vol'jin—Baine's ally and friend against Garrosh, who had urged the tauren to take the responsibility and defend Hellscream to the best of his ability.

Baine had done so, and was continuing to do so. And he, no doubt, would attack Go'el as he had the troll.

How have we come to this place, all of us? Go'el wondered, and steeled himself for the interrogation.

19

Harrowmeiser sighed. Another gorgeous evening in the scenic Howling Fjord, in the lovely continent of Northrend. With those spiffy "northern lights" that everyone just went on and on and *on* about. And the delightful subfreezing temperatures. And an oh-so-appealing lumpy cot and something that sometimes could actually be called "food."

The goblin stood regarding the setting sun. A woman flanked him on either side, and not for the first time he wondered what their faces looked like without their helms.

Yep . . . just another glorious day here at Westguard Keep, a reluctant "guest" of the Alliance.

He had lost track of how long he had been held captive, his beautiful zeppelin, the *Lady Lug*, used now by the enemy to protect the keep from being overrun by nearby pirates. Day in, day out. With no real change of seasons, it was hard to estimate. Years, certainly.

Not even a shirt, he thought sadly as the chill set in. *I'm from Ratchet. A tropical clime, thank you very much. And they have me here, with iron balls strapped to my feet and not even a shirt.*

"You know, Greenie Girl," Harrowmeiser mused, "once word about this cruel practice gets back to the Horde, this could be some kind of international incident. I mean"—and he stretched, working a flex or two into the movement—"I'm practically *naked* here." He showed his sharp yellow teeth in a leer and waggled his eyebrows suggestively at the woman on his left.

The gritting of her teeth was almost audible. The emerald-eyed dwarf loathed the nickname, which of course only reinforced Harrowmeiser's usage of it at every possible opportunity.

"Ach, dinna need to tell me," Greenie Girl muttered. "Talk about a cruel practice!"

"Oh?" he asked. "Could it be that the sight of my glistening green skin, stretched taut against my rippling muscles—"

"—reminds us of plague vats? Why, yes," chimed in Bluebell. Her name was something much less approachable, like Sergeant Somebody-or-other, but the woman's eyes were the hue of the sky itself.

"Come now, ladies, you must have hearts somewhere underneath all that plate armor," Harrowmeiser said. "I've been imprisoned here for a long time now, and I've done everything you've asked of me. You want defense against those pirates down there?" He stabbed a sharp-nailed digit in the direction of the Shattered Straits, where a good half-dozen pirate galleons were harbored. Now and then they made incursions, but for the most part they lingered beyond reach of anyone on the land.

But not, Harrowmeiser thought, his small chest swelling with pride, *beyond the reach of the brilliance and talents of the goblin people!* "You *got* defense against those pirates down there! I've supervised this zeppelin on Alliance orders every single day, ferrying boatloads of adventurers, since you captured my ship, and only *once* has—"

"Seven hundred and thirteen."

"I beg your pardon, Bluebell?"

The human's eyes went a lot less sky-blue and a lot more glacier-blue. "Seven hundred and thirteen times. Your zeppelin has had some sort of malfunction or accident *seven hundred and thirteen times*. And today's not yet over."

"Madam! You wound me!"

A snort from Greenie Girl. "Ha! Don't we wish! Dinna tease, goblin—it's nae kind."

"Me? Tease? Never! You know, they say, once you go goblin . . ." he began, but paused when he realized that neither of them was listening to him.

Their heads were turned to the right, looking in the direction of the main gate, and Harrowmeiser's large ears caught what had gotten their full attention. Guttural sounds of indecipherable war cries rent the air, along with Alliance shouts of defiance. There was the too-familiar clash of steel, and the angry singing of arrows, and the shouts turned into screams of anguish.

"Oh, this is dandy," he muttered. "I got these things strapped to my feet, and here come the vrykul all out for blood."

"Stay here," said Bluebell, and she took off running.

"Wow," said Harrowmeiser, raising an eyebrow in appreciation, "she can move pretty fast in that armor."

"So can I," murmured Greenie Girl. They stood in silence for a moment, and the dwarf twitched. Suddenly she swore a colorful oath. Drawing her sword, she fixed Harrowmeiser with a glare through her visor. "Ye stay right here!" And then she took off to follow her companion, running at a brisk trot toward the commotion.

Harrowmeiser wasted no time. He went as far as the chains about his legs permitted him and reached a patch of earth next to the docking area. Groping frantically about, his fingers closed on a stone. His brow furrowed in concentration, he started slamming it against the locking mechanism. He glanced up toward the gate, trying to figure out what was going on, and then back at the zeppelin.

Hell with the lock, he thought. He hefted one of the heavy iron balls with a grunt and dragged the other with him as he inched toward the *Lady Lug* and sweet, sweet freedom. Ungrateful wenches. They'd miss him when he was gone. He was the only thing that brought a little humor, a little brightness, into their bleak, Alliance-colored world.

He heard the sound of running feet on the deck and froze. His ears drooping, Harrowmeiser saw what looked to be two human males racing toward him. One wore plate armor from head to toe; the other was probably a mage or a priest. His hand kept his hood low over his face. They weren't wearing uniforms, and they were coming around the wall rather than directly from the fort, but it didn't matter. They'd already been part of the fray—the warrior had a bloodied sword drawn.

The goblin gulped. "I was, uh, just getting the ship ready!" Harrowmeiser exclaimed with a ghastly attempt at a smile. "We could mount an aerial attack—really show those vrykul bastids, huh?" He balled his fists and punched the air, making what he hoped sounded like fierce grunting noises.

"Get on board," the mage said in a silky but harried voice. "Hurry. Shokia and the others are buying us time."

Harrowmeiser was completely confused, but hey, they were letting him get on the zeppelin. He started slogging toward the ship. The warrior let out an exasperated grunt, and Harrowmeiser realized he was a she, though wearing a male's armor. To his astonishment and secret delight, she swept him up in her arms—iron balls and all—and carried him on board. She deposited him unceremoniously in front of the wheel, and his hands closed on the handles as if for dear life.

"Wow, you got some good muscles there! Where to, lady?" he shouted.

"Down there, and I am no lady!" the woman yelled back. Her voice was deep and husky, inviting no disobedience. She was looking back at the dock, doubtless wondering when the escape would be noticed.

"Hey, remember, you said it, not me," Harrowmeiser retorted. Then he said, "Wait, wait . . . you mean you want me to take 'er down toward the *pirates*?"

"I did not realize I had liberated an imbecile," the warrior woman snapped, glaring at him through the slits in her helm. Boy, and did she ever have a glare. Harrowmeiser didn't even know that human eyes could look like that.

"There's pirates down there," he repeated. "Oh . . . oh no . . . I get it now. *You're* pirates too, aren't you? This is all about the attacks, isn't it? Listen. I can explain everything! The Alliance *made* me do it!" For one of the few times in his life, Harrowmeiser was actually telling the truth.

The woman grunted and removed her helm, revealing gray skin and tufts of mashed-down, spiky black hair.

"Pirates, pagh," the orc said, and spat. Right on the deck of his lovely zeppelin. "Drunken rum-swilling vermin. Unfortunately, we need their aid right now, and we will have it."

"I'm rescued!" Harrowmeiser crowed. "It's about time! Who are you guys, anyway?"

"I am Zaela, the leader of the Dragonmaw," said the orc, drawing herself up.

"Holy cow," gasped Harrowmeiser. Word of her exploits during the siege had reached him even in Northrend. Some Alliance "heroes" liked to rub in news of Horde defeats. "Warlord Zaela? I thought you were—"

Zaela swore colorfully. "I am alive, well, and burning for revenge, as I imagine are you, goblin."

"Harrowmeiser's the name. Indeed I am, but I am burning more to escape cleanly, and getting recaptured by pirates was not what I had in mind. What do you want with them?"

"We need people to fight for our cause, and they will do so. If we pay them well enough. My sources tell me you were once well connected, and may yet have access to significant funds. You will help us create an army."

Suddenly it all made sense. This, he was comfortable with. "Oh yeah, sure, I got some good business partners and have made a copper or two in my day. But what's your cause? I might not want to support it." He folded his arms stubbornly.

She whirled. "You will support our cause because it will free you. And keep you alive."

She had a point. "Your negotiation tactics, while not exactly subtle, are convincing. Okay, I'll take you down to the pirates."

"Will they recognize you, goblin?" the tall, slender human said to Harrowmeiser in a silky voice. He flipped back his hood, revealing long white hair and glowing green eyes. A blood elf! "I would be quite vexed if we have gone to all this trouble to save you, and you spoil things by getting your head separated from your shoulders."

"They, uh . . . might?" he hedged.

"Well," the blood elf drawled, "stay out of the way and let us do the talking. Or wait—perhaps we could get a disguise for you as well." Seeming to realize something, he snapped his fingers exaggeratedly. "No, that will not work. You are too short for a dwarf."

Harrowmeiser glared. The mage reached out and patted the top of his head.

Baine Bloodhoof saw a mixture of resignation and determination in Go'el's blue eyes. He respected the orc deeply, and considered asking no further questions. But he knew if he did not question his friend, he would be a coward, and would not be discharging his duty to the fullest. Either Go'el and Vol'jin would understand, or they would not. Baine had accepted the task, and he would complete it.

He inclined his head and held the position for a beat longer than was necessary for courtesy. "Let the record show that the Defender recognizes Go'el, once known as Thrall, as a true hero in a world in which that term is bandied about far too casually. The Defender thanks him for his many years of sacrifice, for the good of the Horde, and indeed for Azeroth. We owe him much."

Go'el's eyes narrowed, but he replied politely, "I did what I was called upon to do."

As do I, Baine wished he could say. "When you stepped up to claim the mantle of warchief, you had a vision of your new Horde, did you not?"

"I did. I wished to have a Horde composed of races and individuals who valued honor, martial prowess, and respect for one another as family. I wanted to leave behind old ghosts of the demon-ridden heritage that so dogged our footsteps."

"And you feel that the Accused threatened this? Even though it was his own father who put the truest end to that demon-ridden heritage?"

"With respect, I protest," said Tyrande. "Grom is not the Hellscream that is on trial here. A son is not his father."

"I agree with the Accuser. Ask the question another way, Chu'shao," Taran Zhu said.

"Did you feel that Garrosh threatened your vision of the Horde?"

"I did, but I also said that I was not sure I had the right—"

"Just answer the question, please, yes or no."

A brief flash of anger showed in those blue depths, but Go'el replied, "Yes."

"You are, as I have said, known for your honor. You are even fair to your enemies, as the jury is about to see."

The image of a human male appeared. He had prostrated himself on the floor, and the earth seemed to be trembling beneath him. His hair was black and he was clad in fine clothing. He seemed terrified.

Kairoz froze the scene. Baine turned to Go'el. "Do you recognize this man?"

Go'el's face was hard. "I do. And . . . I am grateful you did not show what happened before this."

Baine knew what Go'el referred to. Kairoz had insisted it would make the eventual point better if Baine were to show that scene, but the tauren did not have the stomach to do so. "Can you identify him for the court, please?"

"It is—it was—Aedelas Blackmoore." A surprised murmur

rippled through the room as everyone realized that they were witnessing a truly historic moment. "I had come to parlay with him. I offered to spare Durnholde Keep and the lives of everyone in it, if he would only agree to free my people. He . . . refused."

Hating himself, Baine asked, "Would you please tell the court what form that refusal took?" He did not look at Go'el.

There was a moment of silence. Then Go'el said, "I told him my terms. His answer was . . . to throw the head of a murdered young woman, Taretha Foxton, at my feet."

"You are an orc, imprisoned by humans. What would such a death mean to you?"

"You know, Baine." The voice was low and cold.

Now Baine turned, keeping his expression carefully neutral. "I do. The jury does not."

Go'el took a deep breath, composing himself. His voice was precise and controlled. Only the tight clenching of his fists betrayed his emotion. He looked up where the celestials sat, and there was kindness and empathy on their wise faces.

"Taretha Foxton was my friend. She thought of me as a brother. Had she been my own sister, I could not have loved her more. She was kind to me, and had already risked her life once to help me escape. She gambled with it a second time to send me a warning—and that time, she lost. Blackmoore—" He paused, clenching his teeth, then continued. "Blackmoore killed her, cut off her head, and threw it down at me, hoping to break me. He did not."

Baine gestured to Kairoz. A younger version of Thrall now appeared in the scene. He looked every inch the hero that he was—bigger and more powerful than most orcs, clad in the black armor of Orgrim Doomhammer, and wearing the massive weapon that was the late orc's namesake strapped to his back. In each hand, Thrall held a sword, one of which he tossed at Blackmoore. The man screamed and scuttled back, staring up at him. It was plain to see now that Blackmoore's linen shirt was stained with vomit.

"Thrall, I can explain . . ."

"No," said Thrall, in the same unnaturally calm voice he had just used with Baine. "You can't explain. There is no explanation. There is only a battle, long in the coming. A duel to the death. Take the sword."

Blackmoore shrank back. "I . . . I . . ."

"Take the sword, or I shall run you through where you sit like a frightened child."

Blackmoore's hand shook, but he grasped the hilt of the sword and clumsily got to his feet.

"Come for me."

And, surprisingly, Blackmoore did. It was obvious to anyone watching that the human had been drinking, but even so, he was swift and Thrall had to act quickly to parry the blow.

Blackmoore's expression changed. His brows drew together and his lips thinned, and as he feinted to the left and then attacked fiercely on the right, his moves were steadier and had power behind them.

In his day, Baine recalled, Blackmoore had been thought a superior warrior. Indeed, Kairoz had informed Baine that in an alternate timeline, Blackmoore had himself won the kingdom of Lordaeron and had ruled as a tyrant. Thrall was much stronger, but Blackmoore was more agile—and he was fighting for his life.

When Thrall noticed that the human was looking about for a shield to protect his left side, the orc furiously tore the door off its hinges and threw it at Blackmoore.

"Hide behind the coward's door."

Blackmoore twisted out of the way, pushed the door aside, and called, "It's still not too late, Thrall. You can join with me and we can work together. Of course I'll free the other orcs, if you'll promise that they'll fight for me under my banner, just as you will!"

Incredulity showed on the orc's green face; then anger darkened it. In that instant, Blackmoore lunged. Thrall was so taken aback by

Blackmoore's ludicrous words that he failed to parry in time. The human's sword clanged off the black armor.

"You are still drunk, Blackmoore, if you believe for an instant I can forget the sight of—"

Baine had seen this before. He knew what to expect. And even he found himself starting as Thrall exploded into action. Thrall had held back—but he was doing so no longer. He bore down on Blackmoore with speed, power, and lethal grace.

Blackmoore didn't stand a chance, but he refused to yield. The blows on the sword he raised to defend himself must have jarred his bones to the marrow. His strength began to give out; his movements slowed; and one final strike sent his blade hurtling from his grasp. Even then, he did not yield. His hand went down to his boot and he came up with a dagger, springing upward with a shout, teeth bared, ready to bury it in Thrall's eye.

Thrall's bellow reverberated now as it must have done then, and his sword came slicing down.

Baine spared the onlookers the precise moment of Blackmoore's passing. "Stop." The scene disappeared before the fatal blow could fall.

"A fair fight," Baine then said. "More than fair, some would say. Aedelas Blackmoore was a man guilty of many things. The son of a traitor, he had planned all along to turn traitor himself—to make weapons of the orcs, and use them to defeat the Alliance, with himself as the king of all the human realms. Additionally, he was cruel. He beat Thrall, badly, simply for losing a fight in the ring. He seduced young Taretha Foxton for his own amusement, then executed her for attempting to help Thrall. A monster, many, even humans, would say.

"Go'el had every reason to hate Blackmoore. And yet, he gave his enemy a fighting chance. He even brought him a weapon, so Blackmoore could die with honor."

He turned and regarded Go'el. "What I cannot understand, then, is why an orc who so prized honor—even to the point of arming an enemy who had murdered someone he loved mere moments before—was ready to kill Garrosh Hellscream in cold blood. Is that in keeping with the Horde you envisioned, Go'el?"

Many things happened at once. Tyrande had risen, shouting, "I protest! The witness is not on trial here!" Go'el, too, was on his feet, but said nothing—he didn't have to.

Taran Zhu struck the gong repeatedly. "Order!" he shouted. "Chu'shao Whisperwind! Go'el! Resume your seats immediately, or I shall reprimand you both! Chu'shao Bloodhoof, you will cease this line of questioning. I agree with the Accuser!"

Baine bowed to Taran Zhu, and faced Go'el. The orc was no longer standing, but he regarded Baine with a look the tauren had never seen directed at him before—one he had hoped never to see.

"I will get to the heart of the matter," Baine said.

"A wise choice," Taran Zhu said archly.

"Your decisions—both to stay away from Orgrimmar as long as you did, and your appointment of Garrosh Hellscream in the first place—have been criticized by some," said Baine.

"I am aware of that criticism." Go'el deliberately sat back and folded his arms across his chest.

"You have said here in this courtroom that there were reasons why you made these choices."

"I did, and I listed those reasons."

"Do you wish you had done things differently? Do you perhaps feel responsible for what Garrosh Hellscream has done?"

"No. To both questions."

"You are certain of this?"

Go'el's eyes narrowed, but before he could speak, Tyrande was on her feet. "With respect, I protest! The Defender is harassing the witness!" she shouted.

"Chu'shao Bloodhoof," Taran Zhu said, his voice mild as usual, "if you have a point to make, please do so."

"I do, Fa'shua, as you will see. Go'el was once taken by the Druids of the Flame," Baine told the rapt audience. "They used one of his greatest strengths—his affinity with the elements—to torture him. Scattering a part of his essence to each elemental plane. During this time, he was forced to face his fears. I respectfully submit that those fears have a bearing on what happened on the battlefield—and in this courtroom."

He nodded to Kairoz, who fairly leaped to his feet. The bronze dragon had been waiting for Go'el to testify after being forced to, as he had said, "take a backseat while Chromie showcases all the really exciting moments."

Baine had replied, "I think a life hanging in the balance should be excitement enough."

Kairoz had answered, "Then by all means, let us tilt that balance in our favor." And he had found Baine several moments in time that he believed would do precisely that.

The scene that now came to life was a dramatic one—a temple in the sky, with columns as white as the clouds that surrounded it. Blue lightning crackled and jagged throughout the temple, followed by the angry answer of thunder. Revenants, their glowing blue-white, energetic forms encased by armor, whirled about. And in the center, caught in the raging tempest, was what looked to be the shadow form of a gigantic Go'el.

Aggra's image stood, crying out to her mate, attempting to reach him. The words the gray shadow figure uttered were filled with grief and pain.

"*Failed.* I have failed this world. The elements . . . will not speak to me. The Earthen Ring . . . has lost faith in my leadership. My weakness . . . has delivered Azeroth . . . into oblivion."

Her clothing and hair were whipped by the angry winds, and Aggra's voice was all but swallowed up. "Go'el, it's me—Aggra! Don't you know me?"

"Oblivion . . . nothing . . . but oblivion," moaned the despairing shadow. "I have . . . failed the Horde . . . as warchief. Garrosh . . . will lead it to ruin. My people . . . to ruin. Cairne, my brother . . . why did I not listen?"

The image faded, like a ghost with the first light of a new day. Baine quoted, his voice soft but carrying clearly, "'Why did I not listen?'"

And another scene took shape.

20

No, not this moment . . .

Go'el's heart ached deep within his chest, stopping his breath for a few seconds. He looked over at Baine, shocked that the son would so use the image of the father. Baine stared down at his hands. He was unable to watch. *So, it pains him as well. But he still chooses to show this.* Go'el gritted his teeth and called on every tool he knew for calmness.

"You are making a grave mistake," came a deep, rumbling voice. As Go'el knew it would.

Cairne Bloodhoof.

The elderly bull awaited Thrall beneath the dead tree that at that time bore the skull and armor of Mannoroth. Cairne stood with his arms folded, his muscles and erect posture belying his years. A soft murmur rippled through the crowd. Horde and Alliance had both respected and admired this tauren.

They said you were winning the fight, my brother . . .

"Cairne!" the image of Go'el—no, he was Thrall then—said. "It is good to see you. I had hoped to hear from you prior to my departure."

"I do not think you will be glad, for I do not believe you are going to like what I have to say," the tauren replied.

"I have ever listened to what you have to say, which is why I requested you advise Garrosh in my absence. Speak."

Except it wasn't true, was it? He hadn't listened.

"When the courier arrived with your letter," Cairne said, "I thought I had indeed, at long last, finally become senile and was dreaming fever dreams as poor Drek'Thar does. To see, in your own writing, that you wished to appoint Garrosh Hellscream as leader of the Horde!"

Cairne's voice rose as he spoke. Thrall looked about, frowning slightly. "Let us discuss this in private," Thrall began. "My quarters and ears are open to you at all—"

"No." Cairne stamped his hoof, a rare show of anger. "I am here, in the shadow of what was once your greatest enemy, for a reason. I remember Grom Hellscream. I remember his passion, and his violence, and his waywardness. I remember the harm he once did. He may have died a hero's death by slaying Mannoroth; I am the first to acknowledge that. But by all accounts, even your own, he took many lives, and gloried in the doing. He had a thirst for blood, for violence, and he quenched that thirst with the blood of innocents. You were right to tell Garrosh of his father's heroism. It is true. But also true were the less savory things Grom Hellscream did, and his son needs to know these things as well. I stand here to ask you to remember these things, too, the dark and the bright, and to acknowledge that Garrosh is his father's son."

"Garrosh never had the taint of demonic blood that Grom had. He is headstrong, yes, but the people love him. He—"

"They love him because they only see the glory! They do not see the foolishness. I too saw the glory," Cairne admitted. "I saw tactics and wisdom, and perhaps with nurturing and guidance those are the seeds that will take root in Garrosh's soul. But he finds it far too easy to act without thinking, to ignore that inner wisdom. There are things about him I respect and admire, Thrall. Mistake me not. But he is not fit to lead the Horde, any more than Grom was. Not without you to check him when he overreaches, and especially not now, when things are yet so tenuous with the Alliance. Do you know that many secretly whisper that now would be a fine time to strike at Ironforge, with Magni turned to diamond and no leader yet visible?"

"Of course I know this." Thrall sighed. "Cairne—it won't be for very long."

"That does not *matter*! The child does not have the temperament to be the leader you are. Or should I say, you were? For the Thrall I knew, who befriended the tauren and helped them so greatly, would not have blithely handed over the Horde he restored to a young pup still wet behind the ears!"

"You are one of my oldest friends in this land, Cairne Bloodhoof," Thrall said, his voice dangerously quiet. "You know I respect you. But the decision is made. If you are concerned about Garrosh's immaturity, then guide him, as I have asked you. Give him the benefit of your vast wisdom and common sense. I need you with me on this, Cairne. I need your support, not your disapproval. Your cool head to keep Garrosh calm, not your censure to incite him."

"You ask me for wisdom and common sense. I have but one answer for you. Do not give Garrosh this power. Do not turn your back on your people and give them only this arrogant blusterer to guide them. That is my wisdom, Thrall. Wisdom of many years, bought with blood and suffering and battle."

Thrall stiffened. This was the absolute last thing he had wanted. But it had happened, and when he spoke, his voice was cold.

"Then we have nothing more to say to one another. My decision is final. Garrosh will lead the Horde in my absence. But it is up to you as to whether you will advise him in that role, or let the Horde pay the price for your stubbornness."

Go'el watched, his heart heavy with sorrow, as then-Thrall turned his back on his brother and walked into the night. He knew what he had done then—mounted his wyvern and flown to the Dark Portal, to begin his training in Draenor.

He would never see Cairne again.

The image of Cairne stood, his eyes following the departing figure. Then he sighed deeply and lowered his head. After a moment, he looked up at the skull of the demon.

"Grom, if your spirit lingers, help us guide your son. You sacrificed yourself for the Horde. I know you would not wish to see your son destroy it."

"Stop." The image of the old bull faded. Baine faced Go'el and drew himself up. "I ask you now, Go'el, the same question you asked yourself: Why did you not listen?"

Go'el expected Tyrande to protest, but she remained seated, calm, a slight smile playing around her lips. She was giving him the chance to respond, and he took it.

"Because I am not a bronze dragon. I do not flit backward and forward in time, knowing all the possible repercussions of every choice I make at every turn. I am mortal, and can only work with what I have in front of me, just as you do. I made the *best* decision when there was no *good* decision. Yes, I appointed Garrosh to lead the Horde in my absence. And when the Cataclysm struck, you, Baine Bloodhoof, were there with me, and you understood why I left Garrosh in charge. Do I wish I had chosen otherwise? Wishes do not a world make. We do the best we can where we are, every minute, every breath. We make mistakes, and we have to live with them. We try to learn from them. And that is all we can do."

"Garrosh Hellscream made mistakes too," replied Baine. "And his mistakes will be even harder to live with."

"*If* he lives," Go'el said.

"You tried to kill him, did you not?"

"You know that I did."

"If you could go back to that moment—with Garrosh before you in defeat—would you again attempt to kill him?"

Go'el looked deep into his heart. Would he?

The answer surprised him.

"No," he said quietly. "Over these last few days, I have come to believe that this trial is a good idea. Voices needed to be heard, and they would otherwise not have been. I have every faith in the August Celestials to make the right decision."

"I have one more question for you," Baine said. "You have admitted that you have made mistakes in your life." He pointed to where Garrosh sat, blank-faced, arms, legs, and waist encircled by chains. "*He*, too, made mistakes. Shouldn't *he* have the chance to learn from them? To do what he can to correct them?"

"There are some things you can *never* correct," Go'el rumbled, his voice rich with emotion. "Sometimes you just have to stop what is causing the damage before it does more. Your father was wise, Baine. But do we know that he was *right*? Do we know all ends? I don't. Do *you*?"

He locked gazes with Baine, and it was the tauren who looked away first.

"No further questions, Fa'shua," Baine said, and resumed his seat.

Tyrande rose with a rustle of her gown. "You say that we do not know all ends, Go'el, and this is so. May it please the court, I wish to show one possible end, had Go'el made a different choice. An end that was so very likely, so highly probable, that Ysera the Awakened had a vision of it—a vision that prompted her to seek out the witness."

"The Accuser may present this Vision," Taran Zhu agreed.

This scenario took time to form. At first, nothing could be seen or heard. Then, gradually, Go'el could discern the shapes of buildings, mountains, trees. And as they came into focus, he realized that the buildings had no inhabitants; the mountains, no meadows; and the trees were only skeletons. It was so silent because there was nothing left alive to *make* sounds. All he could now hear was the wind, and the crackling of distant thunder.

More things came into sight: bodies, rotting where they had fallen. Bodies of humans and orcs and taunka, of mammoths and magnataur and bears. No carrion feeders came to partake of the feast; the ravens, too, lay still on the dead earth, their black feathers rippling in the dispassionate wind.

No, wait—something yet lived. The discordantly beautiful purple, violet, and indigo hues of a twilight dragon came into view as he and his brethren flew over the abattoir that was now Azeroth. He was joined by another, then another, until the air was so thick with them that Go'el could barely glimpse the final horror the Vision currently displayed. But a glimpse more than sufficed.

Impaled upon the spire of Wyrmrest Temple was the body of the Destroyer, the Worldbreaker—the bringer of death, dead himself, dead in a world where only twilight dragons wheeled and circled.

This Vision would never come to pass. And Go'el knew it was, at least in part, because of him.

"No further questions."

21

I t was well after dusk when Vereesa finally arrived. Sylvanas had all but given up hope and was ready to return to the Undercity when she spied her sister's hippogryph. Relief washed through her, and hard on its heels was anger.

"You are well over an hour late!" she snapped. "I am glad I no longer need to eat, if it takes the living so long to simply finish a meal!"

"I am sorry," Vereesa said. "I wanted to talk with Jaina. To see if she had changed her mind after Go'el's testimony."

It had gone better than Sylvanas had hoped. Many of the Horde, and obviously many in the Alliance as well, had laid the grotesquery that was Warchief Garrosh squarely at Go'el's green feet. Some doubtless would continue to mutter. Such was the way of the discontented. No proof, no explanation or reason would ever be enough to disabuse them of tightly held, deeply cherished grievances. Baine had come close to bringing Go'el down to the level of a mere mortal, but Tyrande's masterful closing Vision had silenced the naysayers, at least for the time being. Even though the orc now said he agreed that the trial was a good idea, everyone still remembered that it had been Varian Wrynn who had halted the execution.

"Change her mind which way?" inquired Sylvanas, curious enough to put aside her anger with Vereesa.

"Any way. I do not know if it was Go'el's testimony or the

conversation she had with Kalecgos, but she seems less certain that she wants blood."

"I thought you said she was behind us!" hissed Sylvanas, alarmed now. "And what did that blue dragon say to her?"

"I do not know. I could not get close enough to hear," Vereesa said. "But Kalecgos is not made of stern stuff; Sister, you know this. He is too close to the Life-Binder to want what we do—or to let Jaina want it, if he can stop it. I do know that when they came back from their walk, they both looked very distressed."

"Do what you can to keep Jaina's heart hard," Sylvanas said. "And in the meantime, it sounds as if we must act more swiftly than we had originally planned."

Vereesa nodded. "As you suggested, I have been talking to the pandaren food vendors who have set up temporary shop near the temple. Mi Shao has said that his sister, Mu-Lam, is one of those working in the kitchens to feed the prisoner and the guards. We talked about what Garrosh eats."

This was better. "Tell me."

Vereesa was not stupid, and she now visibly relaxed. Her hand moved from where it had been resting on the pommel of a dagger in her belt. The sisters walked down the shore to the ocean. "He eats the same thing for breakfast every morning: an assortment of buns and tea."

Sylvanas shook her head. "That will not do. Unless your friend Mi Shao could be persuaded to prepare some 'special' buns for him."

"No. Nor will his sister, I think. There are certainly pandaren who understand poisons, but few who would use it to this purpose."

"Go on." A glint of something in the sand caught her eye, and Sylvanas stooped to pick it up. It was a commemorative medallion, crafted within the last decade, which bore Kael'thas Sunstrider's smirking image upon its golden face. Her lip curled, and she tossed the medallion into the waves.

"Lunch is rice and spit-roasted meat of some sort—chicken, mushan, tiger, whatever the hunters bring in, I imagine."

Sylvanas struggled not to smile. "Not tiger meat, I think."

"But it is served in—*oh!*" Vereesa looked shocked for a second, and then she laughed. It was a laugh of pure, surprised, and delighted mirth, free of any shadow of malice or manipulation. For the most fleeting of moments, Sylvanas was again standing on this beach, but bathed in sunshine and warmed by the sound of her sisters laughing at some antic of Lirath's.

The memory caused her to twitch slightly. But still, she smiled. She couldn't help it.

"No, I think you are right," said Vereesa between giggles. "I do not think Xuen would appreciate that much." She took a deep breath and recovered herself. "I . . . think that is the first time I have laughed since . . . well. That is what they give Garrosh for lunch."

Sylvanas left the warm glow of the past, returning to the task at hand. Murder was much more comfortable than mirth. More familiar, at the very least.

"Again, unless we can manage to poison the animal before it is slaughtered and butchered, there is no window to tamper with it," she mused. "This is more difficult than I had anticipated."

Vereesa had picked up a shell and was idly tossing it from one hand to the other. The humor had gone from her, and she frowned slightly. "Sylvanas . . . how are we going to get the food to him? I mean—I do not think they make special meals for him. The guards eat the same thing he does."

"I fail to see a problem."

"Well—we do not want to kill the guards."

Sylvanas blinked. "Pardon?"

"We want to kill Garrosh, not the pandaren guards who attend him."

Sylvanas shook her head. "It does not matter who dies as long as Garrosh does. He certainly has not lost any sleep over the notion of collateral damage. If a few pandaren die, it is worth it. Or do you not have the stomach for this after all?"

Vereesa stared at the seashell. Back and forth, from one hand to the other. Just like her mind. Sylvanas would take no pleasure in killing Vereesa, but she could not permit her sister to lose her nerve. Not now.

Stay the course, Sister. Stay with me on this.

"I-if others than Garrosh die, Varian will be much more inclined to try to find out how this happened. So will Taran Zhu. That could lead them back to us. If it is just Garrosh—everyone will be much more willing to look the other way."

Sylvanas's red eyes narrowed as she regarded Vereesa. "That . . . is something I had not considered," she was forced to admit. She still suspected Vereesa simply didn't want to take innocent lives. "You realize it makes our task harder."

"I would rather think a bit more now about how to kill him without being detected than think of ways to elude capture," Vereesa said. "From what I have observed in court, even Vol'jin might disapprove. Certainly Varian would."

The wind picked up, playing with their hair. "I thought you were supposed to be distraught with grief," Sylvanas said.

"I am! Do not dare—oh." The anger left as quickly as it had come. "Thank you."

"Well, continue with the menu served for dinner at the Temple of the White Tiger."

"Three different dishes. Rice noodles with fish, some sort of stew, and green curry."

Sylvanas was thinking furiously. It had been so long since she had tasted food. Her mind went back to the festivals and feasts she had shared with her family. Picnics here on the shore, with music from Lirath's flute. Alleria would be curled up with a book, and Sylvanas and Vereesa would splash in the surf and return to shore wild with hunger, and voraciously devour roasted quail and ham, apples and watermelons, cheese and breads . . .

"Sylvanas?"

Sylvanas snapped back to the present. A second time, now, she had drifted away. This was not good. "You will need to learn how to prepare these dishes," she said to Vereesa brusquely. "Once we know the ingredients, perhaps we can find a way to salve your tender conscience and still achieve our objective."

"I shall," Vereesa said. "I will tell Mi Shao that my boys are interested in pandaren foods. That will please him."

"Keep an eye on Jaina as well," Sylvanas said.

"Oh, I will, do not worry about that," Vereesa said.

They stood at the water, and Sylvanas realized that their meeting was over—yet neither Windrunner wanted to depart. The silence stretched between them; then Vereesa said, "Are you speaking to anyone on . . . on your side?"

"No," Sylvanas said. "My dislike of Garrosh is very well known, and I have already run afoul of Baine and Vol'jin. Also, the fewer who know, the better. I think we can trust one another."

Vereesa turned to the Banshee Queen and regarded her steadily. "Can we, Sylvanas?"

Sylvanas nodded. "I will not betray you, Sister. We have suffered enough losses." She realized as she spoke them that the words were true. It was . . . unexpected.

Vereesa smiled. "Good. We had best be getting back."

They fell into easy step with one another, returning to their respective mounts. "When do you think you can talk to Mi Shao?"

"I can do it tomorrow at the first respite, get the conversation started," she said.

"Then let us meet back here tomorrow after court."

"Are you sure that is wise? We do not want to arouse suspicion."

Sylvanas almost stumbled at the thought of not seeing Vereesa again tomorrow. A strange pang she should not be able to feel, like the ache of a phantom limb, stabbed her, and she bit her lip against crying out.

"You said yourself time is of the essence," Sylvanas replied. "And we do not know yet what poison will be required, how it will be administered—"

Vereesa held up a hand, smiling a little. "All right, all right! I will be so glad when this is done. Think of it, Sylvanas!" Her eyes were bright with delight. "Garrosh Hellscream . . . on the floor of his prison cell, gasping out his last breath as he feels cold poison slowly stopping his heart. How I wish there could be some way for him to know who had done this to him."

"You are more bloodthirsty than I remember," said Sylvanas. "It becomes you."

"I have to be. I have thought of nothing else but that orc's death since—" Her voice caught and she glanced away. "Well. I will see you tomorrow, Sister." She smiled with an odd shyness, and suddenly looked less like the harsh, angry woman recent events had molded her into and more like the little sister Sylvanas remembered. "It may sound strange, but . . . I am glad we are doing this. Together."

"So am I, Little Moon. So am I."

"We will not make it in time!" Zaela snarled, pacing up and down the deck of the *Lady Lug*. Harrowmeiser stood, the balls and chains still at his feet, his arms crossed. His glower was truly magnificent.

"Well, lady—"

"Warlord!"

"Warlord, I think the *Lady Lug* is doing a fine job considering I've not been allowed to really tinker with her for a few years. I'm doing the best I can!"

"Do better! All this will be for nothing if we do not get there before the sentencing!"

"It might help if you take these off," snapped Harrowmeiser, pointing to the iron balls.

"I leave them on so that you will fall faster to your death when I throw you overboard for failing me!"

"Actually," said Harrowmeiser, "objects of equal mass fall at the same speed."

"Correct, but you are not factoring air resistance into that equation," Thalen said, inspecting his fingernails. "Or any magical means of intervention. For example, suppose you had a parachute or a slow fall spell cast on—"

"You will help him, Thalen."

The archmage froze. "I beg your pardon?"

"Since you are both so clever, work together. Now. Find a way to get us to Pandaria swiftly."

Until right this moment, Thalen had been enjoying the flight. Zaela was a worthy colleague. She had overthrown a fel orc to seize leadership of a clan hardly known as pushovers, and she had given the anti-Garrosh traitors a good run for their money. It was unsurprising that their draconic ally had appointed her head of the unlikely band. The Dragonmaw had gone on ahead and were currently waiting to regroup with them in Pandaria.

Shokia had been recruited next. The orc sniper seemed to know their leader personally, though she would not mention how. Her understanding of battle tactics, particularly from heights and distances, had helped to refine their strategy.

And Harrowmeiser . . . had stayed out of his way. Until now.

The two went belowdecks, where Harrowmeiser sullenly briefed the blood elf on how the *Lady Lug* operated. Thalen found himself reluctantly impressed.

"This zeppelin is not quite the deathtrap that you lamented it is," he commented. "How did you keep it running so well for so long while you were a prisoner?"

Standing next to a wheezing bellows and a loudly turning crank, the goblin replied, "Taffy, twine, and a troll voodoo fetish."

Thalen laughed. "You are a funny fellow. But, all joking aside, how?"

Harrowmeiser sighed and pointed a grimy green finger at the

engine's inner workings. Thalen found himself staring at the skull of some small, hapless animal that had been decorated with paint and colorful feathers.

"Oh, dear," he said. "I see." He could feel the magic coming off the fetish and mused, "Well, nonetheless, what you have done did seem to be working. Mostly." Gingerly, he reached for the item and peered at it for a long moment. "I have a proposition for you."

"Hey, right now my mind is totally wide open to anything that doesn't end with me plummeting to my death. At any velocity."

"You use some spit and polish and get this running as smoothly as possible." He waved his fingers, and violet mist began to subtly roll off them. "And I will see if I cannot augment our little friend here to give us more speed."

He raised the fetish and blew on it, softly, and smiled as the feathers fluttered.

22

Day Five

Jaina Proudmoore fidgeted in her seat. She looked around the vast arena and spoke quietly to Varian and Anduin about inconsequential matters. Though she and Kalecgos continued to sit next to one another, Jaina knew the strain had to be evident to others. It wasn't over between them—not yet—and she didn't want to send something so precious to an early grave. Not if she could help it, and still look at herself in the mirror.

Chromie and Kairoz had their heads together at the Vision of Time, possibly discussing the order in which the various Visions would be displayed. In an attempt to break the silence that thundered on her ears, Jaina said, "It really is good of Kairoz to offer the use of the Vision of Time. It completely eliminates hearsay. We know that what we see is entirely true."

Kalec, too, was watching the bronzes, and he had a slight frown on his face. "I appreciate the accuracy the Vision of Time is providing, but . . . Garrosh made mention of the Darkmoon Faire, and I worry that these scenes we are watching are becoming more entertainment than evidence."

And so it comes back to that . . . always, ever, back to that. "Garrosh brought this on himself," Jaina snapped.

"I will not argue that, but the theatricality of it all . . ." He shook his blue-black head. "What is happening here is important. It's not sport—it's supposed to be justice. It should not have the air of the gladiator ring."

"People are hurting, Kalec," Jaina said. "Some of us will never really recover from what this monster chose to do. We need this."

He turned to her, and concern was writ plain on his beautiful features. He took her hand, enclosing it in both of his, and said quietly, "To what end? To put the past behind you? To move on? You haven't done that, Jaina. As I said before—I'm not sure you even want to."

Emotions flooded Jaina and she jerked her hand from his grasp.

Taran Zhu struck the gong for silence. Grateful for the interruption, Jaina crossed her arms across her chest, seething and aching both.

"This Pandaren court of justice is open. So shall it be," Taran Zhu said. "Chu'shao, summon your first witness."

Tyrande nodded, rose, and walked to the witness's seat.

"The Accuser summons Alexstrasza the Life-Binder."

Jaina's jaw dropped. This, she had not expected. Alexstrasza, whose true form was of course a dragon, did not usually display much modesty in her choice of clothing when in her humanoid guise. Today, however, she was clad in a shimmering, red-gold gown that covered her from neck to toe. Only her arms and throat were bare. She rose with quiet dignity and made her way to the chair.

A handful of people stood up—her flight, and her sister. Then members of the other flights, and then still others, until the room was filled with the gentle thumping sounds of hundreds of booted feet hitting the floor. Nearly everyone present was standing in silent respect as the former Aspect, who had guarded, protected, and loved all life on Azeroth for millennia, reached the chair. Before she sat down, Alexstrasza tilted back her horned head and looked up at the sea of faces. A gentle smile illuminated her visage, and she placed her hand on her heart in a gesture of gratitude. Her eyes glittered with unshed tears.

Standing beside Jaina, Kalec whispered, "Do you need *this*?"

Jaina did not answer.

Tyrande smiled warmly at Alexstrasza, making a low bow. "Life-Binder. I will endeavor to make your testimony as painless as possible."

"You are kind," Alexstrasza replied. "I am grateful."

Tyrande took a deep breath. "This witness needs no introduction. Even the celestials know of her."

"With respect, I protest," said Baine. "Unless the witness can give evidence directly against Garrosh Hellscream, I implore that she be asked to step down."

Tyrande said, "Fa'shua, Garrosh Hellscream received important and influential assistance from one clan in particular—the Dragonmaw clan. I wish to show you the sort of people with whom Garrosh allied himself in recent times."

"Fa'shua," Baine interjected, "we all have—most of us have, anyway—kept poor company from time to time. What the Dragonmaw clan did in the past is irrelevant."

"Chu'shao Bloodhoof's point is accurate," said Taran Zhu.

"Yes, but it is not the whole story," Tyrande replied. "The Dragonmaw enslaved and *continue* to enslave and torment dragons. They did so under Garrosh's reign, and I think this witness highly appropriate."

Taran Zhu nodded, satisfied. "I agree with the Accuser. You may continue your examination."

"Life-Binder, you and your people were kidnapped and imprisoned by the Dragonmaw at one time, correct?"

"Yes," Alexstrasza said. She was, Jaina thought, remarkably calm.

"Can you tell us how this happened?"

"The Dragonmaw had gotten ahold of the Demon Soul, an artifact that was used to control dragonkind. They followed a wounded male to our home, and used the Demon Soul to capture three of my consorts and me—though not without a fight."

"What happened then?"

"Nekros, the master of the Demon Soul, ordered my flight and me to follow him to Grim Batol."

"What did they want with you?"

"They wished us to serve them as mounts in their war against the Alliance. To . . . ride us into battle, and have us attack their foes."

"Surely, some red dragons fell in these battles. How did the Dragonmaw replace them?"

"They took my children from me, as I laid each clutch."

Jaina bit her lower lip in sympathy. She did not have children, nor was she likely to. She adored her "nephew" Anduin. And she had been devastated at the death of her apprentice, Kinndy. But she knew that even those great affections were nothing compared to the parent-child bond. To be the mother of creatures that were magical, life affirming, and all but immortal, and to see them enslaved—she had no idea how Alexstrasza could bear such a thing. Glancing over at the celestials, she could see that even they, who had listened with attentive and kind detachment, were moved.

"Forgive me for the personal nature of these questions."

"I understand why you ask them."

Tyrande looked grateful, and Jaina realized that astonishingly it was the Dragonqueen who was comforting the night elf high priestess in this moment. Jaina shook her head in wonder.

"You said 'each' clutch," Tyrande resumed. "How was it you laid more than one? Why would you willingly continue to conceive children, knowing they would be taken?"

"I refused, at first," Alexstrasza said. "I told them they had one clutch; I would not give them any more. Nor would my mates agree. Nekros . . . Nekros took one of my eggs, held it before my face, and crushed it between his hands. He . . . spattered me with it."

Her voice broke and she paused, composing herself for a moment, then continued. "I cried out in anguish—my unhatched child, murdered before my eyes, my body adorned with its gore . . . Despite the chains that bound me, I attacked the orcs, wounding several of them before they subdued me."

"So you did what they wanted."

"Not right away. I refused food, trying to die before I would produce more children for them to torture. They destroyed another egg. After that . . . I did what they wanted." She smiled sadly. "You see, if my children lived—I had hope that they could perhaps one day be freed."

Jaina's hand went to her mouth in sympathetic horror. She'd known about this brutal part of orcish history, of course, but hearing Alexstrasza tell it . . .

In this moment, Jaina found she agreed with Kalec about the Vision of Time. Hearing the story was upsetting enough. She was grateful beyond words that Tyrande had refrained from showing it.

"Other lives were lost too, were they not?"

"Yes. Eventually, three of my four consorts were slain."

Jaina glanced over at Vereesa. The high elf sat as if she were carved out of stone. Only her quickened breathing gave away the intensity of her emotions.

"So despite you and your consorts agreeing to these horrific demands, you were not treated with care by your captors?"

"No. I was kept in chains. Even my jaw was in a brace, so that I could not attack them. If any of us resisted or struggled to free ourselves, they would use the Demon Soul against us. It was"—and Alexstrasza gave a faint shudder at the recollection—"unspeakably painful."

"Would you like to take a respite?" Tyrande asked gently.

The Dragonqueen shook her great horned head. "I would prefer to finish and be done with the retelling," she replied. Her mellifluous voice was strained.

"You produced red dragons for them to use, as they demanded," Tyrande said. "How were they so used?"

Alexstrasza gazed down at her hands, neatly folded in her lap. "They were ridden into battle, like beasts, and their abilities were harnessed to kill members of the Alliance. Any rebellion on their part would lead to torment and possibly the deaths of their un-hatched brothers and sisters."

"How would a red dragon, in particular, feel about being forced to perform such acts?"

Alexstrasza lifted her head, and could not disguise the pain in her voice when she spoke. "We revere life, all life," she said. "We abhor the taking of it. The Dragonmaw could not possibly have forced us to do anything that appalled us more."

Tyrande nodded, as if satisfied, and turned to face the spectators. "As leader of the Horde, Garrosh Hellscream willingly and know-ingly allied with the Dragonmaw clan and their methods of ob-taining mounts. You have heard what they have done to the most benevolent race on the face of our world."

She began to walk, counting off on her fingers as she had after Vol'jin's testimony. "Enslavement. Torture. Forced pregnancy. The abduction of children. The killing of prisoners. Five counts are laid against Garrosh, once again, by the evidence of a single witness."

Tyrande spared a moment to regard Garrosh, then turned back to Alexstrasza. "Thank you," the night elf said. Then, to Baine, she said, "Your witness."

Baine rose and approached the Dragonqueen. Jaina frowned and said to Kalec, "Doesn't it bother you that he's going to question her after that?"

"I wish she hadn't had to speak at all," he replied. "But the Life-Binder is strong, and has suffered far worse than words in a court-room. She does what she must. So does Baine."

"He doesn't have to do *this*," Jaina hissed. This time, it was Kalec who did not reply. Jaina leaned forward, watching intently, propping her chin in her hands. She'd thought better of Baine. But watching him during this trial, she just couldn't understand how he could defend Garrosh, especially when it required such cruelty. Couldn't understand any of it.

"Thank you, Life-Binder. I regret the necessity to cause you pain," the tauren said. *As if he means it.* "I will be brief. You have suffered greatly at the hands of the Dragonmaw specifically, and the orcs in general. How do you feel about them now?"

"I have no quarrel with any race on Azeroth," she replied. "I am the Life-Binder, and even though most of my powers as Aspect have disappeared, my heart is still the same."

"Do you like them?"

"I love them," she said simply. Jaina froze, then slowly lifted her head from her hands. Her eyes were wide and unblinking as she stared, shocked, at the Dragonqueen.

"*Orcs?*" said Baine, as if he had read Jaina's mind. "Who did such terrible things to you? How could you possibly love them? Do you not cry out for their destruction? For the destruction, particularly, of Garrosh Hellscream, who restored them to power?"

"Few beings are truly evil," said Alexstrasza. "And even they are not necessarily beyond redemption. Change is inherent in life. As long as something lives, it can grow. It can seek the light, or the darkness. It is only when it chooses the darkness so completely that life *itself* is endangered that I would say there is no hope."

"As was the case with Deathwing and Malygos."

"Yes. To my bitter regret."

Tyrande was searching through documents at her table, her body taut. Now and then she glanced up, frowning slightly.

Jaina kept staring at the red dragon. "What is she saying?" Jaina whispered sharply. "What is she *doing?*"

"With respect, I protest!" shouted Tyrande. Jaina, relieved, closed her eyes.

"Yes, Chu'shao?" asked Taran Zhu.

"I call for a respite!"

"On what grounds?"

"The witness is clearly distraught by these questions!"

Taran Zhu blinked, then looked down at Alexstrasza. "Life-Binder, do you need a respite?"

"No, Fa'shua. It was painful to recount what happened, but I am well enough."

"Request denied. Continue, Chu'shao Bloodhoof."

"Thank you." The tauren inclined his head, then turned to regard Alexstrasza. "I have a final question. If one of the selfsame orcs who so tormented you, who killed your children while they were still in the shell, were to come to you today and ask your forgiveness . . . what would you do?"

The great Life-Binder's smile was small at first, but it grew. Alexstrasza looked over to where Go'el and his family were seated, and held his gaze. When she spoke at last, a light seemed to shine from her, so bright was her spirit.

"I would forgive him, of course." She said it to Baine as if he were a child, as if it were a simple, obvious answer.

There were no further questions.

23

When Taran Zhu struck the gong and announced that court was over for the day, Anduin immediately turned to his father. "I'm going to go see Garrosh now," he said. "I'll probably miss dinner." Usually, he had a meal with his father and often Jaina, Kalec, and Vereesa at Violet Rise, and then excused himself to return to do . . . whatever he was doing with Garrosh. He wasn't sure if it was talking with, listening to, guiding spiritually, or simply being a verbal training dummy for the orc. Sometimes all four. Right now, he wished there was a fifth thing he could be doing—shaking some sense into Garrosh's thick skull.

Varian nodded. "Thought you might want to do that," he said. "There'll be something left."

"It's all right. I'll have some of Mi Shao's dumplings."

"Wait, what?" Jaina said. "*Garrosh?* Anduin, what are you doing with Garrosh?" She looked both angry and alarmed.

"I'll explain it over dinner," Varian told Jaina. "Go on, Son."

Anduin jumped down lithely over a row of seats and hastened to the stairs. Behind him he heard Jaina saying, "Varian, what's going on?"

Anduin winced. He'd been so intent on getting to Garrosh, he'd forgotten about Jaina's presence. He'd deliberately not told Jaina about his meetings with Garrosh. Few knew, and he liked it that way precisely because of the sort of reaction he was getting from Jaina. Everyone seemed to think they had a say in what he chose to do and with whom he interacted, and he was growing very weary of it. Right now, though, that took second place to his need to see Hellscream.

He hurried down the hall to the doors that led to Garrosh's cell. "The prince is swifter than the prisoner today," Li Chu said as Anduin arrived. "He is still on his way."

"I'll wait." Anduin stepped to the side of the corridor and leaned against the wall, his arms folded tightly across his chest. He tried to force himself to relax, had a brief moment of dark humor at the absurdity of *that* particular task, and simply stood there.

Garrosh arrived a few moments later, favoring his bad leg, his approach heralded by the clinking and dragging of the chains that bound him. He was accompanied by Yu Fei and the six guards always assigned to him whenever he left the cell. Anduin saw a flicker of surprise on the brown face, quickly quelled. The Chu brothers opened the door. Yu Fei entered first, beckoning to Anduin to follow her. They descended the ramp and stepped to the rear of the room to stand quietly as Garrosh clanked up to the open cell door. Two of the guards unlocked all his chains save the ones about his ankles, while the other four and the Chus stood by, watching the orc's every move. Garrosh went to the furs and sat down while the door was closed and locked. Yu Fei stepped up and murmured an incantation, waving her paws in a delicate motion. The windows began to glow a soft purple.

"What does that do, specifically?" Obviously it was an extra security precaution, but Anduin realized he didn't know exactly how it worked.

"It is a one-way barrier," Yu Fei answered. "The guards can reach in should it be required, but Garrosh cannot reach out."

"Smart," said Anduin, and Yu Fei colored slightly and bowed.

"You honor me," she said, eyes downcast, and scurried out. Briefly, Anduin wondered at her odd behavior, but was much more interested in having words with the orc. Li and Lo nodded to the prince, then closed and locked the outer door, as per Anduin's request to be alone with the prisoner.

Anduin didn't move at first. He simply glared at the orc, who seemed amused at his obvious anger.

"Speak, Prince Anduin, or you shall burst," Garrosh said. "And I have no desire to be blamed for the mess."

"How could you do that? How could you do *any* of this?" The words tumbled from Anduin's lips, and as if the act of speaking had given him the ability to move once more, he strode forward and stood less than a foot away from Garrosh's cell bars. "You're not crazy. You're not without feelings. So tell me—how can you do this?"

Garrosh was enjoying himself as he leaned back on his sleeping furs, the chains jingling with the gesture. "Do what?"

"You know what I'm talking about. Allying with the Dragonmaw!"

"For all your piety, you are very quick to judge," Garrosh said. "Tyrande played a fine card today; I will give her that. Alexstrasza certainly made more than one eye grow moist with her tale."

"*Tale?* Is that all it was to you?"

Garrosh shrugged. "It is history now, and wringing my hands over it will accomplish nothing."

"Any more than would others wringing their hands over you?" Anduin shot back.

"Exactly. I do not need your sympathy, human."

"So why did you want to talk to me? Me, a priest, someone you tried to kill?"

Garrosh was silent.

"She's the Life-Binder, Garrosh. She's—she's the kindest thing in this world. And your people did *that* to her."

Garrosh's eyes brightened. "Aha, so the truth comes out. You are just like Jaina, aren't you? You secretly think us all monsters."

Anduin made a strangled noise and turned away in frustration. The orc laughed. "You are all alike."

The prince snorted. "Sure we are. Just as you are like Go'el and Saurfang and Eitrigg."

Garrosh grunted and looked away. "They have forgotten or, in Go'el's case, never known the true glory of the Horde."

"Oh yes, there's an awful lot of glory in smashing eggs."

"There is glory in bending a dragon to your will!"

"So, you *do* think that torturing the protector of life is a fine thing to do."

"I did not kidnap Alexstrasza!"

"No, but you're in neck-deep with those who did. With those who still enslave dragons. Because there's 'glory in bending a dragon to your will,' isn't there?" He stepped closer. "What is your vision for the Horde, Garrosh? Because all this world has seen of it is needless violence, torment, and the betrayal of friends."

"My Horde would crush its enemies as a giant crushes an insect!" Now Garrosh was on his feet, shoving his face so close that Anduin could feel hot puffs of angry breath on his cheeks. But Garrosh did not touch the bars.

"And what happens when this Horde you envision crushes all the insects that are bothering you? What happens then? What are you going to do when you run out of enemies? Turn on yourselves? Oh, wait, you've done that already, haven't you?"

They stared at one another for a long moment; then Anduin sighed. The fury had bled out of him, and all that was left was sorrow. Sorrow, and sickness at the ruination Garrosh Hellscream had left in his wake—not the least of which was Garrosh himself.

"I want so badly to understand," Anduin said, his voice barely a whisper. "Because at least some of it, I already do. I understand you want your people to carry their heads high. You want your children to be healthy. You want the orcs to be strong, so you can thrive. You want to do great deeds, so you won't be forgotten when you crumble to dust. This, I do, I really do, understand. But the rest? Alexstrasza? The inn? The trolls? *Theramore?*" He shook his golden head slowly. "I can't."

As Anduin spoke, Garrosh, too, had grown quiet. He watched Anduin raptly, almost transfixed by the boy's words. Now he replied in a voice as calm as Anduin's.

"You never will."

For a moment, Anduin didn't reply. Then he said, "You may be right."

"Prince Anduin, please step back from the cell," came Li Chu's voice. Anduin started at the sound and obliged. Li's gaze was on Garrosh. "Is everything well, Your Highness?"

"As well as it can be," Anduin said. Behind Li stood Lo, carrying a tray. On it was a bowl of steaming green curry, another one of rice, two peaches, a tropical sunfruit sliced into quarters, and a fresh pitcher of water. Garrosh could not, at least, complain of being treated as poorly as he had treated his own prisoners. Yu Fei murmured her incantation, and the glow on the bars faded. Under Li's watchful gaze, Lo placed the meal on a small table right beside the door.

Anduin left Garrosh to his supper. At the entrance to the ramp, he paused for a moment, then turned around.

"Then again," he said to Garrosh, "you might be wrong."

This time, it was Sylvanas who was delayed. By the time she reached Windrunner Spire, Vereesa was already there, pacing back and forth on the beach. When Sylvanas alighted from the bat, Vereesa ran to her.

"We can do it!" she cried. "It is perfect!"

Sylvanas found herself smiling at Vereesa's excitement. If true, this was wonderful news. "Speak quickly. I am eager to listen!"

"One of the rotating meals is green curry," she said. "It is every third day, usually, but Mu-Lam Shao says that the order depends on what is fresh more than anything. They make it in a large pot in the kitchen, and everyone is served from that pot."

They fell into easy, almost perfect step as they walked, both their movements swift and excited. Sylvanas felt as though all her senses were heightened, as though she were awake for the first time in a long while. "Go on."

"When Garrosh's meal is dished up, it is sent down to him on a tray along with rice and some sort of fruit—again, whatever is fresh. They also give him a quartered sunfruit." Vereesa could barely contain herself. "Sylvanas—the preparation of the dish is finished by the diner. You mix in rice with each bite and put a squeeze of the sunfruit juice atop it. The fruit itself is tart, but the peel is sweet, so you can eat the peel at the end of the meal. We do not have to put the poison in the curry—"

Sylvanas stopped in her tracks. "We can put it in the sunfruit," she murmured. "And Garrosh will poison *himself*!"

"Yes!" Vereesa's joy radiated from her like a sun. "All we need to do is swap out the sunfruit right before the dish leaves the kitchen."

Both of them reached out their hands at the same time. Vereesa's gloved fingers squeezed tightly. *She is so happy*, Sylvanas realized. *And . . . so am I.*

"This is brilliant, Little Moon," Sylvanas told her. "*You* are brilliant." Her sister blushed with pleasure. "Will you be able to get into the kitchens to do this?"

Vereesa nodded. "Yes. I am already a regular. I talk with Mu-Lam while she prepares the food. No one has objected so far; I think Mi Shao has told them of my interest. I watched them prepare the curry today. The sunfruit is cut up right before the curry is ladled into the bowl, then placed on the tray. I can bring one already quartered and poisoned and swap the one for the other in a heartbeat's time."

"And you know he uses the sunfruit?"

"Yes. Mu-Lam says he finds it delicious."

"How lovely," mused Sylvanas. "Garrosh, possibly one of the most dangerous orcs to ever live, slain by a fondness for a Pandaren fruit."

"It feels like a gift," said Vereesa. "As if this is destiny."

Sylvanas looked down at their clasped hands. She felt . . . warmth inside. Not physical, no; she would never again feel that. If she and her sister had not been wearing gloves, Vereesa would recoil from the cold touch of Sylvanas's skin.

Or . . . perhaps not.

"Maybe it *is* destiny," Sylvanas murmured. "Maybe you and I were meant to reach out to one another. It could be that Garrosh Hellscream could not be toppled by anything other than the combined forces of the last two Windrunners in Azeroth."

She lifted her head, her glowing red eyes boring into Vereesa's sky blue. "The Horde and the Alliance could barely manage to stop him. But you and I alone, my sister, will make an end of him. And . . . perhaps a beginning of something else."

"What do you mean?"

"We do not have to stop with Garrosh's death," Sylvanas said. Her voice trembled slightly. How long had it been since it had done so? Only once, since her murder. Once, years past now, when an adventurer had given her a sapphire-adorned locket.

"What is there in the Alliance for you now?" she pressed, hoping she read her sister correctly. "Garrosh can be only the beginning. We are powerful, we Windrunner sisters. We have changed the world. And we can *keep* changing it—together. When Garrosh is slain, come join me."

"*What?*"

"Come and rule by my side. You hate the Horde—so did I, until I had a place of power there. We can be our own law, Little Moon. We can reshape the Horde in our image. Nothing could stop us. We will grind our enemies into dust and elevate our allies. I feel this; I think you can feel it too."

Her hands gripped Vereesa's, hard. But the high elven ranger did not draw back. She stared, lips slightly parted, her eyes searching Sylvanas's.

"I . . ."

"I want you with me, Sister," Sylvanas said, and her voice broke. "I have been . . . so very lonely. I did not even realize it until now. I did not think I could—stay with me. Please . . . stay, my Little Moon."

24

Day Six

"Chu'shao Whisperwind, you may summon your first witness."

"Thank you, Fa'shua. I summon Gakkorg, formerly of the Kor'kron."

There were not many Kor'kron left. Most of them had sided with Garrosh, even to the point of engaging in battle with Go'el's forces when he arrived in the Echo Isles. Vol'jin had not yet selected his own special guards, and Baine imagined that there would be more than a few trolls among them. The handful of Kor'kron who had survived were in prisons, save for this one. Gakkorg had defected early on, even before Pandaria had been discovered. There had been a price on his head, but the canny orc had managed to stay underground.

He was younger than Baine had realized, and, as was usual for the Kor'kron, a fine physical specimen. His skin was a deep, almost emerald shade of green, and he walked with a limp as he went to the witness chair to make his vow.

"Please tell us your name and position," Tyrande requested.

"I am Gakkorg. I was, as you have said, once a member of the Kor'kron. I served under Warchief Thrall and then later under Garrosh Hellscream."

"Few survived long if they 'once' served," mused Tyrande.

"With respect, I protest!" shouted Baine.

"I agree with the Defender," said Taran Zhu. "Please ask your questions without commentary, Chu'shao."

"When did you leave Garrosh's service?" Tyrande continued.

"Shortly after his initial campaign to claim the continent of Kalimdor."

"Thank you. Chromie, the Vision, please."

The dragon of the Vision of Time awoke under Chromie's gentle coaxing. The Gakkorg of the past appeared, a bulging, bloodstained sack flung over his back as he approached one of the many ramshackle metal longhouses that were sprinkled over Bilgewater Harbor.

The floor of the longhouse was covered with straw, and it housed captives.

They were asleep at first, but awoke when the door opened. There were four of them, and each had a strong chain fastened to his or her right foreleg. They yawned, knuckling the sleep out of wide, brown eyes and murmuring curiously, their faces larger than an adult human's but still small for their kind. Thick, long hair tumbled in baby's curls of black and brown and gray down their backs. They wore only the most primitive bits of animal skins for clothing, and as they started to sniff the air and realized what Gakkorg was carrying, they clapped excitedly and made sounds of delight. Their small tails lashed and they stomped their heavy feet up and down.

They were the offspring of the magnataur.

"That's it, little ones," encouraged Gakkorg. "Make a lot of noise so your parents can hear you." He removed a hunk of dripping meat from the sack, and the younglings went wild. Laughter burbled from one. The rest cried with desire, tears glistening on round cheeks as they reached out their hands.

The image of Gakkorg regarded them for a moment; then he shook his head and muttered something to himself. He tossed a hunk of meat to one of them, a scant female, who pranced as best she could with her fettered foreleg, then plopped down to devour the sweetened meat. The others clamored all the louder for their own share, and Gakkorg obliged. Soon all four of them, from the youngest, barely a baby, to the eldest, a male with the smallest indication of tusks coming from either side of his head, were chewing on their food.

"Stop here, please." The scene froze. "Who and what are these?" Tyrande inquired.

Gakkorg's face was gray with sorrow. "Magnataur younglings," he said. "Garrosh kidnapped them in order to force the adults to fight for him in Ashenvale."

"Were they tortured in any way?"

"No," said the orc. "My job was to feed and tend to them. When their parents grew difficult, I would give them special treats so they would make a lot of noise all of a sudden. They liked meat that had been soaked in honey. The parents couldn't tell what we were doing to them, and worry kept them manageable. I would not torture younglings, night elf."

"But you tended kidnapped ones," Tyrande said, simply stating a fact.

Gakkorg rubbed his face. "Yes, I did," he said heavily.

"Did the adults fight for the Horde in that battle?" asked Tyrande, although Baine knew that the high priestess had seen them herself.

"They did."

"What happened to them?"

"They were all killed," Gakkorg replied.

"So their little ones were orphaned," Tyrande continued. "The adults died keeping their part of the bargain. What was Garrosh's part?"

"He told the magnataur he would kill their offspring if the adults didn't fight. If they did fight for the Horde, he would release the younglings."

"I see. Did he honor his word?"

Gakkorg didn't answer at once. He simply sat and stared at the images of the youngsters, frozen in time, the gore of their meal offset by the innocent delight they took in the treat.

"Answer the question, please," Tyrande prodded.

Gakkorg shook himself. "Yes . . . and no. The magnataur—well, they are not the sharpest swords in the armory. And Garrosh was very clever in his wording." Now he did look away from the scene and narrowed his eyes at Garrosh. His words were almost spat. "He released the younglings, all right. The magnataur assumed that Garrosh meant he would take them home. Instead, he sent orders that they were to be set loose on the beaches of Azshara."

Baine closed his eyes. He did not dare look at Garrosh, for fear that he would physically attack the orc for this latest atrocity.

"But, they could fend for themselves, could they not?"

"Perhaps they could have, in Northrend, where they understood what was safe and what wasn't. Where they could have found adults of their kind. But they were released on the Shattered Strand."

"And that was not safe?"

"There are naga on the Shattered Strand." Gakkorg's voice was hollow. He said nothing more; he didn't have to.

"And what did you do when you learned this?"

"I took off my tabard and disappeared," he said. "I was not the only one."

"Thank you. And so another count of the abduction—and murder—of children can be laid at Garrosh Hellscream's feet. Chu'shao Bloodhoof, your witness."

Baine couldn't even speak to decline. He simply waved his hand in a negative gesture. He had nothing to say to Gakkorg, and feared if he did address the orc, it would be only to congratulate him for his desertion.

As Tyrande walked back to her seat and Gakkorg returned to his place in the stands, a Sentinel emerged and made a beeline for Tyrande. They spoke quickly, and Tyrande's brows rose. She seemed disbelieving at first, but something the Sentinel said appeared to convince her.

"Chu'shao Whisperwind," said Taran Zhu, "would you care to share with the court?"

"One moment, Fa'shua." The two night elves continued speaking in sibilant whispers, and Tyrande finally nodded. The Sentinel hastened outside while Tyrande composed herself. She appeared to be stunned, pleased, and overwhelmed all at once. Eventually she rose, her robe rustling softly, and for a long moment simply stood at her desk. She made no move to call a witness, instead searching the crowd, then turned her gaze up to the celestials, as if trying to make a decision. Baine was on alert. Tyrande always presented herself as confident and controlled, but now she looked . . . quietly triumphant.

"Lord Zhu," she said, "I submit a formal request to have this trial regarded as irreparably compromised."

The arena began to buzz, and Taran Zhu struck the gong. For the first time since the trial began, Garrosh leaned over to speak to Baine. "What does this mean?"

"Depending on why she wants this, either she thinks you'll be acquitted—which I do not believe for a moment—or she wants to get a new jury."

"Which means I will undoubtedly be executed."

His voice was placid, almost bored. Baine looked at him sharply. "There are only a handful of beings capable of returning an impartial verdict. Four of them currently compose your jury."

"I stand by my statement."

Baine didn't answer. When the furor had subsided, Taran Zhu said, "Chu'shao Bloodhoof and Chu'shao Whisperwind. Will you and your time advisors please approach the dais?"

When all of them stood before him, Taran Zhu peered at Tyrande with irritation. Chromie did not look particularly happy, Baine observed. "Accuser, tell me why at this late point you wish me to declare this trial compromised."

"It has come to my attention, and I must bring it to yours, that Chu'shao Bloodhoof has a conflict of interest in representing the Accused. I do not believe he can do a fair job, and therefore request that the trial be formally declared compromised and that a new Defender and jury be appointed."

"Chu'shao," Taran Zhu said with a combination of gravity and exasperation, "I am dubious that you are unaware of the virtual impossibility of finding *anyone*—Horde, Alliance, or otherwise—who is capable of a completely fair representation of the Accused."

"Well, you will simply have to do so," Tyrande said.

"What is the nature of this evidence?"

Tyrande now had the grace to look a bit uncomfortable. "I have just been notified that a witness has been located who will give testimony that, to say the least, does not reflect well on Chu'shao Bloodhoof. I would prefer not to sully his reputation unnecessarily. I believe that hearing this information will so influence the jury that they will be unable to render a fair verdict."

Taran Zhu folded his paws and scrutinized her at length. "I would not wish to be your enemy, Lady Tyrande."

"I am glad you are not, Lord Zhu."

"And what is the identity of this surprising witness?"

"I would prefer—"

"Right now," Baine interrupted angrily, "I care not one *whit* what you prefer, Chu'shao! *Who do you have?*"

Taran Zhu held up a paw. "Pray silence, Chu'shao Bloodhoof. Chu'shao Whisperwind—Chu'shao Bloodhoof's opinion of Garrosh is nothing new. He has even addressed any potential bias in his opening statement. If you had a protest, it should have been raised then."

"I did not have this witness at that time, Fa'shua."

Taran Zhu was still for a long moment. Finally, he spoke. "Chu'shao Bloodhoof, it is clear what Chu'shao Whisperwind wishes to achieve. I have more faith in the celestials and their ability to render a fair verdict than she does, but I would know your thoughts. It seems as though you would be the one damaged by this."

This was the moment, Baine realized. Taran Zhu would do what he felt was best, of course. Such was his right as fa'shua. But he had asked Baine, and the tauren would answer truthfully. He also understood that Tyrande did not have to do this. If the testimony was as damning as she seemed to believe—and he had no reason to doubt her certainty—then she simply could have brought in the witness and let things fall out as they would. She was attempting to show him respect—and, perhaps, do him a kindness.

"There was a time when I would have welcomed this," he said. "To have conducted my duty as best I could, and yet be relieved of the necessity to continue. The Earth Mother knows I have struggled with my choice. I did not ask for this burden, and I am certain whatever witness Tyrande has found will make public the degree of my feelings toward the Accused. As poor a champion as I might be, I am nonetheless the best Garrosh Hellscream has. I was called to defend him, and defend him I shall. Whatever the risk to me personally. These are my thoughts, Lord Zhu."

To his surprise, Tyrande looked unhappy. She turned to him and said earnestly, "I do not think you appreciate the import of what is about to happen. I have no wish to make this a personal attack."

"And yet, you are."

"I *must!*" She kept her voice soft, but the passion of her words poured forth in every syllable. "I will sacrifice you, Baine Bloodhoof, if need be, in order to present the strongest case possible. I will sacrifice whatever and whomever I must."

Baine took a deep breath and blew it out. He drew himself up to his full height and, looking down on the night elf, said very calmly, "Do so, then."

Taran Zhu was watching them both. Now he said, "So be it. Chu'shao Whisperwind, you are free to present your witness. Based

on the evidence, the Accused may choose whether or not to keep
Baine Bloodhoof on as chu'shao."

Tyrande closed her eyes for a moment. "Baine Bloodhoof, what
happens next . . . be it on your head. Thank you, Fa'shua."

Before Kairoz took his seat, he grabbed Baine's arm and whispered, "I know what she has on you. I don't have time to research a
counter-Vision, and I can't come up with anything off the top of my
head!"

"You will not need to," Baine replied stoically. "If Chromie is
involved, then it is clear that Tyrande plans to show whatever evidence she is presenting, not merely discuss it. I must trust the truth
will speak for itself, and I accept the consequences."

"You're as idealistic as the young prince," hissed Kairoz in frustration.

Baine snorted in wry amusement. "I have been called worse," he
replied, and returned to his seat.

Garrosh again leaned over and asked, "What happened?"

"The trial will proceed. This time, you get to decide a part of it.
You can keep me on, or not. If you choose to have someone else defend you, Taran Zhu will appoint another Defender."

"Why would I wish to do that? You are making my last few days
entertaining ones."

Tyrande stood beside the witness chair, took a breath, and then
said, "Please be aware that I regard the next witness as extremely
hostile to the Accuser's case. I summon Longwalker Perith Stormhoof to speak."

And at that moment, Baine understood exactly how far Tyrande
Whisperwind was willing to go in order to have Garrosh formally
executed.

25

The tauren Longwalker Perith Stormhoof approached the chair slowly, with the air of one going to an execution. He sat down with dignity and waited.

"Please tell the court your name," Tyrande said.

"I will not testify," said Perith. His voice was deep, almost emotionless, but Baine knew better.

"Perith Stormhoof," said Taran Zhu, "you are compelled to give testimony if you are so called."

"I have sworn an oath, to Cairne Bloodhoof and to Baine Bloodhoof after him, to never say or do anything that would harm him. I am the trusted keeper of their secrets. You cannot force me to speak."

"Under Pandaren law, I can hold you indefinitely until you do choose to testify," Taran Zhu stated.

"I will stay in prison and keep my honor to the end of my days rather than betray my high chieftain."

Baine had had enough. He rose. "Perith Stormhoof, I order you to speak. You have more than proved your loyalty, both to me and to my father, and it is for both of us that I tell you I will hold nothing you say against you. This is a place for truth, which Cairne and I ever valued, so speak yours, as Pandaren law requires."

The mask vanished and Perith looked at him, anguished. Clearly, he didn't think Baine fully appreciated the impact of what he might be asked to reveal. But Baine did, and was almost relieved. He nodded. *Go ahead.*

"I will speak, only because my high chieftain has told me I must," Perith said, and his grief was almost palpable.

"May the jury take note—this is a hostile witness," said Tyrande. She expressed no joy in Perith's capitulation, but neither did she show regret. "Please state your name and position."

"I am Perith Stormhoof. I am a Longwalker in the service of Baine Bloodhoof and his father, Cairne, before him."

"Tell us what a Longwalker does."

"We are couriers first and foremost, but more than that. We know the content of the missives we carry. We know the secrets of the high chieftain." His voice was flat, defeated. "We know how to travel safely, in all respects, so that we and our vital missions are not hindered."

"When you are not delivering messages for High Chieftain Bloodhoof, where are you, usually?"

"In his presence."

"As a counselor, an advisor?"

Perith shook his gray head. "No. As a shadow, save when he needs me."

Garrosh leaned in toward Baine and said, conversationally, "She will destroy you, tauren."

"I am rather certain she will," Baine replied.

"Then why—"

"Peace," Baine rumbled, his voice dangerously soft.

"So you are privy to many secrets," Tyrande continued. "The Accuser wishes to state for the record, this testimony is being sought *only* for the purposes of the trial. I have no desire to pry secrets of the Horde to aid the Alliance."

"If I thought you might do so, Chu'shao, I would be seeking to remove *you* from the trial," Taran Zhu said, almost cheerfully.

Baine did not look up into the stands to see the reaction from any Alliance members. He would let this play out. *Please, Earth Mother, let this be the best decision for us all . . . We are so weary of war.*

Tyrande frowned slightly, but nonetheless inclined her head. She returned her attention to Perith. "When did you first enter Baine Bloodhoof's service?"

"The night of his father's murder," answered the Longwalker. "The Grimtotem had taken Thunder Bluff and attacked Bloodhoof Village. Baine received a warning in time and was able to escape, thanks be to the Earth Mother."

"And you were the one who warned him?"

"No. I had accompanied Cairne to Orgrimmar. I was . . . delayed in my return after the mak'gora. The Grimtotem were watching. I caught up with Baine afterward in Camp Taurajo."

"Who did warn him, then?"

"A Grimtotem shaman named Stormsong, who had more honor than Magatha."

"Baine was fortunate. May it please the court, I would like to present a Vision from that terrible night."

Baine closed his eyes for a moment, praying for calmness, as the scene manifested. It was he, Jorn Skyseer, Hamuul Runetotem, and Perith, sitting in the background as he usually did. Perith was deeply respected by Baine, but he preferred to keep to the outskirts of all activity. It was part of his training as a Longwalker.

"Magatha has what she wanted," said the image of Hamuul as food was placed before them. "Control of Thunder Bluff, Bloodhoof Village, probably Camp Mojache, and unless we stop her soon, all the tauren."

"But not Sun Rock," Jorn put in quietly. "They have sent a runner. They were able to repel the attack."

Baine watched himself nod, growl softly, and take a bite out of necessity rather than appetite. "Archdruid," the image of Baine said after a moment, "my father ever trusted your advice. I have never been in more need of it than now. What do we do now? How do we fight her?"

Hamuul didn't answer at once. Finally he said, "From what we can learn, most of the tauren are now controlled by Magatha—willingly or not. Garrosh might be innocent of treachery, but he is most certainly a hothead, and one way or another he wished your father dead. The Undercity is not safe for you, not patrolled as it is by orcs likely loyal to Garrosh. The Darkspear trolls are likely trustworthy, but they are not many. And as for the blood elves, they are much too far away to offer any aid. Garrosh will likely reach them before we could."

Baine's laughter rumbled, though it was bitter. "So it seems that our enemies are more trustworthy than our friends."

"Or at least more accessible," Hamuul replied.

The image of Baine fell silent, lost in thought. At length, he shook his head, ears flapping, having reached a decision.

"I will take an honorable enemy over a dishonorable friend every time. So let us go to an honorable enemy. We will seek out the woman Thrall trusted. We will go to Lady Jaina Proudmoore."

The courtroom exploded.

Jaina stared at Tyrande, the voices all around her as muffled and nonsensical as if she were underwater. She couldn't feel the hand grasping hers, or the one shaking her shoulders. She could only stare at Tyrande, with a terrible, unshakable sense of betrayal. The night elf looked back at her with a combination of implacable determination and deep compassion.

"How could she do this?" murmured Jaina. She had half expected this sort of thing from Baine, but from Tyrande—

"Jaina!" Kalec's voice was stronger and fuller than she had ever heard it before. He shook her shoulder. The movement snapped her spell, and suddenly everything sped up and grew so loud; everyone was shouting, and Taran Zhu was banging the gong. Jaina dragged her eyes away from Tyrande to regard Varian. He too was shouting.

"Jaina, why didn't you tell me about this?"

Anduin's eyes were as big as gold coins. He too had apparently decided that silence was the best option when it came to helping the deposed tauren high chieftain.

Light help her and Anduin now. "It's all falling apart," she murmured. "Everything. It's all just falling apart."

"Jaina," said Kalec. "Taran Zhu has just called for a ten-minute respite. We can leave if you wish. You do not have to be here for this."

"What is it that she doesn't have to be here for?" demanded Varian. He visibly struggled to calm himself and was only partly succeeding. "This is just like what happened with the Sunreavers. Jaina, you should have told me. Tell me what I have to prepare for next."

Jaina shook her head and squared her shoulders. "I have no doubt but that you'll see it," she said. "I can't tell you everything in ten minutes."

"Then tell me what you *can*! Light blind me, Jaina, I just found out someone I regarded as one of my best friends had secret meetings with Baine Bloodhoof!" he snapped, folding his arms across his broad chest—perhaps in an effort to keep from attacking her. "Your constant sneaking off to meet Thrall was bad enough, but . . ."

"Father," said Anduin quietly. "I have something to tell you too."

Baine sat quietly, feeling oddly at peace while the world went mad around him.

Taran Zhu had called for a ten-minute respite, but it took at least twice that long to stop the fighting and remove the combatants to their new "quarters." Tyrande could not know that he had not attempted to hide his initial contact with Jaina Proudmoore. Baine had been so angry at Garrosh's decision to wait and see who won the conflict between Grimtotem and Bloodhoof that he made it

common knowledge that an Alliance leader had been more sup-
portive than his own warchief. He had gone so far as to use Jaina's
support of him as a reason to not attack Theramore during a large
assembly of Horde leadership and their people. No one had thought
him a traitor. Jaina had some who respected her among the Horde,
and she was not nearly as despised as Varian or Tyrande.

At least, not then.

Garrosh gazed at him with a bemused expression. "So, it appears
you might be joining me in prison, Bloodhoof," the orc said.

"Possibly," said Baine. "But I would request a different cellmate."

"Perhaps Jaina?"

"No. But perhaps Anduin."

Taran Zhu struck the gong again, and this time people seemed to
be ready to resume their seats.

"I debated ending the trial for the day," Taran Zhu said, his voice
harder than normal and his eyes bright with a rare display of outrage. "But it is my hope that by the end of this witness's testimony,
we will all be in a more civilized place. If not, know that I will immediately put any witnesses or persons named in this court under
Shado-pan protection if I feel they are in any danger. This is not the
Darkmoon Faire, nor is it a gladiator ring. It is a courtroom. It is a
place for justice, and for truth. And I *will* have it so."

No one spoke. He took a moment to glance around the seats;
then his gaze traveled back down to Tyrande. "Chu'shao, you may
resume your questioning."

"Thank you, Fa'shua." Taking her time, she rose, smoothed her
gown, and walked over to Perith. "I believe where we left off," she
said, as if they had merely paused for an ordinary respite, "we saw
that Baine Bloodhoof was planning to meet with Lady Jaina Proudmoore."

All eyes went to Jaina. She sat straight and calm, her hands folded
in her lap, but her flushed face and quickened breathing belied her
cool exterior. Beside her, Kalec looked ready to spring into action

if he felt the need to, and Varian's face was thunderous. His gaze darted from Perith to Tyrande, and Baine couldn't tell which one the human king was angriest with.

"That is correct."

"Were you present at that meeting?"

"No, I was not."

"But you know what happened?"

"I know what my high chieftain told me."

"And that was?"

Perith glanced at Baine, deep sorrow in his eyes. "Lady Jaina would not bring the Alliance into war with the Horde, but she did agree to personally offer aid."

"And what form did that aid take?"

"She gave him gold."

Disapproval rippled through the audience. "How much gold?" inquired Tyrande.

"I was not privy to those details."

"Was this the only time your high chieftain had dealings with the lady Jaina?"

Baine tensed. This second visit was *not* common knowledge. Perith's voice was ragged as he answered.

"No, it was not."

Tyrande nodded to Chromie. "May it please the court, I have a second Vision to present."

26

Jaina was still numb from the revelation. It would wear off, she knew, but for the moment, she welcomed it. Her emotions were so conflicted, so knife-sharp, she did not wish to examine them—not here, not now, certainly. Varian had not immediately whirled on her—or his son—as a traitor, and right now, that was enough. He was waiting to see how the rest unfolded.

So, truth be told, was she.

Jaina's cozy little parlor appeared, its fireplace flanked by two chairs and rows of books, and she grew dizzy for a moment. A simple thing, her parlor. Just a room. And it was gone, blown to violet dust along with everyone and everything in Theramore. The crackle of the fire, the clink of teacups on saucers, the sound of laughter or lively, intellectual conversation—never to be heard again.

She couldn't tear her eyes away from the scene, but reached out blindly to Kalecgos. He caught her hand and held it tight.

And the sight of herself, in a hastily thrown-on robe—

Golden hair, kind eyes, a face that bore a single furrow in its brow, lips that knew more of gentle words than shrieks of pain.

It was an alien face.

Jaina's heart was shattered at the visible evidence of how truly innocent she had been not that long ago. She did not want to break down, not in front of everyone, and Kalec knew that. So he made no move to wrap an arm around her or comfort her other than to grip her hand, steady as stone.

The Vision-Jaina paced, then turned to greet her visitor. How small she looked next to a tauren—Jaina thought the pedestrian observation a little oasis in the midst of her personal emotional hurricane. He wore a cloak and stood quietly, not protesting the roughness displayed by the guards who led him in.

"Leave us," Jaina said.

My voice . . . Did I truly sound so young?

"My lady? Leave you alone with this . . . creature?" one of the guards protested. She glanced at the guard sharply.

"He has come to me in good faith, and you will not speak so of him."

The guard blushed a little, embarrassed. Then, bowing to his mistress, he and the other withdrew.

Perith pulled off his hood. "Lady Jaina Proudmoore. My name is Perith Stormhoof. I come on orders from my high chieftain. He asked me to give you the mace. He said . . . it would help you to believe my words are truth."

Fearbreaker. An exquisite and ancient dwarven weapon, given by Magni Bronzebeard to Anduin Wrynn, who had in turn given it to Baine Bloodhoof in that selfsame parlor. Only now did Jaina remember that she had held it during this meeting. It was clutched in the then-Jaina's hands, as pristine and perfect as the day it was forged. It bore a head of silver wrapped in bands of gold, and was etched with runes and dotted with small gems.

"I would never mistake Fearbreaker," the then-Jaina said. Nor would anyone else. Those who knew Anduin would know Fearbreaker, and so now Tyrande had exposed the prince of Stormwind as well as the lady of Theramore.

"He knew you would not. Lady Jaina—my high chieftain thinks gratefully and highly of you, and it is because of the memory of the night when he received Fearbreaker that he has sent me with this warning. Northwatch Hold has fallen to the Horde."

Angry cries started to come, some directed at Jaina, but most at Baine. Jaina understood why. Going to Jaina for aid against Magatha—an internal conflict—was not the same as warning her about a Horde attack against the Alliance. For the first time in what felt like ages, Jaina found herself concerned for the well-being of a member of the Horde.

Taran Zhu struck the gong, and while the tension did not subside, the spectators fell quiet. No one wanted to be expelled from the courtroom at this juncture.

The image of Perith continued speaking. "It further wounds him that this victory was won with the usage of dark shamanic magic. He despises these actions, but to protect his people, Baine has agreed that the tauren will continue to serve the Horde as they are needed. He wishes me to emphasize that at times, this obligation brings him little joy."

Some of the anger abated, but the room still fairly crackled with fury.

"Well do I believe that," Jaina heard herself say. "Still, he has participated in an act of violence against the Alliance. Northwatch Hold—"

"Is only a start," Perith said, interrupting her. "Hellscream would reach much farther than a simple hold."

"*What?*" Even now Jaina recalled feeling as if she had been punched in the stomach.

"His goal is nothing less than the conquest of the continent. He will shortly be ordering the Horde to march on Theramore. And mark me well, their numbers are strong. As you are now, you will fall. My high chieftain remembers the aid you gave him and asked me to warn you. He has no wish to see you caught unawares."

"Your high chieftain," she said, her heart full, "is a truly honorable tauren. I am proud to be so highly regarded by him. I thank

him for this timely warning. Please tell him it will help save innocent lives."

"He regrets that a warning is all he can give you, my lady. And . . .
he asks you to please take Fearbreaker, and return it to the one who
so kindly gifted it to him. Baine feels that it is no longer his to keep."

There, Jaina thought, *surely Vol'jin will understand; perhaps he even
knew about this—*

"I will see to it that Fearbreaker is returned to its former owner,"
the image of Jaina said. Her voice was rich with warmth and gratitude. *I was . . . good,* Jaina realized. *I was good, then . . .*

She could tell that Perith saw that as he bowed deeply to her.
Quickly Jaina scribbled a note, sealed it, and gave it to the Longwalker.

"This will ensure your safe passage through Alliance territory, if
you are caught."

His voice rumbled with laughter. "I will not be, but your concern
is appreciated."

"And tell your noble high chieftain there will be no rumors of a
tauren Longwalker visiting me. To all who would ask, I will say that
word reached me from an Alliance scout who managed to escape
the battle. Take refreshment, then return safely."

"May the Earth Mother smile upon you, Lady," said Perith. "I understand my high chieftain's choice even better now that I have met
you."

"One day," the Jaina of the past said earnestly, "perhaps we will
fight on the same side."

"One day, perhaps. But that day is not today."

Nor was it today, here in the present, Jaina thought. "So, Your
Majesty," she said, addressing Varian and keeping her gaze forward
as the scene faded. "Are you going to arrest me for treason?"

"I have one question."

She turned and looked at him. His scarred face was in profile, and
his angry gaze was not on her, but on Baine. "Do you believe Baine

knew about the mana bomb? Do you think he was part of the plan to bring all the generals to Theramore?"

"No." The answer came swiftly, certainly, and there was a strange easing in her chest at the single word.

Varian nodded slowly. "Good," he said. "And I haven't decided yet. When this is over, you and Anduin are going to tell me everything." Now he did look at her, his blue eyes showing the banked fires of his emotions. *"Everything."*

"Chu'shao Whisperwind," said Taran Zhu, "do you have anything further to ask of this witness?"

"No, I do not, Lord Zhu," Tyrande said.

"Chu'shao Bloodhoof, you may have a moment with the Accused and—"

"I do not need a moment," Garrosh interrupted. It had been so long since Garrosh had done anything other than sit and listen that Jaina was startled to hear his voice. It was loud, and powerful, and it carried, but it was not the arrogant bellow she was accustomed to hearing from the orc. "I have made my decision."

"The Defender should speak—" Taran Zhu began.

"*I* will speak," Garrosh said, raising his voice even louder, "and I will keep Baine Bloodhoof."

Baine's ears swiveled fully forward at that. Clearly he, like everyone else, Jaina supposed, had assumed that Garrosh would be outraged at the tauren's fraternization with the enemy.

Tyrande seemed unable to believe it. "Fa'shua, I—"

"The Accused is happy with his chu'shao," said Taran Zhu. Even he seemed a bit surprised, but he recovered almost immediately. "I suggest you accept that with good grace, Chu'shao Whisperwind. Do you have any further witnesses to summon?"

"Only one more, Fa'shua."

"You shall do so on the morrow. Chu'shao Bloodhoof, are you prepared to subsequently bring your witnesses?"

"I am indeed," said Baine.

"Very good. I think we have had enough surprises for one day. I will remind everyone as you depart—this temple is a place of peace. Whatever your feelings are regarding the events of today, speak of them gently, and act on them not at all." He struck the gong three times, to formally end the day's activities.

Jaina rose to leave, but Varian put a hand on her arm. "Not yet. We're going to have a little talk."

27

It was not a "little talk."

It was a long talk; it was an uncomfortable talk; and ultimately, Anduin found it to be not really a talk at all, but a full-on shouting match.

His father was understandably furious. Both Anduin and Jaina had known Varian would be, which was why they had never mentioned Anduin's participation in the talks Jaina had with Baine, or even that they had occurred in the first place.

"How could you aid Baine, Jaina? How could you give him *funds?*" Varian exploded as soon as they reached Violet Rise. Varian had erected a large canopy near his tent, where he conducted whatever business he needed to. There were chairs provided, the seat of the king of Stormwind no grander than any other, but no one sat. Rain beat a steady tattoo on the fabric.

"I gave him my own personal funds, not Theramore's, and not the Alliance's. And you cannot possibly think that having Magatha Grimtotem as leader of the tauren would have been a good thing for anyone, including the Alliance!" Jaina shot back.

"I didn't have a chance to say what I thought, because you never consulted me!"

"He didn't come to you; he came to me. And Theramore has"— Jaina turned pale and then gulped—"*had* gotten quite used to taking care of itself! Besides, you would not have been inclined to listen anyway, just as you are not inclined to listen now."

Varian rubbed his eyes. "I did listen," he said. "Today in court. I listened to a tauren Longwalker inform me that you had engaged in talks of a very delicate political nature with a race of people who were the enemies of the Alliance."

"We were not in conflict then with the tauren or the Horde," Jaina said.

"We are *always* in conflict!" Varian cried. "Somewhere, someone is doing something to cause strife. You're too smart not to know that. That's why things of this nature are so key—everything matters. This was important, and I shouldn't have had to find out about it the way I did."

"You know as well as I do that you wouldn't have listened to Baine no matter what he said, no matter what his reasons, because he was Horde. And it was because I *did* that I was able to at least get the children of Theramore to safety!"

"And *you're* doing the same thing now," said Varian. "You're the one who won't listen to anything the Horde has to say." Before Jaina could protest, he raised his hands in a preemptive gesture. "Let's take a step back." He forced himself to speak calmly. "Let's leave Baine, and you, out of it. What I really want to know is why in the name of the Light you thought it was a good idea to drag my child into it!"

"I kind of—just stumbled on it," Anduin said, inserting himself into the argument in an attempt to smooth things over. "I escaped Ironforge using Jaina's hearthstone and popped right into the middle of the conversation. Don't be angry with her, Father; it's not like she had much of a choice."

"I've a good mind to put you both in prison for a while," Varian snapped.

"You will not address me in this manner. I am a leader in my own right, *not* your lieutenant, and not your child," Jaina said, her voice like ice. Thunder rumbled as if in response. She trembled with anger.

"You are a member of the Alliance," Varian retorted, stepping closer to her.

"Do you know," said Jaina, biting off the words, "the more I think about it, the more I think the former leaders of the Kirin Tor were right—that it's better to be independent. Do not push me, Varian Wrynn. Because I will push back if I have to."

"Jaina—" Anduin began, but Jaina shook her head.

"Forgive me, but I think I've had my fill of Wrynn men for the time being. I will see you all at dinner." She moved her hands deftly, with the practice of many years, teleporting herself to who knew where, her features appearing unkind and harsh in the purple-blue light. Then she was gone.

Father and son stood in silence for a while. The rain continued to patter over their heads. "So," said Anduin when the pause became awkward. "Are you going to send me to prison without any supper?"

"She shouldn't have dragged you into it," Varian said, not smiling.

"She wouldn't have if I hadn't just, *poof*, appeared in her parlor," Anduin said. He sat down, absently tracing a pattern on the chair's arm with his finger. "Baine is a good person, Father."

Varian took a seat and rested his face in his hands. "Magni . . . he was your friend, Anduin. Fearbreaker was a precious thing for him to give to you. Why did you give it away to a *tauren*? For him to just—throw back in your face?"

There it was—the hurt beneath the anger. "Because it felt like the right thing to do. The Light liked Baine. And he gave it back to me because he was honorable. He had chosen his side, and the last thing he wanted was to have to use Fearbreaker against Jaina in battle."

Varian closed his eyes for a moment. "I hadn't thought about it like that. I'm still very angry with Jaina, Son."

"She knows why. She's hurting now, though. I think . . . seeing her old home today was difficult for her."

"Of course it was. This trial . . ." He shook his head. "I will be glad when it is over. Whatever the outcome, Garrosh is no longer in power. I don't think it matters anymore if he dies or languishes in prison, as long as he was stopped."

"Your Majesty?" It was one of Varian's guards calling from outside the tent. "I have a missive for you."

"Enter," Varian called. The guard entered, saluted smartly as rainwater dripped everywhere, and gave the king a rolled-up scroll that had somehow remained dry. It was sealed with wax and bore the Pandaren characters that marked it as an official court document. Varian slid a finger beneath the seal, cracked the wax, and read. He looked absolutely furious for an instant, and then started to laugh.

"What is it?"

For answer, Varian tossed the scroll to Anduin.

To His Majesty, King Varian Wrynn:

YOU ARE SUMMONED to appear at the Temple of the White Tiger to testify for the Accused in the trial of Garrosh Hellscream.

It was signed with a tauren hoofprint.

After dinner, Anduin went down to the beach. The rain had stopped, at least for the moment, and he did not want to be around his father or Jaina. He sat on a boulder and looked out over the ocean, at the rocking ships in the harbor, at the violet light of the tower.

He heard the flapping of wings. Alert, he jumped to his feet, Fearbreaker in his hand, then relaxed when he saw a shape about the size of a large dog hovering a few yards over his head. In one forepaw, the creature carried a leather satchel.

"Care for company?" Wrathion asked.

"You know," Anduin replied, "Jaina and my father would just as soon I not talk to you anymore, so by all means, please *do* come down and keep me company."

Wrathion let out a laugh and dropped easily onto another rock near the prince. Swifter than a blink, he had changed into his human-shaped form. He was still grinning.

"I don't see Left and Right," Anduin said, referring to Wrathion's nearly omnipresent bodyguards.

"I gave them the evening off. I came to see if you were all right after the rousing adventure that was today's testimony," he said. "I was quite prepared to break you out of prison if your father was so inclined as to put you there. I just wanted to make sure you knew that."

"Very kind of you," Anduin said. "That's been bypassed for the moment, at least until after the trial. I think Father would like to see me locked up until I turn thirty-seven."

"I am given to understand that is a sentiment shared by most human parents at times," replied Wrathion. "You did not go see Garrosh today, I assume."

"How did—never mind." He hadn't exactly tried to hide it, but he had not volunteered the information, and he was certain that no one else had. But Wrathion always seemed to find out whatever he wanted to. "I'm . . . not sure I'm going to see him again."

"Don't tell me you've given up trying to bring the fellow into the Light!" Wrathion put a hand on his heart and recoiled melodramatically. "I confess I should be rather sad to hear that, although I've long maintained your naiveté will be your undoing."

Anduin rubbed his chin and sighed. "I don't know. I'm just tired, I think. Tired of all of this. And I'm stuck here, especially now."

"When I am a little older," Wrathion announced, "I shall, if asked politely, take you on my back and ferry you to fascinating places, where we will have adventures that will age your father ten years in one night."

"You have no idea how wonderful that sounds," Anduin said morosely.

"In the meantime," the black dragon said, "I see driftwood for a fire, to keep out the chill and provide illumination for—" With a flourish he withdrew something from the satchel. "Jihui."

Anduin's spirits lifted. A game whose goal was to have both parties in balance sounded like the perfect way to spend this particular evening.

"You're on," he said.

28

Day Seven

"Accuser, you may summon your final witness," said Taran Zhu.

Tyrande looked tired, Jaina thought.

"May it please the court, I summon Lady Jaina Proudmoore to speak."

Jaina rose and without haste descended the steps to the temple floor. She questioned the wisdom of what Tyrande had done yesterday for many reasons, not the least of which was the fact that the night elf had besmirched the reputation of her best witness. No matter, thought Jaina. There was, surely, more than enough evidence of Garrosh's horrendousness that even such compassionate beings as the celestials would see the need to lock him up somewhere dank and dark—and then forget he was there.

Kalec had tried to talk to her last night, but she had told him she was fine, and very tired, and she would see him in the morning at court. She then had nightmares, both in reaction to Perith's testimony and in sick anxiety over her own.

"First, let me say, Lady Jaina, that I am truly sorry to force you to relive certain things."

Jaina looked Tyrande directly in the eye. Bluntly, she said, "Chu'shao, I relive Theramore every day. Ask your questions."

Tyrande nodded, looking somewhat chastised, and began to walk and speak. "Lady Jaina, as we heard yesterday from Perith Storm-hoof, you had warning about the attack on Theramore."

"I did."

"What did you do after receiving that warning?"

"I gave instructions that the civilians of Theramore were to be notified. Those who wished to leave were free to do so. As it turned out, most of them wanted to stay and fight. Later, we sent a full ship of civilians, including all the children, to Gadgetzan. I then contacted King Varian."

This was not as difficult as she had feared. *Simply answer the questions*, she told herself. *Keep it impersonal.*

"And what was his response?"

"He told me that he would send the 7th Legion's naval fleet, and would recall several of his generals from their stations in various parts of Azeroth. He would also contact Genn Greymane, and I would speak to the other Alliance leaders for aid."

Tyrande kept walking, her hands clasped in front of her, her gaze not on Jaina but on the jury. "What happened after that?"

"I was later informed that several Horde ships arrived. They anchored just out of Alliance waters."

"When you learned this, did you attack?"

Now Jaina did start to feel something, a sick, queasy sensation in the pit of her stomach. She shook her head. "No."

"Why not?"

"Because they were not in our waters. And I did not want to be the one to provoke a war." *I should have. Light help me, I should have. Maybe if we'd struck before the generals arrived . . .*

"You said you sought help from the other Alliance leaders. Did you ask anyone else for aid?"

Jaina licked her lips. "Yes," she said. "I went to Dalaran and spoke with the Council of Six. They responded to my request by sending Rhonin himself, along with several other prominent magi. Rhonin's wife, Vereesa Windrunner, ranger-general of the Silver Covenant, also accompanied him."

"What did you do then?"

"We awaited the reinforcements promised by King Varian. We became a city preparing for war—stockpiling food, weapons, bandages. The soldiers trained every day. We expected the Horde to come sailing into our harbor at any minute." Her heart rate sped up as the questions drew her inexorably closer to speaking of the Destruction of Theramore itself.

"Did the promised aid arrive?"

Jaina bit back a retort. Everyone knew these events. Everyone knew what had happened at Theramore. Surely, even the celestials did. But this was what she had been waiting for, was it not? To make Garrosh Hellscream pay. And if it meant reliving the events of that horrible day again, she would do so.

She cleared her throat. "Yes, it did. The 7th Legion arrived with twenty ships and half a dozen of the Alliance's finest generals . . . and one great admiral." Aubrey, who had barely survived the attack on Northwatch Hold, only to die in Theramore . . .

"Lady Proudmoore?" Tyrande asked.

"I-I'm sorry. Could you repeat the question?"

"I said, the attack from the Horde did come, did it not?"

"Yes."

"And were you prepared?"

"Yes. We won, eventually, but it was hard earned, and we had a significant number of casualties. In the midst of everything that was going on, we uncovered a traitor. Thalen Songweaver. A member of the Kirin Tor—one of the Sunreavers." Jaina tried to speak dispassionately, but she snarled the last word. Her fists clenched. Why hadn't she realized then they were not to be trusted?

"Did you lose anyone close to you?"

"Captain Wymor. He was a friend of many years' standing."

"Anyone else whose loss you felt especially deeply?"

Jaina shook her head. "No. Not . . . not then."

"Did you have any inkling that the Horde was doing anything other than its level best to destroy Theramore through conventional means?"

"No. They fought fiercely and took many casualties. We had every reason to believe that they were giving their all, as we were."

"So you thought it a genuine victory."

Jaina nodded. "Yes."

"What did you do after the Horde retreated?"

"What must always be done," Jaina said. "We tended the wounded. Buried the dead. Comforted those who had lost loved ones. Held those who had survived."

Kinndy . . .

She swallowed. "We discovered that during the battle some of the Horde had liberated Thalen Songweaver. Vereesa and Shandris Feathermoon set off to see if they could find the trail before it went cold. So they weren't—" Her throat closed up.

"So they were not there when the mana bomb fell," said Tyrande, with deep sympathy.

Jaina was glad that she had thought to tuck a handkerchief in her sleeve. She pulled it out and dabbed at her eyes. "No," she said, "thank the Light, they survived."

"Chu'shao," said Taran Zhu, "would you like to call a respite?" Tyrande looked at Jaina. The archmage shook her head. It took everything she had to be here, in this moment, saying these things, and she was not sure she could do so again if she stopped now.

"No, we will continue," Tyrande said. "So you thought the battle was over and the Alliance was victorious. You began to take care of your people. When did you realize that something was wrong?"

"Kalecgos had come to Theramore before any of this happened." The "if onlys" would not be ignored. They galloped through her mind like a herd of talbuk, never one at a time, but many. If only they had tried harder to find the Focusing Iris. If only it had not been stolen. If only . . . "A precious artifact known as the Focusing Iris had been stolen from the blue dragonflight, and Kalec had sought my aid in locating it. Shortly after the battle, he informed me that he was able to sense the Focusing Iris—and that it was rapidly approaching Theramore."

"The Focusing Iris," Tyrande mused. "Can you tell us more about this?"

"It had lain dormant for millennia, until Malygos began to use it to direct surge needles. These needles pulled arcane magic from Azeroth's ley lines and channeled it into the Nexus," Jaina explained. "After Malygos died, the Focusing Iris was utilized to animate Chromatus, the only chromatic dragon experiment that was successful. It took all four of the Aspects, along with the assistance of Go'el holding the power of the element of earth, to defeat him." Once again, Jaina was forced to recall what the former warchief had contributed to the world. Angrily, she pushed the thought away.

"A powerful artifact indeed, and obviously devastating in the wrong hands," Tyrande said. "What happened next?"

"Kalec went to find it," Jaina said. "And Rhonin—" Her voice cracked. She poured a glass of water with a hand that trembled and took a sip. Her heart was beating as fast as a rabbit's.

Tyrande made a movement, as if she wanted to put a hand comfortingly on Jaina's, but did not complete the gesture. Instead, she turned to Chromie and said in an almost reverent voice, "May it please the court—with great respect, I present a Vision of that event."

Chromie looked more solemn than Jaina had ever seen her. The little gnome gently placed her hands on the Vision of Time, and then began to weave the spell that would awaken the slumbering metal dragon.

Jaina bit her lip, hard. An image began to form, and she recognized herself and Rhonin, who had given everything. Her eyes stinging with tears, she looked up in the stands to see Vereesa. The high elf's hands were clenched into tight fists, and she did not appear to be breathing. Jaina did not know whether to be sorrowful or joyous that Vereesa was to witness this moment. It would be devastating, but she would see, really *see*, the true heroism of the man she had loved. And so would everyone else.

The scene took place in her tower—her beloved tower, filled with books and scrolls and little seating areas where one could read, with potions brewing away and bottles of elixirs of this and that scattered about with cheerful haphazardness. A window was open, letting in light and air—and showing the sky galleon of the goblins, as of yet only a small dot. This was the place where she and Pained and Tervosh had spent countless hours. And now, where Rhonin, so very vibrantly alive, awaited the Jaina of the past as she hastened up the stairs, followed by some volunteers who had been helping her and, she realized belatedly, whose names she did not know.

"Is it the Focusing Iris?" asked the image of Jaina.

"Yes," said Rhonin. "It's powering the biggest mana bomb that's ever been made. And putting out a dampening field so that no one can get away. I can divert it. But first, help me—I can hold back the dampening field long enough to get these people to safety."

"Of course!" The image of Jaina began to cast a portal. Stormwind, Jaina remembered; she'd been planning to send her companions there. But she saw, and now everyone else did as well, that the portal was going to open on a small, rocky island in the Great Sea.

"Why are you redirecting my portal?"

"Takes . . . less energy," grunted Rhonin. His efforts to hold back the dampening field were clearly draining him. Jaina started to protest, but he cut her off. "Don't argue. Just—go through, all of you!"

Jaina's companions obeyed, but she didn't. She watched herself turn a shocked expression to Rhonin. "You can't defuse it! You're planning on dying here!"

"Shut. Up. Just go through! I have to pull it here, *right here*, to save

Vereesa and Shandris and as . . . as many as I can. The walls of this tower are steeped in magic. I should be able to localize the detonation. Don't be a foolish little girl, Jaina. Go!"

"No! I can't let you do this! You have a family. You're the leader of the Kirin Tor!"

"And you're the *future* of it!" Rhonin snapped. He looked as if he was about to collapse, as if he stayed on his feet only by an act of sheer will.

"No! I'm not!" the image of Jaina insisted. "Theramore is my city. I need to stay and defend it!"

"Jaina, if you don't go soon, we will both die, and my efforts to drag the cursed bomb here instead of letting it strike the heart of the city will be for nothing. Is that what you want? *Is it?*"

The sound of the approaching sky galleon increased. "I won't abandon you!" Jaina shouted. "Maybe together we can divert it!" Jaina watched herself turn to look at the nearing ship—to see Kalecgos fall, to see the bomb being dropped. The Vision adjusted, and suddenly it was as if everyone present was seeing what Jaina had seen. There was a collective gasp in the courtroom.

What had followed had been a blur in Jaina's mind, but now she saw it all. Rhonin paused in his spellcasting long enough to physically grab Jaina and shove her into the portal. She struggled, but was caught within the portal spell's grasp.

Jaina was looking right at Rhonin when it happened.

The leader of the Kirin Tor stared toward the window, his arms outstretched, on his goateed face an expression of complete and total defiance.

And then—

Her world went white. Rhonin's entire body turned violet—the hue of utterly pure arcane magic. Then it exploded in a sickening cloud of lavender ash.

Before she even realized what she was doing, Jaina's throat was suddenly raw from her scream. She was not alone—not here in the courtroom, and not in the past, where those who watched the mana bomb descend were crying out in hopeless horror.

Dimly, she heard the reverberating tone of Taran Zhu's gong and his call for respite. Jaina was grateful that Vereesa's torment was over, although her own was just beginning.

Anduin hadn't spoken directly to Jaina about what she had personally witnessed. He had heard about it, and had thought he understood the nightmare of what she had undergone. He realized now he had only the barest comprehension. He didn't know what else Tyrande was planning on showing, but after what she had done yesterday, he expected the worst. She'd already shown the jury and the spectators the horrific sight of Rhonin's sacrifice. She was not, Anduin guessed, about to hold back.

He had to admit, the night elf's brutal, take-no-prisoners, spare-no-feelings attitude was working. Anduin stared angrily at Garrosh as the orc sat, crippled, sha-scarred, and chained within an inch of his life, next to a Baine who had his head in his hands. Anduin knew that it was not the threat of prison that kept the angry mobs from taking over in the temple. It was that of not being allowed to see the next Vision, hear the next witness, or vicariously experience the next atrocity.

The respite was only for twenty minutes. Vereesa had gotten up and left without a word. Anduin didn't think she would return, and couldn't blame her. Jaina too had left almost immediately with Tyrande, although by their body language, Anduin could see the relationship was strained. He'd expected Kalecgos to accompany the two, but instead, the blue dragon remained in his seat.

"Aren't you going to Jaina?" Anduin asked. "It's a brief respite, but I'm sure she'd be glad to see you."

Kalec gave Anduin a halfhearted shake of his head. "I'm not sure she would," he said.

Anduin shifted awkwardly in his seat. Varian was paying no

attention. The king leaned back in his chair, his arms folded against his chest, and stared fixedly at Garrosh.

"I'm sorry to hear that," Anduin said quietly. "She's been through so much . . . You two seemed really right for each other."

"So I had hoped," the dragon said. Then, as if he had said too much, he clapped Anduin on the shoulder with too-boisterous good humor. "Going to go stretch my wings."

"Might do the same," Anduin said.

"What, stretch your wings?" It was a poor joke, but it made Anduin smile despite himself.

"Ha, I wish. I just have legs. See you in a bit, Kalec."

Three lotus buns and a cup of yak milk tea later, Anduin found himself questioning just why he was trying to help Garrosh Hellscream at all. And if Tyrande showed what he thought she would, Anduin didn't think he would continue.

Jaina was pale, but more composed than she had been earlier. She and Tyrande seemed easier around one another as they entered and each resumed her seat. Taran Zhu announced that court had resumed session, and instructed Tyrande to continue.

"As we saw in the Vision of Time, Rhonin did succeed in portaling you to safety, and in drawing the mana bomb directly to the tower," said Tyrande. "What happened then?"

Jaina sat straight, hands folded in her lap. Her eyes were red, but when she spoke, her voice was calm. "I regained consciousness on the island. Kalecgos found me, and I told him that I was going to return to Theramore, to see if there was anyone left I could help. He offered to come with me, but I insisted on going alone."

Out of the corner of his eye, Anduin glanced at Kalecgos. The dragon's lips were pressed together in a thin line and he wasn't looking at Jaina. Anduin guessed that the conversation the two had actually had was nowhere as civil as she was describing.

"And did you?"

"Yes."

"I would like to show the court what Jaina Proudmoore saw upon her return to the city she had founded, had loved, and was willing to die for." She nodded to Chromie.

A collective murmur of horror rose from the spectators, and Anduin saw that even the August Celestials, usually so impassive, looked distressed. The mana bomb had left a huge crater, yawning in front of the rubble that was all that remained of the great tower. The sky had been rent and wounded, with the insane colors that Anduin had heard one could see in Northrend.

And the bodies—

Anduin swallowed hard, tasting bile. There were so many. Some of them looked normal—well, as normal as a corpse could look, he supposed—while others floated in midair, bleeding *upward*. Still others were a uniform shade of violet. There seemed to be no rhyme or reason as to which form death took.

He watched the image of Jaina, her face drained of color and blank with shock, walk about the ruins. Her hair—white, now—almost seemed to be floating about her, and he could hear the hum and crackle of still-viable arcane energy.

The detritus of ordinary life stood in sharp contrast to the overwhelming scale of the destruction. Anduin glimpsed things like goblets, hairbrushes, leaves from a book that crumbled to purple dust when Jaina picked them up.

The enormous temple was quiet as everyone watched Jaina sort through the ruinations, looking for life, for any sign of hope. The only thing that broke the silence was the soft sounds of grief as Jaina came across bodies that someone recognized and mourned. Pained, who had survived so many battles, still clutched her sword as Jaina bent to stroke her long hair. The strands shattered beneath the mage's touch.

Anduin recognized others—Admiral Aubrey, Marcus Jonathan,

for so long a fixture at Stormwind's main gate. He found himself wishing selfishly that the then-Jaina would just leave, so that he wouldn't have to see the horror anymore, even secondhand.

There was a small shape on the ground, about the size of a child. He turned to look at Jaina, and saw that she had buried her face in her handkerchief. She couldn't bear seeing this again, and he didn't blame her, not one bit.

The image of Jaina stared at the small corpse, lying face down in a scarlet puddle. The blood had matted her pink ponytails. Tenderly, Jaina reached out to the body of Kinndy Sparkshine, the gnome who had been her apprentice.

It crumbled into violet sand, and the Jaina of the past screamed in agony.

Anduin tried to look away, but he was transfixed, unable to tear his gaze away from the sight of Lady Jaina Proudmoore, one of the finest magi of this age, shrieking and weeping, picking up handfuls of the arcane dust as if she could piece the girl back together.

Beside him, Kalecgos took a sharp intake of breath. Anduin wanted to leap to his feet and yell at Tyrande, *Stop this, please, stop!* As if somehow Tyrande had heard that silent cry, she nodded to Chromie. The scene, mercifully, disappeared. Anduin exhaled a breath he hadn't realized he had been holding.

Tyrande turned, her eyes blazing triumph bought at a dear price. Her voice strong and bell-like, she said, "Your witness, Chu'shao Bloodhoof."

29

Baine Bloodhoof did not rise at once. He was too stunned at what he had seen. He could not imagine inundating Jaina with a series of questions after this, let alone attempting to say anything positive about Garrosh Hellscream. He couldn't even bring himself to look at the orc. He said a quick, silent prayer to the Earth Mother for guidance, rose, and approached the one-time lady of Theramore.

"Lady Jaina," he said quietly, "I would be happy to ask for a respite, if you so desire."

She looked at him with a mixture of unreadable emotions, and her voice was flat. "No. I'd like to get this over with."

"I am sure no one in this room can blame you." He did not offer sympathy. She did not want it—not from him. "And while we in this room struggle with our own reactions to what we have just seen, we can only guess at how you felt after this cowardly attack." He did not shrink from the word. Baine was a tauren who called things what they were. No one who had just witnessed the Destruction of Theramore could possibly call it anything else. "Could you please tell us, in your own words, how you felt?"

She stared at him, then started to laugh. It was harsh, bitter. He flattened his ears, taken aback. Jaina struggled to get herself under control. "I don't think the words exist for how I felt."

"Please try, Lady Jaina."

"Angry. So very angry. There was so much . . . *rage*. I couldn't breathe; I couldn't eat; I could barely move, I was so angry. What you saw here? Yes. It was horrible. I see many of you weeping. But you still weren't *there*. You didn't see your friends . . ."

She pressed her lips together and grew silent. Baine gave her a moment, then prodded gently, "You were angry. What did you want to do?"

"I wanted to kill him."

"Garrosh Hellscream?"

"Yes. Garrosh, and every single orc I could get my hands on. I wanted to kill every goblin, every troll, every Forsaken, every blood elf, and every tauren, including *you*, Baine Bloodhoof. I wanted to wipe out the Horde the way Garrosh Hellscream had wiped out my home. Had wiped out my *life*."

Baine was not angry. His voice and mien continued to be gentle as he spoke. "What did you do?"

"I went to King Varian, and told him what Garrosh had done. That he had been right, about his distrust and hatred of the Horde, and I had been wrong. I told him we needed to make war on the Horde—and we should start by destroying Orgrimmar."

"How did King Varian react?"

"He agreed that we needed to go to war. But he didn't want to strike right away, as I did. He said we needed to have a strategy, to rebuild Northwatch Hold. I promised him the Focusing Iris, and said I knew how to use it to destroy Orgrimmar as Garrosh had destroyed my home."

"What was his response?"

Jaina looked down at her hands again. "He said . . . we couldn't risk adding to the Alliance's losses by acting precipitously. And Anduin said he thought even some of the Horde might be angry with Garrosh for his cowardly actions. I told them it was too late for that."

"What exactly did you say?"

"I don't remember."

"Lady Jaina, I can produce a Vision of this encounter if you cannot tell me what you said." His voice was kindly, but nonetheless her head whipped up, and he saw . . . shame in her face.

"That won't be necessary," she said quietly. "I told Varian he was a coward, and I . . . apologized to Anduin for any part I had in creating his gullibility. And . . . I walked out."

"What did you do then?"

"I went to Dalaran. I told Vereesa what had happened. How brave her husband had been, that he had been the one to save me, and her, and everyone else he possibly could." Baine did not look up to see Vereesa's reaction; she had not returned after the respite. "I begged the Kirin Tor for aid. I wanted them to uproot Dalaran, as had been done before, and use it to raze Orgrimmar. They refused."

"So no one, it seemed, wanted to wipe out an entire city. Even after what had happened in Theramore," said Baine.

"No, they didn't."

"What did you do then?"

"I had recovered the Focusing Iris before the Horde could do so. And when no one else would aid me, I learned how to use it."

"With no army, no flying city to assist you?"

"That's correct."

"What was your plan?"

Her eyes didn't move from his. She stuck her chin out. "To send a tidal wave composed of water elementals to wipe out Orgrimmar."

"I think it safe to say that we all know that you did not do so," Baine said. "Were you prevented? Or did you change your mind?"

"I . . . a little of both."

"Can you explain that?"

Jaina's brow furrowed. "I . . . had everything worked out. I knew exactly what I planned to do." She paused, perhaps trying to choose her words carefully, perhaps trying to remember just how she had felt at the time. Kairoz had found this precise moment and was quite irritated that the tauren had opted not to show it. Baine did not think it would help Garrosh's case to show a raging, broken Jaina carefully crafting vengeance, nor did he think it would bring anything but further pain to a woman who had had more than her share foisted upon her in one day.

"I was on Fray Island, and I had created the wave. I was only a few moments away from sending it north, to Orgrimmar, where it would gather even more strength along the way."

"Why did you not release it, Lady Proudmoore?"

"Go'el interrupted me."

"How did he know where to find you?"

"He had had a vision, from the elements. They called out to him and asked him for help. He said he would not let me drown Orgrimmar. We . . . fought for control of the wave."

Baine looked over at Go'el. He was with Aggra, leaning forward, watching intently, his blue eyes sad. The friendship between human diplomat and orc leader had been unique. Garrosh had destroyed that, too.

"Who was winning?"

Jaina followed Baine's gaze, then glanced down quickly. "I was," she said. "I was about to kill him."

"What happened?"

"Kalec found me. He joined with Go'el in trying to dissuade me from my path."

"Did they? Or did they overpower you?"

Jaina's expression was troubled. "They . . . told me that I would be no better than Garrosh. No better than . . . Arthas. And I realized . . ." She lifted her face. "I realized they were right."

"And that Garrosh would also be like you?"

"With respect, I protest!" said Tyrande.

"Fa'shua, I am attempting to make sure we all understand the witness's words correctly," Baine said.

"I agree with the Defender," said Taran Zhu. "Witness may respond to clarify."

"Yes," said Jaina. "We would be alike."

"And you didn't want that."

"No. Never."

"But for a moment, you understood how he could want to do such a thing. To destroy a whole city, even civilians."

"I—yes. Yes, I did."

Baine inclined his head. "Thank you, Lady Jaina. I have no further questions."

"Do you, Accuser?" asked Taran Zhu. His paw went to the mallet; apparently he assumed the answer would be no.

"Yes, Fa'shua, I do," said Tyrande, rising and walking to Jaina's chair. "Lady Jaina . . . you also later discovered that, had you released the tidal wave, you would have destroyed the Alliance fleet. Would you say that is the reason you are glad you refrained?"

Baine held his breath. It would be easy for Jaina to simply say yes. That was the answer Tyrande wanted, and Jaina would be free to leave, and to try to do what she could to salve wounds that had been so brutally reopened. He knew that the betrayal of the Sunreavers in Dalaran—her new city, her new Theramore—had cut deeply. Many said it had catapulted her right back to where she was emotionally after Theramore fell, and there had been rumors that she had pushed Varian to actually dismantle the Horde.

Jaina did not answer immediately. She gave the question the consideration it was due. "Of course, I was relieved to hear that I hadn't inadvertently wiped out the fleet. But no—that wasn't why I was glad." She looked at Garrosh, and there her gaze remained. "I am glad I refrained, because I would never, ever want to be like him."

Later, Baine would think that Tyrande should have accepted that. But the night elf could not leave well enough alone. Jaina was Tyrande's final, best witness. The Accuser would henceforth be confined to follow-up questioning, and it was clear she wanted to end on a strong note. And so, she asked one question too many. "Or like the Horde?"

Jaina went very still. Tyrande waited. After a moment, she prompted, "Lady Jaina? My question was, do you wish to never, ever be like the Horde?"

And Jaina—battered, angry, wounded, devastated, honest Jaina—replied simply, "The Horde isn't Garrosh."

Tyrande's eyes grew wide as now, too late, she realized her error. "No further questions, Fa'shua," Tyrande said quietly, gave Jaina a long look, and returned to her seat.

When Sylvanas arrived at Brightwater Lake in Tirisfal Glades, near the Undercity, she found her sister waiting.

"I got your note," Sylvanas said, "and I brought horses for us." Sylvanas had not expected Vereesa to return to the courtroom after the respite. She had just watched her husband die—or, more correctly, watched her husband be turned into a pure arcane manifestation, *then* die. But Sylvanas had been surprised at the note, which said only, *Brightwater Lake. I want to ride.* Sylvanas took it as a good sign that Vereesa had suggested meeting at a place so deep in the Forsaken lands. She was proud of her sister for even knowing about the site, and for getting to it unspotted and unscathed. The Windrunner "Moons" were both superior rangers. Vereesa's requested activity, though, was not a surprise. They had loved riding together as children; Vereesa especially had taken to it.

Vereesa sat with her back against the trunk of a dead tree. She turned her head slowly. She looked haggard, fragile, and Sylvanas was glad she could, she hoped, offer something pleasurable to her sister. Vereesa's eyes widened at the mounts. The dead things regarded her steadily. One of them bent its long neck, devoid of flesh, and bit at a patch of grass. The grass fell back to the earth as its teeth ground it, but the being did not appear to notice, and bent its vertebrae for another mouthful.

"They are . . . skeletons," Vereesa murmured. "Horse skeletons."

"Few living things will bear me willingly, Sister, or even bear being near me. You will need to learn to ride these, if you are to come live in the Undercity. I promise you, they will obey."

"Yes, I imagine they will," Vereesa said.

She made no move to get up. Sylvanas dropped the reins of the two horses, knowing they would go nowhere, and sat beside her sister. Awkwardly, she asked, "How are you?" It had been so long since another's welfare mattered.

Vereesa closed her eyes, but tears slipped from beneath her lashes. "I miss him so much, Sylvanas. So very much."

Sylvanas had no comfort to give. She couldn't even reanimate Rhonin's corpse for her sister. So she sat quietly.

"I am so, *so* happy we are killing Garrosh," Vereesa said. "I hope whatever poison you have is slow and painful. I want him to suffer— suffer as he has made me suffer. I am glad I saw what I did today. It is fuel for my fire. I never want to have to see that again—even think about his death again. I want nothing to do with that world anymore."

"Well," said Sylvanas, withdrawing a small vial from her pouch, "I think I can make all your dreams come true. This tiny vial contains enough poison to kill twenty orcs. And yes . . . it is everything we both want—slow, agonizing, and utterly without a cure."

Vereesa reacted as if Sylvanas had just given her a birthday present. Her face lit up, the sorrow retreated, and she accepted the vial almost reverently. "So small, to be so lethal," she murmured.

"One drop on each segment of the sunfruit, and Garrosh Hellscream will be no more."

Vereesa clutched the vial tightly, her other hand closing around the locket that draped her slim throat. Sylvanas had returned Vereesa's necklace to her, and both sisters now routinely wore the jewelry during their time together. "Thank you, Sister. I knew I could turn to you."

Sylvanas smiled. "You have no idea how much it pleases me that you did. And as for leaving that world—I open mine to you. Is that why you wished to meet here?"

Vereesa nodded. "It was . . . becoming too sad to keep meeting at the spire," she said. "I wanted to start investigating where I will soon be living."

Sylvanas hid a smile at the choice of words, but said nothing. The strange phantom pains were increasing, but Sylvanas ignored them with the same steely will that had won her freedom from Arthas. For the first time since he had marched on her people, leaving behind the Dead Scar like the trail from a slug, Sylvanas was . . . *happy*. She had lost so very much, and it seemed to her that fate had delivered this unexpected gift—both for her personally and for any attempt to obtain more power within the Horde. She and her sister would indeed be unstoppable. Violence and horror had brought Sylvanas to the place she was today, and the same had driven Vereesa to seek her out.

How good it would be, she mused, to have someone she trusted. Truly trusted, who did not merely obey her orders out of fear or personal gain. Someone who thought, felt, as she did. And it seemed as though Vereesa longed for this as well.

Sylvanas had not told Vereesa everything, of course. One could not be equal to the Banshee Queen unless one was oneself a banshee. Her people would resent having to obey a living thing. But she would make her sister's death so much gentler, easier, than her own had been. Kind. Vereesa would merely go to sleep, and awaken beautifully transformed, reborn with insight and ambition that one who breathed could never fathom.

"It may amuse you to learn that I now know how to make green curry fish," Vereesa said, carefully tucking the precious poison into a bag.

"You are more than trusted in the kitchens, it would seem."

"Yes. Another day or two, and then . . ." She frowned. "Sylvanas—can it truly be this easy? I keep feeling that something will go wrong somehow."

"Nothing will go wrong, Little Moon," Sylvanas reassured her. "We have not been given this moment—we have bought it with sweat and tears and torment. We have earned the right to this victory."

"We have. My only regret is we cannot watch Garrosh Hellscream breathe his last."

"Ah," Sylvanas said, "but we can certainly imagine it, and that will have to do. What we *will* see is his corpse, and the chaos that his death will cause. And when one day we are able to claim credit for our kill, those who were too slow or too timid will envy us."

Vereesa gazed out over the lake, arms wrapped around her knees. "I had always thought these lands dark and . . . sad," Vereesa said. "But there is a strange kind of beauty in the darkness, is there not?"

"There is," Sylvanas replied. "I am no night elf, but they understand this. There is a sweetness and a purity in night, in the time when the moons shine and the sun hides its face. There is beauty in death."

"Do you . . . think they will accept your decision? To bring me in, to rule alongside you?"

"The Forsaken, or the Horde?"

"Either. Both."

"Perhaps not at first," Sylvanas said. "They will need a little time to grow accustomed to the idea. But soon, they will learn to value you, and be glad of your presence in the Undercity."

"I am not worried about myself," Vereesa continued. "I am concerned for the boys. It will be . . . very strange to them."

Sylvanas was taken completely by surprise at the statement. Was Vereesa really thinking of—no. That was impossible.

She chose her words carefully. "It would," she agreed, as if the idea had just occurred to her. "They would have no friends their own age, and it would be difficult to explain to them why. They might be very unhappy. The Undercity . . . is really no place for children, Sister."

Vereesa looked away. Sylvanas watched her like a hawk, cursing herself that she had not appreciated that Vereesa was not just a widow, but the sole parent to two children. This was the first time Vereesa had mentioned them since the sisters had begun their secret meetings. It was as if, with their father's death, Vereesa could not think of anything other than revenge.

"No," Vereesa sighed. "No, I suppose it is not." Her hand dropped to the grass and she picked up a pinecone absently.

Something in her voice alerted Sylvanas. "Of course, if you really want them to come along, I would do my best to make them welcome. They are, after all, my closest kin—other than you."

She shook her white head. "No, you are right. I cannot imagine it would be a good place for them. They are better off where they are." Vereesa laughed without humor. "I have not been the best of mothers to them anyway." Abruptly Vereesa crushed the cone in her hand. The scales cracked and fell off as she tossed it away.

Sylvanas was reassured. Vereesa understood. Sylvanas was glad—she would just as soon not have to murder her own nephews. Nonetheless, she would feel easier when her sister was safely dead. Then they could be together.

Forever.

30

Day Eight

"I summon King Varian Wrynn to speak," said Baine.

Anduin couldn't resist. He leaned over to his father and whispered, "Stick to the questions. Don't volunteer anything."

"Ha, ha," muttered Varian as he rose. Anduin saw Jaina's shocked expression and realized that he was likely the only one Varian had informed that Baine wished to present him as a witness for the Defender. Her blue eyes went from father to son; then she pressed her lips together and stared stonily ahead.

She was not alone in her surprise, of course. It would have seemed odd to have the king of Stormwind speaking in favor of the leader of the Horde under any circumstances, even if that leader had been Go'el. But Garrosh? Anduin sat back, wondering what Baine had in mind.

Varian made his vow, and then looked expectantly at Baine. "May it please the court," Baine said, "before I begin asking the witness questions, I would like to present an evidence item. Most of you know King Varian Wrynn as the one who counseled against an outright execution of the Accused. But he was not always so moderate."

"With respect, I protest," said Tyrande, rising. "King Varian is not on trial."

"No, he is not," agreed Baine, "but without a choice he made, Garrosh would not be alive, and none of us would be assembled here today."

Jaina muttered something under her breath about *mistake*. Kalec frowned unhappily, and, seated behind Jaina, Vereesa looked smug. She was a beautiful woman, but the expression was ugly. Anduin bit his lip, then returned his attention to his father.

"While that is undeniably true," said Taran Zhu, "it is not a sufficient argument for me to ignore the protest."

"Fa'shua, as odd as it may seem, I wish to establish King Varian's credibility as a character witness for the Accused."

"Even if your request were not reasonable," said Taran Zhu, "that would be something I would wish to see. I agree with the Defender."

Tyrande accepted the decision with grace, but her lips were thin as she sat back in her chair. She began making notes.

"Then if it please the court, I will show a Vision that establishes this."

Kairoz strode toward the Vision of Time. Anduin noticed that the hourglass had been inverted, and the top bulb, which had all but run out with Tyrande's presentation of the Destruction of Theramore, was now full. Gently, the flesh bronze dragon wove the spell around the artifact, and the metal-crafted one came to life to send the glowing sands flowing downward.

At first, the scene was dark. Then came the sounds of muffled battle—angry shouts, screams, the clash of steel on steel.

"What was that?" a frightened female voice demanded—one that only recently had begun taking on the more typical accent of her people.

Moira Thaurissan. Anduin knew now what was coming next. What he didn't know was whether it would strengthen the Defender's case—or if he even wanted it to.

A lamp was lit and Moira peered about fearfully. She was not alone in her quarters in Ironforge. Next to the bed, a cradle contained a sleeping infant, and two Dark Iron dwarves stood at the door. One of them started to open it.

"No!" hissed Moira. She rose, standing up on the bed, staring at the door. She was clad in a nightgown, and her hands crept up to her throat. "I order you, do not go outside! They might not find us!"

They drew their weapons, just in case. They did not have to wait long. There was a massive *thump* on the door, and Moira gasped. A second, and a third time someone on the other side tried to break in. The door bowed and then gave way completely on the fourth try.

Moira shrieked in terror. The baby, startled awake, added his piercing, frightened wail to the din. The three intruders burst into the room and began attacking the guards. The Dark Iron dwarves fought fiercely, but they were outnumbered. The intruders' masked leader expertly wielded two swords, quickly dispatching one dwarf with a thrust so powerful that the killer could not immediately pull his weapon free, and he left it in the body.

He whirled to face Moira and, panting, tugged off his mask. The spectators, and the image of Moira as well, gasped when they realized it was Varian. Anduin had known, but found himself still grieving at the violence. If only he had arrived sooner. His eyes went to where the real Moira was seated, and he saw her looking composed, if uncomfortable. Anduin regretted that she was being forced to watch this—and angry at Baine for showing it.

Varian seized the terrified dwarf, hauling her off the bed and dragging her out of the room as she struggled to escape. The Vision followed them as Varian took his captive to the open area near the Great Forge. Dwarves and gnomes were beginning to cluster, watching in frightened incomprehension. Varian pulled Moira to him by the collar of her nightgown and pressed his sword against her throat.

"Behold the usurper!" Varian shouted. "This is the child Magni

Bronzebeard wept countless tears over. His beloved little girl. How sickened he would be to see what she's done to his city, his people!"

He turned his head to look into Moira's wide eyes. "This throne is not yours. You bought it with deceit, and lies, and trickery. You have threatened your own subjects when they have done nothing wrong, and bullied your way to a title you have not yet earned. I will not see you sit upon this stolen throne one moment longer!"

"Stop here," said Baine. Anduin could feel the spectators collectively returning to the present, all eyes trained on Varian. "We recognize you and Queen-Regent Moira Thaurissan, who obviously has survived the ordeal. Can you please tell us what is happening?"

"This took place right before the Cataclysm," Varian said. "It was after King Magni had attempted to perform an ancient ritual, hoping to connect with the earth and discover what was going on. Something went wrong, and Magni literally became part of the earth. Queen-Regent Moira appeared out of nowhere, claiming the throne. She put Ironforge on lockdown and held my son hostage. Fortunately, he escaped."

"What did you do then?"

"I infiltrated Ironforge."

"To what end?"

"To neutralize Moira and to liberate Ironforge."

"How did you intend to neutralize her?"

"I don't think I knew, really. Kill her, I suppose, if she resisted."

"There were casualties."

"Yes."

Anduin glanced at Tyrande. She leaned back in her chair, arms folded, face carefully blank. Anduin knew she wanted to protest, but she had already been denied on this point. Baine looked at Kairoz, and nodded to continue.

"*Father!*"

Anduin watched himself push through the crowds, desperate to reach Varian. *I look so young,* he thought distractedly.

"You shouldn't be here, Anduin. Get out. This is no place for you."

"But it *is* my place!" the image of Anduin replied. "You sent me here! You wanted me to get to know the dwarven people, and I have. I knew Magni well, and I was here when Moira came. I saw what turmoil her arrival brought. And I saw that things got far too close to civil war when people reached for weapons to solve their problems with her. Whatever you may think of her, she *is* the rightful heir!"

"Maybe her blood's right," snarled Varian, "but her mind's not. She's under a spell, Son; Magni always thought so. She tried to keep you prisoner. She's holding a bunch of people for no reason. She's not fit to be leader! She's going to destroy all that Magni tried to do! All that he . . . he died for!"

Closer to his father now, the Anduin of the past reached out a hand. *I was scared to death,* Anduin thought. *Scared I'd say the wrong thing, and he'd slice open her throat, and it would be my fault. How far we have come, all of us. Most of us, anyway.*

"There's no spell, Father. Magni wanted to believe there was rather than the truth—that he drove Moira away because she wasn't a male heir."

"You spit on the memory of an honorable man, Anduin."

"You can be an honorable man and still make mistakes."

"Stop," said Baine. "King Varian, what do you think Prince Anduin meant by that?"

"He was referring to some of my own actions in the past," Varian said. "I had done and said many things I wasn't proud of. I had made threats, lost my temper, displayed intolerance—well, that's a polite way of saying it—toward other races. As I think is fairly evident, Anduin doesn't think or behave that way."

The scene continued. Anduin watched himself make the argument that it was up to the dwarves to decide if they wanted to accept Moira or not. And for the rest of his life, he would remember what Varian had said.

"*She held you hostage, Anduin!* You, my son! She can't be allowed to get away with that! I won't let her hold you and a whole city prisoner. I won't, do you understand?"

"Stop," said Baine. "It sounds as if you wanted to kill Moira not for usurping Ironforge, but for endangering Anduin."

Varian nodded. "I . . . was angry. My son and I had a strained relationship at that time, and I . . ." He struggled with the words, clearly conscious of how many ears were listening. "I was surprised to discover how much I didn't want to lose him. And when he was safe, I wanted to punish Moira for my being made to feel that way."

His eyes sought out Anduin, and warmth passed between father and son. The scene went dark. "How did the situation finally end?" Baine asked.

"Anduin argued, quite rightly, that the dwarves had the right to decide their own fates."

Baine nodded again to Kairoz. Now, the Varian of the past seemed to reach a decision. "Much as I wish it weren't true," he said to Moira, whom he still held captive, "yours *is* the rightful claim to the throne. But just like me, Moira Bronzebeard, you need to be better than you are. You need more than just a bloodline to rule your people well. You're going to have to earn it."

"Stop. And thus was founded the Council of Three Hammers, which is currently how the dwarven people are content to have it, correct?" continued Baine.

"That's right, yes."

"And when she agreed?"

"I let her go, and my people and I stood down."

The scene resumed a few moments later. Varian went to Anduin and hugged him tightly. All around them, the dwarves, relieved and ready as always to celebrate with a fine brew, were shouting and whistling, calling out, "Wildhammer!" "Bronzebeard!" "Dark Iron!"

"See, Father?" the Vision's Anduin said. "You knew exactly the right thing to do. I knew you did."

Varian's image smiled. "I needed someone to believe that for me, before I could," he replied.

Baine gestured to Kairoz, and the scene froze.

"Do you think you have changed, Your Majesty?"

Varian's gaze flickered to Anduin. The young prince grinned. Varian looked back at Baine and nodded.

"Yes. I have."

"Would others agree with you?"

"Others seem to see it more than I do myself, so, yes."

"Why did you try to change?"

"Because those parts of myself stood in the way of becoming the man I truly wished to be."

"You were, quite literally, a man divided at one point," Baine continued. "The reintegration was not an easy one, and your entire remembered history for a time consisted of nothing but violence. Those are steep odds to battle, for a man trying to change his nature. How did you manage to do so?"

"It . . . was not easy," Varian admitted. "And I was—I am—far from perfect. I . . . backslid from time to time. I first had to come to the realization that I truly wished to change, and then, it took will and discipline, and reasons that made the struggle worth it."

"Will. Discipline. Reasons to even engage in such a difficult struggle," Baine repeated. "Where did you find the will, the discipline, and the reasons?"

"I had people who wished to help me, and I listened to them," Varian said. "They—well, they were able to get through my thick head how I really was behaving, and it wasn't in line with what I envisioned. I wanted to be the best father I could to a son without a mother. The best ruler of a people who were enduring very hard times. I felt as if I owed it to them to make my time on the throne about what they needed—to make their lives better—and not spend it tending to my own petty impulses."

"So would it be accurate to say that it wasn't because someone threatened or forced you into changing, but that you changed because you wanted to be better for those who depended on you?"

"That is absolutely accurate, yes."

"Do you think Garrosh Hellscream cares for his people?"

"I protest!" shouted Tyrande.

"I agree with the Defender," Taran Zhu said, and nodded to Varian.

Varian, clearly conscious that he was under oath, took a moment to compose his thoughts before answering, fixing Garrosh with sharp blue eyes.

"I believe he did, once. I believe he still cares for the orcs, but not the Horde as a whole."

"So, that is a yes."

"If by 'his people' you mean 'orcs,' then yes."

"Would you say Garrosh is intelligent?"

"Yes, very."

"So here we have someone who even you, his enemy, say cares for his people. Who is, in your own words, very intelligent. Some might say that about you, Your Majesty. Do you think it is possible for such a person to change?"

A sound that might have been a slight laugh escaped the king. "I *highly* doubt that Garrosh—"

"Just answer the question, please. Yes or no? Is it possible for a person who cares for his people and who is very intelligent to change?"

Varian scowled, opened his mouth, then closed it again. He took a breath, then said, quietly, "Yes. It's *possible*."

"Thank you, Your Majesty. I have no further questions for you."

Tyrande had appeared to be struggling with staying seated, and now practically leaped up to question Varian, who looked almost as relieved as she.

"Your Majesty," she said. "I only have a few more questions. First—are you genocidal?"

"What?" Varian stared at her, and Baine shouted, "With respect, I protest!"

"Fa'shua," Tyrande said smoothly, "I am not accusing the witness of anything, merely asking him to define himself."

"To what end, Chu'shao?" asked Taran Zhu.

"The Defender has brought in King Varian as a character witness for Garrosh. He has had the opportunity to establish the witness's expertise, and now I am doing the same thing."

"I agree with the Accuser. As long as I determine that you are not harassing the witness, you may proceed. Witness may respond."

Tyrande inclined her head and returned her gaze to Varian. "Are you genocidal, Your Majesty?"

"No," Varian stated, his brows drawing together. Anduin wondered where in the world Tyrande was going with this questioning.

"Do you crave, and have you ever craved, power?"

"No," Varian said. "I would go so far as to say that the mantle of power and responsibility is a heavy one." Anduin knew that at one point, his father would have preferred the simpler life as Lo'Gosh the gladiator to being King Varian.

"The Defender just showed us a scene of you and members of SI:7 infiltrating Ironforge, attacking the Dark Iron portion of the population, and threatening an unarmed female. Would you say this is something you do on a regular basis?"

"Of course not! This is ridiculous," Varian began.

"Please, Your Majesty. Just answer the question." Tyrande was completely unruffled.

"No!"

"At your angriest, darkest hour, did you ever calculatedly plan and execute a plan to exterminate the entire population of a major city?"

And then Anduin understood. "No," replied his father.

Tyrande turned calmly to Taran Zhu. "Fa'shua, the Defender has brought King Varian in as an expert witness on the issues that Garrosh Hellscream must deal with. I submit that while King Varian may indeed have dealt with similar challenges, he is not, has not been, and will *never* be the same as Garrosh Hellscream. Therefore, he cannot be considered an expert on what Garrosh will or will not do. And in turn, I ask you to strike from the record everything this witness has said."

"With respect, I—"

Taran Zhu held up a paw. "I see your point, Accuser, but I will not strike the witness's testimony. I believe that both your line of questioning and that of the Defender are valid and appropriate ones."

"But, Fa'shua—" Tyrande began.

"You have made your point, Accuser. Do you have any more questions for the witness?"

"No, Lord Zhu."

"Very well. Court is now over for today. Tomorrow we will present closing arguments. Chu'shao Whisperwind, Chu'shao Bloodhoof, it will be your last chance to appeal to the jury. I suggest you do not squander it."

31

Day Nine

I t was the final day of the trial, and tension crackled in the air. As Sylvanas walked into the temple, she passed one of the goblin bookies who had thus far managed to elude the pandaren guards.

"Hey, Lady," he said, his spectacles perched on his broad, bald head and the buttons on his waistcoat polished to gleaming perfection, "sure you don't want to place a bet?"

Sylvanas was in high spirits, and the thought amused her, so she paused and smiled down at the little green cheat. "What are the odds?" she asked, a grin quirking her lips.

"Even money and dropping for swift execution, two to one for life imprisonment, and some truly fascinating odds for the crazier scenarios."

"Such as?"

He consulted his notes. "Let's see . . . twenty-five to one for a split jury, eighteen to one for an escape attempt, fifty to one for sudden unfortunate demise of the Accused, and two hundred to one for full and total repentance, including, but not limited to, volunteer work at the Orgrimmar Orphanage." He peered up at her, the spectacles making his tiny eyes look disturbingly enormous.

"Does anybody really bet on that one?" she asked, amused.

"Hey, you'd be surprised. Long shots come in every day. I once saw a spit-and-polish gnomish drag car that was leading by fifteen lengths at the turn fail to finish on the old Mirage Raceway."

Oh, the temptation. But Sylvanas could not risk the goblin remembering the bet, so instead she patted his shiny green head and went inside.

Tonight, after closing arguments, the August Celestials would withdraw to debate, and Garrosh would have his last meal. She knew it would be the green curry fish; it was Garrosh's favorite, and Vereesa had confirmed it would be served. Whatever happened in the courtroom today, it was nothing more than inconsequential entertainment. Let others worry and wrinkle their brows in concern, debate and argue and fret. Sylvanas and Vereesa were the only ones who understood how marvelously pointless it all was.

Taran Zhu had to strike his gong a few more times than usual to quiet the buzz of chatter. "As I am certain all of you know by now, today is the final day of the trial of Garrosh Hellscream." He peered at Tyrande. "Chu'shao Whisperwind, are there any witnesses you care to summon again to speak?"

Sylvanas noticed the night elf was wearing a more formal robe than she had previously, no doubt in anticipation of a victory. Which under any other circumstances Sylvanas would be delighted to have her celebrate. "There are none, Fa'shua."

"Chu'shao Bloodhoof, are there any witnesses *you* care to summon again?"

Baine shook his horned head. "No, Fa'shua."

"So noted. Before the closing arguments begin, in what is likely a vain effort to prevent the last few hours of this trial from turning into a carnival, I wish to inform all present what they may expect to see. Today will unfold thus: The Accuser will give her argument for the execution of the Accused. The Defender will then speak his argument for life imprisonment. We will take a respite for two hours, so that the Accused may eat what could potentially be a last meal before making any final statement, should he so choose."

Sylvanas went rigid. What? She had thought the curry would be served tonight, after the jury had gone to deliberate, not in the middle of the afternoon! All their plans . . . Her gaze went to her sister. She could not make out Vereesa's expression from this distance, but her sister suddenly seemed to develop a great interest in her bag. Vereesa rummaged through it, then nodded and turned to look over in the direction of the Forsaken seating area.

Elation replaced momentary panic. *My dear sister,* she thought, fighting back a smile, *what a team we shall be!* Vereesa was keeping the poison on her person at all times, it would seem. They would not fail, no matter when the cursed orc was supposed to shovel food into his boastful mouth.

Disaster averted, Sylvanas returned her attention to the judge. He looked over the crowd, his face stern. "I trust there will be no disruption at that point. His fate is about to be decided before us all. He has a right to say whatever is in his mind and heart and be heard, and to speak for as long as he desires. If this is not understood, I will be more than happy to make it clear by giving anyone who lacks clarity a month in the heart of the Shado-pan Monastery."

Sylvanas did not doubt for a moment that the pandaren would do so, and apparently no one else did either. Taran Zhu seemed satisfied with the gravity that met his statement and resumed.

"After the Accused has spoken, the jury will deliberate. We will all reassemble when the jury returns with its verdict. Chu'shao Whisperwind, we are ready to hear your closing statement."

Jaina watched closely as Tyrande rose, taking a moment to look over her notes before rolling them up neatly and placing them aside. The night elf knew that this was what many of those who had come here had been waiting for. She had everyone's full attention, and she took her time. Tyrande placed a runecloth bag, a simple thing, on the desk, reached inside, and withdrew a stone about the size of a hen's egg.

"In my opening statement," she began, her lyrical voice carrying clearly, "I told you that I had received the easier task. My job as Accuser was to produce evidence that Garrosh Hellscream did not deserve a 'second chance,' did not deserve to 'make amends,' or any other phrase the Defender might have trotted out to play upon your sympathies. Even before I spoke, Garrosh admitted to committing the crimes he has been charged with, and . . ." She smiled a little and shrugged. "I have no doubt you recall his attitude."

Her pacing brought her back to her desk again. Tyrande carefully placed down the stone, reached into the bag, picked up a second rock, and continued speaking.

"The Defender asks, can people change? Of course they can. It is the nature of things to change. But sometimes, things do not change for the better. A tree grows, certainly. But so does a malignancy." Once again, she put down the stone, and this time picked up two.

"I made you promises in my opening statement," she said. "I told you you would watch Garrosh Hellscream plot, you would listen to him lie, and you would witness him betray."

She paused and looked directly at Jaina. "I regret the terrible necessity that compelled me to show many of these scenarios. But I would be deeply remiss in my duty if I did not do everything in my power to make my case as fully and convincingly as possible." And she bowed, bringing the stones in her hands to her heart.

Jaina understood. She swallowed hard and nodded. Tyrande did not overtly react, but Jaina thought she looked relieved. Yet again, the high priestess placed down the stones and drew two more. Four of them formed a small line along the edge of her desk now, and more than one person was eyeing them curiously.

"There were ten charges, all in all," Tyrande said. "Multiple counts of many—most—of those charges." She reached for more stones as she spoke, placing them down next to the others, all in that same tidy row.

"Genocide. Murder. Forcible transfer of population. Enforced disappearance of individuals. Enslavement. The abduction of children. Torture. The killing of prisoners. Forced pregnancy. The wanton destruction of cities, towns, and villages not justified by military or civilian necessity."

Tyrande paused. She perused the stones, made a show of counting them all. "Nine stones here." She gazed up into the stands, her radiant eyes searching the faces. "Perhaps you are wondering why there are only nine, when I have just said that there were ten charges against Garrosh. That is because these stones do not represent the charges."

She turned back to her desk and picked up the first rock, examining it. "These stones," Tyrande said slowly, "are more than representations. They are pieces of the very land that will forever bear the memory of Garrosh Hellscream. For instance . . . this was taken from the Stonetalon Mountains. Overlord Krom'gar murdered an entire village of innocents, following what he believed to be Garrosh's philosophy for the new Horde. How did he do so? By dropping a bomb on them. Garrosh killed him for his . . . dishonor."

She slammed the stone down, hard, and Jaina jumped, startled. A small gasp of surprise rippled through the arena. Tyrande looked up with her fierce, beautiful eyes and picked up the next stone.

"There are dark red patches on this one . . . it has seen much bloodshed. It was taken from the arena in Orgrimmar." Tyrande fingered it thoughtfully. "The place where the mak'gora is fought. The place where Baine Bloodhoof's father died by treachery." This one, she placed down gently, and she moved to the third.

"This mossy stone is from Gilneas. Where Garrosh Hellscream attacked . . . and so many fell. And another—from Azshara, beautiful, autumnal Azshara. It is not so beautiful now, is it? Not when Garrosh Hellscream gave the land to the goblins, who carved it with machines into a giant symbol of the Horde. Who rendered the water unfit to drink in the capital city itself!" She slammed this one down as she had the first, and Jaina saw true pain in her face.

That pain deepened when she gently picked up the next stone, which had striations of blue and green. "Ashenvale," Tyrande said. "Rich with forests and streams and life. Ashenvale. Ravaged by the orcs on Garrosh's command, the site of a battle fueled by the abduction of children and the deaths of their parents."

Jaina, enraptured, braced herself for the slamming down of the rock. But instead, the night elf softly placed it down, stroking it sadly before turning to the next. This one looked different from the others—like a piece of lava from a volcano—and suddenly Jaina realized where it had come from.

"Not content with plundering Azshara and Ashenvale, not given pause by having the deaths of innocents on his hands, Garrosh wanted more. Much more. He believed not only that the Horde had a right to survive and thrive, but that *he* had a right to do anything he wished to achieve that goal, regardless of what harm he might do." She held up the piece of rock for all to see. "This is a piece of a molten giant! A powerful elemental being forced into brutal submission, used by dark shaman who cared not if the earth cried out in pain and anger at being so abused. And this . . . was *after* the Cataclysm!"

Three more left. Jaina looked at the one next in line. It was gray, and—smooth, the way a rock that had been worn down by centuries of water was smooth. Tyrande picked it up, with the care with which one might handle a delicate egg, and gazed directly at Jaina.

The archmage's breath caught. She felt Kalec's hand close, so lightly, on her own, so willing to withdraw if she did not wish comfort. Jaina didn't look at him. She couldn't tear her eyes away from that simple piece of rock. Instead, she opened her hand and entwined her fingers tightly with his.

"Theramore," Tyrande said, her voice deep with emotion. She did not need to say anything further.

She pressed the stone to her heart before placing it back down onto the desk. "Darnassus," she said softly, touching the next to last stone. "The night elf home, violated when the Sunreavers betrayed Dalaran and used their magic not to help this world, but to steal the Divine Bell."

And the last . . . "The Vale of Eternal Blossoms," she said, and her voice broke. Jaina knew this was no act. "An ancient place, hidden away for so long. Only recently have we been able to behold it. And now, it is so gravely damaged it may take another eternity for it to again reach full flower. All for Garrosh Hellscream's unspeakable, unstoppable lust for power for one faction of the Horde!"

She whirled, her anger and passion etched in every taut line of her strong, lithe form. "What would such a one as he do with a second chance, other than use it to wreak more damage? To gather more power, to betray more allies? August Celestials! You are wise beyond our ability to truly comprehend. I urge . . . I implore you. Sentence Garrosh Hellscream to death for what he has done—to his enemies, to his allies, to the very land. He will not change. He cannot change. All there is of him is pride and hunger. As long as his heart beats, he will plot. As long as he breathes, he will butcher."

She took a deep breath and rose to her full, elegant height.

"End it. End *him*. Now."

32

The courtroom was silent when Tyrande returned to her seat. Jaina could almost feel the intensity with which everyone regarded Garrosh Hellscream. So many lives. So much pain. So much destruction—all by one orc. *One!* Was it possible for an individual to do more damage than his entire race?

One—who was sitting right here. One clean sword strike, one perfectly aimed fireball, and it would be over. Garrosh Hellscream would never harm anyone ever again.

Her fingers itched to perform the motions of such a spell.

After a moment, Baine Bloodhoof rose. The sound of his hooves was very loud in the still chamber. Jaina felt a rush of pity for the tauren and his impossible task.

He stood, gathering his thoughts as he addressed the solemn, attentive celestials. "I know that you are expecting a passionate plea for mercy, an appeal to your wisdom and compassion. I may still make such a plea; I have not decided yet. What I wish to share with you now is not about Garrosh Hellscream. It is about me."

He clasped his hands behind his back and began a slow walk of the circumference of the arena floor. "When I was asked to defend Garrosh, I very definitely had no desire to do so. I envied Chu'shao Whisperwind, for not only was she more likely to win, but I wanted the chance to do what she has done." He stopped in front of Tyrande's desk. She looked at him, curious but wary. Baine picked up the second stone—the one from the mak'gora arena. It had, Jaina was certain now, spatters of blood on it, which was probably the precise reason Tyrande had selected it. It could very likely be Cairne's blood.

Tyrande narrowed her eyes, but did not stop him. Baine continued his ambling.

"What a satisfying thing it must have been, to collect these stones. To permit herself to think about what had happened in these places, and how tragic and needless those events were." His hand closed tenderly around the small rock. "To sit with Chromie, and peer through time itself to find evidence of each count, and say to the jury and the spectators, 'Here, see this! See it; feel it! This—this is what Garrosh Hellscream has done!'"

What is he doing? Jaina wondered. *Is he just giving up? Admitting that defending Garrosh was a hopeless task from the beginning?*

"So I went to Thunder Bluff. To the home my father and Warchief Thrall had founded for my people. I went to breathe its air, and sit on its red stone, and ask my father, what do I do?" Baine gestured to Kador Cloudsong, seated in the stands. "I asked for a vision. And it came."

Now, Baine's voice trembled slightly, and his hand tightened around the stone that possibly bore spatters of his father's lifeblood.

"My father knew I could not indulge in my hatred, and my pain, and still hold my head high. He knew that I needed to say yes, to truly defend Garrosh to the best of my ability, no matter what the outcome, or there would be no peace. He knew this because he knew me—and also, because my father, who died at Garrosh's hand, would have done the same had he yet lived.

"And so I agreed to represent Garrosh. I spent many hours with Kairoz, researching events, as Tyrande has done. And I found that there is no way to truly *defend* Garrosh Hellscream. There simply isn't. The only 'defense' is to go beyond the events and into what truly matters."

Baine looked again at the rock nestled in his large palm. "Tyrande has gone to great lengths to find these stones for her closing argument. I do not belittle that, or the pain I am certain she felt as she gathered them and thought about what they signified. But I must tell you, poignant as her presentation was, it was exactly that. A presentation. A show, just like the Visions of Time were, and in a way, just like the Darkmoon Faire—to which this trial has been unfavorably compared—most certainly is."

Looking right at the jury, he crushed the small rock with his powerful fingers.

"It means nothing."

Jaina felt a rush of anger, of offense—how could he do this? Destroy so callously what should have been a precious memory of his father? Other ripples of displeasure surged through the room. Taran Zhu picked up his mallet, and the murmurs quieted.

Baine, unperturbed by the reaction, opened his hand and let the dust trickle to the floor. "In the end, this is what all becomes. We are all dust. Rocks, trees, creatures of field and forest, tauren, night elf, orc—this is what we become. And it does not matter. It does not matter that we die. What matters is that we *lived*."

He looked about the arena, slightly challenging now. "It is only when there is life that things can change. Only while we live can we comfort a friend, or raise little ones, or build a city. My father *lived*, and did so fully and well. He taught me many lessons."

Now Baine looked straight at Jaina and Anduin. "He once said destruction is easy. But creating something that lasts—that, my father said, was a challenge."

He reached for another stone—the one from Theramore, where he, Jaina, and Anduin had talked about so many things. "I could smash Garrosh Hellscream's skull with this rock. Or . . . I could use it to build a city. I could grind corn upon it, or heat it for cooking. I could cover it with bright paint, and use it in a ceremony to honor the Earth Mother. Whatever we do or do not do with this stone, it will become dust one day. All that matters is what we do with it while we live. And I believe that if we truly look into our hearts, past the fear and wounds that guard them, we know this to be true.

"We have all done things we are ashamed of. We have all done things we wish we could take back. We all carry within us the potential to become our own versions of Garrosh Hellscream. As I watched the Vision of Time display events in this trial, I began to see this. I saw it in Durotan, who attacked Telmor, but who later was exiled by his own people for his beliefs. In Gakkorg, who left an envied position as a member of the Kor'kron because he was so sickened by what he was ordered to do to innocent younglings. King Varian"—and here Baine pointed—"you once held a sword to the throat of a woman clad only in a nightgown, who had no defenses. And now, the two of you are friends and allies. Alexstrasza, so terribly abused—she forgives as deeply as she suffered, because she knows, as all of us should know, it is the only way."

He looked at Jaina again, and his eyes were full of compassion. "The lady of Theramore, which is no more, has suffered loss and betrayal. She is no Aspect, imbued with extraordinary patience and purpose to sustain her, and we have seen and heard her grief and her fury. But even she understands. She does not wish to be like Garrosh."

Baine turned back to the celestials, who watched him intently. "Tyrande speaks of true justice. I believe that you know what it is. And I believe that we here today will see it done. Thank you."

Baine had perhaps not won everyone over, but he had said many things that struck home, for Jaina, at least. So much was going through her head and heart as she left for the two-hour respite. Kalec had asked if she wanted to have a meal together, but she gently declined. "I . . . I need to think about things," she said, and he nodded, his eyes sad even as he smiled.

Jaina bought a bowl of noodles and found an out-of-the way area outside to eat, perched beneath a cherry blossom tree. She was fond of noodles and the view was splendid, but she ignored both as she mechanically placed food in her mouth and chewed.

She did not envy the celestials their task. She thought about what she had heard, and seen, and been forced to say. She thought about Kinndy, her perkiness sharply at odds with the seriousness with which she took things and her steadfast, vital will. She thought about Kalec, and the choice that he was wrestling with. That he loved her, she had no doubt. But his heart—better, stronger, kinder than hers, she understood with a flash of bitterness—could not bear the virulence of her rancor. It wounded him, she realized. He could stay and remain wounded, or leave and be whole.

Some choice, she thought. But Baine was right about one thing. She didn't want to be like Garrosh. And if their roles were reversed— what would Garrosh choose to do to her?

"Lady Jaina?" It was Jia Ji, one of the court couriers. He bowed low. "Forgive my intrusion on your solitude. I have a message for you."

He extended a scroll. Frowning, Jaina took it, and paled when she saw the seal. In the red wax was the unmistakable mark of the Horde.

A thousand thoughts tumbled through her head, all horrible, as she broke the wax with shaking fingers, unrolled the scroll, and read:

> *It took some time for me to learn what happened in Dalaran. You used to be a woman of peace; you be that no more. Garrosh scorches earth, and the dead ain't the only victims. You got no blame or hate from me, no matter what you feel toward Garrosh—or the Horde.*
> *We all got our ghosts.*
>
> —V

She reread it several times, and then slowly smiled. "Do you wish me to convey a response, Lady Jaina?" asked Jia.

"Yes," she said. "Please tell the warchief that I thank him for his understanding."

"Of course, my lady." Jia bowed low and turned to bear her message. Jaina watched him go, the smile still on her face, warming her. From her vantage point, she looked at the milling throng below. Only one among them had blue-black hair. He was talking with Varian and Anduin, and as she watched, he shook hands with both of them and started to walk away, looking downcast.

He's leaving.

Clutching the missive from Vol'jin, Jaina began to run.

"Kalec!" she shouted, heedless of the heads turning in her direction. *"Kalec!"*

Her feet flew over the path, and she jumped nimbly over a root here, a missing step there. The crowd parted at her approach. She didn't notice or care. Her gaze was fixed on Kalecgos, and she said a quick prayer to the Light that he wouldn't get swallowed up by the crowd.

"Kalec!"

His steps slowed, then stopped. He cocked his head as if listening, then turned, his gaze scanning the sea of people. Their eyes met, and his face lit up like the sun. Her heart surged with gladness. She closed the space between them and flung herself into his outstretched arms.

Right there, in front of all eyes, they kissed, joyfully and longingly, and Jaina was fiercely grateful.

Garrosh Hellscream had taken enough.

He would not take this; he would not take *her.*

33

"Vereesa!" Mu-Lam Shao greeted her friend warmly. "I did not know if I would see you today, since it is the last day of the trial."

Vereesa smiled at the pandaren, who was busily chopping ginger, onion, and other items so fast the knife was a blur. "Oh no, I wanted to make sure that I got the recipe for this. It is very popular here, it seems, if even an orc will eat it."

Mu-Lam chuckled, a warm rumble, her eyes bright. "Some might say, even an elf," and she winked. "But yes. I would be remiss if I did not make sure you knew how to prepare it. You are always welcome in my kitchen, you know. You will come back to visit?"

She looked up hopefully. Vereesa suddenly, unexpectedly, felt a pang. No, she would not be back. She would not be anywhere she had ever been before. Only the dark places would be hers soon, and the dusty lands of Orgrimmar, and the smoggy shantytowns of the goblins. But that was not entirely true. She could go to Silvermoon, and relive how very different things were there now from when she had lived there, and visit her family's spire . . .

"Oh, of course," she lied easily. "I have gotten fond of you, Mu-Lam." That, at least, was the truth.

Mu-Lam beamed. Then, as if slightly embarrassed, she said more brusquely, "Here . . . make yourself useful. Chop this basil and cut up the sunfruit."

The sunfruit. There they were, their fragrance tangy and luscious without even being sliced yet. Vereesa moved the knife with extra deliberation, so as not to cut herself accidentally.

There would be eight diners, and Mu-Lam had put out eight small ceramic dishes. Vereesa cut the sunfruit into quarters as Mu-Lam described everything that went into the fish curry, including the curry paste. Vereesa didn't hear much of it. All she could think about was Garrosh Hellscream, dead, despite Baine Bloodhoof's final plea. Rhonin was dead . . . now, Garrosh would pay.

"Which one is Garrosh's?" she asked, hoping her voice sounded casual.

"His tray is the brown bamboo one," Mu-Lam said, pointing with a spoon. "Give him an extra quarter. It might be the last thing he eats, and I know he likes it so."

"You are very kind toward a killer." Vereesa snapped the words before she could censor them. But Mu-Lam knew of Vereesa's loss, and looked at the high elf with sympathy.

"I will awaken tomorrow to this beautiful land, to wholesome food and loving friends and family, to work that is worthy and makes a difference. Garrosh Hellscream, whatever the August Celestials decide, will never have that. Knowing this, I find it easy to be kind."

Shame, hot and electric, washed over Vereesa. Anger followed hard on its heels. She merely nodded and took another segment of sunfruit. Mu-Lam wiped her paws and turned away to ladle up the curry.

Now.

Vereesa slipped the vial out of her pouch and unstoppered it. Her hands no longer shook as she placed three drops—one would have been sufficient—on each section. The liquid quickly dissolved in the juices of the mouthwatering fruit. No one could ever tell. Vereesa slid the stopper back into the bottle, pressing firmly to seal it, then washed her hands with soap.

The deed was done.

"Thank you, Vereesa," Mu-Lam said. "I will miss you, until our next visit."

Vereesa gave her a wan smile. "Thank you, Mu-Lam. For everything. Until we meet again."

She turned to leave. Mu-Lam called after her, "And when you come, bring your little ones! They must be beautiful boys!"

Her boys.

The reaction hit Vereesa all at once, and she started to tremble. She kept walking, lifting a hand in farewell, exited the room below the temple that had been transformed into a temporary kitchen, and hurried into the corridor.

She leaned up against the cool stone, breathing hard. Vereesa was no stranger to violence. She had taken lives before. But that had always been in battle, when she had been fighting for something, or someone. This was different. This was deliberate, calculated, carefully planned murder, using the weapon not of a ranger, but of an assassin. It was worse than an arrow in the eye, worse than a knife in the dark.

They must be beautiful boys.

She had not thought of them, not really, in a long time. First she had to deal with the Sunreavers and Lor'themar, then the Siege of Orgrimmar, then the trial. She had barely spent any time with them in recent years, not even right after—

They *were* beautiful, with Rhonin's red hair and her eyes: Giramar, eldest only by a few moments, and Galadin. Vereesa suddenly realized how much she had missed their laughter. How wild they both used to be, but kindhearted, her boys, and their father would be so proud of how bravely . . .

She tried to picture them in the Undercity, and . . . couldn't. Where would they run and play and laugh? Turn their faces up to the sky for its kisses? How could they learn anything about life in a city of the dead?

"Vereesa?"

Lost in the images of her vibrant children in the gray, dark Undercity, Vereesa started violently.

"Anduin," she said, laughing a little. "I am sorry—I was lost in thought."

"No, *I'm* sorry. I didn't mean to startle you. Are you all right?"

She came back to the present, face to face with another beautiful boy, though this one much older than the twins. But he had the same kindness and good heart, this fair-haired prince. "I am fine, just fine," she said. "What are you doing down here?"

He looked a little sheepish. "Going to see Garrosh. He asked for me, a while ago, and we've been talking after court each day. After Alexstrasza's testimony, I didn't want to see him again, but . . . well, this might be the last opportunity I ever have. I feel I should go, even if he just yells at me again."

Vereesa stared at him, and thought of her laughing boys. Before she could change her mind, she suddenly lunged for Anduin and grabbed his arm. He peered at her, confused.

"Vereesa?"

"I believe the Light is at work here," she said, the words tumbling out quickly, quickly, before fear and hatred closed her lips. "I surrender my choice to you. Garrosh's food is poisoned. Do with the knowledge what you will."

Without waiting for an answer, she raced down the corridor. She would find Yu Fei, and go to Dalaran, and hug her boys—her warm, lovely, *living* children—tightly, and never, ever think of forsaking them again.

Anduin stared after the high elf ranger, his mouth open with astonishment.

Poison? Vereesa had been about to poison Garrosh? He could scarcely believe it. Then he thought of how bitter and harsh she had been since Theramore, and how she and Jaina had fed off of one another, and painfully realized that, yes—he *could* believe it.

He was jolted into action with a sudden thought—what if the food had come already? He sprinted down the hall, sliding to a stop in front of the door to the ramp.

"Dinner," he panted. "Has it come yet?"

"No, Prince Anduin," Lo said. "Perhaps you should go eat yours and return when you are calmer."

He felt weak from relief and laughed shakily. "Sorry. Can I see him?"

The brothers eyed one another. "He is . . . in a very disagreeable mood," Lo said.

"Very," Li agreed.

Anduin's giddy relief that he had been in time was replaced by solemnity. "He is facing death," he said, "and not the sort of death he ever envisioned for himself. He has acted brave, but now, all he can do is wait. I can understand being . . . disagreeable. I would like a few moments alone with him, perhaps?"

"As you wish, Your Highness," Li said with obvious reluctance, and opened the door.

Garrosh was not seated on the furs, as he usually was. He was pacing the short length of his cell, his feet only able to move a few inches at a time. He looked up angrily as the door opened, and his face grew even darker as he saw who it was. Anduin braced himself for a verbal barrage, but the orc said nothing, merely continued his constrained pacing.

Anduin took his chair and waited. *Clink-clink-shuffle-drag, clink-clink-shuffle-drag . . .*

After several minutes, Garrosh halted. "Why are you here, human child?"

It was not what Anduin had expected. Garrosh sounded not bitter, not raging, but—resigned. "I came in case you nee—wanted to talk to me."

"Well, I do not. Run along, now." Contempt began to replace the resignation in the orc's voice. "Go back and play your little games with the Light and wave your little mace Fearbreaker. At least Baine was enough of a tauren to return your toy."

"You're trying to anger me," Anduin said.

"Is it working?"

"Yes."

"Good. Now, go."

"No," Anduin said, surprising himself. "You asked for me once. Some part of you wanted a priest, but you couldn't face talking to someone from the Horde. Because then that desire, that *need*, would be too real. Better to ask for me, your so-called enemy. Better to play word games and trade insults than to really face the fact that guess what, you might just be *executed*. But what you don't understand, Garrosh, is that I believe in what it means to be a priest. I'm going to stay with you, whether you want me here or not. Because there might come a minute, just one minute, when you might be glad of my presence."

"I will rot in the darkest reaches of the Twisting Nether before I will *ever* be glad of your puling presence!" Garrosh changed, right in front of him, and Anduin realized how much the calm façade must have cost the orc. It was gone, now, dropped like a cape Garrosh no longer felt suited him. His eyes did not glow red, but the rage inside them was visible nonetheless. He was seething, his manacled fists clenching and unclenching.

"You sit there each day, all smug and sanctimonious," Garrosh continued, the words dripping disgust. "You and your precious Light. So certain that by enduring my words and watching my fate play out in front of you that you'll be able to make me change my ways. Everyone wants something from me out there, *boy*, and you do too."

"I'm only here to try to help you—"

"Help me what?" His voice rose. "Help me die? Help me live like a pet wolf, whimpering for pats and the occasional scrap of meat? Is it not enough for you that I cannot even stride like a warrior, but must be chained like a beast? Is that what you want your Light to do to me?"

Anduin felt as if he were being physically bombarded by the words. "No, it's not that at all. The Light doesn't work that way—"

"Because of course an adolescent human *boy* knows all about the Light," the orc sneered, and he started to laugh.

"I know enough," Anduin said, his own temper rising. He fought for patience. "I know that—"

"You know nothing. *Boy.* You are still wet behind your ears, so recently did you leave your mother's womb!"

Anduin jerked as if stung. "My mother has nothing to do with this, Garrosh. This is about you, and the fact that you've likely got just a few hours to go before you know—"

"This is about what I *say* it's about! And I say it's about your arrogance, your cursed *Alliance arrogance*, that you know what's best, and you know what's right, for everyone, including me!"

Anduin was breathing quickly now, and his own fists clenched. The door opened, and Yu Fei and the Chu brothers entered, looking as serene as if they had heard nothing of the orc's ranting. Garrosh snarled at them.

"Stand back, Garrosh. You know we have no wish to harm you," Lo said. Little Yu Fei stood by, and Anduin suddenly knew that she was the threat in this situation, not the Chu brothers. Garrosh stared at them and bellowed impotently, then retreated while the mage deactivated the spell and his tray of green curry fish was placed inside. Yu Fei reactivated the spell, and with no other word, the three pandaren left. The door closed and locked behind them.

"Garrosh, listen to me—" Anduin began, intent on warning him about the poisoned dish.

"You listen to me, boy. I hope you live to be king. Because whether or not I am here to see it, the day you take the throne, the orcs will celebrate. And we will come for Stormwind. Do you hear me? We will race through your streets, and kill your people. We will place your soft little peace-craving body on a pike, and burn your city down around your still-wet ears. And in whatever afterlife your precious Light grants you, your parents will wish Queen Tiffin had *miscarried.*"

Anduin had stopped breathing. He felt as if he was about to burst with white-hot wrath. He wanted to stop Garrosh from speaking, ever, to blast his mind and wipe all that it was to be Garrosh Hellscream from it. He knew how to use the Light. He could use it now, not as a shield to protect, or a balm to heal, but as a weapon.

Maybe Vereesa had been right—maybe the Light *was* at work. It was going to take care of Garrosh Hellscream. All Anduin would need to do was stay silent. He'd been an idiot to think he could help. That he could somehow reach Garrosh. The orc had been correct about one thing. Nothing good could ever, ever reach him.

He tried to kill you, he thought. *He'd kill you now, if he could. Let him die. The world really would be better off without him.*

Garrosh watched the prince of Stormwind struggle against his rage, and laughed. He squeezed a sunfruit quarter over his curry and picked up the bowl, raising it to his lips.

With an anguished sob that was half a snarl, Anduin darted forward, reaching his arm through the ensorcelled window and knocking the bowl from Garrosh's hands. It clattered to the floor, its contents spattering the furs.

Garrosh seized Anduin's arm and yanked, slamming the prince's face against the hard iron. He twisted the arm sharply, taking it to an almost impossible position, and Anduin gasped.

"Roused you to anger, have I, *boy?* Then I have won!"

"Your food—it's poisoned," Anduin hissed, clenching his teeth against the pain.

"You lie! I can't squeeze your skinny little throat through the bars, but I've got your arm, and I can rip it out of its socket!"

Anduin let the Light fill him, and the pain fell back before him. Calmness replaced the agitation in his spirit, and he offered no protest. He simply regarded Garrosh. The orc was right. He could tear off Anduin's arm as easily as ripping a plant from the earth. Anduin was at the orc's mercy, and he surrendered his concern. He had done the right thing, and that was what mattered. Whatever would happen, would happen.

Garrosh stared at him, panting in fury, but Anduin's gaze never wavered.

A small motion near Garrosh's feet drew both their attention. It was the rat that Anduin had seen before, drawn out of hiding by the tantalizing aroma of fish curry. It scurried forward, whiskers twitching as it sniffed, then plucked out a morsel with its forepaws and began to eat.

It jerked, sat very still, then resumed eating. Again, its body shook, and this time it began to convulse. Blood and foam appeared on its muzzle, and it thrashed about in agony, trying to crawl back to its hole with limbs that refused to obey. It made grunting, wet breathing noises as its lungs labored for air, and then, mercifully, it ceased to move.

Anduin swallowed, hard, fixated on the rat, then raised his eyes from the wretched creature to see Garrosh staring intently at him. The orc glanced away, and he shoved Anduin back so hard the prince stumbled.

Anduin hesitated for a moment, rubbed his now-healed arm, then turned and ascended the ramp. With a steady hand, he knocked on the door. It opened to him, and he left without another word to Garrosh.

He had made his peace. It was time for Garrosh to do the same.

Before he headed back down the corridor, he turned to Li Chu. "When Garrosh is brought in to hear the verdict," he said, "please . . . remove his bonds."

"We cannot do that, Prince Anduin," Li said.

"Then—at least take off the leg chains. Let him walk as a warrior. Surely six guards will be enough if he tries to flee. I . . . don't think he will. He knows he's probably going to die."

They exchanged glances. "Very well. We will ask Taran Zhu," Li said. "We make no promises."

It had been a busy day for Jia Ji. As one of the court's couriers, he was oath-bound not to speak of his missives or who had sent what to whom, and his services were much in demand. Today seemed to be the busiest day yet.

First, there was the letter from Warchief Vol'jin to Lady Jaina, then a verbal response from the lady to the warchief to be conveyed. Then there was a note from the ranger-general Vereesa Windrunner to her sister. He had waited for a reply, and had been told to "Get out!" in a very loud and angry voice. Even so, he did have a verbal message for the ranger-general—from Prince Anduin, not Sylvanas. Yu Fei portaled him to Dalaran, where he found Vereesa sitting by the fountain, watching her two boys. They were all making wishes and laughing, each with fistfuls of coins.

"Ranger-General," he said, bowing politely, "I have a message for you." He looked meaningfully at the two red-haired, half-elven children.

The ranger-general paled a little and rose from where she had been sitting next to the fountain. The boys stopped and fixed her with worried looks. "I will be right back," she promised them, and walked out of earshot.

"Yes?" She was polite, but wary.

"The message is from His Royal Highness, Prince Anduin Wrynn of Stormwind. It is as follows: 'He lives. I will not make two children both fatherless and motherless. What you do now is your choice.' Shall I bear back a response?"

Her face softened and became beautiful again with peace. "Yes," she replied. "Tell him . . . Rhonin thanks him."

The dead horse galloped as swiftly as it had in life, and never tired. Its rider killed as swiftly as she had in life, and she, too, never tired. The corpses were starting to litter the forest: wolves, bears, stags, spiders. Whatever had the bad luck to cross her path died, not always quickly and seldom clean.

The Banshee Queen uttered the horrifying shriek of her kind, infusing it with all the sickening sense of betrayal and raging, insane grief that filled her. A bear fell, weakened and panicked by the sound alone. She peppered the thick brown hide with arrows, and the beast bellowed in pain and churned up the mossy earth. Sylvanas drank in its suffering. She leapt off her skeletal mount and charged a wolf, which met her snarl for snarl until she tore off its head with her bare hands.

The pain was unbearable. It was the same phantom agony she had experienced over the last several days, when she had felt so happy with Vereesa. Except now, even the joy that had accompanied the pain was gone, and there was nothing left but torment.

Torment, and hate.

Her leather clothing was now spattered with blood, but she did not care. The only way to stop hurting was to hurt something else, to vent her anguish and sorrow and despair on something living, since she could not vent it on Vereesa, sister, Little Moon—

She staggered, clutching the wolf's head, blinking eyelashes sticky with crimson fluid. She dropped the head, and it bounced hollowly. Sylvanas fell to her knees, buried her face in her hands, and wept, wept like a broken child who had lost everything, everything.

Little Moon . . . !

Gradually the sobbing ceased, and the familiar peace of coldness drove out the heated hurting. Sylvanas rose, licking blood from her lips.

She should have known. The pain she had felt at first, when she dared foolishly permit herself to hope for something different from what she had now, to feel something for another . . . to feel love again . . . It had been a warning. A warning that she was no longer made for feelings such as hope, or love, or trust, or joy. These things were for the living; these things were for the weak. In the end, they would slip through her fingers, trickling away like the violet remnants of Jaina Proudmoore's apprentice Kinndy, and she would be left alone. Again, and always. Calmed now through tears and slaughter, she remounted her horse. Sylvanas Windrunner, the Banshee Queen of the Forsaken, would never again make the mistake of believing she could love.

34

G o'el was surprised to see that Sylvanas's seat was empty. Of all the Horde leaders, he had thought she held the most personal, most virulent hatred of Garrosh. What had Baine said? Vol'jin had told the tauren, *Ain't nobody knows more of hate than the Dark Lady. And she like her hate dished out icy cold.*

And yet, on the day when Garrosh was to finally break his silence, she was not here to lap up his suffering. Strange.

The spectators filed in, filling the seats, though no one would dare take Sylvanas's. Kairoz stood alone at the bronzes' table, tinkering with the Vision of Time. Go'el assumed he was deactivating it, seeing that its purpose had been served. He found himself annoyed that Kairoz chose to do so now rather than last night, or even before then. There had been no need for the device in closing arguments; all the evidence had already been presented. Although he had no love for Garrosh, Go'el still thought it discourteous that Kairoz was doing such a mundane task. He wondered why Taran Zhu had allowed it, as it smacked of disrespect for the court proceedings, and reasoned that it must be important in a way only a bronze dragon would know. Chromie, no doubt, would join Kairoz in a few moments. Go'el was certain that neither bronze dragon, each of whom had played such a pivotal role, would miss hearing Garrosh speak.

This trial had strained more than it had solved up to this point. Many in the Horde had expressed anger toward Baine for his apparently sincere defense of Garrosh. The tactics the Defender had used with Vol'jin and Go'el himself had certainly stung. Baine's closing argument, however, clearly showed the reasons why Baine had felt it necessary to do what he had done, and Go'el understood. Still, he was glad to see the end of this. Whatever decision the August Celestials reached, it would be a relief.

The arena hummed with the sound of voices talking excitedly, even more today than usual. The chatter subsided when Taran Zhu entered, walking toward his seat with the same unhurried step as he had every day before. He struck the gong and announced, "Court has now resumed. Please bring in the jury."

The four celestials took their customary positions, serenely unreadable, ready to hear what the Accused might have to say. Beside Go'el, Aggra tensed. "Here he comes," she murmured.

Garrosh Hellscream was still flanked by six guards, but today the chains around his legs that made his steps short and halting were gone, though he still walked with a limp. Gone too were any chains other than a single set of manacles that bound his hands. He stood straighter than he had before, with a weary but stoic mien.

"I am glad Taran Zhu permitted this," Go'el said to Aggra. "Whatever else he is, he is a warrior. He should face death like an orc, not like an animal."

"Hmm," said Aggra. "You are more charitable than I. I do not think he deserves any show of respect, for if he ever had it from anyone, he has more than squandered it."

"And that," said Go'el, "is a tragedy too."

Anduin had been schooled from his earliest years in how to sit calmly at formal occasions. "No wiggling for a prince," he had been told. But today, after his encounter with first Vereesa and then Garrosh, he was jumpy and had difficulty not shifting in his seat. Fortunately, everyone else seemed as anxious as he, though he hoped no one else had experienced the sort of respite he had. By the way they were acting, Jaina and Kalec had actually had a pretty good one. They were holding hands and looked happy. Anduin was glad. He wanted something to go right for a change.

"How are you holding up?" Varian asked.

"Me? I'm fine," Anduin said, too quickly.

"I didn't like it when you started talking to Garrosh," Varian said, "but . . . I think it was the right thing. It's all up to the celestials now."

"Do you think if he asks for mercy, they will grant it?" Anduin couldn't help but ask.

"I can't begin to guess what a celestial might or might not do," Varian said. "What concerns me is that you're all right."

"I am," Anduin said, and he realized he was. He'd done all he could for Garrosh, and was content. Though still a little jumpy. He detected movement at one of the doors. "There he is."

As Garrosh walked forward, Anduin saw that Taran Zhu had agreed to Anduin's request to reduce Garrosh's chains. The orc had even been given a clean tunic. He seemed better than when Anduin had left him, calmer, more . . . dignified.

"Huh," said Varian. "Where's Chromie? I thought she'd want to be here for this."

Anduin glanced over, and sure enough, only Kairoz was at the bronze dragons' table, still fiddling with the Vision of Time.

"No idea," he said, then returned his full attention to Garrosh. The guards marched him into the center of the room; then four of them dropped back. Only two remained, and even they stood a few steps behind the orc as he faced the fa'shua.

"Garrosh Hellscream," said Taran Zhu. "You have been tried in a formal court of Pandaren law. Before the jury begins its deliberation on your fate, is there anything you wish to say, to me, to the jury, or to any spectators?"

Garrosh regarded the crowd as if seeing them for the first time. He turned in a tight circle as he looked around the ring, pausing here and there for a moment. At one point, he locked gazes with Anduin, and something flickered across his face.

"Yes," he said, his voice strong, carrying easily in the large space. "I do have something to say. Honorable Taran Zhu. August Celestials. Spectators from all across Azeroth. I have heard everything you have heard. I have seen what you have seen."

He moved to face Tyrande, who sat quietly, perfectly composed. "Tyrande Whisperwind has presented a strong and damning case against me. A case that has roused some of you to anger, and thoughts of revenge. Thoughts of my death. I do not blame you for hungering for that."

He gave Tyrande a slight smirk, then turned to his Defender. Baine too looked composed, though somewhat more grim than Tyrande. "Baine Bloodhoof, who has little enough cause to do so, has with great earnestness presented a case not protesting my innocence, but asking for your understanding. For your compassion. For you, the jury and the spectators, to look within your own hearts, and see that no one is completely free from blame."

Then, to Anduin's surprise, Garrosh turned to face him. "And Prince Anduin Wrynn, who by all rights should be foremost among those clamoring for my death, has chosen to spend hours in my company. I attempted to slay him, in a brutal, cruel, and painful manner. And what does he do?" Garrosh shook his head, as if in disbelief. "He speaks to me of the Light. He tells me he believes that I can change. He has shown me kindness when I offered hatred and violence. It is because of him that I stand before you, facing what I expect to be a pronouncement of my death, as a warrior, not as a broken slave."

He lifted his shackled hands, and gave Anduin a slight bow before turning to face the crowd once more. "Oh, yes. I know full well how much blood is on my hands. I know exactly the magnitude and the consequences of what I have done." He took a deep breath and seemed to be gathering his thoughts. Anduin leaned forward, not wanting to hope, but hoping wildly, beautifully, anyway.

"And now, here at this moment, when I am free to speak my mind and heart, I tell you true: I regret . . ."

His laughter rang through the arena.

"Nothing!"

Anduin forgot to breathe. He felt cold, numb. He sat, staring at Garrosh, for a moment unable to mentally process the words. Sound hammered on his ears, the outraged cries of a furious public. Taran Zhu struck the gong futilely, calling for order.

But Garrosh, it seemed, had only begun. He lifted his shackled arms and bellowed, "Yes! *Yes!* I would destroy a *thousand* Theramores, if it would bring the Alliance to its knees! I would hunt down every night elf whelp that bleats on the face of this world and silence their mewling forever! I would banish *every* troll, *every* tauren, *every* simpering blood elf and greedy goblin and shambling walking corpse if it were within my power—*and it almost was!*"

Anduin realized his father had been repeating his name. He looked over at Varian unsteadily, overwhelmed with shock and disillusionment. "Anduin," Varian said for perhaps the third time. "Come on. Go'el wants to talk to us and I think I know why."

Go'el stood near the entrance. As he met Anduin's gaze, he jerked his head slightly toward the corridor that led outside. Anduin nodded, licking his lips and shaking his head as he and Varian threaded their way to the stairs. On the floor below, Garrosh continued. Anduin clenched his jaw. How could he have believed Garrosh could change?

"The only 'atrocities' I regret are the ones I did not perform!" the orc shouted, grinning ferociously at the turmoil his words had caused. "The only thing that preys on me is that I was stopped before I could see the true Horde live again!"

Anduin and his father went to one of the doors, where Go'el was awaiting them. "Chromie?" asked Varian.

"Chromie," confirmed Go'el.

"What about her?" asked Anduin.

Go'el turned to him. "She helped Tyrande with the Accuser's case, and yet she's not here?"

"Something must be wrong," Varian said.

"I can go try to find her," Anduin offered at once. "I know this place pretty well after so much time." His voice was bitter. He did want to help, but more than that, he didn't think he could stand listening to Garrosh a moment longer.

Anduin ran lightly down the stairs to Garrosh's cell area, thinking he would ask the Chu brothers if they had seen Chromie, and tell them to be on the alert if they had not. He rounded the corner and skidded to a stop.

The two pandaren lay limply on the floor, looking like black-and-white sacks of grain someone had carelessly tossed aside. The chains that hitherto had been used to bind Garrosh were now fastened securely around their stout bodies, and gags had been thrust between their jaws.

"Oh, no," Anduin moaned, hastening to them. Both of the brothers had suffered blows to the head, and their fur was sticky with blood, but they yet breathed. Anduin placed a hand on Li's heart and murmured a prayer to the Light. A soft yellow glow enveloped his hand, making it feel warm and tingly. The Light's blessing flowed through him, cleansing him like a gentle fall of rain, spreading from him to Li. The pandaren opened his eyes as Anduin removed the gag.

"Two . . . females," Li muttered as Anduin turned to Lo Chu and prayed to the Light to heal the other twin. "They had crossbows— they should not have, but they did." Beneath Anduin's hands, the huge lump on Lo's skull receded and he, too, blinked to consciousness. Anduin tugged off that gag as well.

"If they had crossbows, you are lucky to still be alive," said Anduin, wondering who these warrior females were and why they had come. "Let me get you out of these chains." He knew that Lo Chu carried the keys to both the chains and the door in the ever-present pouch that hung at his side. Anduin reached his hand in for them, then frowned. "Lo, where are the keys?"

"The females must have stolen them!" Lo squirmed in impotent irritation.

"Did you recognize them?" asked the prince. Both brothers shook their heads. "But . . . this doesn't make sense. Garrosh was already out of the cell. Why would they want to—" He jumped up and banged on the closed door. "Chromie?"

He thought he heard something and pressed his ear to the door, concentrating. "Anduin!" It was faint, but the high-pitched, gnomish voice belonged to Chromie. He sagged in relief.

"Someone tied up Lo and Li and stole the keys, but we'll get you out!" Anduin reassured her, yelling in order for Chromie to hear him. "Don't worry. What happened?"

"It was Kairoz!"

"What?" Anduin's jaw dropped.

"Please, just listen; we don't have much time! I think he's going to do something with the Vision of Time. I caught him tinkering with it and asked him why, and he made some excuse about 'shutting it down.' I started questioning him, and then—then I woke up locked in here. You have to stop him from doing whatever he's planning! Please, you have to hurry!"

"Go!" shouted Li.

"We will meditate and cultivate patience," added Lo.

"That will serve you well," came a smooth, silky voice. "Li in particular could use it."

Anduin whirled, sickened as his heart contracted at yet another betrayal on this dismal day. "Two females with crossbows," he said, bitterly. "One orc, one human, weren't they, Li? I should have known."

"Perhaps you should have, but it is not yet within you to suspect treachery, Anduin Wrynn," said Wrathion with a sad smile. "If it is any consolation at all, I am deeply sorry for what I now must do."

Anduin laughed scornfully. "Sure you are."

The Black Prince shrugged. "Believe what you will, but it is the truth. We are friends, you and I."

"Friends? Friends don't kill each other!"

The dragon's glowing eyes widened and he looked almost hurt. "Why would I do that? Look at the Chu brothers. They are alive, though admittedly with rather terrible headaches, and I care far less about them than I do you."

"Wrathion, what is going on here? What are you *doing?*"

The young black dragon sighed. "You once asked me to watch and listen, and to make up my mind as to what is best for Azeroth. I have done exactly as you bid. You are the heir to the throne of Stormwind. You have a duty—to keep your kingdom safe. You do what you believe is best for it and its people. As the last black dragon, the former charge of my flight—to keep Azeroth safe—falls solely to me. I must honor that charge."

"Don't listen to him, Anduin!" cried Chromie.

Anduin gestured toward the still-chained pandaren. "*This* is keeping Azeroth safe?"

"In this case, I assure you, the end does justify the means. It is my deep hope that one day you will understand. And on that day, you and I will face a terrible enemy. Perhaps we shall even do so as brothers."

Desperately, Anduin reached out his hand. "You don't have to do it this way. Tell me what's going on. We can work together. We can find some way to—"

"Farewell for now, young prince," said Wrathion. He lifted a hand, and Anduin knew no more.

35

"Nothing—*nothing* in this world can stop me!" Garrosh roared, raising his still-bound fists and shaking them in a gesture of triumph.

At that moment, Jaina realized what had been bothering her. Everyone was upset—Garrosh, Taran Zhu, the guards, the spectators. But Kairoz simply stood by the table, a slight smile playing about his handsome face. From one heartbeat to the next, everything clicked into place. Even as Jaina drew breath to shout a warning to Taran Zhu, the bronze dragon languidly reached out an elegant hand and, eyes still on the ranting Garrosh, pushed the Vision of Time just far enough off the table.

"No!" Jaina cried out, her voice lost in the furor as, almost in slow motion, she watched the Vision of Time topple to the unforgiving stone. As it fell, turning end over end, the sands inside began to glow—and both decorative, tiny metal dragons affixed to the hourglass woke up, stretched their wings, and flew.

It crashed with a discordant yet musical sound, the globes shattering and the sand they contained spilling outward—and upward. An almost blinding storm of energy rose up, a tornado of golden, whirling light. The sounds of the crowd turned to shrieks of terror instead of anger, and Jaina felt a change in the air—the frisson of magic. The dampening field that had blanketed the temple was gone. The only magic that had been excepted was that of the bronze dragons—magic that now eliminated the field. Before Jaina's numbed gaze, an enormous slice in time and space yawned open. Garrosh and Kairoz seemed to drop straight through the floor—and other beings surged out of it.

They were not demons, or elementals, or anything so ordinary. As Jaina recognized these beings who shook their heads, looked around, and brandished their weapons, shock rendered her unable to speak for a moment.

Her gaze was riveted to the woman with a single golden streak in her white hair, clad in flowing white, purple, and blue, and bearing an ornate staff. The woman's mouth was set in a hard, angry line, and her eyes glowed pale blue. Hovering over her, large enough to grasp her in his foreclaws, was a blue dragon, splendid and all the shades of ice and sky, laughing insanely. Standing beside the white-haired woman was a night elf, her features cruel and cold, and next to her—

"Kalec!" Jaina cried. "They're us!"

But he was already on his feet, racing toward the open floor to find a large enough space in which to transform. Jaina dropped into battle mode, her mind clearer and sharper than it had been for the duration of the trial. She and Kalec had an advantage many others did not. With the dampening field down, they had their weapons back.

And she intended to use hers. The woman on the floor, targeting the races of the Horde and sending fireballs in their directions, was no stranger. Jaina remembered all too well how that woman felt. This was not merely a possible Jaina—this was one she had *been*, in this timeline, and she was grimly determined to stop that woman in her tracks. She summoned a crackling ball of whirling fire and hurled it at her other self.

That Jaina turned and met the fireball with a blast of pure arcane energy. A cold smile twisted her face, and Jaina had an instant where she wondered, *I know exactly what I will do, and so must she—how do I fight myself?*

Go'el and Varian leaned against one of the stone pillars that flanked the entrance to the temple, listening to Garrosh Hellscream rave. "He digs his own grave with each word he speaks," Go'el said, shaking his head. "What a waste."

Varian started to nod, then cocked his head, frowning slightly. At once, Go'el was alert, and turned from the frenzied display inside the temple. He heard it now too, still faint but growing louder, a steady but erratic beat, as of many—

"Wings," snapped Varian. Even as he spoke, another sound became audible, this one more regular and thrumming, a rhythmic *whump-whump-whump.*

"Zeppelin!" shouted Go'el. Two skilled warriors with decades of experience between them, they acted in perfect concert with no more words. Varian sprinted down the corridor and outside, shouting out a warning while snatching up a sword from the paw of a surprised guard. Go'el spun on his heel and turned to the temple floor. He had just opened his mouth to call the fighters out to do battle when he saw Kairoz, so very casually, so very calculatedly, tip over the Vision of Time, and the floor of the Temple of the White Tiger was engulfed in chaos.

Go'el lifted a hand to shield his eyes from the energy storm, swirling and emitting a noise that almost, but not quite, drowned out the screams of the crowd. A massive temporal rift burst open. Squinting, Go'el watched in impotent fury as Kairoz and Garrosh, both grinning victoriously, disappeared through the floor. Go'el expected the aperture to close, but Kairoz had left nothing to chance. Where once two had stood, now there were ten, and Go'el knew them all. His eyes went at once to the powerful orc clad in traditional human plate armor. Across his gleaming chest was a tabard of red and gold, bearing the crest of a black falcon. The orc swung a gigantic battleaxe as, swifter than his fellows, he charged straight for the seats filled with screaming spectators.

Go'el knew that crest. An enemy out of time who had come to kill him had worn it. Go'el had killed that enemy. He would kill this one as well.

"Thrall!" Go'el screamed, and the mighty orc, wearing the tabard of Aedelas Blackmoore, whirled to face himself with a hungry grin.

Zaela laughed as the infinite dragons, with loyal Dragonmaw orcs crouched atop their backs, approached the Temple of the White Tiger. Inside, her warchief was making his escape, thanks to Kairozdormu. She recalled that first meeting with the bronze dragon in Grim Batol, in the same room where Alexstrasza had been held captive by the Dragonmaw of years past. "I will give you, the leader of the Dragonmaw, a draconic army to command," he had told her.

"Bronze dragons?" Zaela had asked.

He shook his head. "The bronze dragonflight would have time unfold as it wills, no matter the consequences. The infinite dragonflight and I believe in altering time to suit *our* will."

There had been no leak, no warning, nothing to distract from the glory of this certain victory. The most important of Garrosh's foes were gathered in one place; she was sure that when Kairoz revealed everything to him, he would appreciate the tribute to his own brilliant strategy at Theramore. Striking from both within and without the temple would pin those who sought to quench their ugly obsessions with Hellscream between death at the hands of the Dragonmaw and death from their own alternate selves.

It was an elegant plan. Zaela was untroubled by the thought of killing members of the Horde in this attack. As far as she was concerned, the only members of the real Horde were with her now.

She had difficulty restraining her normal, casual violence toward the dragon she rode. The infinite dragon was no dominated beast of burden, but a willing ally provided by Kairoz. She leaned to the left, and the dragon, the membranes of his wings the pleasant color of the metal of guns, banked and brought her alongside Harrowmeiser's somewhat repaired zeppelin.

"Is your jolly crew ready?" She shouted to be heard over the rattling noise.

The goblin glanced over his shoulder at his shipload of pirates, all of whom bristled with weapons, and gave Zaela a thumbs-up. Some of the pirates had initially wanted to slaughter Harrowmeiser, but the promise of gold had mollified them. "Yeah, though some of 'em don't quite trust the chutes. I am deeply offended. Shokia's in position in the bow, ready to pick off stragglers and key targets, and Thalen is in the stern prepared to do the same. So"—and he pointed to the ball and chain that still encircled each foot—"when can these come off?"

Zaela threw back her head and laughed, freely, joyfully. To think that she was lost in despair but a few days ago!

"You will dance at our victory celebration, goblin. I promise you!"

"I better—I've sunk a lot of money into this venture," Harrowmeiser said.

"I will go on ahead and see if Kairoz has been successful!" she shouted, and again, with just a squeeze of her right thigh, the dragon banked and resumed course. She heard Harrowmeiser's fading voice yelping, "Hey, hey, don't *touch* that—no, no, don't *drink* it, for the love of . . . !"

Though there had been no means to create another mana weapon even approaching the power of the one that had reduced the once-proud Alliance city to a sinkhole, Thalen had managed to craft several dozen smaller ones. Exploiting their newfound respect for one another to the fullest, Harrowmeiser had rigged some of Thalen's mana grenades with random timers. They would appear to be duds, only to explode erratically and, hopefully, at the worst possible moment. Each dragon rider was equipped with at least two or three, and they would boost morale with each victim they claimed. Zaela could see the temple now. It spread out before her, its serenity about to be rudely interrupted. Its bridges, walkways, and little pagodas were filled with pandaren; its center arena, with the enemies of Garrosh Hellscream.

She led the flight, bringing her mount down closer. He knew what to do. Folding his wings, he dove, and she clung to him like a burr on a wolf. He jerked his head sharply and exhaled a dark tornado of scouring breath down upon the cluster of pandaren merchants who were pointing skyward and shouting.

Zaela howled her delight. Kairoz, as he had assured her he would, had removed the dampening field. She reached into her pouch and drew out a tiny sphere. The leader of the Dragonmaw threw her first mana grenade, and grinned at the small lavender explosion.

Anduin blinked, peering through a haze of pain. He heard Chromie calling his name, and other sounds coming from above—more than just the shouting he had heard before. He couldn't quite identify the clamor, and gingerly touched the back of his head. He hissed as the pain shot up by several degrees. He felt a lump about the size of an egg, and his hand came away red. The din continued, and abruptly comprehension clicked into place.

He recognized the clash of steel and the sharp song of magic. Anduin was suddenly overcome with a wave of nausea that had nothing to do with his injury. Because of him, Garrosh had gone into the hall wearing only the lightest of restraints. *If he hurts anyone, it's my fault.*

"Anduin?"

"I'm all right, Lo," he lied, nearly blacking out again from the act of simply sitting upright. He was drained from healing the Chu brothers and didn't have much strength left, but he asked the Light for aid, and the pain subsided to merely excruciating. "I gotta get up there . . . stop Kairoz. I'll send someone down for you and Chromie."

"You are too injured to join a fight," Li said firmly.

Not when I'm responsible for it, Anduin thought despairingly, but did not say. Ignoring their protests, he got up the stairs through an effort of sheer will, and when he stumbled through the door, he wondered if he was hallucinating.

He recognized the combatants, and at the same time, they were strangers: The blue-skinned troll with a necklace made of human and elven ears, who cackled as he tried to add more to his collection. The mighty tauren, wielding a massive mace, who wore a warchief's armor . . .

And the golden-haired human boy in the coronation robes of a king of Stormwind, who huddled on the ground, knees pulled tightly to his chest, frozen with horror. He clutched, ironically enough, Fearbreaker.

Wrathion's words rushed back to him: *"I worry you may be too soft to wear your kingdom's crown, Prince Anduin."* In another timeway, at least, the double-crossing dragon had been right. Anduin's paralysis broke and he rushed toward the other boy, his hand outstretched, when the young king of Stormwind yelped, "Behind you!" and covered his head.

Anduin darted to his left and tumbled, tedious hours of hand-to-hand combat training instinctively kicking in, and he heard the whizzing sound of a glaive barely missing him. He sprang to his feet and whirled to see the huge troll leering at him.

"Ya be quick, little prince, but I be wearin' yah ears just da same," said Vol'jin.

Anduin stared at the gigantic troll as he straightened to his full height, glaive raised. The prince dove toward the other Anduin, grabbed Fearbreaker from his grasp, and swung the mace upward. A brilliant yellow light shone from it, making Vol'jin grunt in pain.

That pause gave Anduin enough time to swing Fearbreaker in a smooth, almost leisurely arc, and for a wild moment it seemed as if the mace was moving itself. Its silver head struck the troll's left side. The leather armor prevented the blow from being a deadly one, but Anduin felt ribs give beneath it nonetheless.

Vol'jin stumbled, grunting, and turned a cruel face toward Anduin. "For dat, you gonna suffer, little prince," he promised. "Bwonsamdi gonna have to wait a little while for ya spirit!"

He came at Anduin like a madman, shrieking in his own guttural language, and Anduin realized to his horror that the troll wasn't going for a kill, but reaching out for his right ear.

Crying out incoherently, Anduin brought up Fearbreaker, the glowing mace again saving his life by knocking the glaive away from his face. Vol'jin countered at once, getting in a blow to Anduin's unarmored shoulder that made the prince stagger backward. Fearbreaker fell from his fingers. He clapped a hand over the bleeding wound and looked up just in time to see Vol'jin draw back for the killing blow . . .

And then stumble, a shocked look on his tusked, white-painted face, as young King Anduin launched himself at Vol'jin.

It was futile, of course.

Vol'jin recovered at once, twisting and easily throwing off the slight King Anduin as a dog might shake off a rat. Almost brusquely, the troll stabbed the youth in the chest, pulled out the dripping glaive, and bent to slice off the human's ears.

A giant golden claw descended from nowhere, grasped Vol'jin, and hurled him across the arena. Chromie brought her huge head down to Anduin. "Are you all right?"

He was fine, and he was dying, and he didn't know how to respond. Anduin went to his other self, hoping somehow he would be in time. Quickly he murmured a prayer and the wound stopped bleeding, but he could tell by the king's chalky face that death had been only delayed, not averted.

"He leaped on Vol'jin without even a weapon," Prince Anduin said, his voice rough. "He saved my life." He peered at Chromie, as if seeing her for the first time.

"You got out," Anduin said stupidly. "I forgot. I'm sorry." He cradled the king, feeling warm blood seeping out onto his shirt. Vol'jin's glaive had gone all the way through.

"Guards found us," she said. "I must do everything I can to destabilize this rift. It's the only way to send them all back."

It was quite surreal, Anduin thought, to be holding yourself as you died. "What do you need me to do?" He couldn't seem to tear his gaze away from that pale, still face . . . *his* face . . .

"You are doing it," Chromie said, with infinite kindness. "Acceptance will help their reality in this place grow tenuous. It's easy for you to accept your alternate. The others," she said, lifting her great head and looking about at the violence, "will have a harder time."

She changed into gnome form, scurrying to the broken shards of the Vision of Time, which still lay on the floor, and began to cast a spell. Anduin returned his gaze to the king, who was looking up at him with oddly peaceful blue eyes.

"You're . . . all right," said the king.

"Yes, I am," the prince said. "You saved me."

"I . . . did?" The voice was softer now, but the king looked pleased. He chuckled, then winced in pain. "I was so scared . . . I couldn't do anything, just watch him—"

"But you did," Anduin interrupted him gently. "When it counted—you came through."

The king fell silent, then said, "'s cold in here."

Anduin gathered the boy tighter, careful of his wound. "I've got you."

The fighting continued, but it felt dim and far away to Anduin. There was another long pause, and Anduin thought that perhaps it was over. Then the king said, so softly Anduin had to strain to hear, "I'm afraid . . ."

Anduin swallowed hard. "Don't be," he said. "You'll be with Mother and—and Father."

"Is . . . Father alive? Here?"

"Yes, yes he is."

The dying Anduin closed his eyes. "I'm glad. I wish I could see him."

"You will. Just—hang on, all right?"

A ghost of a smile. "You're as bad a liar as I am." The smile faded. "Tell him I love him."

"I will."

The king sighed softly, and his chest did not rise again. His skin grew pale, paler than it should be from the simple but solemn touch of death. To Anduin's surprise, the king's body began to emit a soft, pure radiance, and then it dimmed.

King Anduin Wrynn had gone home.

Slowly, Prince Anduin Wrynn stumbled to his feet, grasped Fearbreaker, dragged a sleeve against his wet face, and started to heal those still locked in battle.

36

Guards rushed in carrying weapons. One pandaren tossed a small axe toward Baine. The tauren caught it smoothly in one hand as he ran toward the two Thralls locked in combat. He was grateful Go'el was clad in shamanic clothing, for there was nothing visually different about these two other than what they wore and what they wielded. Just as he reached them, he found himself frozen in midstride and struggled to keep his balance. He heard the bellow of draconic laughter and glanced up to see the mad Kalecgos grinning at him. This incarnation of the blue dragon was quite insane; it was the only reason there were not more dead inside the arena. He appeared to be targeting friend and foe alike, and had nothing resembling a battle strategy.

His counterpart did, though, and charged his other self, drawing the mad Kalecgos's attention away from Baine. The two orcs fought on, but the other Thrall appeared to have the disadvantage. *Of course*, Baine thought. The alternate Thrall never had the chance to undergo shamanic training, whereas Go'el was a master shaman in addition to his battle experience.

Baine had almost gotten to the two when he sensed more than saw the attack. He barely turned in time to deflect the blow from the huge mace wielded by what seemed like an armored mountain come to deceptively quick life, and he stared into his own eyes. His other self seemed surprised, and backed off for a moment, long enough for Baine to remember that he was clad only in light clothing, while his alternate was in full armor.

Out of the corner of his eye, Baine noticed that the celestials had not moved, and he became furious. Could they not see that people were dying? Were they too "high above" it all to help?

At that moment, as if they had heard his thoughts, a shout went up, piercing through the haze and cacophony of battle. It was a strong voice, deep and rich and now coming from a tiger's jaws, as much a plea as a warning, the voice of he whose temple this was—Xuen.

"Remember the sha! *Remember the sha!*"

And suddenly Baine understood.

These alternate selves he, Go'el, and others were battling—they were not random incarnations. Kairoz had deliberately selected the darkest, the most broken, the most bellicose versions he could find. Kalecgos was insane. Thrall was the champion of the hated Aedelas Blackmoore. Baine himself was the warchief of the Horde, and somehow he knew the other had gained that position by murdering Garrosh Hellscream to avenge his own Cairne Bloodhoof.

No wonder the celestials did not join the fray. Anything they did would do nothing more than add fuel to the fire.

"You killed Garrosh, didn't you?" he asked his other self. "Because he killed our father."

The other Baine's eyes narrowed and he snarled. "I tore Hellscream apart with my own hands," he said, "and the bronze dragon tells me you—you *defended* him!" With a bellow, he charged, but Baine parried, his axe's blade clanging against the head of the mace. Baine's own words came back to him, sharp and clear as any of the draenei's crystals: *"We all carry within us the potential to become our own versions of Garrosh Hellscream."*

Wisdom—the gift of Yu'lon. "This is what we all could be! They're not the enemy; they're *us!*" he shouted to the crowd. "We cannot fight them. Only accept them!"

A sudden certainty flooded Baine: fortitude, bestowed by Niuzao. Baine's arm felt stronger as he deflected another blow. The more he opened to what the celestials were trying to tell him, the more he could accept their gifts.

Again the other Baine attacked, and this time the mace struck his counterpart's shoulder. Baine grunted, but did not retaliate.

"Is my other self a coward?" shouted Warchief Baine.

"No," Baine said. "We are the same. You chose another path, Baine. But I understand how you felt—why you wanted to kill Garrosh."

"You lie, else you would have done the same." And the other bull charged. This time, though, his anger made him careless. Baine got in a blow—but used the blunt end of his small axe.

"I will not harm you," he panted, "but I will defend myself!"

Warchief Baine hesitated. He was listening—but who knew for how long?

Yu'lon's wisdom again brushed the tauren's heart, and he knew all at once what he needed to say, how he could reach his wounded, pained self. Baine spoke quickly. "Our friend Go'el, known perhaps to you as Thrall, told me that even in another timeline, we are always ourselves at our core. And our father, Cairne, believed that it was harder, but better, to—"

"—create something that lasts," murmured the warchief.

And Baine felt hope.

Kalec knew that of all the out-of-time combatants, his doppelganger posed the greatest threat. Not only was he a dragon, but the alternate Kalecgos was clearly quite insane.

And that terrified him.

Only Kalec knew how close he had skirted madness born of deep grief when Anveena had died; only Jaina knew how he had almost lost himself while reliving the dawn of the Aspects through the eyes of Malygos, himself lost to insanity. This alternate timeline version was far, far too possible.

Baine's words reached him, but how could he ever accept *this*? Even as he had the despairing thought, the blue dragon dove and lashed his tail, scattering a huddled crowd of onlookers. Some of them did not rise.

"No!" shouted Kalec. He blasted Kalecgos with ice, slowing the great dragon, but not stopping him. Kalecgos swiveled his head and laughed and sobbed.

"Why not?" he pleaded. "Let them hate me. Let them finish me! *Please!*"

Kalec had had his dark moments. But he had never felt what the dragon before him was feeling. "What happened? What could have done this to you?" he asked, his voice breaking, even as he dreaded the answer.

"They're gone. All of them!"

They were talking, at least. Kalecgos, for this moment, was not killing. "Who is gone?" Kalec asked.

"*All of them!*" bellowed Kalecgos. "Anveena! Jaina . . . all the blues, *all* of them, even Kirygosa—"

"*What?*"

"After Orgrimmar fell, they died in the war—all except me . . . all *because* of me. I couldn't stop her, and they're all gone now . . ."

Kalec couldn't believe it—except, horrified, he could. This broken Kalecgos had not been able to dissuade his timeway's Jaina from destroying Orgrimmar, and the war that ensued had wiped out the entire blue dragonflight. For a moment, Kalec could do nothing but reel at the shock, and felt the brush of madness himself. Then, his thoughts cleared, and he understood how to reach Kalecgos.

"It's not your fault," he said. "Jaina made the choice, and she chose not to listen to you, or to Go'el." Clarity filled him as he spoke the words, realizing exactly how true they were. How could he himself not have seen this?

"I should have stopped her!"

"She is not yours to command!" Kalec cried. "She is her own woman! I am so sorry, Kalecgos, so very sorry for what you have lost, but this is not your burden!"

"So easy for you to say such things! *Your* Jaina lives! She loves you!" Kalecgos shouted, then hesitated. "She . . . does, doesn't she?"

Kalec's chest ached at the question. "She does. But she still walks under a shadow. And only she can make the choice to step away from it. Don't you see?" Kalec implored. "We're the same. We did the same thing. The difference lay in what *Jaina* chose to do. Not in anything *you* did or didn't do."

Kalecgos looked stunned. "And . . . Anveena?"

The other he had once loved with his whole heart. "She chose, too."

Kalecgos did not instantly return to sanity with his comprehension. But he paused, and his face relaxed as his expression turned contemplative.

And then, he was gone.

With mixed feelings, Varian realized he was looking forward to the coming battle. The trial had been more of an ordeal than he had expected, and he welcomed the chance to do something physical, useful, and unequivocally right.

He paid little attention as spectators came tumbling out of the arena and the monks sorted them into two groups—those that could fight, and those that needed to be kept out of the fighting. The monks swiftly began to usher the noncombatants down the steps from the flagstone courtyard, toward the grassy training area and then over the bridge. Most of them seemed terrified. He couldn't blame them, if what—who—he suspected was coming was indeed on its way. It had to be the Dragonmaw. Who else would storm the temple on the final day of Garrosh Hellscream's trial?

It would be a long, harrowing race to safety—if there could truly be any. The temple was largely undefended from the air. It was a place to train to fight, where strength was appreciated—but it was strength of the body and the will, not magic or engines of war. This, he thought, was Pandaria's greatest weakness, and in a way, what made it so special.

He was willing to die to protect it.

Those who had brought flying beasts took to the skies, ferrying hunters, magi, shaman, and others. Varian didn't know if these spellcasters would even be able to attack. He had no sensitivity to magic, and thus couldn't himself tell if the dampening field had been removed. The sound of wings came nearer. Varian tensed. If the hunters were good at their job, they'd kill some right away, or at least knock off a few of the Dragonmaw. Once riderless, the proto-drakes would flee if they could.

He stood beside the brazier in the courtyard, adjusted his grip on the two-handed sword, and shifted his weight to the balls of his feet. Battle lust was rising in him, and he invited it. Beside him were several pandaren monks, whose names he didn't know. They appeared tranquil, but Varian knew that they were ready for the fight.

Their enemies were small dots at first, drawing closer and closer. Varian squinted. "The silhouettes," he said to the pandaren. "It's hard to tell from this distance, but . . . they look wrong."

"What do you mean?" one asked.

"The Dragonmaw orcs ride proto-drakes, not dragons, not anymore. And these . . ." The words died in his throat.

"Are dragons," the pandaren finished. "Therefore, they *do* still ride dragons."

A terrible suspicion began to grow in Varian. No more black dragons, surely. And the twilight dragonflight was gone as well . . . "Inside—what happened?"

"I was given no clear explanation, but I was told something went wrong with the Vision of Time."

Varian swore. "The infinite dragonflight," he said. "My pandaren friends . . . we are in trouble."

At that moment, the leader's dragon dove, breathing a black cloud of swirling sand. The field was down! A brutal grin twisted Varian's lips. "Things just got more even," Varian said.

"Even? They have dragons!" protested the pandaren.

"And *we* have warlocks!" A cheer went up as several people from all different races began casting summoning spells. Felhounds— ugly, red, spined creatures from the depths of the Twisting Nether— shimmered into being. Nearby, a human warlock, a woman whose young face belied her white hair, bent to absently stroke the beast, calling it a "good puppy." These particular demons fed on magic, Varian recalled. He found himself grinning, and the lovely young woman who dealt so affectionately with demons gave him a wink.

Magi began hurtling fireballs, ice shards, and missiles of arcane energy. The Dragonmaw leader threw something down several yards away. A small globe of violet-white light encircled the area, with the incongruous beauty of an opalescent bubble. Varian knew what it must be, and the appalling proof became evident a moment later. Three corpses lay sprawled on the flagstones, their bodies turned purple with the arcane energy of the mana grenade. Others recognized it too, and panic again began to ripple through the crowd.

Righteous fury rose in Varian. "Bring them down!" he shouted to the spellcasters. "Get them on the ground where the rest of us can have a piece of them!"

His words heartened the spellcasters, who began their attacks anew. One or two of the orcs tumbled from their mounts, hurtling to crash into the waters below if they were lucky, to break on the stone if not. One Forsaken mage sent a solid, powerful fireball to burn clear through an infinite dragon's membranous wing. The dragon cried out in pain, flapping erratically and finally crashing to the ground in front of the main temple steps, where those without magic fell upon it mercilessly.

But other dragons came. Over a dozen flew in a V-formation over the temple and its environs. Powerful wing beats knocked dozens off their feet. Varian, rushing toward a downed and injured orc, moved as if he were trying to run through mud. He heard the sharp sting of arrows and hissed as one of them found its target, piercing his shoulder. He wore no armor. No one did. They had been attending a trial, not preparing for a battle. He was lucky; a nearby orc shaman collapsed, a black-fletched arrow in his throat.

Arrows weren't the only things that the Dragonmaw used as missiles. Two more mana grenades struck, sending up their unholy globes of instant arcane death, and now their own magi were raining down fire and ice.

The dragons banked and turned upward, veering off from their strafing run, and now a goblin zeppelin chugged into position. For a brief, awful instant, Varian thought that somehow the Dragonmaw had cobbled together another true mana bomb like the one that had obliterated Theramore, but the zeppelin appeared to be carrying no payload. Then why—

Dozens of figures leaped off the flying vessel, their parachutes blossoming behind them. The hunters and the spellcasters needed no urging from him to attack the incoming enemy. Many would be dead by the time they hit the ground. But not all.

The arrow had lodged where his left arm joined his shoulder, and the pain was white hot. Varian left the arrow in rather than risk pulling it out, ignoring the wound's shriek of protest as he lifted his two-handed sword and started charging the parachutists, incredulity and dark pleasure filling him as he realized that the Dragonmaw had hired not only mercenaries as cannon fodder, but pirates at that.

"You're making this fun, Dragonmaw!" he shouted defiantly, and charged the first pirate. Still struggling out of the parachute, he was an easy kill, but others had gotten free and now converged on Varian. The king's blood was hot, and he swung the great broadsword as if it were a child's toy, decapitating the troll who came at him with a cutlass and following through to cleave the black-haired human woman almost in two. The mammoth tauren, no less fierce for the fact that he had one eye, was more of a challenge. Varian harnessed his momentum and twisted his torso, bringing the blade upward and slicing off the tauren's right arm.

But the left had a weapon too, and this one bit deep into Varian's side. Dizziness filled him and he stumbled back, abruptly unable to lift the sword to defend himself. But the blow never came. Something even bigger than the tauren, gray-skinned and wearing red and yellow armor, rushed forward. With a single slice, the tauren's horned head was cleanly separated from his body. The felguard fixed Varian with tiny, glowing eyes and rumbled, "Your fate will be the same."

Varian couldn't summon the energy for a witty retort. He blinked, trying to focus. His legs gave way and he fell to his knees, wondering if perhaps the felguard had been right.

Gentle hands touched him. There was an abrupt sear of agony as the arrow was tugged from his shoulder, replaced immediately by warmth and a sense of well-being. He gave a grateful look to the night elf priestess, a slip of a thing with long, dark purple hair and lavender skin. She ducked her head shyly and turned, lifting her hands in supplication to pray for the white-haired warlock whose felguard had saved his life.

Varian rushed again into the fray, launching at a cluster of five pirates who were ganging up on a young orc shaman. Together, he and the orc defeated the pirates, nodded in acknowledgment, and looked for more enemies.

Shadows again passed over them. Varian expected another attack, but this time, seven dragons wheeled away from the immediate area of the temple. For a moment he wondered why, and then he knew. They were heading for the bridges. Almost nonchalantly, a dragon struck at one with a massive tail, snapping the ropes and sending the pandaren reinforcements unlucky enough to be crossing hurtling to their deaths. Another grabbed the ropes of a second bridge in a great foreclaw and simply yanked.

Everyone who had not already reached safety was now stranded in the courtyard and training ground.

More pirates dropped from the sky. Varian had thought that they had been sent to occupy the guards outside, but now he saw that while some of them were engaged in combat, most of them were heading for the temple interior.

His son was in there. Growling under his breath, Varian took off in that direction. He heard the crack of rifle fire and then felt as though his left side had been hit by a hammer. Grimacing as pain followed almost at once, Varian pressed a hand over the wound and kept going. But before he covered more than a few yards, an enormous shadow fell over him. Varian stopped in his tracks, whipping up the broadsword.

"Zaela!" he grunted in disbelief.

She was crouched atop the great infinite dragon, grinning maniacally, an axe in her hands. "King Varian Wrynn! I free my warchief and take your head all in one day!"

"Come get it then!" he shouted. Springing into action and ignoring the increasingly sharp, white-hot agony of the bullet wound, he leaped up as high as he could, seized her ankle, and yanked her off the dragon.

She had not been expecting that, and landed badly. Her dragon had to veer and rise abruptly or risk slamming into the temple wall. If Varian had been wielding a smaller sword, that would have been the end of her, but he had to pull back to use the broadsword. As he did so, Zaela snarled, bit his ungloved hand, and wrapped one leg around his. He didn't fall, but he stumbled. The orc warlord scrambled to her feet and raised her more maneuverable axe, about to bring it down on his midsection.

She screamed as a blast of fire exploded into her.

Still on the flagstone, Varian turned to see Jaina Proudmoore, her extended hands already forming the motions to make a more lethal spell, a fireball beginning to manifest between her palms. A crack rang out and Jaina twitched, her eyes going wide, the nascent fireball suddenly snuffed out as red began to blossom across her chest.

"Jaina!" Varian shouted.

Stumbling, her torso scorched, Zaela began to lurch down the corridor into the temple. Varian could still catch her, still kill the orc and end any threat she would ever pose. But he did not follow.

Others would stop her, or not. But someone needed his help more than he needed to kill.

Varian reached instead for Jaina.

37

Despite the excruciating pain of the burns along her torso, Zaela dearly wished she had the time to spare to take Varian Wrynn's head, as she had promised. Garrosh would no doubt have displayed the trophy to loud cheering, and she, Zaela, would be the one who had scored the kill. More important than her ego was to make sure that Garrosh had been able to escape cleanly, and at first, when she entered the temple, it was impossible to tell. It was a battlefield condensed into a small, confined arena. She saw at least one blue and one bronze dragon hovering over the fray, doing what they could to attack the enemy without harming their allies. A few of the smaller infinites had actually come into the temple, and they had no such restrictions. Elsewhere, the pirates were shouting joyfully as they gave vent to their bloodlust, pausing in their slaughter only long enough to rifle through the pockets and pouches of the fallen—friend or foe.

Zaela's nostrils flared with contempt. She did not charge into the fight, though her racing heart longed to do so. Instead, gritting her teeth against the agony of her burns, she threaded through the combatants, searching for her warchief. There was no sign of the mighty Garrosh, or the slender high elf his time-walking friend had pretended to be, and joy flooded her. Her mission was now both successful and complete. There was no more need to linger here.

"My Dragonmaw!" she shouted, lifting her gore-stained axe without revealing the pain the action caused. "The infinites await us outside, to bear us to safety and victory! Leave the pirates to their fate!"

A cheer went up among her people, and she took pleasure in the look of betrayal on the stupid faces of their onetime allies. Fools. Not one of them had ever asked how they would be leaving the battle. They would now either die or rot in prison. They would not be missed—by anyone.

It seemed to end as soon as it began. The pirates, somehow taken by surprise at Zaela's casual abandonment of them, were quickly rounded up and turned over to the pandaren. More frustrating was the escape of most of the Dragonmaw on the backs of the infinite dragons. Those that remained behind either were already dead or fell within minutes.

Once the fighting was over, Go'el searched for Aggra. He found her holding their child, standing over the corpses of three pirates who had apparently been foolish enough to attack her. She appeared tired, probably, Go'el thought, from healing as well as fighting. Aggra turned to him as he approached. Go'el wrapped mate and child both in his powerful arms.

"You have fought against yourself ere now, my heart," Aggra said as she stepped back to gaze up at him fondly. "But always before, it has been more . . . metaphorical."

His eyes were somber as he looked at her. "I pray to the ancestors to never have to do so again." To have seen himself as Blackmoore's obedient pawn had been unnerving. He had struggled to accept this part of himself, per Baine's wise words, instead of killing this Thrall—a thrall in every sense of the word. And in the end, it was the name that enabled him to do so. He had been Thrall, and so he understood what he had left behind; this orc had never known he could become Go'el. It seemed as though all the others had also won their difficult personal battles.

"Go'el!" The voice was Varian's, but weakened and hoarse. Go'el turned and his blue eyes widened in horror.

Jaina . . .

Varian, himself bleeding from several wounds, staggered in, carrying the archmage's frighteningly limp body. He made it a few more steps before his legs buckled, but he did not drop his precious burden. Go'el was there, cradling Jaina and lowering her with care to the ground. Aggra handed the baby to Eitrigg and followed Go'el.

"She has lost a great deal of blood," Aggra said, but even so, her brown hands were reaching into her ever-present pouch of totems. Go'el imitated her, grasping the totem for water and asking for its healing touch, but he felt hope slipping away with every breath. There appeared to be only the single bullet wound, but it was close to her heart, and he was drained. There was a waxy pallor to Jaina's skin, and Go'el couldn't even see if her chest rose and fell.

Varian snarled as others tried to help him. "I'll be all right," he said, grimacing. "Her first."

"Jaina!" Anduin pushed his way through, his heart on his young face. He dropped his knees beside the woman he called "aunt." Without hesitation and with utmost care, he covered the wound with his hands. A dim glow began to suffuse them, and the red-saturated fabric made a soft, squishy noise.

Go'el could not feel the elements responding. His call to them was too weak. He had struggled against himself and against other foes, and both he and Aggra were exhausted. So too was the young prince, as was evidenced by the dark circles under his eyes and the slump of his shoulders. Even Tyrande, who prayed to her Mother Moon in a voice that trembled, and Velen, ancient and wise as he was, appeared to have arrived too late.

Kalec raced up, his face almost as pale as Jaina's, as the archmage exhaled a red, frothy bubble. The dragon fell to his knees, taking her face between his hands. "Jaina," he whispered. "Don't. Don't go. You've faced so much more than this. You're so strong, Jaina. You hang on. Do you hear me? *Hang on!*"

"Jaina," Anduin urged. "Please . . . please, don't leave us. I already watched myself die today. I can't watch you too . . ." Tears poured down his face, and even as he uttered the words, the Light faded.

Her chest barely rose and fell. A few more breaths and she would be gone. Go'el's friend for so long would be lost to him forever. There would be no chance to repair what had been damaged. Jaina would have died his enemy, and Go'el could think of nothing worse than that. Unable to speak, he gently placed a hand on Aggra's shoulder, interrupting her spell. She looked at him, and he shook his head. Her face contorted, not with her own pain, but with empathy for her mate, and she embraced Go'el fiercely.

Anduin lifted his hands. They were drenched with Jaina's blood. Beside him, Kalec had gone very still. He looked stunned, utterly disbelieving.

"Anduin," said Varian, in the gentlest tone Go'el had ever heard from him, "come away. There's nothing you can do."

Even those who had opposed Jaina seemed shaken. There was no expression of glee or triumph on any face, just shock that one who was so legendary, so much bigger than life to so many, was still subject to its rules.

"No," Anduin whispered. "I can't . . ."

"And so, the student remembers the lessons of my temple," came a voice that was at once young and ancient, eager and solemn, and unspeakably kind. "Hope is what you have when all other things have failed you. Where there is hope, you make room for healing, for all things that are possible—and some that are not."

Go'el looked up to see Chi-Ji, the Red Crane, hovering in the air above them. The wind from his wings was cool, so refreshing after the heat of battle and the warmth of tears. It smelled of spring, and new beginnings, of life and hope. The orc's aching heart eased, and filled instead with peace. The bruises to body and spirit, the wounds and hurts both great and little, melted away like snow beneath the sun. Calmness and contentment settled upon him, and when he looked down at Jaina, the bleeding had ceased and the archmage's flesh was once again glowing with health. Jaina opened her eyes, looking at the sea of faces—human, dragon, orc, and so many others—gazing at her with wonderment and joy. She reached for Kalec, and he pressed her hand to his cheek.

To Anduin, she said in a voice still somewhat weak, "You're getting pretty good at this." The prince laughed shakily. Kalecgos gathered her in his arms, holding her tightly and pressing his face into the soft crook of her neck for a moment. Go'el realized that Jaina looked . . . happy. Perhaps she had been healed in more than body, and he wondered how she had been able to accept her raging alternate self. He supposed he would never know. Their eyes met, and he smiled at her. And when she stretched out a hand to him, he took it. She squeezed it once and let go. Elsewhere, others too were rising, hale and whole and looking not a little bewildered.

"Thus is the blessing of Chi-Ji," the crane said. "No more shall die this day. Take this second chance, and use it wisely."

"I thank you, Red Crane," Varian said, and he bowed deeply. He turned to look at Chromie. "Garrosh is gone. It was Kairoz, wasn't it? How did that happen?"

Chromie looked as angry and defeated as Go'el had ever seen her. Pale, her brown and golden tabard spattered with blood and dust from the Sands of Time, she addressed them.

"We once knew the timeways inside and out," she began. "We could see the past and the future with perfect clarity. Our flight's charge, from the moment Nozdormu became our Aspect, was to protect the sanctity of the timeline. And we were given vast power to do this. Now . . . things aren't quite so clear. We can still travel the timeways, but we don't have that perfect knowledge anymore.

That's why we've enlisted mortals to help us keep the timeline safe. But there have been some mutterings. Some of us think that perhaps we should use what skills we have left to manipulate the time-ways. Alter the past, change the future to something better."

She smiled sadly. "Of course, who's to say what is 'better'? Especially when we don't have the perfect insight we once did. That's what's held most of us back. But it's obvious now that Kairoz was among those who thought that the bronze dragons could and should change things. He always did like to tinker . . ." Her voice trailed off.

"How could this have happened? You told us that the Vision of Time had limited abilities," Tyrande said. It was clear that she was trying not to attack Chromie, who was obviously as devastated—perhaps more so—as they were, but the high priestess was extremely frustrated and angry. "That it could only show images of things past or future, not manifest them or alter them in any way."

"That was true until this morning," Chromie said. "Nozdormu was adamant about that. But the Vision of Time was Kairoz's creation. He must have constructed it with a way to bypass the safety measures."

Varian frowned and looked at Go'el. They both remembered finding Kairoz's behavior odd. "He did it this morning," Varian said. "Right out in the open, in front of us all. He's a bold one, I'll give him that."

"Wrathion's in on it," Anduin said. "He was the one who knocked out me and the Chus."

An uneasy silence settled on everyone. Vol'jin broke it. "So now we got a high and mighty bronze dragon inventor, the last black dragon, and the son of Hellscream all working together, and we don't even be knowing where or *when* to look for 'em." He shook his head.

Go'el turned his attention to the celestials. Other than Chi-Ji, they had remained silent and somewhat distant. "You did not join us during our fight against ourselves physically, but you granted us the gifts of insight. I understand why you did not do more," he said. "And all of us are grateful beyond words to you, Chi-Ji, for the life of Jaina and others. But I would have thought you would be more"— he strained for the word—"distressed that Garrosh is gone, since it was your duty to pronounce sentence."

"August Celestials, please sate this pandaren's curiosity," said Taran Zhu. "Do you know what verdict you would have rendered?"

"Indeed we do," rumbled Niuzao. "We knew from the very beginning."

Everyone stared at the celestials. Go'el struggled against his anger, and Tyrande looked stunned.

"And . . . what would you have decided?" asked Taran Zhu.

"Garrosh Hellscream would live, so that he would continue to learn," said Yu'lon, undulating her graceful green form. "Dear ones, wisdom, fortitude, strength, and hope cannot be learned in death."

"Life is not about reward and punishment," said Xuen. "It is about understanding, accepting who oneself is right now, in order to know what to change, and how."

"We feel that justice has been done," said the Black Ox, stamping a hoof and shaking his shaggy, gleaming head.

"Then why have a trial at all?" demanded Tyrande. "If you knew at the outset what his sentence would be at the end of it? Were you simply toying with us?"

Yu'lon said, very gently, "Never, passionate Accuser. Your efforts were vital to the outcome of the trial. You see . . . It was not merely Garrosh Hellscream who was on trial." For a moment, Go'el did not understand. Then comprehension dawned.

"We were too," he said. He was surprised that he was not furious at having been manipulated, but a deeper part of him, a wiser part—the part that blended with the Spirit of Life—completely accepted it. He saw in the faces of the others—tauren, human, troll, elf, even dragon—that they did as well.

Chi-Ji bobbed his head. "The young prince and the tauren Defender grasped it earliest. But now, all of you understand. You have been judged and sentenced both. With all of our blessings, and the knowledge you have obtained of your own hearts and minds and those of others, your task is to go back into the world and do what you must."

They looked at each other. Varian, fit and strong, with one hand on his son's shoulder. Kalecgos and Jaina, their fingers entwined. Tyrande and Baine, Accuser and Defender, standing side by side. Vol'jin, nodding and looking thoughtful. Chromie, and Lor'themar, and so very many others.

Go'el was no longer in a position of leadership among them. Even so, he found that all of these faces eventually turned toward him. Humbly, Go'el, son of Durotan and Draka, spoke for them all.

"We will find Garrosh."

Epilogue

Garrosh stepped out of the timeways portal, Kairoz at his side. "What do you think?" asked the bronze dragon. He looked extremely pleased with himself, as well he might be.

Garrosh didn't answer at once. He stood, feeling the soft wind caress his skin, and gazed at the rolling green hills of Nagrand. He planted his feet in the waving grass, and felt a healthy, strong earth beneath them.

"This is not my home," he murmured, squinting up at the sun. "This is not my sky."

"Yes, and no," said Kairoz. "You are home, Garrosh Hellscream. But no . . . This is not the sky you grew up with."

A herd of clefthoof thundered past, not too far in the distance, strong, glossy-coated beasts. This was where his people were born. He saw the same earth, the same sky, that his father had. This was the gift of the bronze dragon—a world that was no more, but that could become . . . anything.

"Hellscream!" shouted a rough, orcish voice.

Garrosh started at the sound of his name, thinking that somehow his allies must have followed him and Kairoz.

"Who—" he began, but Kairoz, his smirk more mischievous than ever, simply pointed. Utterly confused, Garrosh turned his head.

The call was for another Hellscream.

Standing atop a hill, wind blowing through his black hair and sun gleaming on his muscular brown body, a fierce, tattooed orc whose blood ran in Garrosh's veins replied to the greeting with an ear-splitting cry, and raised—

—Gorehowl.

ACKNOWLEDGMENTS

I would like to acknowledge, as ever, the truly astounding folks at Blizzard who make my work so joyful and nurture the projects all along the way: Chris Metzen, Micky Neilson, Dave Kosak, Jerry Chu, Sean Copeland, Matt Burns, Cate Gary, and Joshua Horst.

NOTES

The story you've just read is based in part on characters, situations, and locations from Blizzard Entertainment's computer game *World of Warcraft*, an online role-playing experience set in the award-winning Warcraft universe. In *World of Warcraft*, players create their own heroes and explore, adventure in, and quest across a vast world shared with thousands of other players. This rich and evolving game also allows them to interact with and fight against (or alongside) many of the powerful and intriguing characters featured in this novel.

Since launching in November 2004, *World of Warcraft* has become the world's most popular subscription-based massively multiplayer online role-playing game. The current expansion, *Mists of Pandaria*, takes players to a never-before-seen continent filled with new quests and adventures. More information about *Mists of Pandaria* and the upcoming expansion, *Warlords of Draenor*, can be found on WorldofWarcraft.com.

FURTHER READING

If you'd like to read more about the characters, situations, and settings featured in this novel, the sources listed below offer additional information on the story of Azeroth.

* Further details about former warchief Garrosh Hellscream can be found in issues #15–20 of the monthly *World of Warcraft* comic book by Walter and Louise Simonson, Jon Buran, Mike Bowden, Phil Moy, Walden Wong, and Pop Mhan; *World of Warcraft: The Shattering: Prelude to Cataclysm* and *World of Warcraft: Jaina Proudmoore: Tides of War* by Christie Golden; *World of Warcraft: Beyond the Dark Portal* by Aaron Rosenberg and Christie Golden; *World of Warcraft: Wolfheart* by Richard A. Knaak; *World of Warcraft: Vol'jin: Shadows of the Horde* by Michael A. Stackpole; and the short stories "Heart of War" by Sarah Pine, "As Our Fathers Before Us" by Steven Nix, and "Edge of Night" by Dave Kosak in *World of Warcraft: Paragons*.

* More information concerning High Chieftain Baine Bloodhoof, including his turbulent relationship with Garrosh Hellscream, is revealed in *World of Warcraft: The Shattering: Prelude to Cataclysm* and *World of Warcraft: Jaina Proudmoore: Tides of War* by Christie Golden; *World of Warcraft: Stormrage* by Richard A. Knaak; and the short story "As Our Fathers Before Us" by Steven Nix in *World of Warcraft: Paragons*.

* High Priestess Tyrande Whisperwind rises to a position of leadership among the night elves in *Warcraft: War of the Ancients Trilogy* by Richard A. Knaak. Other events in her life are portrayed in *World of Warcraft: Stormrage* by Richard A. Knaak; issue #6 of the monthly *World of Warcraft* comic book by Walter Simonson, Ludo Lullabi, and Sandra Hope; the *World of Warcraft: Curse of the Worgen* comic book by Micky Neilson and James Waugh, Ludo Lullabi, and Tony Washington; and the short story "Seeds of Faith" by Valerie Watrous in *World of Warcraft: Paragons*.

* Prince Anduin Wrynn possesses a unique ability to forge bonds with members of both the Alliance and the Horde. You can read more about his life in *World of Warcraft: The Shattering: Prelude to Cataclysm* and *World of Warcraft: Jaina Proudmoore: Tides of War* by Christie Golden; *World of Warcraft: Wolfheart* by Richard A. Knaak; the monthly *World of Warcraft* comic book by Walter and Louise Simonson, Ludo Lullabi, Jon Buran, Mike Bowden, Sandra Hope, and Tony Washington; and the short stories "Blood of Our Fathers" by E. Daniel Arey and "Prophet's Lesson" by Marc Hutcheson in *World of Warcraft: Paragons*.

* King Varian Wrynn's early years are depicted in *World of Warcraft: Arthas: Rise of the Lich King* by Christie Golden, *World of Warcraft: Tides of Darkness* by Aaron Rosenberg, and *World of Warcraft: Beyond the Dark Portal* by Aaron Rosenberg and Christie Golden. More recent events that have shaped his life can be found in the monthly *World of Warcraft* comic book by Walter and Louise Simonson, Ludo Lullabi, Jon Buran, Mike Bowden, Sandra Hope, and Tony Washington; *World of Warcraft: The Shattering: Prelude to Cataclysm* and *World of Warcraft: Jaina Proudmoore: Tides of War* by Christie Golden; *World of Warcraft: Stormrage* and *World of Warcraft: Wolfheart* by Richard A. Knaak; and the short story "Blood of Our Fathers" by E. Daniel Arey in *World of Warcraft: Paragons*.

* Lady Jaina Proudmoore's past is explored in the *World of Warcraft* comic book by Walter and Louise Simonson, Ludo Lullabi, Jon

Buran, Mike Bowden, Sandra Hope, and Tony Washington; *World of Warcraft: The Shattering: Prelude to Cataclysm*, *World of Warcraft: Jaina Proudmoore: Tides of War*, and *World of Warcraft: Arthas: Rise of the Lich King* by Christie Golden; *World of Warcraft: Cycle of Hatred* by Keith R.A. DeCandido; *World of Warcraft: Dawn of the Aspects* by Richard A. Knaak; and *Warcraft: Legends*, volume 5, "Nightmares" by Richard A. Knaak and Rob Ten Pas.

* Tales concerning Kalecgos and his past heroics are chronicled in *World of Warcraft: Night of the Dragon* and *World of Warcraft: Dawn of the Aspects* by Richard A. Knaak; *World of Warcraft: Thrall: Twilight of the Aspects* and *World of Warcraft: Jaina Proudmoore: Tides of War* by Christie Golden; *Warcraft: The Sunwell Trilogy* and *World of Warcraft: Shadow Wing*, volume 2, "Nexus Point" by Richard A. Knaak and Jae-Hwan Kim; and the short story "Charge of the Aspects" by Matt Burns (on www.WorldofWarcraft.com).

* The Banshee Queen, Sylvanas Windrunner, is featured in *Warcraft: The Sunwell Trilogy*, volume 3, "Ghostlands" by Richard A. Knaak and Jae-Hwan Kim; *World of Warcraft: Stormrage* by Richard A. Knaak; *World of Warcraft: Arthas: Rise of the Lich King* and *World of Warcraft: Jaina Proudmoore: Tides of War* by Christie Golden; and the short stories "In the Shadow of the Sun" by Sarah Pine and "Edge of Night" by Dave Kosak in *World of Warcraft: Paragons*.

* The earlier adventures of Go'el—also known as Thrall—are detailed in *Warcraft: Lord of the Clans*, *World of Warcraft: Thrall: Twilight of the Aspects*, *World of Warcraft: Jaina Proudmoore: Tides of War*, and *World of Warcraft: The Shattering: Prelude to Cataclysm* by Christie Golden; *World of Warcraft: Cycle of Hatred* by Keith R.A. DeCandido; issues #15–20 of the monthly *World of Warcraft* comic book by Walter and Louise Simonson, Jon Buran, Mike Bowden, Phil Moy, Walden Wong, and Pop Mhan; and the short story "Charge of the Aspects" by Matt Burns (on www.WorldofWarcraft.com).

* Vereesa Windrunner has played a role in many events throughout Azeroth's history. Her past exploits are revealed in *Warcraft: Day of the Dragon* and *World of Warcraft: Night of the Dragon* by Richard A. Knaak, and *World of Warcraft: Jaina Proudmoore: Tides of War* by Christie Golden. She also makes brief appearances in *Warcraft: War of the Ancients Trilogy* and *World of Warcraft: Stormrage* by Richard A. Knaak, and *World of Warcraft: Tides of Darkness* by Aaron Rosenberg.

* Major events in Warchief Vol'jin's life, including those from before he became ruler of the Darkspear trolls, are presented in *World of Warcraft: Vol'jin: Shadows of the Horde* by Michael A. Stackpole; *World of Warcraft: Jaina Proudmoore: Tides of War* by Christie Golden; and the short story "The Judgment" by Brian Kindregan in *World of Warcraft: Paragons*.

* Taran Zhu, staunch defender of Pandaria and revered leader of the secretive Shado-pan order, is also featured in *World of Warcraft: Vol'jin: Shadows of the Horde* by Michael A. Stackpole.

* Velen stands as one of the wisest and most ancient members of the Alliance. His time living on the world of Draenor is depicted in *World of Warcraft: Rise of the Horde* by Christie Golden. Other details regarding the draenei leader are featured in *World of Warcraft: Wolfheart* by Richard A. Knaak and the short story "Prophet's Lesson" by Marc Hutcheson in *World of Warcraft: Paragons*.

* You can find more information about Alexstrasza the Life-Binder in *World of Warcraft: Thrall: Twilight of the Aspects* by Christie Golden; *Warcraft: War of the Ancients Trilogy*, *Warcraft: Day of the Dragon*, *World of Warcraft: Night of the Dragon*, *World of Warcraft: Stormrage*, and *World of Warcraft: Dawn of the Aspects* by Richard A. Knaak; and the short story "Charge of the Aspects" by Matt Burns (on www.WorldofWarcraft.com).

THE BATTLE RAGES ON

War Crimes portrays shocking events from the rise and fall of Garrosh Hellscream, one of the most infamous and hated figures in the world of Azeroth. *World of Warcraft*'s fourth expansion, *Mists of Pandaria*, allows you to witness the depths of his depravity and even take part in deposing him as warchief of the Horde.

Yet Garrosh's tyranny is only a harbinger of a much darker storm approaching Azeroth. In the upcoming fifth expansion, *Warlords of Draenor*, the leaders of the Horde and the Alliance will call on heroes to traverse time itself and brave an alternate version of the orcish homeworld, a savage and unforgiving realm filled with strange new allies and ferocious enemies. There, a merciless army of orcs known as the Iron Horde is gathering for an invasion of Azeroth . . . and *you* can help stop it.

To discover the ever-expanding realm that has entertained millions around the globe, go to WorldofWarcraft.com and download the free trial version. Live the story.

WE ALL SCREAM FOR HELLSCREAM

Represent your faction in style as you take on Garrosh Hellscream
and the Iron Horde with the World of Warcraft Siberia Elite

WWW.STEELSERIES.COM/BLIZZARD

steelseries